YO-CBA-089

Praise for the novels of Jaclyn Reding

White Magic

"This very satisfying historical romance runs the gamut of emotions; it also leaves just enough unsaid to make you want to read the next book in the quartet." —*Rendezvous*

White Heather

"A fabulous storyline. . . . This is a must read for fans of historical romances." —Harriet Klausner

Stealing Heaven

"Heroes to die for, unforgettable courtships, and unique, entertaining plots make this a winning series." —*Rendezvous*

Chasing Dreams

"A wonderful romance rich in details . . . fast-paced, pleasurable." —*Romantic Times*

Tempting Fate

"A breathtaking read from page one . . . will remain with its readers long after they have closed the book." —*Rendezvous*

"*Tempting Fate* keeps readers turning the pages. Strong characterizations and good plotting make this tale come alive." —*Romantic Times*

"[*Tempting Fate*] gives you everything: a wonderful story, rousing adventure, and courageous characters you'll never forget. Don't miss this splendid new novel." —Catherine Coulter

WHITE
KNIGHT

Jaclyn Reding

A SIGNET BOOK

SIGNET
Published by New American Library, a division of
Penguin Putnam Inc., 375 Hudson Street,
New York, New York 10014, U.S.A.
Penguin Books Ltd, 27 Wrights Lane,
London W8 5TZ, England
Penguin Books Australia Ltd, Ringwood,
Victoria, Australia
Penguin Books Canada Ltd, 10 Alcorn Avenue,
Toronto, Ontario, Canada M4V 3B2
Penguin Books (N.Z.) Ltd, 182–190 Wairau Road,
Auckland 10, New Zealand

Penguin Books Ltd, Registered Offices:
Harmondsworth, Middlesex, England

First published by Signet, an imprint of New American Library,
a division of Penguin Putnam Inc.

First Printing, November 1999
10 9 8 7 6 5 4 3 2 1

This novel is dedicated to
thousands of Scottish Highlanders
who lost their homes, their heritage,
and oftentimes their lives
during the period of time known as
"The Clearances"

~

And for Diana,
Princess of Wales,
and what might have been

Yet where so many suffered one more wail
Of anguish scarce was heeded! Rang the dale
With lamentation and low muttering wrath,
As homestead after homestead in the strath,
As hut on hut perched tip-toe on the hills,
Or crouched by burn-sides big with storm-bred rills,
Blazed up in unison, till all the glen
Stood in red flames with homes of ousted Highland
men.

From *The Heather on Fire: a Tale of Highland
Clearances*
by Mathilde Blind (1841–1896)

PART ONE

No bird soars too high,
if he soars with his own wings.
—William Blake

Chapter One

It is a truth universally acknowledged, that a
single man in possession of good fortune,
must be in want of a wife.
—Jane Austen, *Pride and Prejudice*

London, 1820

Lady Grace Ledys stood in the midst of her uncle's study, a room so scarcely used that the newspaper sitting on the desk was dated six months earlier. The servants, underpaid as they were, rarely bothered dusting the place and had even taken to using the room for storage, knowing it would never be noticed. For this occasion, though, the draperies that were usually closed had been drawn back and a fire burned happily in the hearth that had previously been home to a family of house mice.

Appearances, after all, were everything to the Marquess of Cholmeley.

He sat before her now, her uncle, looking quite at ease in this place he never frequented. His hair had been styled à la Brutus, brushed carelessly forward and curled over his forehead. His boots wore a fresh polish and his waistcoat was one she'd never seen before. He'd summoned her there a quarter hour before, but his attention wasn't focused on her. Not at all. Instead, his entire focus was wholly taken up with the man sitting beside him.

The renowned Duke of Westover was a man who must surely have already known his sixtieth year. His

thinning hair, pulled back in a waspish-looking queue,
showed white against the darkness of his coat. His fingers held loosely to the golden knob atop his polished
Malacca cane and the fourth finger of his other hand
was adorned by a ruby the size of a small walnut. Two
gold fob watches hung over the top of his breeches and
he was grinning at her—more precisely he was grinning
at her breasts, as if the dark mourning silk that covered
them had suddenly grown transparent.

"Tell me, girl, are your breasts genuine?"

He was trying to unsettle her, she knew, and if he had
directed such a question at her just six months ago, he
would indeed have left Grace wide eyed and gasping
with astonishment. Adverse circumstances, however,
often had a way of dulling one's sensibilities.

Before coming to live at the London home of her
uncle and guardian, Grace had known a blissful, refined
existence at Ledysthorpe, her family's ancestral estate in
Durham. She had been raised there since a babe under
the gentle care of her grandmother, the Dowager Marchioness of Cholmeley. Her life had been touched only
by softness and light. She hadn't yet seen the smoke-
clouded spires of London's churches, had never known
the noise and stench and filth of living amongst the other
million or so souls in England's capital city. The farthest
she had ventured had been the short, tree-shaded buggy
ride to the village of Ledysthorpe where everyone knew
her and greeted her with waves and smiles and inquiries
after her health.

On her first day in London, Grace had nearly been
run down by a passing carriage and just missed having
the hem of her skirts spat upon by a strange little man
selling brick dust.

The duke's voice came again then, returning her from
her thoughts to the unavoidable here and now.

"Did you not hear me, girl? I asked if that is your
true bosom."

Grace stared at the duke, determined not to allow him
the satisfaction of her anger and said calmly, her voice
as chill as a winter wind, "Would you have me open my
bodice to prove it, Your Grace?"

The duke looked momentarily taken aback. Her uncle's voice, however, came sharp as a rap on the knuckles.

"Grace!"

Grace turned to where the Marquess of Cholmeley sat in his carved chair just the other side of the Axminster carpet. The Irlandaise knot on his cravat looked to have slipped a degree off center and his mouth was fixed most unpleasantly amidst his bushy side whiskers. But instead of directing his hostility at the man who had just insulted her, his only niece, he was staring with displeasure at *her*.

Surely even Uncle Tedric must recognize the impropriety of this interview. But he wasn't moving. He wasn't even speaking. In fact, he was smiling, damn him, smiling at her in the same way that wily clerk at the glovemaker's shop had when he'd tried to fool her into buying that pair of gloves with the overlong pinky fingers. *They'll shrink with age,* the clerk had said—as if he had actually expected she'd believe him. Grace frowned again, looking from her uncle back to the duke; *shrunken with age, indeed.* Suddenly the clerk's words couldn't have rung any truer.

"I assure you, Your Grace," her uncle said, giving Grace a smile that held so little warmth it made her shiver, "there is no artifice. Everything you see of my niece is indeed what the good Lord endowed her with."

"Indeed," the duke repeated as he shifted from one buttock to the other in his seat, "although she certainly wouldn't be the first chit to have puffed out her bodice with a wad of stuffing to wheedle a man into marrying her."

With a sniff, he returned his attention to her. "Walk here to me girl."

Grace shot one last look at her uncle, silently begging him to stop this unprincipled humiliation. But instead of speaking out and protecting her as he should in his role as her guardian, he simply nodded, his eyes telling her his thoughts more clearly than any words.

He was determined that the duke should offer for Grace's hand and bless them all with his guineas in the process.

How had she never before realized the truth of her

uncle? Grace could remember as a child how her grandmother had *tsk'd* and shaken her head over her youngest
son. *Self-indulgent,* she'd called him. *An epicure.* But to
Grace, from the time she'd been old enough to walk,
her "Uncle Teddy" had been nothing short of the most
handsome, most distinguished man she'd ever known,
the closest thing on earth to his elder brother, her father.

Until now.

In the time since she had come to live under his guardianship, Grace had come to see Tedric Ledys, Marquess
of Cholmeley, undistorted by childhood adoration. In reality, her uncle was everything anyone else had ever
termed him. It was he and no other who had brought
her to standing as she was before the Duke of Westover,
feeling like a mare on the block at Tattersall's.

"Take a turn now, my girl."

Grace lifted her chin, fixing on the stare she'd seen
her grandmother employ so many times during her childhood, most often whenever Grace had misbehaved. It
seemed to succeed, too, this particular look, for the duke
actually knit his brow in a moment of confusion. Bolstered by his reaction, Grace took a short turn, then
stood stiff as a lamppost before his chair.

At this nearness, she could see that the duke was even
older than she'd first thought, perhaps nearing his seventieth year. He stood nearly half a head shorter than she,
cloaked in the heavy clove scent of his cologne. Grace
closed her eyes. *Good God, in the name of all that is
holy, please do not allow Uncle Tedric to marry me off
to this man.*

"You've spirit," the duke said on a half smile that
revealed decaying teeth. "I like that."

Grace swallowed, calling on every ounce of fortitude
she possessed to remain still and hide her revulsion at
the mere thought of sharing any form of marital intimacy
with him. She schooled herself to hold her tongue until
after the duke had gone, when she would inform Uncle
Tedric as firm as she could that no amount of wealth
was worth having to wed the Duke of Westover.

"Thank you, Your Grace," she said, fighting to keep
her voice cold and detached.

The duke took her chin between his fingers, turning it to stare at her profile.

"Your teeth."

"What of them?"

"I should like to see them."

Grace frowned, peering at him from the corner of her eye. "And shall I whinny for you as well, Your Grace?"

Tedric cleared his throat behind her. "You may take your seat, Grace."

Her uncle was frowning with displeasure as she headed for her seat. He would take her to task later, she thought—or perhaps he'd just sign the marriage contracts now in front of her, consigning the rest of her life to this horrible man.

Damn Uncle Tedric, Grace thought as she sat stiffly on a bench between the two men, to the right her past, to the left—God forbid—her future. Why, oh why had her uncle handed her the sole responsibility of restoring the family coffers? His part, of course, had been to empty them through whatever foolish means he might find, be it gaming, drinking, or philandering—talents he had come to perfect—leaving them to live under the very real threat of debtor's prison.

It had taken him six months to reach his present crisis—the span of time since her grandmother had passed away leaving the government of the Cholmeley finances to him. While Nonny had lived, Uncle Tedric had been given an allowance which he'd always managed to spend long before he should receive the next, necessitating a quarterly trip to Durham seeking more. Grace could remember the visits throughout her childhood, listening as he catalogued his expenses for her grandmother over their supper, bemoaning the state of wretched thrift under which he was forced to live. Occasionally Nonny would relent and release additional monies to him. But on those occasions when she refused, Grace had recognized a dangerous light in Tedric's eyes and watched the muscle on the side of his jaw stiffen against the words he so obviously would have liked to say. He was left to bide his time until the dowager would no longer hold the authority over the family finances. And it hadn't taken long.

After Nonny's death, while Grace had dressed herself in mourning black and avoided any amusement save her books and drawing, Tedric had gone like a fox henhouse wild, squandering his way through his substantial inheritance before running up debt on the Cholmeley estate he had no hope of ever repaying. He soon turned his sights upon Grace—or more accurately upon her inheritance, which was held in trust until she wed or reached her twenty-fifth year, a portion of which was to become his as her guardian. Standing before the duke as she was, it was clear to Grace that Uncle Tedric had decided the eighteen months before she reached five-and-twenty was too long to ask his creditors to wait. Surely, though, there must be some other way for them to raise the funds he needed. Grace quickly decided she would do everything to convince her uncle to it as soon as the duke was gone.

Tedric spoke up then. "There is no history of illness, either physical or mental, in our family, Your Grace. My niece's parents, my brother and his wife, were tragically lost while at sea when she was a child, leaving my mother responsible for her upbringing. The marchioness saw to it that Grace received her education from the best ladies' tutors. Grace hasn't yet entered society. She was raised solely at our family's country estate in the North, thus her character is sterling. And as I think you will agree, she is quite lovely to look at."

"Her age," said the duke, studying her again. "Three-and-twenty, you say? A bit long in the tooth to have not yet been introduced to society."

"I shall turn four-and-twenty in the fall," Grace added quickly.

Tedric shot her a quelling stare before saying to the duke, "My niece gave up a coming-out before now so that she might pass the last years of my mother's life at her side, seeing to her care. You may have heard Lady Cholmeley left us this past winter, just after she reached her seventieth year."

The duke's severe expression seemed oddly to soften. "I had heard tell of Lady Cholmeley's passing." He paused a moment, almost as if offering a prayer to her memory and then said, the crustiness returning, "I would

suspect, however, the reason for your niece's delay in
coming to society is due more to your habit of gaming
beyond your means." He leveled her uncle a hard stare.
"Yes, Cholmeley, I have done a bit of digging into your
affairs. It would appear you are nearly twenty thousand
pounds in arrears."

Twenty thousand!

Tedric's face blanched. The duke watched him, brow
aloft as if he awaited a denial. There came none. Only
a lengthy and telling silence.

Grace could but stare. How? How had he amassed
such an enormous debt? She had thought perhaps a
thousand pounds, even two, but this? Her chances for
convincing Tedric to abandon his ideas of her marriage
were futile in the face of such a figure. Still, the fact that
the duke knew their circumstances offered one consola-
tion. Surely he would never marry her now. In fact,
Grace made to rise from the bench, thinking his departure was surely imminent.

"Lady Cholmeley . . . ," the duke murmured then to
no one in particular. ". . . We were acquainted once.
Many years ago. She was a lady in every sense of the
word."

The fondness in his voice, the affection, was unmistakable, and it brought Grace to dropping back onto her
seat. It seemed he wasn't totally discounting her as a
prospect. Tedric wasted no time in using whatever affin-
ity the duke held for her grandmother to his advantage.

"Grace was named for my mother, you know. I believe you can see that my niece resembles her closely."
He motioned across the room to where the famed
Gainsborough portrait of her grandmother hung above
the hearth. "Did I mention they were quite close?"

Grace, Lady Cholmeley had been the truest reflection
of an age when elegance had reigned, when women had
been cherished, and when honor had meant everything.
Her stance regal, her hair perfectly coiffed, she stood
surrounded by her spaniels on the riverfront lawn at
Ledysthorpe. Even with her present situation, Grace
found herself smiling at the portrait, longing for the days
when it had been just the two of them—before Uncle

Tedric, before London, before the Duke of Westover had come to assess her as a prospective bride.

The duke turned, regarding Grace once again, comparing her, she knew, to her grandmother's image before he returned his attention to her uncle. After a moment of silent contemplation, he made to rise, thunking his cane once on the floor before him.

"I shall take the matter of a marriage under consideration, Cholmeley." He turned for the door. "My man will write to you should the need arise."

As she watched the duke leave, Grace quickly began a mental catalogue of the Cholmeley silver, wondering how much she might fetch for it in sale.

Chapter Two

Christian Wycliffe, Marquess Knighton, alighted from the steps of his shining yellow barouche even before his coachman could reach the door to open it properly for him.

The coachman's name was Parrott, one that suited him well for both his peculiar habit of always repeating the last words of what was said to him and for his nose, which did indeed resemble a hooked beak.

"I've got it, Parrott," said the marquess, nodding to the man as he swept toward the front door of the Georgian town house shaded by elms before him.

"Got it," repeated Parrott, bowing to the marquess's backside. "Got it indeed, my lord."

Parrott had been in Lord Knighton's employ ever since his cousin Willem had vacated the post upon leaving England for America five years before. Willem had recommended Parrott as his replacement before he'd gone, a day the coachman would never forget no matter if he lived to see one hundred years.

How nervous he'd been as he had tooled his lordship about the streets of London, demonstrating his skill with the horses; how struck by the young marquess's affable and unruffled demeanor. In his efforts to impress his prospective employer, Parrott had nearly run down a wealthy-looking matron who was crossing the street. He'd managed to turn the horses before striking her, knocking her instead on her bottom upon a patch of grass. Crestfallen, Parrott had thought his chance for the post immediately lost, but Lord Knighton hadn't so much as batted an eye as he'd tipped his tall hat to the affronted madam while congratulating Parrott on his success at finding her such a soft place on which to land.

From that moment, Parrott had thought the marquess the most pleasant, most generous man he'd ever met, able to conquer any obstacle put in his path. A gentleman, a hero, a veritable god.

It hadn't taken long, however, after he'd been assigned the coachman's position, spending part of most every day with Lord Knighton, for Parrott to discover that the marquess was really a man who wore two different, very contrary faces.

To most, Christian, Lord Knighton was the handsome and courteous lord, wealthy and self-assured, a man who had the very world bowing at his feet. Most anything he desired was his for the taking. Even the clouds seemed incapable of lowering when the marquess was about.

It was only when he was away from the scrutinizing eyes of society that Parrott came to know the other side of the marquess, the one most everyone else never saw—the one who seemed to bear the full weight of the world upon his shoulders.

It was the face that Lord Knighton had begun to wear far more frequently of late.

To the rest of the world, the marquess was the heir to the wealthiest man in the land, his grandfather, the great Duke of Westover. Wherever Lord Knighton went people knew it. You could see it in their eyes when they begged his acquaintance, or sought his opinion out of false flattery, or even pushed their unmarried daughters in his path—as often happened when the marquess was about. A room immediately hushed at his entrance. Traffic stopped at the sight of him. The pleasure of a solitary walk in the park was something denied him, for inevitably some romantic miss would devise a plan to gain his attention—the last one had even trained her lap dog to bring the marquess her shoe so that he'd be made to return it to her, just like Cinderella and her fateful glass slipper.

In the past year or so the marriage-minded misses and their mamas had become doubly bold, as if they had somehow decided his lordship's bachelorhood had gone on long enough. *"He is approaching his thirtieth year,"*

Parrott had once heard one of them say, *"long past the time when he should be presenting the old duke with an heir."*

Lord Knighton was what most ladies would call "handsomely cut." His features were strong; his dark hair cut short and worn naturally. He wore his face clean shaven and his suit of clothes seemingly without effort. Coupled with the vast fortune he was set to inherit, it was no wonder the man never had a moment's peace.

"Would you be wantin' me to await you here in front with the coach then, my lord?" Parrott asked, bowing his head as the marquess rapped at the door.

Christian nodded, adjusting the cuff of his coat. "I would expect this to prove a visit much like any other I have made to my grandfather's house, Parrott. The sooner cut short the better."

"The sooner, the better. Indeed, my lord," said Parrott, ambling away.

Of the countless places Parrott had driven the marquess, Westover House here on Grosvenor Square was certainly the one at which he spent the least amount of time. It looked a fine enough establishment from the outside—weathered red brick and gleaming windows behind an iron fence topped by finials that shone golden even on an overcast day such as this. Parrot could only guess at the finery inside; he'd never once been admitted nor had he so much as glimpsed the stables in the mews at the rear, although he'd heard from some of his acquaintances that they were equally fine.

The young marquess, however, seemed oblivious to it all. He came to this place only when summoned and emerged just as quickly as he could, always in a far worse humor than he'd been upon arriving. There was bad blood between the marquess and the duke, his grandfather—bad blood, indeed.

"Pull the coach around the square and park it under that large oak on the corner, Parrott. I've a notion a visit to my club will be in order once I leave here."

"In order. Aye, milord."

Christian remained at the door as Parrott made off, watching as the coachman climbed onto his seat and clicked his tongue to the horses to urge them forward.

He knew a sudden desire to walk back down the steps and disregard the summons that had brought him to this place even as he realized it would do him little good. Eventually he would find himself back at this same spot, waiting before this same door, for this same purpose. It was patently unavoidable.

Christian turned when he heard the sound of the latch opening behind him. The door swung open and he nodded to the butler, Spears, a man who'd been at his station in the Westover household as long as Christian could remember.

"Good day, Lord Knighton," said Spears, bowing his head dutifully as he immediately secured Christian's gloves, beaver hat, and many-caped carrick, brushing a hand over the fine wool to dislodge an offending bit of lint.

Christian mumbled his response and headed directly for the study, the usual setting for these nonsensical meetings. What would it be today? A lecture on his responsibilities at the northern properties? A justification of the invoices for Eleanor's new wardrobe? No doubt the old man had forgotten that his granddaughter, Christian's sister, was to have her long-awaited coming-out. Or perhaps the duke sought to delay it another year and make Nell's chances for a safe and happy future all the more difficult. If that were his aim, Christian was fully prepared for a confrontation.

Instead he was brought up short by the butler's call.

"I beg your pardon, my lord. His grace is not in his study this morning. He wished me to inform you he awaits you in the garden instead."

The garden? Christian wondered that his grandfather even knew the house had such a thing, for he ate, slept, and even relieved himself within the paneled walnut walls of his ducal study, a place just as gloomy and severe as its most frequent occupant. As a child, Christian could recall sneaking into the place at night to see if the marble busts of the various historical personages that were set about the room actually did come to life as his father had once told him.

"The garden?" Christian queried, unaware of his Parrott-like response.

Spears nodded once, offering no further explanation. Christian simply took a turn and headed off for the rear of the house.

As he made his way through the lower chambers, past furnishings and ornaments that were meant to impress more than to enhance, Christian tried to shake away the foreboding that had greeted him with his morning coffee. No matter how he tried, he could not shake the sense that something was terribly wrong. He'd felt it in his gut the moment he'd found his grandfather's summons sitting atop his newspaper on the breakfast tray, instructing him to make this urgent and unscheduled appearance. While this wasn't the first, second, or even twentieth time his grandfather had sent such a request, somehow this time just *seemed* out of the ordinary.

Whatever it was that had brought the old man to calling for him, Christian knew it could not be for any good. Through most of his nine-and-twenty years, it never had been. The duke seemed to spend his waking hours devising new and inventive ways to plague his unfortunate heir, as if he felt it his sole duty to assume the tradition of enmity that had previously existed between the king and his heir, the then Regent, before the old king had died earlier that same year. It shouldn't have come as any surprise. After all, the duke had certainly modeled his life after old George in more ways than one, periodic insanity seeming sometimes among them.

But the nearer Christian drew to the garden, the more that feeling in his gut began to burn. He hated the fact that he should feel this way at all, that his grandfather should be allowed to have this effect over him. By the time he reached the double doors leading outside, Christian had convinced himself that the reason for the summons had to be Eleanor's coming-out. The duke was going to refuse it again.

He found the duke sitting in a cane-backed chair beneath the feathery boughs of a large willow tree. The drooping branches nearly shrouded him from view. His pale hair was undressed, falling about his shoulders in thinning strands, and he wore a brocade dressing robe over his shirt and breeches, slippers of red morocco on his feet.

He had not yet noticed his grandson's arrival.

Christian delayed a moment in the doorway. He hadn't been to these gardens since he'd been a boy, since shortly before his father had died, taking him immediately from the innocence and freedom he had known in childhood to the penitentiary role he now held as ducal heir. From then on, Christian's imaginative games of pirate and adventurer, even his interest in the wars taking place overseas, were forbidden, for these were pursuits deemed unnecessary for a future duke. After all, as heir to the Westover fortune, he would never be granted the officer's position he had so often dreamed of as a boy. His grandfather had made certain of it, filling Christian's days instead with studies of Latin and philosophy.

Stepping further into the garden, Christian noticed a glass of lemonade and a book—*a novel?*— sitting on the table beside his grandfather. It appeared that the duke's attention was wholly taken up with watching a bird picking at the ground a space away. Christian wondered if his eyes were deceiving him. A novel? Bird watching? His grandfather, the distinguished Duke of Westover? The burning feeling in his stomach began to curdle. There was no longer any doubt about it; something was definitely wrong.

Christian came to a halt several feet away from the duke's chair, stood tall and straight, and bowed his head respectfully as he'd been taught as a boy.

"Good day, Your Grace."

Elias Wycliffe, the fourth Duke of Westover, turned in his chair to regard his grandson and only living heir.

"Christian," he said in his usual dispassionate tone. When Christian made no attempt to converse further, he added, "You received my message, I see."

Again Christian remained silent, which prompted the duke to say after an awkward moment, "Thank you for taking the time to come."

Christian abandoned his stance for another, one slightly more defensive. "Haven't I always come when you've summoned me, sir? I wasn't aware I had any choice in the matter."

Christian watched his grandfather's expression darken as it always did whenever they were together, and he wondered how they had come to be such adversaries. It had been this way so long now, he no longer could recall it being any differently between them.

"I will make this brief and come straight to the point. Christian, I have summoned you here to tell you that it is time for you to fulfill your part in our agreement—the first part of it, that is. I have made the necessary arrangements for you to marry."

It was a statement Christian had always known he'd one day hear from the duke, still he couldn't quite temper the breath-stealing impact that came immediately after the words had been spoken. For nineteen years he had known this day would come. At twenty, even at twenty-five, he had anticipated it. But as time had passed on without mention of it, Christian had begun to think that perhaps the old man had forgotten the bargain he'd made with his grandson so long ago. He should have known better; the duke had simply been biding his time, waiting until he knew Christian would be occupied with the arrangements for Eleanor's coming-out before delivering the blow he had been waiting so long to give.

Christian didn't move for several moments as he stood waiting for the feelings of anger and impotence that he so often felt before this man to subside. He would not allow his grandfather to detect even the slightest hint of emotion in him. He couldn't allow him the satisfaction.

"Indeed? A marriage?" Christian finally said, managing to hide his response behind a mask of nonchalance. It was a method he had come to master well during the past twenty years.

"Yes. She is of fine stock, a nobleman's daughter, good character, unsullied. I would allow no less for you."

Christian's jaw tightened at the duke's cutting comment, one that implied he should be grateful. The notion of Christian choosing his own wife had never once been a consideration. From birth he had known this, a fact that had become all the more apparent since his father's death. While he could do nothing to change this part of his life, this role he'd been born to, Christian would at least make certain the duke met his obligation in their agreement.

"And Eleanor's coming-out?"

"What of it?"

"If you think to refuse—"

"It will be taken care of just as we agreed this season. Your sister will be given every opportunity to wed a man of her choosing under the protection of the Westover name—without any fear of the truth coming out." He added, "Of course, that is *if* you are agreeable to the match I have made for you."

Bastard, Christian thought, hating the duke for speaking as if he actually had a choice, as if he might actually refuse. Perhaps he would, had Christian not decided long ago to sacrifice his own future for that of his sister's happiness. In order to protect Eleanor, Christian would have made a deal with the devil himself if he'd had to; indeed he already had.

Christian pulled in a steadying breath. As he stared at the pendulous blooms of the snowdrops blowing in the morning breeze at his feet, he remembered Eleanor as a child—how she would bring him flowers, how she had followed him wherever he went. *For you, Eleanor. I do this for you, even though you can never know of it.* His feelings of anger began to subside as they always did when he thought of his sister. Only then did he return his attention to the duke.

"I assume some sort of public announcement is forthcoming."

"*No!* There will not be an announcement made until after you are already wed. I want no possibility of any trouble."

The duke's expression had grown agitated, causing Christian to wonder if some sort of threat had perhaps already been made. *Dear God, Eleanor . . .*

The duke went on. "I have made arrangements for a special license and have already settled the terms of the marriage with your intended bride's family. You have only to sign the contracts before you are to wed on the twenty-ninth."

April the twenty-ninth. Less than a fortnight away, Christian thought, and on so significant a day.

The very anniversary of his father's death.

How his grandfather must have planned this—every detail seen to, every precaution taken. No doubt even

Christian's suit of clothes had been chosen for him. The duke had spent the past twenty years waiting for this day, for the glory of his final domination over his grandson's life, so embittered had he been since the death of his only son, Christian's father. Even now, Christian could hear the duke's words that fateful morning so long ago.

Now your life is mine.

Christian stood, ready to leave before he revealed to the old man just how very right he'd been in that prophecy.

"I assume you will send some sort of missive to me instructing the pertinent time and place."

The duke nodded.

"Then I shall take my leave, sir. Have one of your footmen bring the necessary paperwork to Knighton House and I will see to the signatures. I bid you good day."

Christian didn't wait for an acknowledgment as he started for the door. Truth be told, if he didn't leave at that moment, he might possibly end up slamming his fist through a pane of one of the French doors.

"Christian."

He halted at the threshold, lingering a moment before he turned to face his grandfather's profile. The duke stared outward at the garden, neglecting to look at him as he spoke.

"Do you not even wish to know her name, this woman who is to be your wife?"

Christian hesitated but a moment in his response. "What does it matter, sir, when you have spent nearly my entire life assuring me that one wife is as good as any other?"

And with that, Christian departed, his mood definitely blacker for the visit.

Chapter Three

"Westover."

Grace felt her legs immediately go soft beneath her, her consciousness blurring as if she might actually faint. She quickly grabbed onto the back of the chair she stood behind. It was the only thing she could think of to keep herself from falling to the floor.

Dear God, no, she thought as she struggled to gather her wits, *of all the names her uncle could have given, why, oh why had he spoken that one?*

Simply the memory of that man sitting in this same room, in this very chair, questioning her about the authenticity of her anatomy, made her shudder. It had taken all her will to make it through that day without getting physically ill. And now Uncle Tedric was telling her she was to be the man's wife? To live under the same roof? Share his home? Even—she closed her eyes against the thought—his bed?

Grace shook her head in denial, knowing that no matter the consequences, she could never, *ever* agree to it, and she said as much to Uncle Tedric a moment later, her voice oddly lucid for thoughts so much in chaos.

"I won't wed him, Uncle."

Tedric's face went rigid over the cheek-high points of his collar, the fingers he'd been drumming on the rosewood tabletop going suddenly still. "I beg your pardon, my dear Grace? I fail to recall having asked for your consent in this."

Grace frowned, standing her ground, thankful for the chair in front of her lest her uncle notice the trembling of her legs. "No, Uncle, you did not ask me, but I repeat: *I won't wed that man.* He is old enough to be my grandfather. I don't care what he has offered you. I won't do it. Threaten all you like. Forbid me from leaving the house. Take away all my things, if you must. But if you think to force me to wed him, I promise you now I shall refuse to speak the vows. I will scream hysterically even as you have to carry me bodily down the aisle to him. I would rather live in the streets of . . . of . . ."

"Westminster," Tedric said, knowing perfectly well Grace knew about as little of London as would a foreigner landing on her streets for the first time.

"Westminster! I would live in the streets of Westminster before I will ever become wife to that disgusting man."

"Consider that the streets there are named such things as Cut Throat Lane, Rogue's Acres, and Pickpocket Alley. Believe me, Grace, marriage to Westover is far preferable."

Grace wasn't to be deterred. "I don't care if he is the wealthiest man in England—or the entire world, for that matter. I will not marry him!"

Tedric, Lord Cholmeley simply stared at his niece, no doubt taken aback by her dogged determination, she who had meekly accepted whatever Fate had doled out for her through the first three-and-twenty years of her life. Well, let him stare till his eyes turned to dust. She would not sit idly by and accept *this*.

But instead of arguing with her as she had expected, Uncle Tedric did the most peculiar thing. He began to laugh, a chuckle first that quickly progressed to a side-splitting, shoulder-shaking roar. Tears sprang to his eyes even as he looked at Grace, hands poised at her hips, chin thrust forward. He only laughed all the more as she stared at him in growing disbelief.

What the devil was he about? Grace had expected a quarrel, even threats—but mirth? Not when the rest of her life depended upon this very moment. Regardless of his current financial predicament, did he feel nothing for her, his only niece, his sole blood relation?

Helpless tears came to her eyes, causing him only to laugh more. Unable to bear his hilarity any longer, Grace turned to flee the room.

"Grace! Wait a moment. You don't understand."

But she was already at the stairs, wondering if the Cholmeley coachman knew the swiftest route to Pickpocket Alley.

"Grace, no, you are mistaken. It isn't the present duke who is to be your husband. It is his grandson, Christian, Marquess Knighton."

Grace stopped cold halfway up the stairwell. It was not so much at the news that it wasn't the old duke who was to be her proposed husband, but at the name her uncle had given her in his stead.

Christian, Marquess Knighton.

Knighton.

Knight.

She suddenly thought back to a day months earlier, not long before her grandmother had died. The two of them had been sitting together on the terrace outside the dowager marchioness's bedchamber at Ledysthorpe, a quiet and peaceful place that faced onto the banks of the River Tees several miles inland from the restless North Sea. It had been a lazy summer afternoon—chilly, Grace remembered, for her grandmother had urged her to wear a shawl. Grace had been reading Chaucer's *Canterbury Tales* aloud while the dowager had been sitting in her chair, eyes closed, listening. The memory of that day was suddenly so vivid, Grace could hear the words now . . .

> *A Knight there was, and that a worthy man,*
> *That from the time that he first began*
> *To riden out, he loved chivalry,*
> *Truth and honour, freedom and courtesy . . .*
> *And though that he was worthy, he was wise,*
> *And of his port as meek as is a maid.*
> *He never yet no villany had said*
> *In all his life unto no manner wight.*
> *He was a very parfit gentle knight.*

Grace remembered that she'd looked up while reading to see that Nonny had nodded off, as she so often did. She had set the red ribbon marker between the book's pages to mark her place, thinking to work a bit on her drawing while Nonny dozed. Just as Grace had moved to set the book aside, with an abruptness that had unsettled the spaniel nestled in her lap, the dowager had sat up, suddenly awake.

"You know you will have to marry."

Grace remembered wondering if perhaps her grandmother had been dreaming. "Yes, Nonny, I know that. Someday I will marry just like you did, but I do not wish to think on it just now. I do not wish to think of ever leaving Ledysthorpe. This is my home. I love it here."

"I came here a young bride from what had always been my home, dear. A lady makes her husband's home her own when she is married. It isn't so very far off for you, either, my dear, this marriage I speak of. Once I am gone, you will be unable to avoid it any longer."

"And where are you off to, then?" Grace had asked, coming to her side. "A jaunt across the Continent, perhaps?"

Her grandmother had smiled, reaching to rest a hand against the side of her granddaughter's cheek. "My dearest, I am not long for this life. I feel it in my heart. And once I am gone, I will be unable to do much in the way of protecting you. Tedric will have charge over your future, at least until you reach five-and-twenty. I had hoped to remain long enough to see you to that anniversary of your birth and past that restriction in your inheritance, however I fear now I will not. But know that should I die before you have reached that majority, even though I shall be gone, I will do whatever is within my power to bring you a good husband."

"But however will I know who is the right husband if you are not here to advise me?"

The dowager had smiled again, saying only, "You will, child, because you are of my blood. I had only to dance once with my true love and I knew I would spend the rest of my life loving him. It will be the same when you have found your own one true 'very parfit gentle knight.' "

Her last words whispered like the soft summer wind through Grace's thoughts. *Gentle knight. Knight . . .*

Was it possible? Could this Marquess Knighton be the one her grandmother had spoken of? Had Nonny somehow sent him to protect her as she had promised, or was she being silly and the significance of his name merely a coincidence?

"Grace?"

At her uncle's summons, Grace came into the doorway of the study where he yet sat. She thought again of her grandmother, whose own marriage had been arranged and which had still brought her great happiness. Her mother and father had met only days before their wedding and, according to Nonny, they could not have been more in love. All her life, Nonny had read Grace countless tales of the great lovers—Tristan and Isolde, Heloise and Abelard—whose loves had survived against great, almost insurmountable odds. Nonny had promised her granddaughter that one day she would have the same, that she would be given her own knight in shining armor.

Grace thought then of what would happen if she didn't agree to the marriage. Where would she go, what would become of her should her uncle end up in debtor's prison? She had no acceptable means of supporting herself; few ladies of her social standing did. She had never been to Westminster before, but from the sounds of it, it likely wouldn't be a pleasant place. The way things presently stood, it seemed she really had no choice in the matter. She would have to marry eventually. It was the role she had been raised to fill, all she had been taught to expect. Why not, then, marry the duke's grandson? At the very least, he was nearer her own age.

"I would see him first before I could ever agree to wed him."

Tedric looked as if he might refuse. His mouth flattened into a thin line and his brow drew close over his eyes. After a moment, though, he nodded. "I will see what can be arranged. But I cannot promise anything."

Several evenings later when Uncle Tedric was on his way out—probably for his club, Brooks's—he stopped a moment at the parlor door where Grace sat playing at the pianoforte. She had often heard it said that music had a way of uplifting one's spirits—especially, Grace had found, when one vented one's spleen upon the keys.

From the corner of her eye, she could see her uncle

lingering in the doorway but she continued to play her piece, striking the keys with renewed vigor. When she had finished, he came into the room, applauding softly.

"That was lovely, Grace. You are growing more and more accomplished each time I hear you."

It was quite a compliment, considering that on the last occasion he had listened, she had been twelve. Grace looked at him over her music sheet. He was smiling at her, his eyes filled with a contrived warmth.

"You shall make a fine duchess some day, Grace. Your name portends it."

Grace took little solace from his comment. Instead she turned the music sheet over for the next piece. Ah, perfect—*fortissimo*. She glanced at him. "I'll take that as indication that you have arranged for me to meet the marquess?"

Tedric nodded, obviously pleased with himself as he adjusted his kid glove. "In a manner of speaking, yes."

Grace lifted her fingers from the keys. She folded her hands in her lap, waiting.

"*Meet* is perhaps the wrong choice in words. You see, there can be no introduction, no conversation between you. His grace the duke expressly forbids it."

"He forbids me to meet the man I'm to spend the rest of my life with? What does he seek to conceal?"

"There is nothing to conceal, my dear. Lord Knighton is considered to be *the* bachelor among the *ton,* quite the buck about town, sought after for his wealth and title as well as his looks by every suitable young lady with a mind toward marriage. It is precisely because he is in such demand that the duke doesn't want the marriage between you made public until after the ceremony has been performed. It is really for your benefit as well as the marquess's, Grace. An announcement beforehand would create a public stir. Any hope of peace in your life would be gone. Your every move would be watched, your every gesture criticized. Some desperate miss might even attempt to prevent the wedding from taking place altogether. Thus it will be a private ceremony, in an obscure church in the country somewhere, arranged by special license."

"I am not even to be allowed a formal wedding ceremony?"

As a girl, Grace had always dreamed of a grand wedding. In fact, when Princess Charlotte had wed Leopold of Coburg, she and Nonny had read every news report and had pored over every engraving they could lay their hands upon. Grace had always known that she would wear the dress both Nonny and her mother had worn before her in a church that would be filled with fragrant flowers. It would be a day she would never forget, the day on which she joined her life with her husband's—that nameless, faceless *knight* Nonny had always assured her would be hers.

She now had a name, yes, but the face was yet unknown. And if she could not meet him, speak to him, how would she ever know for certain he was *the one*?

"I'm sorry, Uncle, but I have already told you I cannot wed a man I have never met."

Tedric shook his head. "On the contrary, my dear, you said you would 'see' him before you would agree to wed him—and see him you shall."

"You know that is not at all what I meant when I—"

He held up his hand to silence her. "There is to be a ball, Grace, at the Knighton town house. It is to introduce Lord Knighton's sister to society and is certain to be a crush. You will attend this ball; I will escort you. Since you haven't yet been introduced to society, no one will know who you are. We will go, you will see the marquess—you can even watch him for a while if you'd like—and then we will leave. This is the best I can offer."

Grace looked at her uncle, hearing again the words of her grandmother. *I had only to dance with my own true love and I knew I would spend the rest of my life loving him . . .*

"But for one last thing, Uncle."

"And that is?"

"I would share a dance with him."

Tedric shook his head. "Impossible!"

"Why, sir? It is a single dance. You have already said no one will know who I am, including Lord Knighton."

Tedric fell silent in contemplation of her request.

After a moment, he appeared to smile. "I think perhaps the marquess is in for a bit of a surprise from his wife."

"*Potential* wife." Grace drew a breath, wondering why her pulse had suddenly quickened, but decided that a clandestine dance with one's *potential* future husband without his knowing did have a measure of excitement to it.

"Then you will do it?" she asked. "You will arrange for me to share a dance with Lord Knighton?"

Tedric turned and headed for the door. "I don't quite know how I'll accomplish it, but yes, Grace, I will find a way for you to have your dance with the marquess."

Chapter Four

Grace passed the next three days trying not to think about the Knighton ball. She forced herself to concentrate on thoughts of the weekly menu or the furniture that needed polishing even as she forged through her wardrobe for something suitable to wear. By the time the morning of the ball dawned, she had thrice convinced herself to abandon the venture, then even again as she was walking down the front stairs with her uncle to leave.

When all was said and done, she did go and their coach arrived at the Knighton town house shortly after ten. For the first moment or two, Grace thought surely she must be dreaming, for as they came into the ballroom, she could only think that it was like stepping through a magical door into the legendary land of Cockaigne, where the rivers flowed wine, the houses were made of cake, and the pavements were lined in honey-iced pastry.

Music and laughter rang out in this enchanted setting that was indeed every bit a fairytale. The ballroom was bathed in brilliant candlelight from chandeliers whose crystals winked like diamonds. Flowers the likes of which she had never seen spilled from ornate china and ormolu vases that were set about the room, filling the air with an exotic mixture of their various perfumes. Liveried footmen stood off to one side, awaiting any request, while numerous other servants wove their way among the throng of guests bearing silver trays filled with every sort of delicacy imaginable. Brightly colored chiffon festooned each window opening and doorway, and one could have sworn that the tables set in the supper parlor were groaning beneath the weight of their delights. Jewels glittered about necks, ears, and fingers. Elegant satins glowed against the candlelight. Everywhere she looked gaiety and opulence were evident. Everywhere except—

Grace glanced down, took one look at herself, and blanched.

The pale blue-gray silk she had chosen was one of her best gowns, but its modest design indelibly marked her a rustic from the country. The styling of her hair—a simple topknot of curls that bounced clumsily about her ears when she moved—made her lack of style even more apparent. Uncle Tedric had arranged it so that they would arrive at the ball deliberately late in order to make their entrance as inconspicuous as possible. Grace was certainly thankful for that now.

These noble people had been born to the life of privilege, had never known a day of choosing their own clothing or dressing their own hair. Grace had been born the daughter of a marquess, yes, but it was distinction made only in name, for she had been raised in the country more like a milkmaid than a noblewoman. Nonny had believed that simple living gave one character. How the ladies present this night would gasp were they to learn Grace didn't have her own ladies' maid, but instead relied upon her uncle's housekeeper, Mrs. Bennett, to fasten the hooks at the back of her gown when she couldn't reach them. How could she even pretend to assume the role of Marchioness Knighton, much less that of the future Duchess of Westover?

Just as Grace convinced herself to have her uncle take her home and forget the entire affair, a young lady of perhaps nineteen separated herself from the masses, coming forward. She smiled politely at Grace before presenting her gloved hand to Uncle Tedric.

"I'm so happy you could come, Lord Cholmeley. It is a pleasure to see you again."

She was everything a lady should be—slender, perhaps an inch or two shorter than Grace, with her cocoa brown hair caught up in a graceful sweep beneath an ornamented ostrich plume that drifted softly as an angel's wing when she moved. Her gown was made of white embroidered net that draped over pale rose-colored silk set with sparkling brilliants that winked in the candle-light. It was quite the most elegant creation Grace had ever seen.

Tedric took the lady's hand and bowed over it. "The pleasure is all mine, I assure you, my lady." He turned toward Grace. "Lady Eleanor Wycliffe, allow me to introduce my niece, Lady Grace Ledys."

Grace bowed her head, wishing she had something more ornate than the simple ribbon fillet laced through her curls. "It is a pleasure to make your acquaintance, my lady," she said quietly.

"Grace," Uncle Tedric said, "Lady Eleanor is Lord Knighton's sister. This evening's ball is being given in her honor."

"Yes, it is to be my coming-out. Such a peculiar term, do you not think? Makes one think of a pillow that's been overstuffed!" Lady Eleanor linked her arm through Grace's, whispering, "Your uncle has informed me of your wish to share a dance with Christian. I'm sure Lord Cholmeley wouldn't mind letting me have you to myself for a bit first to get better acquainted." She squeezed Grace's hand. "Especially if we are to be sisters."

When Grace had been a girl, she'd dreamed of having a sister, someone she could talk to and share secrets with, or discuss books over tea as she and Nonny had done. And now, suddenly, here was this lovely young lady offering herself for the role and she hadn't even noticed that the shoes Grace had worn were too dark for her gown.

Grace smiled at Lady Eleanor, immediately and utterly charmed. Tedric wisely took his cue to leave.

"I shall be in the gaming parlor should you have need of me, Grace." He bowed his head. "Lady Eleanor."

"Oh, I'm so sorry, Lord Cholmeley," Lady Eleanor said, stopping him short, "but there is to be no gaming at the ball tonight."

"No gaming?" Tedric looked horrified, as if she had told him that his beloved tailors, Schweitzer and Davidson, had just that morning closed shop.

"It was at my request, my lord. I didn't want anything tempting the gentlemen away from dancing with all the ladies tonight." Lady Eleanor smiled sweetly, leaving Tedric little choice but to quietly agree.

"Might a gentleman then find a glass of port somewhere without fear of having it knocked against his shirtfront?"

"Of course, my lord." She motioned through the door. "Down the hall there is a parlor where you will find port and brandy being served."

When he'd gone, Lady Eleanor directed Grace away from the doorway, taking her slowly about the periphery of the vast ballroom. As they walked, she asked Grace about her childhood at Ledysthorpe, how she liked living in London, and how she had come to live under her uncle's guardianship.

"My parents were lost in a boating accident when I was a young child. I was raised by my grandmother and it was with her that I lived at Ledysthorpe until she passed away late last year."

"I am so sorry. Our father died unexpectedly too, although I am told his death was due to an illness. I was not yet born, but Christian was very attached to our father and took the loss very hard."

Lady Eleanor spoke her brother's name with such an obvious affection, it was evident that they were quite close. Before Grace could think to question her more about him, his taste in reading, or odd bits about their childhood, a trio of young ladies caught her attention. They were staring at her from the corner of the room, whispering their disapproval behind their jeweled fans.

"Pay them no mind, Grace. They do not yet know it, but once you have become my brother's wife, they will be falling over themselves for the favor of your attention. They will mimic every detail of your dress even if you wear a flour sack, and they will pray you won't remember their behavior toward you here tonight."

"I hardly think I shall ever fit in," Grace said. "I have spent all my life in the country, where we lived a very simple life. I'm afraid I am quite a fish out of water here in London."

"Do not be too distressed, my dear. Any one of them would sell their grandmother's jewels for a chance at catching my brother's eye. You should count yourself fortunate that you are unschooled in the ways of the *ton*. I, on the other hand, have been surrounded by this hypocrisy since birth. They lay claim to refinement while they shamelessly throw themselves at Christian in hopes of inducing him to marry—as if he would even consider wedding someone who would do such a thing."

She glanced around the room. "Look there, near the door. Do you see that group of ladies crowding together? Do you know why they are all huddled there and are not out among the other gentlemen present? They are watching the stairs for my brother."

Grace spotted the flock of young ladies congregating near the foot of the stairs. Some appeared to be elbowing others for a forward position, while others stole furtive glances up the stairwell.

"Oh, dear."

"It is truly embarrassing. Once at a musicale, a girl even blacked the eye of another fighting over an empty seat beside him. Quite troublesome. It's become the farce of the past several seasons. Hostesses at any ball he is rumored to attend must be on constant watch for these ridiculous annoyances. It has gotten so that he doesn't go out much socially at all. I cannot tell you the number of ladies who have claimed to be my 'dearest friend' in effort to get close to him. I vow that once everyone learns he has wed you, I shan't have any acquaintance left in town."

Lady Eleanor chuckled, but Grace found herself wondering why the marquess would consider wedding someone he had never before seen, especially someone so unpolished, when he had the very crème of London society from which to choose. She was also beginning to understand why the old duke had insisted on such secrecy about their betrothal. If women were blacking one another's eyes for a chair beside him, what would they do to her if they knew she might actually marry the man?

"Now, since my brother hasn't yet braved this crowd, I shall have to go and search him out so that you may have your dance. I must admit, I think I shall enjoy watching him dance with the lady he doesn't yet know he's about to marry, especially in front of all the 'helpless hopefuls.' " She inclined her head toward the cluster of ladies waiting at the foot of the stairs. "That is what I call them. Appropriate name, do you not think? May I beg your leave for only a moment or two while I go and find him?"

Grace wordlessly nodded, watching as Lady Eleanor departed through the crowd. When she had requested the dance with the marquess, Grace's only thought had been the memory of her grandmother's words to her. It would be a romantic waltz that would tell her the moment her eyes met his whether this man was indeed her "very parfit gentle knight," the one she was meant to share her life with. Grace hadn't considered what else this dance might entail, and had no idea that everyone's attention would be focused upon them.

What if Lord Knighton were dreadful? But if he were, why would all these ladies be clamoring over one another for his attention? No, he must be perfect, and if that were the case, then she certainly was not the lady he should be wedding. He should have a wife of refinement and polish, someone more like his sister, not some countrified mouse who had never before set foot in a ballroom, and who had only just learned to waltz. What if she did something absurd like step on his foot? Or worse, what if she completely forgot the steps of a dance she'd never actually performed with anyone save the Cholmeley footman Henry?

She only felt all the more inadequate when she looked down and noticed that the seam on her glove had begun to come apart even as she felt her hair slipping from its knot. In that moment, Grace knew she could not go through with it. She would find Uncle Tedric and beg him to delay the marriage. Better yet, he could simply thank the old duke for his consideration, but decline the marriage offer and beg his pardon a thousand times over. She, Grace from Ledysthorpe? A future duchess? It was too ludicrous to consider.

Grace turned, remembering that her uncle had gone to the parlor, and started to skirt the room. It was no easy task. The ballroom, it seemed, had grown doubly crowded since her arrival. The musicians were seated and were preparing to play. The dancing was set to begin and the crowd thickened in anticipation.

No matter how Grace tried to work her way through, an unyielding wall of humanity prevented it. She was swept along with the tide of the others and soon found herself on the opposite side of the ballroom. She looked around, chewing her lip. There must be another way through the house, and so she stood on her toes a bit to survey the various doorways surrounding her. No doubt the best choice would be the one closest to her, so she sidestepped two gentlemen involved in deep debate, smiling politely as she headed for the door.

It didn't lead to the parlor, but to a narrow corridor used for getting servants from one side of the house to the other without notice. It would indeed serve her purposes very well. She started walking, hoping to find a doorway that would lead her to the parlor. Halfway down the length of the hall, however, the door she had come through suddenly closed behind her. What followed was the rather disquieting sound of the latch being turned on it. Oh, dear, she thought, this wasn't at all a good thing.

Grace stood a moment in the dark, contemplating her next move. She had but two options. She could go back and knock on the door in hopes of summoning someone, but then she'd be no closer to finding her uncle than she had been when she'd started. Even worse, she would look very foolish for having gotten herself locked into a servants' corridor. Her other option, of course, was to proceed a bit further down the passageway to see where she might end up.

Grace prudently chose the latter.

With one hand against the wall to guide her, she made her way slowly in the darkness. But there didn't seem to be any openings at all, just smooth wall along a corridor that seemed only to grow blacker with each step she took. She stumbled on some stairs and slowly she made her way up. At the top of the steps, she flattened both hands against the wall, moving along until, blessedly, her fingers found an opening in the wall. It seemed to be some sort of panel. Grace felt around the edge of it, but could find no mechanism, nothing that might release it.

She listened but didn't hear any sound coming from the other side. She tried to fit her fingers around the outside edge, but the seal was too tight. So Grace placed her palm flat against the panel and gave it a push. The upper corner seemed to give a bit, so she slid her hands upward and gave it another try, and then another, this time putting the weight of herself against it and—

The panel gave way and Grace tumbled through head-first, landing with a thud on her hands and knees. The fall set the weight of her coiffure forward. She looked through the fallen mass of curls to see the polished toes of a pair of boots standing directly in front of her—boots that were most assuredly attached to a body.

Chapter Five

Grace drew her breath and held it as she looked up past long legs and a trim waist to a chest that was both broad and—

—Bare. Surely this couldn't be real. *He* couldn't be real. Grace blinked, but he did not vanish. Good God, it *was* real.

"This is certainly a first."

His voice was deep and rich and he had the most startling pair of eyes she'd ever before seen. They were silvery blue and the way they were looking at her so candidly made her feel as if it was she who was unclothed, not he. Grace had never before seen a man in any state of undress and was appalled to find herself staring at the muscles that lined his abdomen as he took up his shirt and slipped his arms inside.

"Oh my goodness!" was all she could manage to say. Her next mistake was in wondering how the situation could possibly get worse.

She soon had her answer.

"I suppose, given the circumstances, I should introduce myself," he said as he fastened the buttons on his shirtfront. "I am Lord Knighton, your host this evening. And this"—he smiled, a half-grin that was anything but warm—"is my dressing room. But then you already knew that, didn't you?"

Good God—of all the dressing rooms she could have fallen into in this vast house, how had she managed to choose his? With anyone else, she could quickly beg their pardon and leave, knowing she would likely never see them again. But this was the man she was supposed to marry, the man who didn't yet realize that the woman

who had just come tumbling through his dressing room
wall was his intended bride. Could she dare to hope
he would forget this night and this meeting within the
next fortnight?

The marquess turned and folded his neckcloth with an
ease Uncle Tedric would have applauded, all the while
staring at her as if it were perfectly reasonable for a
woman to have come popping out of the woodwork.
Grace, on the other hand, felt utterly humiliated. It
wasn't until Lord Knighton lowered before her, resting
his forearm on his thigh while he held out his other
hand to her, that she even realized she was still sprawled
ignominiously upon his carpet.

"Unless you have acquired a sudden fondness for my
carpeting, might I suggest we find more equal footing?"

Cheeks burning, she placed her gloved hand into his,
coming as quickly as she could to her feet. She opened
her mouth to speak but no words would come out. She
couldn't quite decide if it would be considered proper
in such situations to thank a half-naked man for assisting
a lady to her feet. So Grace merely stood, her curls
askew, silent as a candlestick while Lord Knighton finished dressing. She was suddenly reminded of Eleanor's
words earlier that evening, telling how the other ladies
had been so bold and relentless in their pursuit of her
brother's attention. She had just fallen through the wall
into Lord Knighton's dressing room—where Lord
Knighton was presently dressing. Somehow she didn't
think there would be a more undignified manner for one
to "throw oneself" at a man.

There was one thing that was certain: Seeing him now
only brought Grace to understanding exactly why ladies
were blacking one another's eyes to get near to him.
Christian Wycliffe, Marquess Knighton was, quite simply, the most beautiful man she'd ever seen. Hair that
was a deep chestnut brown swept back from his forehead
to fall about the stark white of his high collar. He had
the sort of face that sculptors committed to marble—
clean, strong, inherently powerful. Tall and lean, he carried himself with an air of noble distinction. One need
not be told he was the heir to the wealthiest dukedom
in England. Everything about him declared it.

"I . . . uh . . ." Grace faltered, somehow suddenly unable to speak. How in heaven's name was she going to explain her appearance there? "I was looking for my uncle . . ."

He quirked a brow. "Your uncle, is it? Well that's as good a tale as any. It happens all the time, although I would say you are certainly more inventive than the others. This is the first time I've ever had anyone come through my dressing room wall."

Grace watched then as he took up his coat—elegant black—and put it on, taking his time in adjusting his cuffs. *He is angry. He thinks I have come here in hopes of catching him as a husband, like one of the "helpless hopefuls,"* she thought to herself. *If only he knew the truth.* But it was too ridiculous a notion to even laugh at.

He was watching her, quite obviously awaiting her name, a thing she wasn't about to give. Instead she intended to get out of there as quickly as she could manage.

Grace started for the door. "Truly, I was looking for my uncle and I got lost . . ." The thought of sharing a dance with him now was beyond comprehension. "I'm sorry for the intrusion. I shouldn't have come here."

As she made for the door, the marquess stepped directly in her path, effectively preventing her from leaving. Grace's heart was pounding as she stared up at him. His eyes, she noticed, had changed from silver blue to smoky, dangerous slate.

"Surely you don't expect to leave so soon after you went through such effort to get here."

His smile had changed, too, into something infinitely more predatory. Grace swallowed against a sudden nervous tightening in her throat. "I'm afraid I do not understand, my lord."

"That, Miss Whoever-You-Are, is precisely my point. Didn't your mother ever warn you against the dangers of entering a man's bedchamber?"

Grace frowned at his sarcasm, a small part of her pulling deep inside. "My mother died when I was a child."

For a moment, she thought she saw a softening in his expression, but it didn't remain that way long. "Allow me to instruct you on the finer points of propriety." He took a step toward her. He was standing so near, Grace had to cock her head back to look at him, for he was at least six inches taller than she.

"There is a reason ladies of good breeding do not sneak their way into the bedchambers of men. A very good reason." He took her by the arms. She suddenly found it difficult to breathe. She wondered fleetingly if her feet still met the floor. She couldn't feel them. "A lady can never know for certain if the man in question is a gentleman or a blackguard who would seize the opportunity to ravish her."

"But you are a gentleman, sir. Your grandfather is the Duke of Westover."

His hands tightened on her arms and any light to his expression was instantly gone. "A fact, my lady, that should have been warning enough."

Before Grace realized what was happening, the marquess lowered his head, taking her mouth completely with his as he drew her hard against the length of his body.

Christian felt the girl stiffen against him and he tilted her head back to deepen the kiss, tasting her with his tongue, running a finger along the slender column of her throat until he felt her begin to tremble against him. He had had enough of female wiles and machinations to last a lifetime. These antics had been amusing at first, but this latest invasion of his privacy had gone far beyond the bounds. Had she arrived but five minutes earlier, she would have discovered him at his bath and he would now be embroiled in a mess he would have no hope of extricating himself from. He intended to teach the lady a lesson she would not soon forget. Only there was one problem. She didn't seem to realize he was punishing her. She wasn't resisting him. Instead she melted against him, taking his kiss and releasing a soft pleasing moan into his mouth.

Punishment be damned.

Christian kissed her back, forgetting for the moment who he was, where they were, how she'd come to be there. He indulged in the moment and in her—the softness of her skin, the faint herbal scent of her pale hair, the total innocence of a gesture she so obviously knew nothing about. A heat begin to kindle within him—more precisely within his groin—something he hadn't felt in a very long time. Even as he tightened his arms around her, Christian wondered that he should feel this way, with this woman, when no other had been able to stir him in quite some time. Perhaps it was the fact that in less than a fortnight, he was going to be marrying a woman he'd never even set eyes upon. He shouldn't be doing this, he knew, but in the very next moment, she pressed her hips forward against him. Christian nearly lost his mind.

The thought to drag her to the carpet and take what she was so obviously offering nearly overcame him. Every inch of him begged to know her, to test the softness of the skin along her belly. Instead he abruptly pulled away from her, even taking a step back. He watched her, her eyes half-closed, her breathing coming quickly, her mouth so damned desirable. One errant curl twisted over her forehead just above her brow, a twirl of amber honey. Slowly her eyes drifted more fully open and he suddenly knew the color of blue fire. She said nothing, just stood there, lips glossed from his kiss, and the way she was looking at him could only be termed one thing—

Dangerous.

Was she truly as innocent as her kiss hinted? Or was she simply playing the part of the unschooled maiden? She had to be a practiced seductress, he decided. What virgin would ever think to sneak her way into a man's bedchamber?

Christian stared at her hard. Who was this mystifying creature? She was lovely, yes. Her nose was small and straight, her lips a very becoming shade of pink—darker now that he'd kissed them. The silk of her bodice strained against the fullness of her breasts, breasts that were neither too small nor too large—but perfect. Honey-gold hair curled about her head; her eyes, wide and staring, were the brightest blue he'd ever seen. Still, any number of the other young women who had attempted to attract him before could lay claim to similar loveliness. How had she been able to arouse him so thoroughly when no other had?

He realized then there was something to her—a difference, a uniqueness he could not quite define. How else could he explain how he had gone from seeking to teach her a lesson in one moment to being the one who was overcome in the next? How had she managed to defeat the untouchable self-control he had spent most of his life perfecting?

He wondered who she was, but then told himself it was better to keep her a stranger. Once he was wed, any assignation between them would be impossible. He would not tolerate adultery in his marriage. He would demand fidelity from his wife and would practice the same. It could be no other way. So better to get her out of his dressing room as quickly as possible.

Christian crossed the room in two strides and opened the door. He stuck his head out and shouted "Jackson!" to the empty corridor. He stood, watching her askance as if he didn't quite trust she would stay on the other side of the room. In truth, it was himself he couldn't trust; he didn't think he would be able to restrain himself a second time from taking her.

When no response came to his summons, Christian went out into the hall. He was readying to call out again when a liveried footman appeared at the top of the stairs—a very large liveried footman who had become quite adept at handling occasions such as these. Lord knows he'd had plenty of experience.

"My apologies for not having come sooner, my lord. There was a *situation* belowstairs that required my attention."

Christian frowned. "There is a *situation* here that requires your attention as well."

The footman exhaled loudly. "Another one?"

Christian motioned toward his dressing room door. "Please escort the young lady back to the fête. And then make certain that all the doors on all the servants' passageways are securely bolted."

"Aye, my lord." Jackson headed for the door. "Miss, if you'll come with—"

But the footman turned back toward Christian with a look of confusion. "My lord?"

Christian made for the door, knowing even before he got there what he would find.

She had indeed gone, vanishing just as quickly as she had come, leaving Christian to stare at the vacant wall panel she'd fallen through moments earlier, far more befuddled than he cared to admit.

Lord Cholmeley dozed in the coach after they left the ball, leaving Grace to stare out the window at the rain-slick London streets and the hazy glow of the lamplights through the swirling fog. She was thankful for the solitude, for it allowed her to better come to terms with the unbelievable events of that evening.

She still wondered how she had made it out of that house after what had taken place in Lord Knighton's dressing room. She had taken the back stairs, slipping through the wall panel when Lord Knighton had gone into the hall. This time, however, she had found the way straight to the parlor as if her feet had always known the path. There she found her uncle and quickly asked him to take her home, telling him she was unwell—"a female ailment," she'd added. A well-worn excuse, she knew, but it was the only thing she could think of that wouldn't have had him instantly interrogating her. Instead he flushed pink and quickly set off to summon the coach and retrieve their cloaks.

As they had come through the entrance hall on their way to leave, Grace had spotted Lady Eleanor standing on the opposite side of the ballroom. At the sight of her, Grace had been filled with a feeling of regret. Eleanor had been so kind, so encouraging, and Grace felt she owed her some sort of explanation. But at that moment, she hadn't known if she would be able to frame a coherent sentence. Her heart had still been pounding from the thorough kissing Lord Knighton had given her.

All her life Grace had dreamed of her first kiss as something tender, soft, infinitely romantic. It would take place on a flowery river bank or on a ballroom terrace with the moonlight filtering down through the trees. The man who would deliver her this awe-inspiring tribute would be kind and handsome and filled with adoration for her. He would be the man of her dreams.

Lord Knighton was unquestionably handsome, but any further comparison to her dream after that was lost. When he had kissed her, her response had only been turbulent and she'd felt giddy, breathless, and utterly chaotic inside. Nothing about their meeting had been as Nonny had said it would be. There had been no enchantment, no gaiety, no blissful realization of having come face to face with her life's intended mate. There had been only fire and suddenness and a total clashing of beings, and something else she didn't quite understand— something that had shaken her to her very core.

The worst part of it was that she had utterly humiliated herself in front of the man she was to have called husband. She would never forget the darkness of his expression, the thinly veiled anger that had sparked in his eyes when he'd spoken to her, so very contrary to the light and softness she had always envisioned. He didn't adore her. He didn't even like her. And that was a far from propitious preamble to a marriage.

Grace waited until they had arrived back at the Cholmeley town house, retiring to the study for a claret, before she informed her uncle she could not possibly wed Lord Knighton.

Tedric responded with something a little less than familial understanding.

"The devil you won't wed him," he said as he poured himself a brandy. "I don't care if you do scream all the way down the aisle. You are going to wed Lord Knighton.'

"Uncle, please, surely there must be some other way to—"

"It is too late, Grace. He has already assumed the debt."

She stared at him. "What did you say?"

"The duke has paid my creditors in full. It was part of the agreement of the marriage. Westover wanted any outstanding annoyances seen to before news of the wedding came about. Twenty thousand pounds is a great deal of money, Grace. There will be ramifications if you refuse to marry Lord Knighton now. Legal ramifications. The Duke of Westover is not a man to be trifled with. He has already promised to bring a breach of promise suit against us both if you do not go through with the wedding."

"I did not take his money!"

"True . . . but you did sign the marriage contract. It will look as if you agreed to wed Lord Knighton strictly to get rid of my debts and then broke the agreement. You would have a very difficult time explaining to a jury that you had a change of heart about wedding Lord Knighton without having even seen the man."

But she had seen him, Grace thought to herself—quite a lot of him, in fact. An image of him standing over her in all his half-naked glory flashed through her mind before Tedric went on. "The duke will paint you an extortionist in a very public court proceeding. And he will win his judgement. In the end, the Cholmeley family will be ruined. Honor and respect hundreds of years in the making will be lost—the same honor and respect my mother spent her life trying to preserve."

And which you have spent your lifetime doing everything to destroy.

Grace looked to Nonny's portrait above the hearth and she knew that her uncle was right, even though he said these things for his own advantage. Nonny would have fulfilled her duty no matter the cost, no matter the circumstances—she would have wed Mephisto himself if she'd had to.

And because she had raised her granddaughter to follow that same ethic, Grace knew she would have no choice but to do the same.

Chapter Six

The vicar was grinning like a contented fiend—and well he should be. This was likely the most momentous event to have swept through his village since 1669, when one of Charles II's many mistresses had gotten waylaid by an unprecedented blizzard, causing her and her considerable entourage of servants to bed down with the locals for three days and three nights.

Little Biddlington was about as sleepy a hamlet as could be found, made up of Tudor-style timbered houses with overhanging upper storeys that lay hidden from the main London road by a steeply sloping vale and a tangled wall of trees. The Duke of Westover couldn't have chosen the location for the wedding of his heir with more care. Its inconspicuous locale had saved the village nearly two centuries earlier when invading Roundhead troops had been unable to find the place. A decade later, even the plague had missed it, though it struck every other village around them. Thus it would serve as the perfect setting for the wedding nobody knew was about to take place.

The church itself was quite ancient, various parts of it dating back to before the Norman conquest. Crosses cut into the stone doorway of the inner porch were said to have been made by the crusaders blunting their sword points as a dedication to peace on their return from the Holy Land. This, and the gravesite of Mary Pottinger, who had died aged one hundred and seven in 1722, had been pointed out by the vicar, Mr. Weston, upon their arrival; they were, it would seem, the two most distinctive features of the village.

Within the space of the next few hours, though, Little Biddlington's anonymity would be forgotten and Mr. Weston's tiny place in history would be secure. He would no longer fall to obscurity—living, preaching, and then dying in this hidden place, unknown to the rest of the world. Instead he would be known to history as the man who had secretly wed the heir to the wealthiest peer in England. Perhaps they would erect a monument to record the occasion for posterity's sake, right next to the headstone of one-hundred-and-seven-year-old Mary Pottinger. At the very least it would give Mr. Weston and his flock something to gossip about over tea for years to come.

And so the vicar grinned.

Christian, his grandfather the duke, his mother, and his sister had left London before dawn, traveling in an unmarked coach rented just for the occasion. If not for Eleanor's lively chatter about the various landmarks they passed, there would not have been a word spoken at all.

Immediately upon their arrival in the village, the Westover footman had roused the vicar from sleep, presenting him the special license granted and signed by the archbishop himself. "It would be an honor to perform this service, Your Grace," he proclaimed to the old duke from beneath his slouching night cap. He then performed his ablutions and donned his vestments with an alacrity that had surprised them all and stood now at the chancel, still grinning at his good fortune. The young lady—Christian's intended wife—was to arrive with her uncle by a separate route. She had yet to make an appearance.

Christian stood at the end of the church's narrow center aisle, awaiting his bride's arrival. He glanced at the duke, who sat alone on the first bench with his hand fisted tightly around the ball of his cane. How triumphant he must feel, Christian thought, at having lived long enough to see this day, the day he'd waited so patiently for through most of Christian's twenty-nine years. If he had ever wondered before why his grandfather hadn't sought to claim his due part of their bargain earlier, it was patently apparent to him now. He need only look to the emptiness of the seat beside the old duke and consider the significance of the day. His father had died twenty years earlier on that same day. Christopher Wycliffe had been twenty-nine. It was only fitting that at the same age and date the duke had lost his only son, he should exact his terms of the bargain he'd made with his grandson. *Eye for an eye . . . tooth for a tooth . . . life for a life . . .*

Long-hidden memories of that horrible day began to come to light despite Christian's resistance. Even now he could still see the throngs of mourners who had come all the way from London, huddling together beneath the dripping branches of the great Westover elms to pay their last respects. He would never forget the cold that had numbed him to his bones, the wet dripping from the trees, the thick misty fog that had shrouded the Wycliffe family cemetery. Nor would he ever escape the memory of the haunting toll of the church bell that had rung out the traditional nine times and then another nine-and-twenty for each year of Christopher Wycliffe's short life.

An ague had taken him, the family had said, and everyone had believed them. No one could ever have suspected the truth as they looked at the newly titled nine-year-old marquess standing beside his grandfather the duke, shivering in the rain.

Christian looked away from his grandfather to where his mother and his sister sat on the bench across the aisle. Frances, Lady Knighton, had been the celebrated beauty of her time, inspiring volumes of poetry and setting a style that had been emulated throughout many a social season. Once a brilliant sable brown, her hair had since grayed and the pale skin of her face was not quite as smooth as it had once been. Still she continued to attract notice whenever she went out as a figure of elegance and grace and beauty.

Since the death of her husband, though, most of her time was spent hidden away from society, reading her Bible or passing her days in silent prayer. The past twenty years had done little to remove the taint of sadness from her eyes and Christian often thought that that day had not only seen his father killed, but his mother's spirit destroyed as well. For months afterward they'd worried she might do herself a harm. The only thing that had kept her from it, Christian knew, had been the child she'd carried within her—her daughter, his sister, Eleanor.

From the moment she was born, Eleanor was everything that was gentle and good in the world. Christian had watched her grow, blossoming from a silly little tomboy with ragged-hemmed skirts and dirt beneath her fingernails to the refined, accomplished young woman she now was. He had seen her through scraped shins, quinsy, and a rivalry with the neighboring earl's daughter, Lady Amanda Barrington, that had ended with one unruly tangle in the midst of a trout pond. And he would see her safely wed, he said to himself, not in an arranged match like his, but with a man she both loved and respected, one who would love and respect her in kind.

It was for those two women and none other that Christian would see this day through; he would do anything—even marry a stranger—to protect them.

Eleanor, ever the optimist, had tried to ease what she perceived to be Christian's premarital apprehension at their arrival in the village early that morning.

"She will be lovely," she'd said, straightening his neckcloth and brushing a hand over his coat. "You will see."

Christian had simply nodded, but inwardly he had wondered what it would matter whether his bride was or wasn't lovely. He would still have to wed her. He'd signed his name to the contracts. Even now he couldn't believe he'd done it, agreeing to wed a woman he had yet to set eyes upon. But he had seen her name indelibly written on the contracts. *Lady Grace Ledys.* A relation of some sort of the Marquess of Cholmeley, for he'd also seen that name listed as the girl's guardian. A lovely name, yes—but who was she? And what sort of girl would agree to wed a man she, too, had never seen?

There came a stirring at the back of the church then. The time had come for him to face his bride. Christian turned. Now to be done with it.

A slight figure gowned in pale blue stood at the end of the aisle on the arm of an older man, no doubt Lord Cholmeley. The light shone in brightly behind her and Christian wasn't able to clearly see her. As she started walking toward him he thought for a moment he recognized something familiar about her. But that was impossible, he told himself. They'd never met.

He watched her approach. Golden hair shimmered beneath a charming halo of flowers in the morning sunlight that was beaming down through the ancient church's stained-glass windows. Christian didn't even realize he was holding his breath until she walked out of the light and he finally saw her. His breath left him in a rush as he took in her delicate features, pale complexion, and her eyes—the same eyes that had peered up at him from the floor of his dressing room the night of his sister's come-out ball.

Before Christian could wonder what to think, she was standing beside him and the vicar began the service. While Mr. Weston spoke, enunciating as if an entire congregation filled the church, Christian looked again to his bride. Her eyes were fixed on the vicar, and she was listening attentively to his words. Christian noticed her hands shaking slightly beneath the posy of flowers she held. She must have sensed Christian watching her, for she looked at him warily before returning her attention to the vicar.

What the devil had she been doing that night, creeping about through the servants' passages? His initial confusion at the sight of her began quickly to tighten into distrust. Had she been spying on him? What else could have been her purpose? He rather doubted she had been seeking to acquaint herself with the layout of the house.

When the vicar asked if the couple had come both willingly and without reservation, Christian hesitated only a second before giving his assent. On through the liturgy he barely heard the vicar's words, but managed to respond when prompted. He slid the ring—a Westover heirloom sapphire surrounded by diamonds that had been both his mother's and his grandmother's before her—onto the lady's slender finger. In the space of a moment they were suddenly and permanently joined. It didn't seem possible that it could be over so quickly.

After the ceremony closed, the duke stood from his bench, thanked the vicar, and rewarded him with a pouch of coins before turning to leave. His duty was done, his utmost wish fulfilled.

Christian and Grace each quickly signed their names to the parish register, exchanging thanks and farewells with the vicar. Christian then looked to his bride, this stranger—his wife—and offered her his arm. "Madam?"

Outside, beside the gravestone of one-hundred-and-seven-year-old Mary Pottinger, Eleanor and his mother were smiling. When Christian and Grace emerged from the church, Eleanor came forward, embracing her brother with a kiss on his cheek.

"Congratulations, Christian. I am so happy for you. You see, I told you she would be lovely."

He scarcely managed a nod before she then turned to Lady Grace, welcoming her to the family with a kiss and an embrace. "You are a beautiful bride, Grace. And it is just as I said to you. We are now sisters."

Christian stared at Eleanor. She already knew his wife? Why the devil hadn't she told him? Was everyone in on this deception?

Lady Frances came forward and took her son's hands. Her voice was soft with emotion. "Thank you, Christian. I know how difficult this day must be for you. I want you to know you are more than any mother could ever hope for in her son."

For a moment, he swore he caught a glimpse of the woman she had once been before the emptiness came to darken her eyes once again. "If there is any good to what I am, Mother, it is only due to you."

Lady Frances looked quickly away from him to where Eleanor and Grace stood. "She seems a lovely girl, Christian. I know it seems impossible, given the circumstances, but I hope you will find happiness together."

Christian could only nod before the duke stepped toward him, shattering the moment between mother and son with a thunk of his damnable cane.

"Did you think I'd have you wed a gorgon?" When Christian didn't respond, he said, "I've arranged for a coach to take you to Westover for the night. The staff has been alerted and is prepared for your arrival. One night, Christian. That was our agreement. By the time you return to London, the announcements will have been made in the papers."

Christian simply nodded at the reminder that he had one more task to perform in order to fulfill his part of their bargain. And the sooner he saw to it the better. He turned to Grace, who stood waiting beside him, and offered her his arm. "Shall we depart, my lady?"

He handed her inside the coach then climbed in to sit opposite her. They waited while the coachman made his way to his seat. Christian watched as Grace waved out the window, calling farewells to her uncle and Eleanor just before they began to pull away. A riot of questions were galloping through his thoughts. Who was she? Where had his grandfather found her? Just how much money did she and her family stand to receive from this alliance?

It wasn't until the church had disappeared behind them that Grace turned to face him. She looked uncomfortable, to say the least, alone now with a man who was both stranger and husband. She said in an effort to break the awkward silence between them, "I know what you must be thinking, my lord."

"Do you?"

"The other night at the ball. It isn't at all what it seems—"

"No? And just what was your purpose in coming to my dressing room, madam? Did you wish to view the goods before exchanging the vows?"

"As I told you that night, I was trying to find my uncle."

Christian smirked. "And naturally one would think to look first in another man's dressing room. I promise you, my lady, I'm not in the habit of entertaining gentlemen in my private chambers."

"It wasn't supposed to happen as it did. We were just supposed to share a dance. That's all. My uncle had arranged it with your sister. You wouldn't even have known who I was. But I had second thoughts, so when Eleanor went to look for you, I tried to find my uncle so we could leave before you came back with her. Only I got confused in the crowd and somehow ended up in the servants' passage, which wouldn't have been any trouble, except that someone locked the door behind me."

Christian didn't want to believe her, even though her explanation sounded plausible. Either that or she had worked very hard at making it up. "You said you had wanted a dance. Pray, why?"

Grace didn't immediately answer. Instead she looked out the window a moment or two, her brow drawn close in thought beneath the rim of her straw bonnet.

"I had been forbidden to meet you," she said softly. "I thought that perhaps by at least dancing with you, even if you didn't know who I was, I would somehow be able to reassure myself that I was doing the right thing in becoming your wife. It sounds silly now I know in the face of it all, but at the time, it was all I had."

Her eyes shone only with a vulnerable sincerity. She was telling the truth.

Christian had anticipated so many things in the woman his grandfather would choose for his wife. He had expected she would be inspired to wed him for his title and the Westover wealth, those two qualifications that had made him such a coveted prize on the marriage market. He had even been prepared for someone as ruthless and devious as the duke. But Grace seemed to have none of these qualities. Her honesty and absolute candor startled him. They were things to which he was wholly unaccustomed. They were things the Dukes of Westover had been taught since time immemorial to suspect.

He looked at her, hiding his thoughts. "You said you changed your mind. About having a dance with me."

She nodded.

"Why?"

Her reluctance kept her from answering a moment. When she finally did speak, her voice was barely above a whisper. "It was the way they all kept looking at me, like I didn't belong there."

Surely this vulnerability, this innocence could not be real, especially in one hand-picked by his grandfather. How long ago had the duke decided upon her as the chosen bride for the Westover heir? Long enough for her to rehearse every word she would say, every gesture she would make? Perhaps somehow the duke had realized Christian's own secret plan, one that would foil his grandfather's final triumph in their lifelong battle of wills. It was a battle Christian could never allow himself to lose; the risk was too great. Even as he found himself intrigued by her, he knew he must never lower his guard, no matter how lovely, no matter how exceptional his new wife might prove to be.

Chapter Seven

"We have arrived at Westover, madam."

Grace slowly opened her eyes onto a darkened coach interior and the shadowed silhouette of Lord Knighton sitting across from her. She glanced out the side window. The sky outside was dark, starless, the moon a hazy gleam of light behind a thickening fog. Goodness, it was night. How long had she been sleeping?

"Two hours," the marquess said as if clearly reading her thoughts. "Since Wexburgh." He then opened the coach door and alighted, offering his hand to assist Grace down.

She was confronted on the outside by an immense structure that was part castle, part manor house, even part dungeon, issuing from the twilight shadows like the eerie backdrop of the gothic tales she so enjoyed reading. It was surely the most imposing domicile she'd ever seen—twice the size, if not more, of Ledysthorpe. However, its vastness did not in any way signify comfort. At Ledysthorpe, from the moment they arrived, visitors were embraced by a feeling of unmistakable welcome from the servants who came at once to wave in greeting or the numerous dogs yapping excitedly at their heels. Cast in the gray and mist of dusk, this place only gave an impression of cold, austere foreboding. It seemed almost to warn the visitor away rather than draw them in.

They stood in a courtyard surrounded on four sides by somber stone walls that frowned sternly down upon them. Two of the walls were cornered by tall ivy-covered towers and, except for the gated archway their coach had entered through, there appeared no other way out.

After speaking briefly to the coachman, Lord Knighton started across the graveled drive toward wide front steps set beneath an imposing door surely three times the height of him. Grace followed. As they reached the top of the stairs, the door crept open to reveal a grim-faced, elderly butler.

"Good evening, my lord."

Lord Knighton barely acknowledged the man's greeting except to say a curt "Ambrose" as he walked past on his way into the main entrance hall.

He noticed that Grace hadn't followed. He turned. "My lady?"

"You aren't going to carry me across the threshold?"

He stared at her a moment. "I beg your pardon?"

"I thought it was a rule that all grooms carried their brides across the threshold."

"A rule?"

Grace nodded. "To neglect to do so could bring dire consequences to the marriage." Well, that is, consequences more dire than the fact that the bride and groom were utter strangers.

"I suppose that would be an issue for one who believes in that sort of nonsense."

Grace merely looked at him. She didn't move from the other side of the threshold. "I would hate to be responsible for tempting ill fortune."

Christian stared at her. Ambrose, she noticed, stood watching the entire exchange.

"My lady, unless you think to sleep in the doorway, I suggest you walk yourself through that door.'

"But I—"

"Oh, good God, woman, all right!"

Grace took a startled breath as Christian suddenly swept her up and into his arms. It was the closest she had gotten to him all day and she could smell the clean, male scent of him, sandalwood and something else— something spicier. The sudden sense of being held by him, the warmth of her body against his, was new and oddly comforting and when he brought her inside and set her on her feet, she instantly missed it.

He, however, seemed wholly unaffected by it.

"I hope that will set fortune at ease," Christian said and turned to walk further inside.

The outside of the building had intimidated her; the inside, however, was utterly overwhelming. Marble Roman statuary were set around the circular chamber in alcoves cut into the granite walls. Rather than being set where they might be better viewed and appreciated, they had been placed at such a height as to give anyone entering the sense of being stared down upon by a crowd of overlords. Thick alabaster columns measured off the perimeter of the room and the Westover ducal coat of arms, carved in stone, was emblazoned above the arched central corridor. As they walked, their footsteps echoed on the marble floor and carried upward to the lofty heights of the ceiling, a ceiling that was buttressed with oaken beams the size of ship's masts.

A figure emerged from the shadows at the far end of the hall holding a branch of flickering candles, a housekeeper in dark skirts and a white linen mobcap who surprisingly attempted a small smile as she curtsied. She came to a standstill beside Ambrose's rigid posture.

"Good evening, Mrs. Stone," Christian said.

The housekeeper bobbed. "Lord Knighton, 'tis good to see you again."

"Allow me to introduce my wife, Lady Knighton, to you both."

The butler bowed his head dutifully, murmuring "Madam" while the housekeeper dipped quickly into another curtsey. "Welcome to Westover, my lady."

"You will show Lady Knighton to our chambers and assist her with her things. We've had a long journey and we will be leaving first thing on the morrow. Anything her ladyship desires, please see to it."

The two answered in unison, "Yes, my lord."

Grace looked at Christian. "You aren't coming?"

"I have some business to attend to. Ambrose and Mrs. Stone are quite capable of directing you, unless there is some other rule that requires bridegrooms to carry their wives over every threshold in the house."

Grace shook her head, uncertain as to whether he was mocking her. Instead she wondered at his sudden neglect. Did he mean to leave her alone in this vast cavern of a house for the night—on her wedding night? "I just thought that—"

But Christian wasn't listening to her. Instead he turned and began issuing orders to the butler. "Please instruct the cook to have our dinner served in the dining hall. A footman can show Lady Knighton there when she has finished upstairs."

Grace stared up at Christian, wondering if he would ever shed the mantle of cold, armored indifference he seemed to wear. He had been polite all during their journey, and though not overly interested in conversation, she had figured him tired and had thought they would get further acquainted once they reached their destination.

Apparently that was not to be.

But before Grace could voice any agreement or disagreement to these plans, Christian turned and strode toward a side door, the sober echoing of his bootsteps the only sound in the hall. Grace merely stood and watched him go as he closed the door firmly behind him.

"My lady?" Mrs. Stone said finally.

Grace looked at her.

"If you would be so kind as to follow me, I will show you to your chambers."

She gave one last look at the door where Christian had disappeared before she simply nodded and followed in the wake of the light from the woman's flickering candelabrum.

Mrs. Stone led Grace up a cheerless flight of stairs to an upper corridor, paneled in dark walnut and lined with portraits of Westover ancestors bearing expressions as austere and menacing as the house they inhabited. They glowered at her from their shadowed and gilded perches and once she even imagined she had seen the eyes of one of them, a most severe-looking Tudor fellow in jerkin, hose, and cartwheel ruff, move to follow her progress down the hall.

She put it off as a play of the candlelight on the walls, but as they continued, Grace found herself glancing at the binding of the novel she'd carried in with her from the carriage to make certain its title still read *The Mysteries of Udolpho* and not suddenly *The Mysteries of Westover Hall*. This night certainly had all the trappings of a tale worthy of Mrs. Radcliffe, complete with the ancient castle and the somber butler who looked as if he himself might be of the netherworld.

Once they were a fair distance from the entrance hall, Mrs. Stone's demeanor seemed to ease a bit. Soon she even began to chat. "We hope you will enjoy your stay here at Westover, my lady, even if 'tis to be for the one night. 'Twill be your home one day when Lord Knighton becomes the new duke. If there is anything you need, please do not hesitate to ask."

The thought of making her home in this solemn place was most unsettling to her and brought her to remembering something Nonny had once said to her. *A lady makes her husband's home her own.* Grace wondered if her grandmother could have foreseen the gloom of this chilling place.

"Thank you." Grace thought for a moment, then said, "I wonder if you might answer something for me, Mrs. Stone?"

The housekeeper stopped before a massive oaken door, took up the vast ring of keys that hung at her waist, and fitted one inside the lock. "Of course, my lady. Anything."

"Have you been in service here at Westover very long?"

Mrs. Stone turned the handle and pushed the door wide, stepping back to face Grace on her answer. "Oh, quite some thirty years or more." She entered the room and began lighting the numerous sconces and candle stands that were set about the room, continuing as she did. "My mother was in service here before me and married my father, who worked in the stables, so I grew up here at Westover. I started as a scullery maid, then became an upper chamber maid, a nursery maid, and worked my way through the ranks to housekeeper these past ten years or more. My own daughter and nieces are maids here now, too."

Grace nodded. "Then you have known the Wycliffe family very long?"

"Oh, indeed, my lady, very long. I was a nursery maid to Lord Knighton when he was a child."

Grace tried to imagine Lord Knighton as a boy, playing along these same halls, his laughter echoing throughout the lofty ceilings, but an image just wouldn't present itself. She returned her attention to the housekeeper. "Since you have béen here so long, perhaps you can tell me if this house and this family have always been so filled with the misery they are now."

Mrs. Stone stopped immediately and turned to face Grace. Her mouth was fixed, her eyes suddenly clouded.

"I'm sorry," Grace said. "Perhaps I shouldn't have asked."

"It is all right. You've every right to know." The housekeeper glanced to the door, her voice quieting. "No, my lady. It has not always been thus. Westover used to be a happy place filled with much laughter."

"What is it, then, that has brought such sadness to this family?"

. Again Mrs. Stone glanced to the door. "It is only since the death of the previous marquess—your husband's father—some twenty years ago. Lord Christopher's passing brought such a terrible sorrow to them all, one that has lingered even now. 'Twas his lordship's passing that brought along the rift between the old duke and his lordship, your husband. A terrible rift it is, too, one that has never been breached. And poor Lady Frances. Such a ray of happiness she once was. She has never gotten past losing her husband. It was as if when his lordship died, so did life for everyone else in the family." She said then, her voice lightening, "But not every Wycliffe has been so touched by it. You've met Lady Eleanor?"

Grace smiled. "Oh, yes, and I like her very much."

"Ah, such a sweet child she is, Lady Eleanor, so very different in temperament from the others. She is a true blessing and so dear to your husband the marquess. Without her, I should think his lordship would have—"

"That will do, Mrs. Stone."

The housekeeper turned wide eyes across the room, staring with obvious dismay at the doorway where Ambrose had suddenly appeared. The butler's face was fixed most unhappily.

"His lordship has asked me to inform Lady Knighton that dinner is ready to be served in the dining hall." He looked to Grace. "Mrs. Stone can see to the further unpacking of your things, my lady."

His manner was insolent, yet polite enough to avoid any suggestion of insubordination. From Mrs. Stone's expression, though, it was easy to see she was terrified of the man, a terror that was obviously rooted in years of experience.

"Thank you, Ambrose," Grace said. "You may tell his lordship I will be down shortly."

The butler remained at the door. "I am to show you to the dining hall *now,* my lady." His eyes settled on her. "His lordship requests it."

While she would have preferred having Mrs. Stone direct her belowstairs, Grace didn't wish to be the cause of any unneeded trouble for the housekeeper. Thus she decided to go with the stoic Ambrose, although she wasn't much pleased about it. She didn't like him, not at all, and she sensed he didn't much care for her either.

"Very well. Mrs. Stone, if it wouldn't be too much trouble, I should like to have a bath before going to bed to wash away the dust from our journey."

"Indeed, my lady, I will have the bath ready for you when you finish." Mrs. Stone dipped into a curtsey, smiling despite Ambrose's sullen frown.

Grace walked in silence behind the butler along the darkened corridors she had just come through. The only light came from the single candlestick Ambrose carried before him. In his company, the house had grown even gloomier than before, like a lowering stormcloud on an already overcast day. He said nothing to her except to give a warning to her to watch her step once as they turned. Even then he seemed to have spoken more out of custom than any concern for her. When they reached the stairs to descend to the lower floor, Grace finally spoke out.

"Ambrose, a moment if you will."

He stopped, turning to regard her.

"I hope you will not fault Mrs. Stone for my curiosity earlier. It was I who initiated the conversation you overheard, not she."

The butler's face took on a ghoulish quality in the light from his candle, the sharp angles of his face more pronounced. "I am aware of that, madam, and I see no reason to discuss the matter further with Mrs. Stone. However, in the future, should you have any questions that concern either the marquess or the members of his family, I feel certain that his lordship would prefer that you direct them to him rather than the servants. We of the household are not privy to anything more than conjecture about the events of the past."

"Indeed, Ambrose. However, may I remind you that his lordship's family is now also my family as well?"

The butler looked at her a long moment. Finally he said, "Of course, my lady." He then turned without another word and continued down the shadowed stairwell.

They walked for some time, past suits of armor and ancient objects of weaponry that glimmered with a sinister cast in the candlelight. Hoping to ease the direction of her thoughts, Grace found herself wondering wryly how many heads had been lopped off by the various instruments of torture they passed—and if any of them had been newly wedded Westover brides.

They arrived at an arched double doorway and the butler stepped aside, allowing her to precede him. Grace found herself at the entrance to a vast chamber set with a long polished table that stretched across its center. The table would easily seat thirty and when filled would hold enough to feed the entire village of Ledysthorpe. At the far end of it, nearest the blazing hearth, sat Lord Knighton, looking rather like the king at his court. Only there weren't any courtiers present, no performing troubadours, just the empty chair to his right that had been set with a service obviously meant for her.

"Good evening, my lord," she said at her approach, leaving Ambrose to stand at the door.

Christian rose from his seat. "Good evening, my lady. I trust you found the ducal chambers to your liking?"

Grace took her seat. "What little I saw of them before Ambrose arrived to escort me to dinner was most agreeable."

"My apologies. I had thought to give you more time to ready yourself for dinner, but the cook had been awaiting our arrival. The food was already prepared."

Grace wondered that he had abandoned his pressing

business to share the meal with her, but kept that thought to herself. She unfolded the linen napkin, placing it in her lap. Two footmen came forward from the nethershadows to serve them, ladling out steaming turtle soup into each bowl.

"I was wondering, my lord," Grace said after taking a sip of her claret, "why is it we are only staying here at Westover Hall one night? If you have business to attend to, we could certainly stay longer."

Christian didn't look at her, but instead took up his soup spoon. "There are more urgent matters in London that require my being there. It will not take long for me to see to what needs attending here. We will leave for town on the morrow as planned."

He began eating, as if to say the conversation was at an end. Grace, however, couldn't help her curiosity. "But if we are to leave on the morrow, wouldn't it have been a more prudent choice to simply pass the night someplace between Little Biddlington and London, or perhaps even just return to the city rather than travel nearly a day's ride west?"

Christian laid down his spoon. He looked at her squarely. "Yes, my lady, it would have been a more prudent idea, and had I a choice in the matter, that is precisely what we would have done. But there is a tradition among the Westovers, one of which you are unaware. Call it one of your 'rules,' if you will. You see, all new brides must spend their wedding night in the Westover ducal bed—more precisely, they must lose their virginity in it. It is believed that doing so ensures the next male heir."

And at that, Grace's mouth fell open. A moment later, her soup spoon clattered to the floor.

Chapter Eight

When Grace returned abovestairs after dinner, she found a copper bathtub awaiting her in the withdrawing room set off from the main ducal bedchamber. The water was strewn with soft-colored rose petals and it steamed invitingly, as a freshly stoked fire crackled in the marble hearth nearby. Mrs. Stone had set out everything Grace might need—soap that was stamped with the Westover coat of arms, a washcloth, towels, and a thick robe. She had even placed Grace's nightshift and hairbrush on the dressing table with a note that she should call with the bell pull for assistance in dressing afterward.

Anxious for the bath, Grace quickly began to undress herself, unfastening the buttons at her bodice and slipping her gown from her shoulders. As she stepped from it, she looked at the silk pooled at her feet, the gown she had worn to become a wife. She hadn't truly thought of it as her marriage dress, for it was not the one she had always dreamed of wearing—the gown Nonny and her own mother had worn as brides. *If you wear this dress,* Nonny had promised her, *your marriage will certainly be blessed with the happiness and contentment that both I and your mother found in our own marriages.*

But with the duke's haste for the wedding, her grandmother's gown had not arrived in time from Ledysthorpe. Grace had instead worn the most comely gown she owned, the same gown she had worn to the ball when she had fallen through the wall into Lord Knighton's dressing room. After what had happened that night, she hoped the gown wasn't ill fated.

Grace picked up the gown and draped it carefully

across the foot of the bed—the ducal bed—the Westover
ducal bed. It was a large, heavily carved thing set high
off the ground and draped in dark rich velvet. The words
Christian had spoken to her during their dinner together
that night whispered through her thoughts.

*All new brides must spend their wedding nights in the
Westover ducal bed—more precisely, they must lose their
virginity in it . . .*

Grace was not totally naïve about what took place
between a man and a woman, with the eventual result
of children. She had been raised in the country among
horses and dogs and farm animals. While it all seemed
quite surreal to her, somehow she had always thought
that when *that* time came in her life, she would know
something more of the person with whom she would
share the experience than simply his name.

Grace turned from the bed and pulled the pins from
her hair, letting the weight of it fall to her waist. She
stepped into the tub, slipping beneath the clear water,
its warmth enveloping her body and setting her skin atin-
gle. As she bathed, she considered the idea that this
night might bring about the conception of a child. It was
the reason she had been chosen, she knew, the reason
the duke had come looking for a bride for his grandson.
It was the expectation of most every society bride—to
produce an heir and a spare. What a different mother
she would be she thought—not at all like the ladies who
had come to visit her grandmother at Ledysthorpe during her childhood.

From the time she had turned thirteen, Nonny had
allowed Grace to sit and take tea with her and her
guests, despite the disapproving looks of the other ladies.
Grace had sat quietly, sipping at her cup, listening as
they talked of seeing their own children for naught but
a quarter hour every day as if it were a chore and not
a privilege. How they would proudly boast of delivering
their children from nearly the moment of their birth into
the hands of a hired wet nurse and then, later, to a
nursery maid. How they would then evince astonishment
when their children grew up ill mannered and speaking
in the vernacular of their caretakers. Listening to them
day in and day out had only shown Grace that when the

time came for her to have her own children, fashionable or not, she would embrace her role as mother faithfully. She would sing them to sleep, she would feed them at her own breast, and she would teach them the same ideals Nonny had passed on to her. More than anything else, Grace was determined that she should never give her children cause to believe they had not been wanted.

Grace took up the small ewer that stood beside the tub and leaned forward to rinse herself. As she dipped the ewer into the tub a second time, she heard the faint sound of a door opening and closing in the adjoining bedchamber. She went instantly still. He had come? So soon? She waited but the only sound she heard was the nervous drumming of her heart and the water dripping down around her.

Grace rose from the water and was just stepping out of the tub when the door across the room suddenly swung open. She did the only thing she could think of. She quickly grabbed the robe that had been set out for her, shoving her arms into the sleeves as she said, "Please allow me my privacy, my lord. I'm at my bath now."

But it wasn't Lord Knighton who stood there at all. Instead it was a young maid of no more than eighteen years bearing a tray in both hands.

She bobbed a quick curtsey. "Beggin' pardon, my lady. I was just bringing you your tea. Lord Knighton thought you might like a bit before retiring this e'ening."

Feeling quite foolish, Grace took up a towel and began rubbing the wet ends of her hair. "Yes, thank you. Please just set it there."

"Aye, my lady. Would you be wishing me to help you brush out your hair and dress for bed, my lady?"

Grace looked at the maid, tempted to accept. In the end, she decided it would be better to occupy herself as much as possible while she waited for Lord Knighton's arrival. "No, thank you. I think I can manage."

The maid bobbed again before leaving, closing the door behind her.

Grace walked to the tea tray, dropping into the chair in her favorite way with her feet tucked up beneath her as she took up the teapot and poured herself a cup. It

had been thoughtful of him, she mused, to send the tea
to her. Grace took a sip and instantly coughed. Her eyes
watered and her throat burned. The tea was laced with
something quite strong, spirits more potent than the occasional bit of claret she was accustomed to. She very
nearly abandoned the tea, except that after a few seconds, it began to fill her belly with a most pleasant
warmth.

Grace took up the cup and drew another sip, wishing
that Lord Knighton had thought to have the maid in-
clude a biscuit along with the tea. She realized now she
was quite hungry. Dinner, while fine, hadn't tempted her
beyond a sparse few bites. In truth, she hadn't been able
to eat much of anything after hearing Lord Knighton's
comments about the traditions of the ducal bed. Grace
took another sip of the tea, peering into the pot that
was yet two thirds full. Taking up the tray, she headed
for the ducal bedchamber, thinking she would just have
another cup while she changed into her nightclothes and
brushed out her hair and waited for Lord Knighton to
come.

When next Grace noticed the time, it was nearing midnight. She had emptied both the cup and the teapot. She
had even fashioned a ribbon in her hair, tying it in a
pretty bow atop her head. She wore her favorite nightdress, the white linen one with the small pearl buttons
along the front. She had read three chapters further in
her novel. Still there came no sign of Lord Knighton.

Grace yawned, sinking back against the thick, goose-
down pillows on the ridiculously large ducal bed. She
wiggled her toes, which did not even reach halfway to
the other end of the mattress, and decided that the bed
could easily sleep herself, Lord Knighton, and Ambrose
and Mrs. Stone too. Perhaps even the footmen who had
served them their dinner. Grace giggled at the image
that presented itself, that of sacrificing her innocence on
the great Westover ducal bed while the unflappable Ambrose glared at her from the other side of the mattress.

She stared at the huge tree-trunk-sized posters and
wondered why the figures carved in the dark gleaming
wood suddenly appeared to be dancing. She thought of
the other virginal Westover brides who had lain on this

same spot before her. Had the figures danced for them as well? Perhaps that was part of the tradition. She glanced over the side of the mattress, looking for the floor, but she couldn't see it. No doubt the bed had been chosen for this particular tradition because it was so high, leaving frightened young maidens less willing to flee for fear of a broken neck.

The clock struck half past twelve and still Grace was alone. Perhaps Lord Knighton had perceived her dismay at dinner—surely the sound of her soup spoon dropping to the floor and the sight of her mouth hanging open had given him some indication. Perhaps he had decided to forgo the tradition of this bed and this night. The candle on the table beside her was guttering low; the others had long since gone out. The fire in the hearth was burning more slowly with each turn of the clock.

Grace's vigilance in watching the door started to falter as she fought to keep her eyes open. She touched a hand to the side of her face. The tea and whatever had accompanied it had brought a flush to her cheeks, warming her throughout. She kicked at the coverlet. It was growing very late. She closed her eyes, thinking that Lord Knighton must surely have decided to retire for the evening after all, but to another bedchamber, in another part of this gloomy, spooky house. Yes, that must be it . . .

In what seemed the very next moment, there came a click from across the room, echoing strangely to her ears. Grace opened her eyes with some effort—and even then only managed to pry them halfway—to see a figure hovering at the edge of the wavering shadows given off by the ebbing fire. It was the maid again, she mused on a half-conscious thought, and if she was returning with more tea, Grace hoped that this time it might be with something to eat.

" 'Scuse me," she measured out, "but might I trouble you to bring me a biscuit, please?" Grace wondered why her own voice sounded so odd and woolly to her ears.

There came no answer. Grace blinked, watching as the figure drew closer to the bed. Funny, she thought, but the maid appeared to have grown taller from the last time she had come, and broader, especially across the shoulders.

The figure emerged into the light and Grace saw that it was not the maid after all.

It was Lord Knighton standing in the bedchamber with her. He was wearing a dressing robe, and his feet were bare underneath. He was watching her intently. And he was coming toward the bed.

Grace's last thought before he reached her was that apparently he had decided to uphold the Westover tradition after all.

Chapter Nine

Christian watched Grace as he started toward her. It was late, he knew, and a small part of him had thought perhaps she'd have fallen asleep. He hadn't expected to be so long in coming there.

He'd spent the better part of the past few hours with a bottle of brandy, telling himself he was allowing Grace time to prepare for the inevitable conclusion to the evening, when in truth, it was he who had needed the time. Not since he'd been a boy of fifteen, when he'd confronted his own virginity with Lord Whitby's seventeen-year-old daughter in the hayloft of the Westover stables, had he felt so awkward and uncertain.

He was about to consummate his marriage, while at the same time he would *not* consummate his marriage.

At nine years of age, a boy is not yet fully able to fathom the repercussions of his actions. He does without thinking, never considering what the consequences might be five, ten, or even twenty years later. So when Christian had stood facing his grandfather the duke hours after watching his father die, his only thought had been to protect the family he had remaining, his mother and his unborn sibling. He would have agreed to cut off his left arm if he'd had to, but the duke had had other thoughts in mind.

"You will live the life I choose for you, Christian. You will follow the course I have chosen for you; you will wed when I decide you will; and, when the time comes, you will give me your firstborn son."

How easy it had seemed all those years ago, how far off in the future, how *fair*. Two lives for two lives; his mother and the babe she carried for his own and that of a child that he couldn't even begin to imagine. It had seemed almost as if he were getting the better part of the bargain and even as his mother had begged him not to, Christian had entered into the duke's agreement, scribbling his nine-year-old signature across a contract the duke had hastily drawn up. What choice had he? If he hadn't, the duke would have seen them all destroyed.

So Christian had passed the next two decades living the life that had been chosen for him. He had now married the woman chosen by his grandfather and he would do his duty in making her truly and completely his wife—but he would be damned if he was going to play the role of Westover stud and beget the next unfortunate male heir while that diabolical old man yet lived. So he had made a plan. He would take his wife's virginity, honoring his agreement with the duke, but he would never bring the encounter to its usual conclusion by spilling his seed within her womb. In that, his grandfather would be denied the life of yet another innocent. It was the only way Christian could endure living with the bargain he'd made, the only way he could face himself in the mirror every day. And for that reason above all else, he was determined that he should feel nothing while seeing to the business of deflowering his wife.

Christian came across the room to stand silently at the side of the bed. Grace didn't move, didn't make a sound; she simply stared at him from where she lay buried among the pillows, lost on that huge bed. Her hair was loose and curling about her shoulders, shimmering like liquid gold as it spilled over the bedclothes. Christian checked an impulse to reach out and test its softness. He focused his attention on her wide eyes instead.

Grace blinked. "*Yer* not the maid," she said, her words coming too quickly for her mouth to properly form them. "*Yer* Lord Knight'n."

"Yes, my lady, but I think it would be better if you would call me 'Christian.' "

"*Chrish-dinn,*" she repeated, nodding slowly. She closed her eyes a moment then looked at him again and smiled. "I am *Gra-ce.*"

He resisted the urge to smile in return and said instead, "Grace, would it be an accurate assumption to say that you drank the entire pot of tea I sent up to you?"

"Uhmm," she nodded. "You took a very long time in coming."

"I am sorry. Matters took longer than I had expected."

In fact, Christian had never realized before then just how much thought went into the taking of a wife's virginity. All the while he'd been downstairs, he'd tried to consider the best means for approaching the task, weighing one against the other until in the end it had come down to a sort of preconjugal checklist, a practical plan for a hapless bridegroom. First, he had offered her a bit of brandy to ease her maidenly fears. From the looks of her now, it had worked. Next, he would need darkness to protect her modesty . . .

Christian leaned over and blew out the one remaining candle at the bedside table, casting them in the muted firelight. "You didn't eat very much of your supper this evening."

Grace shook her head. She then furrowed her brow as if she were suddenly troubled.

"Is something wrong?"

"I was just wondering why the room keeps moving even though I am quite certain my head has gone still."

Christian frowned. Perhaps the brandy hadn't been such a good idea after all. She was half-tipped.

"You didn't care for what the cook had prepared for supper?"

"No. I mean yes. I did. It was very good, what I had of it, but I just . . . I just . . . I . . ."

Grace lost her words as she watched Christian walk around to the other side of the vast bed. He sat at the edge of the mattress, right beside where her leg was stretched out from under the bedcovers, and moved on to the next item on his checklist—to discern just how much Grace knew about sexual relations.

"Grace."

She watched him warily as he positioned himself closer to her. "I know what *yer* going to do. *Yer* going to take my 'ginity now, aren't you?"

Christian leaned on one elbow above her. "Yes, Grace, I am."

He put his hand on the knot that held the sash of her dressing robe and slowly loosened the tie. Grace barely gave the maneuver notice. She was far too busy staring into his eyes with an expression that wasn't at all fearful or even nervous, but utterly curious. It disconcerted him, the openness of her gaze. It was not what he had expected from his virginal wife. He had told himself to approach this night simply as a task that had to be done no matter how disagreeable, like so many of the interminable philosophical lectures he'd had to sit through while he'd been at Eton. But how the devil, he wondered, did one liken lovemaking to Descartes?

"Grace, what do you know of the relationship between a man and a woman?"

Grace smiled, blinking slowly. "Oh, I know more than you think I know."

He raised a brow. "Indeed?"

She nodded confidently. "You think I'm *mishish* . . . *misssh* . . . *mi*—" She gave it up, saying instead, "You think I don't know what you are going to do to me . . . to take my 'ginity." She smiled. "But I do."

"You do?"

"Uhmm." She looked baldly down at the sash of his own robe and said quite matter-of-factly, "Needle and thread."

Christian quirked a half-smile. "Did you just say 'needle and thread'?"

She looked at him, seeming startled by his response. "You mean you don't know? Grandmother told me men were born knowing these things." She giggled. "How funny to think that I will have to teach you." She sat up on the bed and looked at him then and said with utter seriousness, "You see the way it works is I am the needle and you are the thread . . ."

Christian stared at her, dumbfounded.

". . . without one, the other cannot create a true stitch."

Good God, he thought, the situation was more hopeless than he'd figured. She hadn't the faintest clue what the sexual act entailed. Needle and thread . . .

"Grace, how many times have you been kissed by a man—I mean, other than an affectionate peck from a family member?"

Grace stared at him, carefully contemplating his question. "Including you?"

The memory of her visit to his dressing room the night of Eleanor's ball flashed through his thoughts. "Yes."

"Once."

He had thought as much. Christian stood from the bed. Perhaps a bit of philosophical inquiry would serve after all. If he educated her on the facts of it all, prepared her for what would happen, it might prevent a fit of hysterics when the moment of consummation was at hand. He reached for her. "Grace, come to stand before me."

Grace moved from the bed until she stood looking up at him in the firelight. Her hair was mussed from the pillows and her nightgown was buttoned all the way to her chin. Her bare toes curled against the thick carpet as she waited for him to do whatever it was he planned to do. Christian tried to ignore the soft floral scent of her as he leaned toward her and touched his lips to hers. She stood completely still, her mouth warm and giving, her kiss chaste and unversed. After a moment, he pulled away.

Grace opened her eyes and blinked. "Was that all? Are we finished taking my virginity already?"

"Not quite."

Determined to keep things on a purely philosophical level, Christian said, "Grace, I am going to assume you have never seen a man's body before."

She nodded silently, then thought the better of her response and shook her head instead.

"A man's body is very different from that of a woman. It is made that way for a reason, so that they may join together—physically." Still she stared at him. "I don't want you to be frightened. So I would like you to look at me, at my body, before we consummate our marriage."

Christian loosened the belt of his dressing robe. Watching her closely, he parted the fabric in front and let the weight of it drop to the floor. He wore nothing underneath, of course, and kissing her had aroused him more than he cared to admit. He watched her eyes as they moved over his chest down to where his sex stood erect from his groin. She furrowed her brow as if confused by him, by how things might work between them. He saw the moment of realization in her eyes when she knew what would soon happen. But she didn't move to back away or look at him in fear. Instead, slowly, tentatively she reached out and touched two fingers to his hardness. Christian's body jerked in response. She pulled quickly away.

"I'm sorry," she whispered.

Christian looked at her, swallowing hard in effort to take control of his quickening pulse. He was thankful for the darkness. "You didn't hurt me, Grace. A man's body reacts sometimes without his meaning it to."

She didn't understand, of course, and he didn't have the ability at that moment to explain, so instead he urged her toward the bed and lay her back against the pillows.

Christian fought to take control of the emotions that were stirring within him. He positioned himself beside her and kissed her again, this time covering her mouth with his and drawing her fully against the length of his body. As he did, he took a journey back in time to Eton, to hour upon hour of dictum and lecture. He deepened the kiss, stroking his tongue slowly against hers. She tasted of tea and the brandy he'd laced it with and her hair fell softly against his cheek. He already knew that Grace had never known such a kiss but still she didn't shy away as he had expected her to do. Instead his virginal little wife kissed him back. He felt Grace open her mouth against his, pressing her body even closer to him. He felt a jolt take him deep inside.

Affected more than he cared to admit, Christian pulled away and looked at her. "We will take this slowly," he said more to himself than to her. He'd come to her this evening set on doing his duty as a husband, but only so far as he would need to leave the proof he knew the servants would be looking for on the sheets, her virgin's blood. He had told himself he could separate his body from his mind. It appeared, however, that this wouldn't prove easy, for already his blood was pounding through his veins—this after he'd only kissed her once.

He began reciting philosophic precepts in his head, anything to occupy his attention as he loosened the buttons that held the front of her nightdress, his fingers slipping them one by one through the tiny closures down to her belly. He pushed the fabric aside and drew in a ragged breath at the untouched whiteness of her skin, the tautness of her rose-hued nipples. She was perfect in every way. She would be tight around him, he knew, when he entered her and the thought of it taunted him. He pushed the fabric upward over her legs to bunch at her waist, taking in the sight of the golden down at the joining of her thighs. Inwardly he contemplated Socratic dialogues in an effort to cool his increasing desire.

Christian told himself it would go easier if she were at least somewhat aroused, so he kissed her again and as he did, he brought his head lower along the swell of her breast before closing his mouth over her nipple. Grace arched her back, sucking in a sharp breath as she was taken by the first sensations of desire. She brought her hands upward, lacing her fingers through his hair as he drew on her, fisting her hands as he took her further and further into the untried world of her own sensuality.

When he pulled away, lifting his head to look at her, she opened her eyes, staring in silent bewilderment at him. The wavering glow of the firelight played across the burnished tawny gold of her hair, her rapid pulsebeat showing at the hollow of her neck. Christian felt his thoughts begin to blur. His hands queried her body with caresses, his mouth with kisses, introducing him to the delight of her collarbone, the thrill of the whispering of a touch against her shoulder.

With every gesture, every stroke of his fingers, Grace sought to return in kind, caressing her fingers over his back, against his neck. With each motion, each touch from her, Christian's need for her grew. He ran his hand over her, smoothing down over her belly along her thigh. Slowly, tentatively he parted her legs, touching her skin, seducing her to readiness for him.

When he touched her more intimately, reaching her in places she'd never known existed, Grace gasped aloud. His own pulse was pounding now like cannon fire in his ears. His eagerness to know her, to satisfy his need, brought him to moving over her, positioning himself between her legs, joining his mouth with hers once again. With first one hand, then the other, he lifted her legs, bending them at the knee. His fingers found her, found her wet and slick, and he was desperate to feel her tightness around him. He stared down at her, hesitating only a second until she looked at him, telling him with her eyes that she had no fear. That look took away the last of his restraint and Christian quickly buried himself within her, his mouth taking her startled cry against the sudden sharp pain of him, her woman's body naturally stretching to accept him.

From the moment he entered her, Christian was beyond anything but feeling the tightness of her around him. She was so tight, so good, he could not control the movement of his body as he groaned her name, his hips moving, thrusting into her, deep and then deeper, his eyes tightly closed. The scent of her body, the warmth and softness of her skin, her passion, her sexuality overtook him. With each thrust his desperation grew, so that only with another and another could he hope to find release from the torment she held him in. He buried his head against her neck, groaning against her hair, breathing her in, working again and again until, when it was almost more than he could bear, he came into her one last time, deeper than he could have thought possible.

He vaguely heard her cry out through the pounding of his heartbeat and his own shout as he climaxed and the need, the fury, the utter torment released him, giving him back to himself as his body shuddered, spilling his seed within her.

It took Christian several moments to regain full command of his faculties. Only then did he realize just what he had done. He pulled away from Grace abruptly, as if by doing so, he could reverse what he had just done. But it was too late.

He moved to sit at the edge of the bed with his back to her. All the passion, the desire he had felt moments before had gone, leaving him empty and numb and disbelieving that he had done the one thing he had vowed

he would not do. He did not know what had happened,
how he had lost such total control over a situation in
which he had intended to be master. It was his wedding
night and he'd bungled it beyond bungling. He had not
withdrawn before spilling his seed inside Grace's womb.
In the end, his grandfather had won once again.

Christian stood defeatedly from the bed. The fire had
died to where a solitary flame now flickered sluggishly
among the glowing embers in the grate. Grace lay still
upon the bed, naked in the firelight, watching him. She
lifted her hand and beckoned to him, but he did not
move to return to her. He simply stared at her, silent,
solemn, and after another moment, she slowly lowered
her hand back to the bed.

Christian reached forward without a word and pulled
the edges of Grace's nightrail closed over her breasts.
He frowned, staring at her a moment more before he
slipped on his dressing robe and started to walk away
from her, saying as he went, "Good night, Grace."

And as he closed the door behind himself, somehow,
wherever he was, Christian knew his grandfather was
gloating.

Chapter Ten

The morning dawned to the gleeful *hweet* of the chiff-chaff in the trees outside and the movement of the servants at various stations throughout the house—the echoing of footsteps, muffled voices, the opening and closing of doors. Lost amid a tumble of sheets and pillows on the ducal bed, Grace slowly opened her eyes to face her first day as a wife.

Sunlight poured through the tall windows across the room, creeping across the carpet and lighting the chamber's interior through the veil of hair that fell over her eyes. Seeing the room now in the daylight, she thought it not nearly so harsh and gloomy as she had remembered it from the night before. The furnishings themselves were really quite nice—Tudor in style, the hangings a rich burgundy velvet with gold. Shadows no longer crept about the walls. The carvings on the bedposts no longer looked like frolicking demons but were in fact cherubs poised amid an enchanted setting of clouds. What a difference the light of day could make.

Grace lifted her head from the scattered pillows just as the door to the bedchamber inched open. A maid peeked an eye through to the inside, and then, seeing her awake, quietly pushed the door to enter.

"Good morning, my lady," she said, bobbing a curtsey. She was the same maid who had brought her the tea the night before.

"Good morning."

Grace's head felt heavier than usual, as if oddly it were weighted somehow from the inside. As she sat up, she noticed a strange soreness between her legs. She immediately thought to the night before. Why, oh why had she drunk all that tea? Even now she could only vaguely remember what had happened—Christian kissing her, and how she had spouted some nonsense to him about needles and threads. She remembered the pain of him entering her body, but not much beyond that until he'd risen from the bed to leave her. The only thing she did know was that whatever it was she was supposed to have done, she had obviously done it badly. Why else would a bridegroom be so eager to leave his marriage bed?

"What is your name?" she asked the maid as she watched her move about the chamber, seeing to her duties.

The maid looked startled at the question. "Eliza Stone, my lady. But everyone calls me Liza."

"Stone. You are related to Mrs. Stone, the housekeeper?"

"Aye. My aunt she is, my lady. 'Twas because of her I was able to find a position in this household."

Grace nodded. She heard the sound of horses on the drive outside and stood, walking to the window. The coach that had brought them there the day before stood waiting, the coachman making a great show of checking the harnesses and fastenings. Grace remembered then that they were to leave for London that morning. "Do you know the time, Liza?"

"Aye, 'tis a quarter hour past nine, my lady." Liza picked the topmost gown from Grace's trunk and gave it a shake to smooth out its wrinkles. "His lordship is a'ready awake. He said to see you up and ready to leave for London by ten. You've a long day's journey ahead of you."

She draped the gown at the foot of the bed, a plain beige bombazine carriage dress, along with the other necessaries she'd taken from the trunk—chemise, stockings, half boots. "Breakfast awaits you in the parlor downstairs. I'll have the boys come to fetch your trunks down after you've dressed."

Grace was pulling on her robe when she noticed the maid staring at the bed behind her, the expression on her face quite peculiar. She turned to see what had caught her notice. Splotches of brownish red marked the white of the sheet beneath where Grace had lain. It was blood. *Her blood.* She drew in a startled breath, covering her mouth with her hand. She knew quite well it wasn't time for her monthly—that had come and gone but a fortnight ago. She remembered the pain from the night before.

"Oh, dear . . . what has happened?" She looked at the maid, eyes wide. "Am I . . . am I dying?"

Liza came immediately to her side. "Oh, no, my lady. Not at all. Do you not know? Didn't you realize? Were you never told?"

"Was I never told what? That one should expect to receive grave injury on one's wedding night?"

Liza shook her head, taking Grace's hand. " 'Tis all right, my lady. It is but your *virgin's* blood. 'Tis natural. When a lady beds with a man the first time, the man takes her virginity."

Grace let go a frustrated breath. "Yes, yes, I know that, and the girl is then suddenly considered a woman and can participate in conversation and no longer is required to have a chaperone wherever she goes. She can even wear her hair differently. But what has that to do with this?"

"It isn't that I'm speaking of, my lady. I'm speaking of what happens when a man comes into a woman's body." Liza looked at Grace directly. "I can't say for myself, since I've never been with a man—other than Jemmie the stable boy who stuck his hand down my bodice and got his nose bloodied for it. But Ma says the Lord has made it so a man knows if he's the first to bed with you. There's a part of you called your maidenhead. I don't know exactly what it is, but the man must break through it and it hurts something fierce and there is often blood, but it is only for the first time, my lady. After that, it never happens again. Ma says 'tis what we must bear for the sins of Eve." Her voice dropped to a near-whisper. "But my sister, Mary, she says that after that first time, the rest of the times after that are like going to heaven without the dyin'."

Grace looked at the girl, so much younger than she, but so knowing of things that had never been spoken of, much less thought about during her childhood. Suddenly she felt very much a fool. She shook her head. "No one ever told me."

Liza smiled, smoothing an errant curl behind Grace's ear. "And they call us of the serving class 'uncivilized.' Least we don't send our young girls off to the marriage bed thinking they've been murdered the next morn."

Grace's cheeks colored at her own ignorance. Liza squeezed her hand. "It isn't your fault, my lady. Those sorts of things just aren't talked about among the quality. My ma had nine of us girls and she takes us aside when we each of us reaches ten-and-five. Tells us everything there is to know about ladies and men and what goes on when they get alone between the bedcovers. And because she did, not a one of us has come home yet with a swelling belly before first getting a husband to care for us."

Grace looked at Liza. It took her a moment to realize what exactly the maid was saying. *A child.* A child that could have been conceived because of what had happened between her and Christian the night before. While at first the notion of it frightened her, after a moment or two, it also gave her an inkling of warmth unlike any she had ever known. Her hand instinctively dropped to her belly. Even now she might be carrying a child of her own. Someone she could love. Someone who would be with her always, who would love her—and who would never leave.

Grace heard the sound of the coachman again on the drive outside and remembered the time. She didn't want to be late and risk annoying Christian. "Liza, will you help me to dress, please?"

They left the ducal bedchamber for the small antechamber where Grace had bathed the night before. At the corner washstand, hidden discreetly behind an embroidered screen, Grace performed her ablutions, washing herself thoroughly before asking Liza for her chemise and stockings.

She sat staring at her reflection in the glass while Liza quickly arranged her hair, twisting and pulling it up in a style that befitted a titled lady, but that left Grace resembling herself very little. She realized then she was no longer Lady Grace Ledys. Her name, her own body, and even her jewelry—she looked at the ring on her hand—were now different. She had lost her innocence, was now completely woman, and thus the unfamiliar styling of her hair seemed appropriate. But what of Christian? Would he present himself differently as well now that he had taken the role of husband?

Grace stood as Liza slipped her gown carefully over her head, arranging the soft fabric before setting to work on the buttons along its back. Somehow the plain color didn't quite complement the more refined styling of her hair, leaving her feeling at contradiction with her two selves—the old Grace and the new.

When she had finished dressing, Grace left the ducal bedchamber and took the steps slowly to the ground floor, wondering what she might say to Christian when she greeted him at breakfast. What exactly did one say to a man after one lost their virginity to him? *Thank you, sir, for performing the task?*

What Grace really wanted was to ask Christian what she had done to displease him—more, what it was she should have done. She knew from her grandmother that a good number of husbands and wives shared marital relations without sleeping in the same bed. It was often considered normal. She also knew from her grandmother that those same husbands and wives often found others with whom to fill the time when their spouses were off elsewhere.

Is that what Christian intended? Did he plan to take a mistress, do those same things he'd done with her the night before with another woman? Would he look for someone who would do things correctly, someone to stay with until morning? Or what if he already had a mistress? He was, after all, a man of the world—she was a girl of the country. Despite what might be accepted in other marriages, Grace couldn't bear to think of Christian doing those same things with another woman. Though her memory of last night was vague, what she did remember had been intimate and precious and utterly divine, a completion of the vows they had taken before God and the world, a culmination of the Fate that had brought them together. Now that she knew what really happened between a man and a woman, she would be better prepared. She hadn't known what to expect the first time. Grace would just try harder to do—whatever it was she was supposed to do—right.

The trepidation she'd felt over how she would greet Christian that morning vanished when she reached the parlor door and found the room empty, with a single setting placed at the far chair. Grace felt her insides tighten hopelessly. Apparently, Christian did not intend to join her for breakfast.

A footman sprang to attention when he noticed her at the door, pulling the chair back for her to sit—alone. Grace remained at the door awash with humiliation, deeply stung by Christian's negligence. She was taking breakfast alone on the morning after her wedding night. The footman stared at her and the expression on his face was almost too much to bear. He pitied her. Suddenly Grace found that the discomfort of an empty stomach was far preferable to the embarrassment of eating alone for everyone in the household to see.

"Thank you, but I do not wish to eat this morning," she said to the footman. She turned from the room and hastened away so that he might not see the tears already springing to her eyes.

Chapter Eleven

Grace had no idea where she was headed after she left the dining room. Nor did she care. She simply turned away as quickly as she could, fleeing blindly down the nearest hall as she dashed away her tears in frustration.

As she walked, she fought to soothe her bruised emotions. She had come to this marriage knowing full well it would be work, but it was work she was willing to take on, especially if it meant that she and Christian would one day have the love and respect and commitment to one another that both her parents and her grandparents had found. Was it foolish of her to have even tried? She had expected to make mistakes but she had also expected to learn from them as she had learned everything else in life—from the proper way to pour tea to the right techniques for making sketches. She had never been one to quit, even against great odds. She had always tried to find a way to make things work, approaching a problem from all directions until she found a solution that put things in order. She had known it would take time to get past their initial unfamiliarity. What she hadn't expected was to be denied the slightest chance to succeed.

From the moment she had agreed to wed him, Grace had made it her foremost wish to be a wife her husband could be proud of. When the vicar had spoken the vows the day before, she had listened closely to every word— better or worse, richer or poorer, in sickness and in health—and she had taken each one of them to heart. Yet here she was, the morning after her wedding, already abandoned by Christian. What in heaven's name had she done wrong? No matter how terrible the experience of their wedding night might have been for him, Grace just couldn't believe that she deserved to be forsaken for all of the household to see. Had he expected that she would wake to find him gone and simply sip her morning tea, eat her toast, and await him in the carriage, saying when they met, "Thank you for seeing to the distasteful task of my virginity, sir; might I offer you the seat with the best view?"

Grace stopped walking and looked about at her surroundings. She didn't recognize anything. She stopped to listen, but when she didn't hear any of the servants moving about, she realized she must have wandered into one of the hall's vacant wings. She wondered what would happen if she were to come up missing, delaying their return to the city. Would Christian simply leave without her? Not wishing to be the cause of further discord between them, she decided she should try to find her way back. She wandered on through unfamiliar hallways and abandoned chambers, each just as cold and forbidding as the last. It seemed as if laughter couldn't possibly have touched these walls, nor could merriment have danced across the rich Turkish carpets. This place wasn't a home. It was a relic haunted by sadness and misery.

She came to a door at the far end of a hallway and quietly opened it. Inside she found a sitting room that was set off from the main house, the furnishings hidden beneath dust covers. She would have turned to leave except that the place drew her somehow, standing out as different from the rest of the house. Grace crossed the room and gave the heavy drapery a yank, allowing the morning sunlight to come pouring in through the grubby mullioned windows that lay underneath.

Carpets of the lightest yellow and blue revealed themselves in the sunlight, set beneath furnishings of delicate fruitwood and rosewood; the walls were covered in elegant pastel Chinese silk. It was a room that spoke of softness and femininity, and Grace wondered at the way it differed from the rest of Westover Hall. It was almost as if the chamber didn't belong there—just like Grace. It, too, seemed to have been left to fend for itself.

Grace lifted the cover from one of the pieces and

found an elegant Queen Anne secretary underneath. It was crafted of the finest cherry and engraved across a brass plate on its top were the words "For Frances, my wife . . . my love."

She decided the room must have once been a withdrawing chamber for the dowager marchioness, Christian's mother. Grace remembered her from the wedding—how polite Lady Frances had been to her. She remembered something else too—the shadow she had seen behind the woman's eyes, as if a part of her wasn't really there.

Grace ran her fingers thoughtfully along the polished desktop as she imagined the marchioness sitting in that room, reading or watching the rabbits at play on the lawn outside. Had she been happy? Or had she felt trapped by the coldness of this unhappy place? The desk had undoubtedly been a gift to her from Christian's father, but why was it here, Grace wondered, forgotten and locked away in this place, instead of with Lady Frances at her own residence in London? It was such a special piece, with its inscription telling of the marquess's regard for his wife. Had their marriage been an arrangement like Grace and Christian's? Or had they married for love? Was such a concept even possible in the House of Westover?

A thick layer of dust had accumulated on the fireplace mantel, revealing it had been some time since the chamber had been put to use. As she turned from it, Grace noticed a painting high on the wall concealed by a cloth. Curious, she stood on tiptoe, tugging at the lower corner until the cover slid away.

Underneath was a portrait of a man, a woman, and a young child of no more than five years of age. Grace recognized the dowager marchioness, Christian's mother, but a younger, more vibrant reflection of her. The child, a boy, was kneeling at her feet, his head resting softly against his mother's full skirts while her fingers played lovingly with his dark hair. The man who stood beside them resembled Christian, particularly in the way he held his head. He had the same captivating silver-blue eyes, which regarded his wife with an unmistakable expression.

He loved her.

Grace moved her attention from the marquess to study the boy's image more closely. It was Christian, but a carefree, innocent boy who bore little resemblance to the man she now called husband. Missing were the cold reserve and the unreachable eyes. This boy had known happiness and laughter. He had known love. Grace could only wonder what could have happened to have changed him into the guarded, inscrutable man he was now.

Her study of the portrait was interrupted when she heard the sound of someone walking on the gravel outside. She glanced to the window, where she caught sight of Christian moving from the house down a narrow path through the trees. There stood a door to her right that led to a terrace. Grace opened it quietly, slipping outside.

The wind rustled through the trees, lifting the hem of her skirts and tugging at the tendrils of hair that the maid had left loose as Grace fell in step behind him. She kept a good twenty paces away so that he wouldn't hear her following. She wanted to see Christian, wanted to watch him without his being aware of her. People often behaved differently in diverse situations and she wanted to see if his indifference was a thing directed only at her.

As she came around a turn in the pathway, Grace stopped, lingering behind the sizeable trunk and thick overhanging branches of an oak. Christian had arrived at a small area shaded by other oaks and enclosed by a twisting iron fence. A number of tall headstones lined the interior, flecked gray against the rich, grassy carpet. Grace stepped off the footpath and onto the lawn so that Christian wouldn't hear her approach. Coming under a curtain of new spring leaves, she watched as he stood in contemplation over one of the headstones, watched him crouch down to pluck away an offending weed from beside it. He smoothed a hand over the lettering, laying his palm flat against the stone as one might set a hand in welcome upon another's shoulder.

As she drew a few steps closer, Grace saw that the

gravestone he knelt before was that of Christopher Wy-cliffe, his father.

Christian remained kneeling, his head bent for some time in silent prayer. As she watched him, Grace thought of the man she'd seen depicted in the portrait, Christian's father. He looked as if he'd been the sort of father a boy of five would have worshipped. She remembered her own grief at the loss of her parents, the disordered feeling even at her young age, as if her place in the world was no longer secure despite the fact that she hadn't really even known them.

Grace's birth had been accidental, an imposition on the lives of two people bent on personally conquering the world. She had been left with Nonny as a babe while her parents had gone away traveling more than they had stayed at home. They would return every so often to visit, never remaining long enough to unpack all their belongings before setting off for some other new and exciting destination. They had come home most often on special occasions—a random birthday, the marriage of a distant cousin, the death of Grace's grandfather, the marquess. Still Grace could remember the last time she'd seen her parents, could even remember the clothes they had worn, the smell of her mother's lavender perfume, the way the wind had ruffled the ends of her father's neckcloth as he'd patted her on the head in parting. She remembered how her mother had bent to kiss her on the cheek, retying the ribbons on her straw bonnet with the promise that soon she would be old enough to join them on one of their jaunts around the world. "Next time," she had vowed to her daughter. "Next time we will take you with us and we will see the lions and the elephants in faraway Africa."

But that promised journey had never come. Instead, a messenger had arrived from London a month later with the news that the ship they had sailed upon had gone down in a storm. There had been no survivors. Ironically in death Grace's parents had become touchable in a way they had never been while living, for from then on she'd had the twin headstones that had been erected in the Ledysthorpe cemetery to visit. She remembered the last time she'd gone there—the morning she was to leave Ledysthorpe forever. She had whispered her good-byes and cleaned away the weeds, just like Christian was doing now.

Grace remembered how Eleanor had told her of her brother's closeness to their father. No doubt such an attachment would make facing the memorial of his death difficult, even after all the time that had passed. She wondered that perhaps their shared loss could provide a way for them to lay the first stepping-stone across the river of unfamiliarity that stood between them. Hopeful, Grace threw caution to the wind and started toward the cemetery.

The gate squeaked as she pushed it inward and the sound brought Christian to lifting his head. He stared at her for a moment, his expression unguarded. In a moment later, however, his eyes turned icier than the bitterest winter.

Grace froze, hovering just inside the gate as he stood. For a moment, she thought she saw the sunlight shine in a tear at his eye. He continued to stare at her without speaking, his face set without expression. He needed no words to convey that he was heartily displeased to see her there.

"You must have loved him very much," she said awkwardly.

Christian turned, tossing the weeds he'd pulled over the fencing. "What are you doing here?"

Grace blanched. "I . . . I saw you come here and I thought you might like someone to talk to. You had been kneeling so long, I—"

"First my dressing room, now this. This is the second time you have stuck your nose where it didn't belong. Do you make it a habit, madam, of intruding on the privacy of others?"

Grace ignored his bitter words. "I know what it is to lose a parent, Christian."

For the barest second, her statement seemed to reach him. His expression softened and the tense lines around his mouth went smooth—but only for a moment. Then the ice returned to his stare, and his voice was clipped and sharp as a blade. "You will do well in the future, madam, to avoid meddling a third time."

Grace brought her arms around herself, chilled despite the warmth of the spring sun. She had only hoped to offer Christian comfort, a wife's tender touch to ease his obvious pain at the loss of his father. She had wanted to talk to him, share with him the memory of her own parents, commiserate in their mutual experience. Instead she had met with his anger and hostility.

Grace turned her face away so that Christian wouldn't see the tears that so quickly came to her eyes at his harsh words. Was she doomed to displease him at every turn? She looked back when she heard his bootsteps on the walkway and simply stood there, watching him leave her again, just as he had the night before, stripped raw of anything but humiliation and despair.

Chapter Twelve

Christian stared at Grace as she sat across from him within the closed carriage. They had left Westover Hall nearly an hour before. Since then she hadn't spoken above two words other than to ask how long their journey might take and if he would prefer the front-facing seat instead of the back. But he would have known she was troubled even without her silence. She had one of those intelligible faces that showed the thoughts going on behind it as clearly as if they'd been written on paper. This, coupled with the book she was reading—and the fact that she was holding it upside down—gave a clear impression that she was still smarting from his harsh words to her in the cemetery.

She was wondering at his indifference, trying to understand why it seemed he was doing everything humanly possible to avoid being in her company when just the night before he had touched her more intimately than she'd ever been touched. Their meeting in the cemetery had taken him unawares. He hadn't expected to find her there, coming upon him so quietly as he knelt before his father's gravestone. The moment he had seen her, the memory of his failure the night before had come back to him like a dousing in Westover's ice-cold fish pond. He hadn't meant to rail at her as he had; he was simply unaccustomed to having someone—most especially a wife—suddenly insinuating herself into the most private moments of his life. Even more so, he was unaccustomed to having anyone affect him.

As Grace sat lost to her thoughts and her upside-down tale, Christian took the opportunity to look at her, truly study her for the first time. When one considered it, the old duke hadn't done badly in his choice of a wife for him. Grace had the loveliness of generations of aristocratic blood. Her hair was the perfect shade of blonde, not too light nor too dark, but the color of honey warmed by the summer sunlight. Lashes framed eyes that were brilliant blue, inquisitive, and full of strength and spirit. Her nose was straight and unobtrusive, her mouth full and pleasingly shaped, her skin unblemished, untouched . . .

Christian had known his wife—whoever his grandfather decided upon—would be an innocent. The great Duke of Westover would never consent to a secondhand maid as the mother of the future heir. Christian wondered, though, if the duke had assumed Grace's delicate features betokened a meek and accepting manner and an easily governed nature. It was a mistake one might make when first faced with her. It had been for that reason alone Christian had sent up the tea the previous night. He had known Grace wouldn't be accustomed to strong spirits and hoped they might ease her fears at giving over her innocence to a virtual stranger. He had prepared himself for her apprehension, even her tears. What he hadn't been prepared for was her trust.

Christian could see Grace now in his mind's eye as she lay beneath him on the bed, clad in that prim nightgown even as her virgin's body awakened for him. Her soulful eyes had told him that while she might fear the unknowing, she would never question anything he might do to her. Though she knew next to nothing about him, she'd had faith in him, something few others had ever shown him. That simple gesture had taken away any thought he'd had of indifference toward her, and his plan to keep her at a safe distance had slipped like sand through his fingers.

But if his reaction to her emotionally had taken him unawares, the physical response of his body to hers had undone him completely. In his life, the position he'd been born to, marriage was as certain and as inevitable as death. It was his duty, his sole purpose in life, to sire the next Westover heir, and he wouldn't have been at all surprised had the old man insisted on standing present to assure that Christian fulfilled his end of their bargain in bedding her. Bedding his wife once had been exactly what Christian had planned on doing, and without spilling his seed to deny the duke the one thing he wanted more than anything else in life.

An heir.

But from the moment Christian first touched Grace, knew the scent of her, tasted the softness of her skin, looked into the bottomless blue of her eyes, he'd been lost. Every thought he'd had of restraint and control had vanished in a haze of lust and passion and need. But what did it mean, this reaction to her, really, truly? It signified nothing, he told himself, nothing at all. So he'd had one night where he'd lost his command over his body. Regardless of Westover tradition, chances were that Grace wouldn't conceive a child from that one encounter. And one encounter was all it would be. The mystery of her was past, her virginity no longer an issue to be dealt with. He had done his part. He would not again visit his wife's bed, not until the time came that he was ready for a child—and that wouldn't be until his grandfather was dead and gone.

For a moment Christian wondered why he shouldn't just tell Grace the truth, explain that he could not be a husband to her in the physical sense because of the agreement he'd made with the duke. But then she would want to know the reasons why he had made such a promise—why he had agreed at the age of nine to give over his firstborn son to the duke. It was something she could never be told, not when the lives of his mother and sister hinged upon it.

Christian could, he knew, through his influence and that of his grandfather, arrange a marriage for Eleanor quite easily and be done with running from the past. As a Westover, she would be sought after by any of the best of society's families. But Christian had vowed he would never do that. He had vowed that Eleanor would be given the luxury of choosing. She would meet a man, talk to him, share her thoughts, know as she should know the man she would spend her life with. She would reveal her love of music, her fondness for lemon tarts and gillyflowers. She would admit to him her distaste for mushrooms. She would discuss her favorite books, would show her talent for poetry. She might meet with a boor or two or maybe even three, but she would eventually find the one man who shared her likes and dislikes and who cherished her. She would be allowed to imagine herself in the role of wife long before his permission as her brother and the family patriarch was sought. And when that time came, when the honor of her hand was requested, she would be given the choice to accept or decline.

Put simply, Eleanor would be permitted the one thing Christian had known all his life he would be denied. Eleanor would be given the chance to fall in love—and then the very ugly truth that put at peril her every chance at this happiness would pose a threat to her no longer.

Christian looked at Grace again. Her brow was furrowed now and her mouth was pressed in a frown. For a moment he wondered that she had perhaps been as much a victim as he in this marriage. Then he wondered where that thought had come from. He wondered at her reasons for wedding him, a man she had only seen once when she had come tumbling through the wall of his dressing room. She was a nobleman's daughter, certainly lovely to look at. He had read the marriage contracts and knew she had brought a sizeable dowry. Surely she could have had any number of noblemen interested in wedding her. What had she gained by agreeing to be his wife? And why had his grandfather chosen her above all others? Had she been bolstered by the myth of who society thought him to be?

She could have no idea what she had agreed to when she had consented to be his wife. Grace thought him honorable, a gentleman worthy of her devotion. Her head was filled with dreams of a white knight on a charger coming to rescue her. She could know nothing of the past. The Westover secrets were long buried, unknown to the rest of the world. She knew only what she had been told, smooth words meant to influence the romantic whims of a fanciful young lady.

Thus, Grace could have no clue she had just married a murderer.

Chapter Thirteen

Knighton House, London

Grace studied her reflection with care in the tall pier glass near her dressing table. The gown was fine and her hair was perfectly coiffed, pulled up high off her face in a crown of golden curls. Not a single flounce showed out of place. Everything appeared to be perfect, but the image that met her critical eye only brought her to frowning.

She turned a bit to view her left side. The frown grew to a scowl. To the right side and the scowl hardened into a furrow at her brow. It would be a blessed miracle if she made it through this night.

She was to attend a ball at the home of a very important society figure, someone whom she had never heard of before but who, it seemed, everyone else in creation had. She would attend with Christian, their first appearance together as the Marquess and Marchioness Knighton. Everyone would be watching, of course, looking their fill at the unknown lady who had married the man everyone else had wanted to marry. They were expecting a goddess and no less, a mortal endowed with immortal beauty. They would be looking for a woman of taste and elegance, refinement and—

grace

—something she was sorely lacking.

Funny how life had a way of mocking you, she thought, bestowing upon you a particular appellation and then taking away any possibility of ever living up to it. Far worse was knowing that her lack of social polish was a flaw her husband had evidently noticed. Grace had overheard as much the very morning after their arrival in London, when Christian had been talking to Eleanor in his study, charging his sister with the task of transforming, as he'd put it, "their country mouse into a proper marchioness."

Mouse, Grace had thought, her heart sinking to the very depths of her soul. *What a disappointment I must be to him.* Later, as she'd sat staring out from her bedchamber window seat, her arms hugging her knees to her chin as tears trailed down her cheeks, she came to realize that hidden within her misery at Christian's words lay a challenge. She would prove Christian wrong and become the marchioness he had expected to wed.

Perhaps even a marchioness he could love.

She'd been given a fortnight, time for the tumult that had erupted following the announcement of their marriage in the newspapers to settle. Once news of their secret ceremony became known, the knocker had begun sounding daily, hourly even. It was just as Eleanor had said—everyone, it seemed, suddenly wanted to make her acquaintance. People she had never before met sought her out. Invitations and calling cards arrived in bundles, but Grace put off accepting them. After all, the transformation from country mouse—ahem, *miss*—to marchioness required careful preparation.

First, she would need suitable clothing, an entire wardrobe of it. Morning gowns, day gowns, dinner and ball gowns, carriage dresses, garden dresses, walking and riding dresses. There were gowns fashioned just for the theatre, others for the opera; some for evening, others for full evening. The differences between them all still somehow escaped her, but Grace knew she must never, *ever* wear one at any time other than its intended one. Along with each ensemble came the necessary trappings—parasols, wraps, gloves, hats, shoes, and stockings for each. It amazed her that the acquisition of a mere husband could triple the size of a woman's baggage.

With the exception of the final fittings, Grace had yet to wear any of her newly acquired wardrobe. No occasion had yet come about that would require anything more than her own comfortable—if somewhat countrified—gowns, made of lackluster colors that helped to keep her inconspicuous. No one would dare think that the Marchioness Knighton would go about in homespun. Bonneted and blandly dressed, she could still manage the occasional sojourn to Hookham's without drawing unwanted notice. But Grace knew she wouldn't be able to hide herself away forever. The time would eventually come when she would have to emerge from her refuge of anonymity, face the curious eyes of society, and present herself as Marchioness Knighton.

Not just *any* gathering would do, she'd been told. It must be neither too grand nor too modest, neither distinctly Whig nor Tory. The choice of it would need to be made carefully. After much consideration, the news, when it had come, had not given her even the slightest measure of excitement. Instead it had filled her with an immediate and utter sense of dread.

Christian had informed her of the event in a manner that was fast becoming custom. He'd passed the word through his valet, Peter, who'd delivered it to Liza, the young maid whom Grace had befriended on her wedding night at Westover Hall. Not long after their return to London, Grace had been advised that her lack of a personal servant would be unacceptable in her new role. It made no matter that she hadn't found the necessity for one through the first three-and-twenty years of her life. A marchioness—and more importantly, a future duchess—required a maid.

When told she would need to begin making inquiries after one, Grace's efforts had extended only so far as to send off a letter to Liza offering her the position. The lively maid had turned up at the doorstep of Knighton House within days, bags in hand. Since then, Liza had become Grace's helpmate, confidante, and collaborator in everything she did. She rode with Grace in the carriage and walked beside her along the Serpentine in Hyde Park early in the mornings when no one else was yet about. Liza suggested styles in which Grace could best wear her hair and colors for gowns that would compliment her complexion. But more than just a ladies' maid, Liza had become Grace's friend, something which, other than Nonny, Grace had never truly had before.

True to her brother's request, Eleanor had come to

Grace's rescue in all matters of society. It was she who had hired the dancing master to spend hours teaching Grace the proper execution of a quadrille. It was she who had educated Grace on the various personalities of the *ton,* riffling through every invitation and calling card to designate the ones Grace should or should not accept. And it was she who had persuaded the most sought-after modiste in London, Madame Delphine, to come to Knighton House for a round of consultations and fittings and last-minute alterations, though it was the busiest time of the season. Grace would never have been able to bring it off without Eleanor's support. Just the arrangements for the gown Grace would wear on this first occasion had taken nearly a week. They had spent days mulling over stacks of fashion publications and engravings. After considering dozens of fabric swatches and numerous bits of trimmings, the gown that had been created was the most elegant one Grace had ever seen.

Made from the palest sea-green silk damask, the gown fell in an elegant line to a hem that was corded underneath in order to make it swing gracefully—quite like a bell—when she moved. The skirts were decorated in a woven floral pattern with varying shades of blue and golden threads, and soft petal-shaped sleeves came off a cross-over bodice that was stitched with gold edging. It was indeed exquisite, certainly not the ensemble for a country mouse.

Its deeply cut bodice however, was causing Grace's present dismay.

Grace had never before exposed this much of her bosom, not even when clad only in her underthings, and she felt as if she were walking about with half a gown to cover her. When she had voiced these misgivings during the round of fittings, all three of them—Eleanor, Madame Delphine, and Liza—had assured her that this was *the* fashion and that every lady at the ball would be envious of how well she wore it. Grace couldn't bring herself to imagine it so—in fact, she was certain that if she didn't tumble out of the thing, she'd surely catch a cold in her chest from it.

But perhaps, she'd thought hopefully, she just might manage to catch her husband's eye with it, too.

Though Eleanor hadn't spoken those words precisely, Grace knew they'd been in her thoughts at the fitting that morning. She had proclaimed how her brother wouldn't be able to keep his eyes from her. She wasn't the first in the household to have noticed the disregard Christian showed his new wife. In fact, it was something that everyone in the household had taken notice of.

A good many times over the past two weeks Grace had overheard the servants whispering to one another, remarking on how soon after their marriage the lord and lady had taken to separate beds, and that the door adjoining their bedchambers had yet to be found unlocked in the morning. Since the first night at Westover Hall, Christian hadn't come to her bed. At first, she thought perhaps he was waiting to find out whether she was with child, and that perhaps it only required one such interlude to conceive. But with so many taking notice of his inattention, Grace could only conclude that there was something wrong between them. The only problem she faced now was how to fix matters, especially when Christian was so rarely at home. He left in the mornings and returned sometimes late at night. When Lady Frances had broached the subject of his absence to her son, Christian had merely replied that he had business to attend to. Hoping to combat her loneliness, Grace had thrown herself into preparations for her society introduction, wanting everything to be just right. *Tonight,* she thought, staring at her reflection. *Tonight I will show him that I can be the wife he had expected.*

Liza came into the bedchamber then, humming a cheerful tune. "Well, I think I managed to get the last of the creases out of this shawl. Took quite a bit of steaming and pressing." She held it up for Grace to see. " 'Tis a pretty thing, to be sure."

Indeed, it was. Pale cream Kashmir-designed silk, tasseled and embroidered with small trailing floral cones along each border, it had been Nonny's when she'd been a young lady, a gift to her from Grace's grandfather on their marriage. Grace had always admired the shawl and it had been among the many things Nonny had bequeathed to her. Since it had always held such loving

memories, Grace had a secret wish that it might bring
her good fortune for the evening.

Grace took the length of fabric up, holding it out a
moment to look at it before she wrapped the width of
it snugly over her bodice. She closed her eyes and for a
moment or two it felt almost as if her grandmother were
softly hugging her, for the shawl still carried Nonny's
unique lilac scent.

Grace turned with a smile toward Liza to display the
shawl. "How's this?"

But Liza was frowning, shaking her head in disapproval.

"My lady, I'd not be doing my position as your maid
any justice if I were to let you leave this house looking
like that."

Grace looked at herself again in the glass. "I know.
That was my thought exactly. The modiste must have
measured the bodice of this gown too small. I don't wish
to fault her—anyone can make a mistake—so that is why
I will be sure to wear the shawl over it."

"My lady—no. If you do that, every lady at the ball
tonight will laugh at you." Liza pulled the shawl away,
setting Grace's arms each at an angle. "There is an art-
istry to the wearing of a shawl just as there is to wielding
a fan. You should simply drape the shawl about your
back, like this . . ." She set the soft fabric over each
elbow and then arranged it so that it was wrapped just
below the tiny capped sleeves of the gown. The position
of Grace's figure thus, with her back slightly arched, only
made her bosom that much more conspicuous.

The maid stepped back to survey the result. She
straightened a flounce and then took up the heated tongs
from the fire to reset a loose curl from Grace's coiffure.
She stepped back to study her figure again. "There,
that's perfect. No, wait—" Liza reached forward,
grabbed the high waistline of Grace's gown and gave it
a quick tug—*downward*. Flesh Grace had never thought
to expose to daylight let alone to a crowded ballroom—
swelled above the dangerously low edge of the fabric.
Liza stood back with a grin. "There. Now that *is*
perfect."

"But, Liza, I am falling out of this gown!"

Liza grinned. "That, my lady, can only be a good thing. Now, let us put on your mantelet before you go down to meet Lord Knighton. Promise me you won't give him a peek until after you've arrived at the ball."

Grace stared at her, doubtful.

"Trust me in this, my lady. I would never tell you to do anything that I wasn't truly certain of."

"All right, but we must hurry. Lord Knighton wanted us to leave at eight o'clock and it is already nearly ten minutes past. I fear he may grow annoyed if I delay much longer."

"Oh, but you are early, my lady. There is no reason to hurry. A lady always makes a gentleman wait for her. Makes 'em appreciate more the trouble you go through to look as pretty as you do. Gentlemen know that, otherwise they think you didn't make the effort to look your finest for them. Ma always said when a gentleman says eight o'clock, he really means half-past."

Grace looked at the maid, feeling not for the first time wholly untutored in the ways of women and men. "Liza, how does your mother know so much about these things?"

"Before Ma married my Pa, she had served as ladies' maid here in London to none other than Miss Harriette Wilson."

It was a name that was unfamiliar to Grace. "Harriette Wilson—she was a popular lady?"

Liza smiled, raising a brow. "You could say a good many of the gentlemen sought her company. Everyone from dukes to some say even princes."

Princes? Well this Harriette Wilson must certainly then know the proper way to wear a shawl. In the face of such expertise, Grace shrugged and left the gown's bodice where it was, even though she felt most indecently exposed. She focused instead on the challenge she had put to herself to become a proper marchioness. Christian's marchioness. It was time she gave up girlhood modesty. It was time she stopped playing the role of The Anonymouse and became Lady Grace, Marchioness Knighton. She squared her shoulders. If this was what it took to make her husband notice her, then by heavens she would do it.

Grace stood while Liza slipped her silk mantelet
around her shoulders, fastening it under her chin. When
she had finished, Grace looked to the clock on the table
beside her. It was now twenty minutes past eight. She
certainly didn't want Christian to think she had rushed
in preparing for such a paramount event. She waited ten
minutes more before heading for the door.

Christian, Eleanor, and Lady Frances were all waiting
for her at the foot of the stairs when she appeared.
Christian looked handsome and quite refined in his evening suit of strict black with just the stark white of his
shirt and neckcloth against it. Grace felt a small tug deep
inside herself; she had missed seeing him the past two
weeks. But tonight, all that would change for the better.
Yes, indeed, she thought, recalling Liza's words, *every
lady will envy me for the man whose arm I will be on.*
She would not be nervous. She would act and speak as
the marchioness she was—Christian's marchioness.

Grace smiled hopefully when she saw he had noticed
her descent. But Christian didn't register any response
to her appearance. Instead he glanced at the hall clock,
barely giving her notice. He frowned. "I had hoped to
avoid having to wait in the carriage line."

Grace's smile immediately flattened and she felt a
tightening deep inside her chest. Liza had been wrong.
She had displeased him by being late.

"Oh, but it is better that we arrive after most everyone else," Eleanor said quickly. "There will be less of a
crush to get in. Do remember the Easterley rout, Christian. We arrived promptly at eight and Mother's hem
was ripped when Lord Calder trod upon it trying to
make an entrance before us. It was most clever of you,
Grace, to consider that."

Everyone knew perfectly well Grace's lateness had
nothing to do with any forethought and there followed
a silent moment before Christian turned for the door,
the cape of his evening cloak sweeping outward as he
went. Grace remained frozen on the stairs, all her hopes,
her plans stricken even before she'd begun. She wanted
to turn and retreat to her bedchamber and never emerge
again. But she couldn't. She had to see this night
through. So she renewed her vow to meet the challenge

of the evening and continued down the steps, following the others outside to the waiting coach.

Eleanor, blessedly, chattered endlessly during their ride to the ball in an obvious attempt to keep Grace's thoughts from both her sullen husband, who sat beside her staring out the window, and the butterflies fluttering through her insides. Grace realized they had nearly arrived when the coach slowed to a lazy crawl, picking its way along the street that was lined on each side with other coaches.

Soon they stopped at a stately house set on a corner across from Hyde Park. Candlelight glimmered through every window as shadowed figures clad in shimmering satins walked along the footpath toward the front door. Their coach halted and one footman opened the door while another let down the two steps, taking Grace's hand to assist her to the walkway where Christian awaited. He offered her his arm and together they started up the stairs in silence.

Once inside the house, Grace waited while first Christian, then Lady Frances, and then Eleanor removed their cloaks. She remembered Liza's words about how surprised Christian would be by her gown. The others had already turned toward the ballroom, seeming to forget her. Grace quickly unfastened her mantelet, handing it to the waiting footman with a smile. She joined the others atop the stairs just as the footman was announcing their arrival.

"My lord and ladies, the Marquess and Marchioness Knighton, Lady Knighton, and Lady Eleanor Wycliffe."

It seemed as if a sea of faces immediately turned their way. Grace looked to where Christian stood beside her and noticed he wasn't staring out toward the crowded ballroom below them. Instead he was staring at her as if he didn't quite recognize her. The sullen look was gone, replaced by one of total astonishment.

Country mouse indeed! Grace thought, with a surge of confidence. Liza had been right. He did like the gown. She gave him a smile and asked, "Is everything all right, my lord?"

But Christian didn't answer her. He was far too occupied with staring at her bosom.

Chapter Fourteen

"Really, Christian, could you endeavor to be perhaps a little less obvious?"

Eleanor's comment broke Christian from his blind distraction long enough to realize that he was standing before a ballroom crowded with London's most elite society, openly ogling his wife's breasts. But *good God*! they were lovely. In the weeks since their wedding night, he'd forgotten just how lovely they were. Even now he found it difficult to tear his gaze away. He was mesmerized, totally taken aback, and even worse, he began to feel himself growing aroused beneath his breeches.

Buffoon! What the devil was wrong with him? What had happened to the unflappable reserve he'd adhered to so faithfully in the past weeks since returning to London? And more importantly, how had his modest mouse of a wife suddenly vanished, leaving this earthly angel in her place?

Christian knew the sudden urge to remove his coat, wrap her under it, and take her away from the leering eyes of every other man present. Either that or take her to the nearest closet and explore just how much farther her bodice could be lowered before it fully exposed her breasts. One thing of which he was now quite certain: This self-imposed celibacy was surely going to kill him.

He noticed that Grace was staring at him, the combined looks of uncertainty, hope, and anticipation shining brightly in her brilliant blue eyes. He could read her thoughts as clearly as if she'd spoken them. She had done this for him, donning the gown, taking care with her hair, all to please him. Why the devil did she have to worship him so obviously? He had virtually deserted her since their arrival in the city, never once walking through the door to her bedchamber or engaging in conversation more meaningful than the state of the weather. He had tried being sullen, hoping to give her a healthy dose of reality to temper that romantic wistfulness, fed by novels and comparisons of sex to the threading of a needle.

But he saw now that his efforts hadn't worked a whit. Christian didn't want to be worshipped. He didn't deserve to be worshipped. And he certainly didn't want to be married to a woman who played on his last noble trait—an admiration he had for that which was innocent amid the depravity of the world. It was this same trait that gave Christian his total devotion to his sister, driving him to do anything he could to preserve it in her. And now, incredibly, he found that his wife possessed it in kind, making it nigh impossible for him to dislike her.

He hadn't been fair to Grace, he knew, avoiding her, ignoring her as he had the past fortnight. He simply hadn't had a choice in the matter. If he didn't do everything he could to avoid her, he knew he would only lose himself to her, to her goodness, her innocence. He might even begin to look for the one thing he'd given up on— hope—even as he knew there could be no hope for him, never again. That was a fact made quite certain one cold spring morning twenty years before.

Still Christian realized that Grace had gone to a lot of effort this evening to look her best when she was presented to society as his wife. She didn't wish to shame him before his peers. The very least he could do would be to acknowledge her trouble.

"You look lovely this evening, Grace," he said, a statement that seemed pale in comparison to the vision she truly was. Her gown was made of a particular shade of green that only enhanced the color of her eyes, the cut of it carrying an air of seduction in the way that the bodice hugged her and in how the skirts swayed enticingly when she moved. Her hair had been swept back from her face into a wealth of tiny golden ringlets that danced about her neck when she moved, bits of it brushing loosely against her temple and ears. He had never realized what a slender and alluring neck she had, nor how fascinating the hollow of her throat could be before now.

Grace beamed under his attention. "Thank you, Christian. I am happy you are pleased."

Christian forced his eyes away from her and set her arm upon his as the two of them started to walk together through the crowd, accepting greetings and well-wishes on their marriage from the various people they encountered. Christian introduced Grace to his acquaintances, less than delighted with the way so many of the men in the room were openly admiring the charms of his wife's décolletage. How ironic, he thought to himself—they want to touch her and cannot; he can more than anyone else, but won't. He'd already made that mistake once, on his wedding night, and he was still waiting to discover if it would prove a fatal one in the conception of a child.

They had come across the length of the ballroom and were standing at the far end beside an overgrown potted palm when a voice suddenly broke through the muted murmur of the crowd. "My eyes must be deceiving me. Can this be England's most *in*eligible marquess?"

Christian turned and his face broke immediately into a whole grin.

"Noah!" he said, taking the outstretched hand of his closest friend, Lord Noah Edenhall. "I didn't know you were going to be here tonight. When did you arrive in town? Why didn't you stop to call at Knighton House?"

It was the first time Christian had seen him since the previous season, when Noah had left London after his own marriage to a lady with midnight hair and smoky eyes who was far too clever by half and equally as lovely. Lady Augusta was a celebrated astronomer and the *ton's* latest fascination. To look at her, one would never think that the petite bespectacled damsel would soon be written of in the history books. She had been credited with a stunning celestial discovery the year before. She was also with child, a fact Christian remarked on happily.

"We arrived just yesterday," Noah said. "Augusta had some work to complete with Lord Everton and I had some business to conduct with my brother. And of course, Catriona would never forgive us if we missed one of the balls she so scarcely hosts. Imagine my surprise when I arrived and heard that you had gotten married."

Christian nodded. "We arrived a bit late tonight and missed seeing Robert or Catriona in the reception line."

"Is that my name I hear coming from the newly wedded Lord Knighton?"

Their host for the evening, Robert Edenhall, the Duke of Devonbrook, came forward as if on cue to join them. Tall and dark, he presented a formidable figure wherever he went. But then a man with a formidable fortune usually did. At his side stood his wife, his lovely duchess, Catriona, a coppery-haired Scot who was another of the *ton's* celebrated figures. It was solely because of her that the ballroom was as crowded as it was; no one in London would ever miss a fête hosted by the infamous Duchess of Devonbrook.

Catriona kissed Christian lovingly on the cheek, embracing him openly, heedless of the risk she took in crushing her lovely tartan-trimmed gown. "We heard the news the minute we arrived in town. Congratulations, Christian. I'm so happy you could come this evening. I assume this lovely young lady on your arm is the new Lady Knighton?"

Christian nodded. "Grace, allow me to introduce the Duke and Duchess of Devonbrook, our hosts this evening. And this is the duke's brother, Lord Noah, and his wife, Lady Augusta Edenhall."

Grace smiled timidly at the quartet of welcoming faces. "It is a pleasure to make your acquaintances."

As Christian would have expected, Catriona and Augusta instantly enveloped Grace. Any danger of social disapproval toward her would now vanish under their protection; it had been his foremost thought in choosing this particular event for introducing his wife to society.

"Lady Knighton," said Catriona, "that is indeed a stunning gown. Is it one of Madame Delphine's?"

"Yes, thank you, Your Grace, but please call me Grace." She pulled a nervous face. "That sounded a bit silly, now, didn't it?"

"Indeed, and it will be doubly confusing when you one day become a duchess and everyone begins calling you 'Grace, Your Grace.'" She chuckled. "Let us avoid any confusion and simply address one another by our given names."

"Splendid idea," said Augusta then, taking Grace on one side while Catriona commandeered the other. "Come, let us leave the gentlemen to their port and conversation in the parlor while we badger Grace into telling us if Christian snores half as loudly as Noah does."

"Oh, then it must be a family trait," added Catriona. "I thought none could be worse than my Robert."

Grace grinned, enjoying the banter. "If Christian does snore, it mustn't be very loud for I never hear him through the door adjoining our rooms."

Both ladies suddenly halted. Their respective husbands turned to stare at Grace, who hadn't yet realized the significance behind her words. Immediately everyone shifted their attention to Christian. It seemed as if it had suddenly grown as silent as a church in the midst of that crowded ballroom. Christian wondered that every other guest present had not overheard the exchange.

Catriona, blessedly, came to the rescue, ending the awkwardness. "Come, Grace, let us find a quiet corner somewhere where we might get better acquainted."

Christian stood and watched them go, silently cursing. He wasn't angry at Grace; how could he be? She could have no notion of just what she had revealed by her innocent statement. Without even realizing, she had just disclosed to his two closest friends in life, men who were openly passionate about their wives, that she and Christian, newly wedded, did not share a bedchamber. He turned to regard his friends again. The stares he received in response saw more than he had hoped they would.

"So what business are the two of you transacting?" he said to Noah in hopes of diverting their attentions elsewhere.

Noah stared at him a moment before saying, "Robert has finally convinced Augusta to breed her mare Atalanta with his stallion Bayard. The only problem is deciding who will take the foal should it prove successful. I have suggested that they draw straws. Augusta is more inclined to a combined ownership where the beast shall live part of the year with Robert at Devonbrook Hall and part of the year with us at Eden Court," he finished on a grin. "With Augusta, of course, retaining possession in the summer months."

The conversation progressed from there with neither Robert nor Noah making further mention of Grace's comment. But then they were gentlemen and gentlemen rarely pried into such personal matters.

Ladies, on the other hand . . .

Catriona had found them a bit of quiet space in the back parlor, far from the noise and crowd of the ballroom. They dropped into a pair of matched brocade-covered settees that faced one another, Grace on one side, Catriona and Augusta on the other. Thus when Grace looked up, it was to dual sets of keen, inquiring eyes.

"So, dear," Catriona said on a smile, "do tell us about yourself."

Grace found herself suddenly tongue-tied before these two refined and elegant ladies. With hair the color of glistening copper and diamonds sparkling from her ears, Catriona was exactly what one would think of in a duchess. Poised and confident, Grace couldn't imagine this woman having ever done anything improper in her life. In contrast, Augusta's hair was a silky black and pulled atop her head in a coronet that gave her the look of the nobility she had obviously come from. She was quite intriguing. Grace had never met a woman who would dare to wear spectacles in public, let alone at a society ball.

Even as they had walked across the ballroom together, Grace had watched as Catriona and Augusta had drawn the notice of the crowd. She could only think that everyone else must have been wondering why she would be with these two most distinguished women.

Finally she said, "I'm afraid my upbringing is not what you would consider fashionable," she began. "I cannot make much of a claim to society. I was raised in the country and—"

"Nonsense!" said Catriona. "I was raised in the country, as well—in Scotland."

"And I was raised on board a ship among nothing but sailors," broke in Augusta. "So much more interesting than strapped to a backboard, pouring tea at a finishing school. So tell us, how did you come to know Christian?"

"I didn't really know him." Grace chewed her lower lip. "In fact, I didn't know him at all. Our marriage was arranged by our families."

The two women looked at one another and then together they nodded.

"You don't care for him?" asked Augusta.

"Oh, no—I mean yes, I do care for Christian very much." Grace hesitated, chewing her lip some more. "I just don't think he cares very much for me."

"Impossible!" said Catriona. "Why on earth wouldn't he? You are obviously sweet and charming and intelligent. He should be proud to have such a lovely wife."

"He rarely talks to me; whenever he does, he just seems angry with me." Grace immediately regretted her loose tongue. She had only just made the acquaintance of these ladies, and here she was telling them the most awful truth of her marriage.

But they didn't seem offended by her candor. Instead they seemed concerned.

Augusta said, tapping a finger to her chin, "Odd. That doesn't sound at all like Christian."

"Indeed, he has always struck me as a most polite and attentive man." Catriona looked at Grace, lowering her voice. "Forgive me, dear, if I intrude in matters of which I have no right to ask. Understand that I am Scottish and we are quite open about such matters."

Grace nodded for her to continue.

"I presume, from your comments earlier, that you and Christian do not share a bedchamber . . . or, for that matter, a bed."

Grace felt instantly awash with shame, her face growing heated. She nodded slowly.

Augusta shook her head. "Most odd indeed."

"One can only guess that because your marriage was arranged, perhaps Christian is resistant to admitting defeat."

"Defeat?"

"Oh yes," answered Augusta. "He is, after all, *a man*."

"Indeed. They can be so pigheaded about things, can't

they?" Catriona shook her head. "I would assume, knowing what I do of Christian's family history, that his grandfather the duke arranged your marriage."

Grace nodded.

"There is much hostility between the old duke and Christian. I would guess it is simply because you were chosen by his grandfather that Christian is behaving the way he is toward you. Were he to show that he were pleased with you, to his thinking, that would be allowing his grandfather to win."

Grace wrinkled her brow in confusion. "It would?"

"I know it makes no sense to a woman, dear, because we are sensible and clear headed and we see things as they truly are. Men, poor dears, can only see things in two respects: winning and losing. If Christian were thinking rationally, he would be instead giving his grandfather the impression that he is blissfully happy with his choice of you, which of course he could only be with you as his wife."

"Yes," Augusta added, "obviously with so much hostility between them, it would only rankle the duke more to think that he had given Christian such a gift when he had intended to give him misery. Mind you, not that you are a misery, dear. You clearly are not." She nodded, sitting up with both hands on Grace's knees. "As I see it, we must *enlighten* Christian."

Grace was only growing further confused. "Enlighten him?"

"Oh, yes, dear. It is your only hope of bringing this situation to its necessary conclusion." Catriona sat taller in her seat and looked across the room, studying the crowd. "We must find a way to make our dear Lord Knighton open his clouded eyes and see what he has right before him. Either that or we shall have to conk him on the head with Augusta's telescope to knock some sense into him."

The two of them laughed, and then Catriona straightened more in her seat, peering past Grace to the doorway. "We must proceed most carefully . . . it is a decision of the utmost delicacy . . ." She smiled then. "And I think I have found just the person to assist us in our endeavor."

Augusta looked to where Catriona was staring, a wide smile breaking across her face. "Oh, Catriona, I know what you are thinking and I must say, dear, it is a perfect solution. Indeed, almost *too* perfect."

Grace turned in her seat to see what it was that had so captured the ladies' attention. But she could see nothing at all because the doorway was blocked by the figure of a man. She turned her attention back to the two ladies. "I'm afraid I do not see what you are talking about."

"Look again, dear. I understand he waltzes divinely."

Grace turned a second time and it was then she realized that they intended her to notice the man standing in the doorway. Furthermore, they intended her to . . .

Grace looked back to them. "Oh, no, I couldn't."

"Oh, but you could, dear. You want to draw Christian's notice, do you not?"

"Yes, but—"

"This will do much better than a conking on his head. And it will serve him right for having neglected you as he has. Trust us, my dear. We know well what we are doing."

"But would it be considered proper? I do not wish to do anything that might cause Christian embarrassment. Shouldn't I dance my first dance as a marchioness with my husband?"

"You would have, had he asked you." Catriona grinned. "Besides, I am the hostess this evening. It is perfectly within propriety—in fact, it is my duty—to find partners for the ladies who aren't already dancing."

Grace remained uncertain. Still she had no better option before her and these ladies seemed so sure of themselves.

Catriona looked to Augusta with a devilish smile. "Shall I do the honors, dear sister?"

"Oh, by all means." She looked at Grace as Catriona stood. "Watch and learn, dear."

Catriona straightened her skirts and glided elegantly across the room. In seconds, she had caught the attention of the man at the doorway and they were soon engaged in conversation, smiling and nodding. Moments later Catriona had taken his hand and was bringing him over to where Augusta and Grace were still sitting.

"Lady Knighton, allow me to introduce a friend of ours—and an acquaintance of your husband. Lord Whitly, please meet our new friend, Lady Knighton."

He was about as close as any mortal could be to a god on earth—blond hair the color of spun gold, lazy hazel eyes, and a smile that could easily melt an iceberg. He was dressed in a coat of navy superfine with a superbly starched neckcloth worthy of Brummell himself. Even as he stood beside her, Grace could see other ladies nearby stopping their conversations so that they might watch him, fluttering their fans quickly before them.

Yet even while one could not dispute that he was indeed handsome, Grace found she preferred Christian's darker, more natural looks to the example of overdone perfection that stood before her. Lord Whitly seemed pleasant enough, though, and Catriona and Augusta obviously liked him, so Grace offered him her gloved hand in greeting.

"A pleasure to make your acquaintance, Lord Whitly."

Lord Whitly took her hand and pressed a kiss softly to it. "It is, indeed, my pleasure as well, Lady Knighton."

"Now, Whitly," said Augusta then, "you needn't waste your charms on Lady Knighton because she is thoroughly smitten with her husband, as any good wife should be. All we require of you is a turn or two about the dance floor. That should serve our purposes quite well."

Whitly grinned. "Happy to be of service, my ladies." He motioned toward the ballroom door. "Lady Knighton, shall we?"

Grace looked at Catriona and Augusta one last time even as she rose to her feet. As they headed off for the ballroom, she sent a silent prayer to the Fates that she was doing the right thing.

Chapter Fifteen

Christian took a draught from his port glass and spied his sister Eleanor through the parlor doorway. She was standing with his mother and another, smiling radiantly and he paused a moment, watching her. He noticed she was talking with a gentleman—a gentleman whom he recognized in the next moment when the man turned with Eleanor to look out over the dancing area.

Christian nearly choked.

"Excuse me a moment, gentlemen," he said to his friends, handing his glass to Noah before he headed steadfastly across the room to where his sister still stood. He approached them silently from behind.

"Eleanor," Christian said, his voice cordial, showing no hint of the turmoil that was churning inside of him as he came to stand beside her. He glanced once at the gentleman with her, then immediately looked to his sister again. "It is time for that dance I promised you, isn't it?"

Lady Frances stood to Eleanor's other side giving Christian a look that only the two of them could understand.

"Oh, Christian," Eleanor said on a smile, "I was wondering where you'd disappeared to. I was just telling Lord Herrick here of your marriage. You know the earl, do you not?"

Far better than I care to admit. Christian turned, giving the man an affected smile that never quite exceeded a cool politeness. "Herrick," he said, his voice empty of any emotion, "you are looking well."

It had been over twenty years since the two men had last faced one another, but it might have only been twenty days. Richard Hartley, Earl of Herrick, still had the same coal-black hair and harsh gray eyes he'd had as a boy. For the moment, it seemed almost as if Christian were standing across from him on the cricket field at Eton with his shirttails hanging out the back of his grass-stained breeches, his cuffs rolled to his elbows.

By the time they had parted on that last occasion, Christian had sported a blackened eye; Herrick had stood with a bloodied and nearly broken nose.

But Herrick simply returned a curt nod that revealed nothing, leaving Christian to wonder what the man's aim in speaking with Eleanor could be. "Knighton, my congratulations on your recent marriage."

Eleanor smiled, blissfully oblivious of the tension that had suddenly thickened the air between them. "Oh, so I was correct in thinking you do know one another."

Christian's eyes never left Herrick's. "Yes, Eleanor, Lord Herrick and I have already been acquainted, although it has been some time. We were at Eton together, actually. It is good to see you again, Herrick. Now if you'll excuse us, I believe I owe my sister this dance."

Christian didn't wait long enough for Herrick to respond, but instead directed Eleanor toward the dance floor and as far away from the earl as possible. As he threaded them a path through the other people in the room, Christian didn't realize the tightness with which he was gripping Eleanor's hand until they had stopped and she pulled away, rubbing her gloved fingers. She stared at him curiously.

"Christian, is something wrong?"

"No," he lied. "Should there be?"

"You just seem agitated of a sudden."

They prepared for the waltz that was about to begin and Christian caught sight of Herrick over the top of Eleanor's head. Lady Frances had vanished and Herrick was standing at the edge of the dance floor, watching them.

Christian frowned. He had hoped the earl would have gone off in search of other company.

"Lord Herrick seems very nice," Eleanor said, drawing Christian's attention away from the side of the room.

"You have spoken of so many of your friends from Eton over the years that I thought I knew of them all. Why have you never mentioned him?"

How in God's name was he supposed to answer her? He had thought he'd been so cautious, safeguarding against every possible situation. Of all the contretemps that could have taken place, he never would have expected this one. "I suppose I never mentioned him because the occasion never called for me to, Nell."

Eleanor smiled as she always did when he used his childhood nickname for her. The music began. As they moved about the floor with the other couples, Christian sought to change the subject. "Are you enjoying the ball this evening?"

"Oh, yes, very much. It has proven a most pleasant evening indeed."

As they danced, Christian noticed Eleanor looking to where Herrick yet lingered at the edge of the dance floor. He noticed the smiles they exchanged and felt his stomach tighten in response. *Damnation!* This could not be happening. Not her. Not him. Not now. Christian quickly turned his sister so that her back was to the earl.

"It is amazing," Eleanor said, "the differences in being 'out' and participating in the season as compared to being relegated to our mother's side to watch on in silence."

Christian looked down at her. She was still searching the fringes of the floor for Herrick. His voice lowered. "You have all the time in the world, you know, Nell. You needn't set your sights on the first buck you run across."

Eleanor looked up at her brother, her face coloring at his having seen straight through to her budding attraction for Herrick. "I am not setting my sights on anyone, Christian—not yet, anyway."

"That is good." He turned her about again. "You shall have a love match. I promise you. No one will force you into a marriage you do not want."

The undertone of his words was obvious.

"Are you so very unhappy with Grace, Christian?"

The question was not one he had been prepared for and he wasn't quite sure how to respond. "I don't really know. I don't even know her; we are truly strangers and that is a sorry beginning for any marriage."

"You certainly don't seem interested in getting to know her any time soon, either."

It was more an accusation than anything else and Christian looked at his sister, but her attention was focused elsewhere. He had to maneuver them a bit because it seemed as if the dance floor was becoming more and more crowded. They moved through several more turns of the dance.

"And I would suggest, dear brother, that you concentrate your efforts on your wife a bit more before others see to the job for you. That is, if it is not too late already."

Eleanor stopped dancing. Most everyone around them had as well. Christian turned to where Eleanor had motioned for him to look near the center of the dance floor. Christian searched for whatever it was she was pointing to, but there were too many blocking his view. Everyone's attention, it seemed, was focused there. He inched a bit closer and could see that there was a solitary couple dancing in the midst of the crowd. As he made his way around the onlookers, he soon saw why. He wasn't surprised. Lord Whitly had a talent for drawing attention to himself, as an accomplished dancer, yes, but more so as a notorious rakehell. But in the next moment, Christian felt his breath give way when he noticed the lady with whom Lord Whitly was waltzing so finely.

It was his wife.

Christian fixed his stare on Grace as she glided smoothly through the steps of the dance. The skirts of her gown swept outward with her movements, her gloved hand resting lightly on Whitly's arm as he held her other hand in his. She moved as if she'd been born to waltz, her curls bouncing gently about her neck, and she was smiling, a smile more brilliant than he had ever seen her wear before. It was the sort of smile that should have been reserved for him, her husband, not this stranger, not this well-known roué.

Christian noticed that several of the other guests around him were watching him for his reaction, whispering conjecture. Conjecture, he knew, often led to scandal. If he didn't proceed carefully, this could furnish the tea parlors of the whole of London with gossip enough for the next several days. Christian relaxed his jaw, which he just realized he'd been clenching, and stood back until the first recess of the dance. When Whitly bent into a bow before Grace, Christian began to applaud. Everyone around him soon followed suit until the entire ballroom was paying tribute. Whitly turned and executed a second flourishing bow to the crowd while Grace smiled tentatively under the crowd's overwhelming admiration.

Christian seized the first opportunity to step forward and lay claim to his wife.

"That was lovely, my dear," he said, taking her hand and kissing it. "I hope Lord Whitly won't mind my taking his place through the next movement of the dance?"

Whitly wisely bowed his head. "Of course not, Knighton. She is, after all, your wife—and a treasure at that. Lady Knighton, it was indeed a pleasure. Good evening, Knighton."

Christian stood, watching Whitly's prudent retreat with a smile that was more predatory than polite. He turned to Grace. "Shall we, my dear?"

Grace nodded just as the music resumed. Christian swept her closer to him, his hand placed possessively at the small of her back, that same fixed smile on his mouth. They waltzed into the first several turns, a spectacle for all to see before the others around them joined in on the dancing. He waited until he was certain they would not be overheard before speaking.

"I wasn't aware you were acquainted with Lord Whitly."

"I wasn't," Grace answered. "Catriona and Augusta just now introduced us. He seems a most amiable gentleman."

"Gentleman, indeed." Christian took her into a turn, leading them closer to the far end of the dance floor near to the terrace doors. "It is a good idea, Grace, to dance first with one's husband after being wed. It can avert unnecessary conjecture."

Grace stared at him. "I would have, my lord, had my husband asked me to."

Touché.

As he spun her into the next turn, Christian caught a breath of Grace's fragrance, exotically unique. He immediately felt the palms of his hands grow hot. He said, "That is an intriguing scent you wear, my lady."

"It is a family recipe, my lord. A secret of sorts."

"Indeed." His heart began to pound as if he had just run the length of the ballroom. He looked down at her, a fatal mistake, for in doing so, he was afforded an open view of her glorious cleavage. No doubt it had been the reason for Whitly's smile. Christian was seized by an overwhelming urge to bury his face against her breasts and fill himself with her essence. His breath caught and he felt his sex begin to swell beneath his breeches. Good God, he was a man of nine-and-twenty, not a randy schoolboy. What the devil was wrong with him?

When next Christian turned, he faltered, taking the wrong direction. Grace had been unprepared for it and so when she stepped right, Christian went left. She lost her footing and fell directly against him, every inch of her pressed intimately to him. His response, or rather that of his body, was immediate.

"Good gracious," Grace said.

An understatement, to say the least.

Thank God they were just beside the door to the terrace, otherwise half of London society would have seen just how aroused Christian was. Instead, he quickly recovered his footing and turned them both out onto the terrace.

As he closed the door behind them, Christian said a silent prayer of thanks that it was a chill night and no one else had ventured from the ballroom. At that moment, he was beyond any thought but wanting her. He backed Grace against the far wall and pulled her hard against him, taking her mouth in a kiss that was fraught with impatience and lust. The curves of her body molded to his and he groaned into her mouth. And the more he kissed her, felt her, knew her, the more he wanted her.

The more he *needed* her.

"Damnation!"

Christian tore his mouth away from hers, staring at

her in the moonlight, searching for some sense of explanation for the effect she had on him.

"Christian?"

"Come," was all he said and he took Grace's hand,
striding across the terrace to the far side. At least he
still had enough sense to know he certainly couldn't take
his wife there against the railing of a moonlit terrace.
He found that blessedly the door to Robert's private
study was unlocked. He opened it, navigating his way in
the moonlight to the opposite side of the room. Grace
said nothing, just followed behind him, the rustling of
her skirts against the carpet the only sound between
them.

Christian's pulse was pounding as he took her up the
back staircase usually reserved for the Devonbrook servants. He went to the first bedchamber he could find,
opened the door, entered, and locked it behind them.
He turned to face her. He was breathing hard. His body
felt on fire. At that moment, he wanted her more than
he'd ever wanted anything in his life.

"Grace."

It was all he managed to say before he took her
against him again. He kissed her deeply, thrusting his
tongue into her mouth while he backed her to the side
of the bed. He laid her down and fell atop her, burying
his face against her neck, breathing in the scent of her,
his hands groping her everywhere, anywhere, all at once.
He fumbled with the fastenings of his breeches, cursing
himself aloud as he did.

"I am not a damned animal, Grace. I don't know why
I can't seem to control myself. I need to feel you. I need
to be inside of you. I just can't help it."

She looked at him, her eyes shining softly in the
moonlight coming through the window behind her. "I
want to be close to you again. I have missed you. It is
all right, Christian."

But it wasn't all right. This was not the way a man of
his age and status in life made love to a woman, most
especially his wife. Nonetheless, his breeches were down
around his ankles and he fell over her again, pulling at
her skirts, searching through the layers and layers of
silken fabric, desperate to find her. When he had suc-

ceeded in pushing them up around her waist, he parted
her legs and came between them quickly. His heart was
hammering now against his chest. He could scarcely
breathe. He thanked the saints when he found that she
was at least partially aroused and then thrust himself
deeply, crying out as he buried himself totally within her.

When next he had regained his senses, Christian was
panting, his forehead damp with perspiration. Even as
he lay there atop her, his face buried against her neck,
he could not believe what he had done. He had just
ravished his wife in a guest bedchamber at the home of
one of his closest friends while half of London danced
in the ballroom beneath them, spilling his seed inside of
her not just once now—but twice. Somehow he knew at
that moment his grandfather was laughing.

Christian took himself away from Grace without a
word. He stood to quickly fasten his breeches. He turned
toward her. She lay there, quietly watching him in the
moonlight. One stocking was down around her ankle and
her hair was a tumbled mass of curls against the pillow.
Her eyes were wide and totally filled with that same
damned adoration she always looked on him with. She
looked incredible, so incredible that he felt a slight tightening in his groin, even after what he had just
accomplished.

Christian lowered her skirts, noting unhappily that in
his frantic assault on her, he had torn the edging of her
gown. He stared at Grace, and she him for several
long moments.

"I'm afraid we will not be able to return to the ball.
I've quite ruined your coiffure."

Grace touched a hand to her disarranged curls. "It
doesn't matter. I don't care about the ball. I just want
to be with you."

Christian stood stiffly. They were not words he needed
to hear right then. "I will notify my mother that we are
leaving. I'll see to retrieving our cloaks and calling for
a carriage." He looked at her. "Grace, I have no right
to expect that you would understand—"

Christian never finished his thought for Grace had
stood and very gently placed her fingers against his lips,
whispering, "Shh. Please don't spoil this, Christian."

Her eyes were shining brightly in the moonlight and her face was taken with a dreamy sort of smile. He took her fingers away. "Grace, you do not realize it, but this is not the way relations are normally conducted between a man and a woman. Men who behave as I have, who perform as I have, are animals. A man should be able to control his impulses long enough to take a woman to a proper bedchamber and long enough so that she might at least remove her gloves."

Grace looked at her hands then as if suddenly realizing she still wore them. She looked at him. "But it wasn't terrible, Christian, not even the first time on our wedding night. I'm sorry for whatever I did wrong to make you leave that night. It is just that I wasn't aware it was going to hurt and it was only for a moment and everything else you had done up to that point—especially the kissing part—that had been nice. And tonight wasn't terrible. It didn't hurt at all this time. It startled me a little, but I think, at least I hope it brought me closer to you."

Christian stared at her. Good God, she was blaming herself. He couldn't believe she was apologizing to him for his having taken her virginity so badly. "Damnation, Grace! You are a dreamer!" He wanted to shake her, knock those fanciful thoughts right from her head. "I cannot tolerate this. I will not stand for this to happen again!"

"Christian, you are angry with me." She set her hand on his arm. "You are displeased that I danced with Lord Whitly instead of waiting for you to ask me. It was a mistake. I know that now. I promise I will not do it again."

Christian closed his eyes, so furious with himself at having given over to his passion once again that he wanted to break something. Simply the thought of what he'd done—dragging her here from that crowded ballroom to a guest chamber in Robert's home, taking her as he did, spilling his seed inside of her again—filled him with a raw anger that threatened to explode inside of him. He was a marquess, heir to an esteemed dukedom. He had been raised to eschew all emotion and feeling, quash it beneath a cold, hard blanket of indifference. It was the way of the Westover men and he had spent twenty years cultivating the icy reserve that had kept him safely apart from the rest of the world. He didn't know what it was about this woman that made him forget completely who he was. But whatever it was, this madness had to stop. He was determined that it would.

As he started for the door to make the arrangements for their swift departure, Christian drew on every ounce of callousness he could, hardening his heart against the memory of her eyes, her sweetness, while he made a silent vow to himself, one in which he would not fail.

If it meant he had to banish her to the country, he was not going to break this vow.

He was not, under any circumstances, going to sleep with his wife again.

Chapter Sixteen

Christian would repeat his vow against bedding his wife twice more during the following fortnight. Every time he made the oath anew, he was just as determined to persevere. And every time he failed, he grew that much more disgusted with himself.

Something must be done about this madness.

Blessedly, for the past week, Grace had been occupied with preparations for hosting her first supper party. It had been Catriona's idea, apparently, a way for Grace to establish herself as a member of society. Other than to ask the advice of Eleanor or Lady Frances when necessary, or consult him on the guest list, Grace had embraced the venture wholeheartedly, taking it upon herself to make all the arrangements. Invitations had been issued to well over a dozen guests—friends and associates of the Knighton family as well as several principal society figures. Not one of the invitations Grace had sent had been refused—a good sign, yes, for it indicated that she had been received well by the *ton*.

As he stood before his dressing mirror preparing for the evening's event, it wasn't the guest list or even what they would be serving that occupied Christian's thoughts. Instead it was a peculiar message he'd received two days before, an anonymous note that the Knighton butler Forbes found lying upon the doorstep.

It was addressed to Christian and sealed with a wafer, a *black* wafer, something customarily reserved for correspondence of mourning. The handwriting wasn't noticeably male or female and the stationary was indistinct, leaving it virtually untraceable. The message contained inside was but a single phrase.

*One can never know what it is to lose something
precious until it is gone.*

Frighteningly cryptic, the words were tinged with a
good deal more meaning than Christian cared to admit.
He had reread the note a dozen times since and each
time it had given him the same sick sort of feeling deep
within his stomach. He would have considered canceling
the supper party had it not already been too late. So
instead, Christian told no one about the message, hoping
he might discover its origin quietly and without causing
alarm to the others. What bothered him most was that
he couldn't know for certain who or what the letter per-
tained to; there were so many possibilities. No one in the
household—Grace, Eleanor, Lady Frances, or himself—
could be excluded from the threat the message posed,
leaving them all at risk and bringing Christian face to
face with the very thing he had spent the past twenty
years running from.

Someone else knew the truth about the past and had
waited until now to reveal it, after his marriage to Grace
had taken place and just when Eleanor was making her
social debut. It couldn't have come at a more disas-
trous time.

Christian turned from the mirror as his valet, Peter,
came into the room carrying Christian's newly polished
boots.

"That coat looks fine on you, my lord. A good choice,
the dark blue." He set the boots on the floor near the
chair. "Will there be anything else, my lord?"

Christian shook his head as the valet bowed and made
to leave, adding as he went, "Lady Knighton asked me
to tell you she would await you in the parlor with the
other guests."

Christian adjusted his cuff. "They've already begun
to arrive?"

"Aye, my lord. The Duke and Duchess of Devonbrook and Lord and Lady Edenhall are here, and
Lady Frances and Lady Eleanor have gone down already
as well. There were two or three carriages stopping at
the front when I started up the stairs."

Christian nodded. He quickly tugged on his boots,

straightened his neckcloth in the mirror, then headed from the room, wishing he could put the menacing words of the mysterious message out of his mind for the night.

As he came down the stairs, he heard the sound of laughter and conversation coming from the formal parlor. He did not immediately go in, but stood just outside the door, looking quietly inside. As he studied the faces inside the room, a terrible thought struck him. What if the author of the message was one of their guests? Surely not Devonbrook or Edenhall, his closest friends, but a good number of the other guests had been acquaintances of his family when his father had still been alive. What if one of them had known the truth all this time?

As he surveyed the room, Christian spotted Grace near the fireplace, talking with Augusta and Catriona. He paused a moment to look at her. The transformation over the past month was remarkable. Gone was the meek, naïve country girl who had stood with shaking hands at the chapel altar in Little Biddlington. In her place was a young woman who was doing everything she could to successfully fulfill her new role as marchioness. He'd spotted the gown she had chosen to wear earlier that evening draped across the foot of her bed when he'd passed her chamber door. Pale lavender silk set with brilliants that glittered in the candlelight—he remembered thinking it would look lovely with her eyes and hair. Indeed, he had been right.

If only he could have been as right about his ability to control his own lust.

Before the delivery of the message, Christian had considered the possibility of sending Grace and her maid away from London to Westover Hall for a while, to put her a safe distance away from him while he figured out how he was going to find his way back to having a marriage in name only. But sending her away would no longer be possible, not when he needed to keep her and the rest of the family close in the face of the ominous message he'd received. If anything happened to any one of them because of it, he would never be able to live with himself.

At the sound of Eleanor's laughter, Christian looked

and saw that his sister was standing off to the side of
the room engaged in conversation. She looked radiant
and Christian was pleased to see that she was enjoying
herself, until he realized that the person she was chatting
so happily with was Lord Herrick. His body went instantly cold at the sight of the earl and the casual, almost
intimate manner in which he was speaking to Eleanor.
Christian didn't recall having seen Herrick's name on
the guest list when Grace had shown it to him. In fact,
he distinctly remembered having looked for it to make
certain the earl wouldn't be attending.

Why, then, had Grace invited him?

Christian entered the room, working his way slowly
toward his wife to question her about it. His progress
was stopped several times by greetings from their guests.

"Knighton, good to see you," said Lord Rennington,
an older earl who had been a member of his father's
club. Lady Rennington was one of the few close acquaintances his mother had left in town. They had been acquainted with his family for two generations. He
wondered, could either of them have been responsible
for the message?

Christian paused a moment to exchange polite conversation, then broke away from the earl to join Grace. As
he made his way around the room, he mentally catalogued the other guests present. Lord and Lady Faneshaw. Viscount Chilburn, newly wedded to his second
wife. The Talbots. The Fairfields. The Sykes. Even Herrick. Any one of them could have sent the note. He tried
to remember if there had ever been anything mentioned
among any of them that might indicate they knew more
about the past than he'd thought. All he met with was
a blank, virulent void.

"Christian," Catriona said, noticing his approach, "I
was just telling Grace that we must have the two of you
up to Devonbrook Hall in the fall. You haven't yet seen
the estate since it was rebuilt after the fire."

Christian smiled, all politeness, in order to shield the
tension stretching through his insides. "We would love
to, Catriona. Set upon a date and we will be there." He
took Grace's arm. "Now I hope you ladies won't mind
if I borrow my wife for a moment? There is a matter to

do with this evening's supper that I must discuss with her."

As Catriona and Augusta nodded, Christian turned and walked with Grace across the room to the entrance hall. As soon as they were out of the parlor, his polite smile vanished. He attempted to subdue the irritation in his voice as he said, "Would you mind telling me just what in perdition Herrick is doing here?"

Grace looked startled, glancing uneasily past Christian's shoulder to where Eleanor stood with the earl near the drinks' table. "I had thought Eleanor would enjoy his company tonight. She talks of him so often."

"His name was not on the guest list you gave to me."

"I didn't think of inviting him until later. I had intended to tell you, but you haven't been at home much in the past several days. Is there some reason why I shouldn't have invited him?"

"I just don't want Eleanor setting her cap on the first man she meets. I would prefer that she meet a number of gentlemen and not devote her attention to one so soon after her coming-out. But it is too late. The damage, at least for this evening, has been done."

Ignoring Grace's immediately wounded expression, Christian turned and left her standing in the hall, hoping that both the delivery of that mysterious message at the door and Herrick's sudden presence in their lives were merely coincidental. Somehow it didn't seem possible, and as he went back into the parlor, he wondered if there would be any other unexpected guests that evening.

Grace sat at the far end of a long mahogany dining table set with various pieces of silver that gleamed in the candlelight from days of polishing. The service was impeccable, the room looked exquisite, and each course of the meal was prepared to perfection. Yet she found herself wondering if the evening could be any more a disaster than it already was.

Everything favorable about the evening had disappeared behind the frown Christian wore over his wine goblet as he sat opposite her down the length of the table. His displeasure at discovering Lord Herrick was nothing compared to that at the guest who sat to his immediate right. Grace had thought that by inviting the old duke and seating him and Christian together, they might somehow be persuaded to talk to one another and perhaps find a way to begin mending their terrible rift. But the murderous looks Christian was sending her way only told her she couldn't have been more mistaken.

To make matters worse, the room was markedly silent. Supper parties were made for sparkling conversation, the reporting of news, the sharing of opinions and ideas. With the exception of the occasional request for salt or more wine, no one in the room was saying much of anything. Instead they stared at one another across the table, occasionally looking her way. Finally, blessedly, Catriona spoke up.

"Robert," she said to her husband, "why do you not tell everyone about the fish little James caught when you took him trouting for the first time last month."

As the duke began to relate the tale of their young son, Grace leaned toward Augusta, who sat at her left, and whispered, "Why aren't any of the others talking to one another?"

Augusta took a sip from her glass—a concoction of milk touched with cinnamon, a treat she found she craved now that she was with child, and which the cook had been all too happy to prepare for her. "I'm not an expert on things pertaining to society—that was always my stepmother's forte—but I would guess they are not talking because before now, they have never been made to spend this much time in each other's company."

"But I don't understand. I made certain to seat all the husbands and wives together."

"That is precisely the problem." Augusta nodded her head toward the other end of the table. "You see Lord Faneshaw there? He will not give his wife even the slightest nod of his attention, but he certainly has been throwing glances in Lady Rennington's direction three seats down and across from him. It is because typically at such events, the two of them are seated together."

"They are?"

Augusta set down her spoon and said quite matter-of-factly, "Of course, dear. She is his mistress."

Grace covered her mouth with her napkin just quickly enough to stifle her gasp.

Augusta nodded. "And Lady Faneshaw is usually seated with Viscount Chilburn whose new wife, Lady Chilburn, is usually seated with Lord Sykes for much the same reason. Among the society set, a good many hostesses do not think it fashionable to seat a husband and wife together, which is why Catriona and I don't normally attend such functions. We actually enjoy conversing with our husbands, but we are never seated together and thus are stuck with either a boor like Rennington, or a lecher like Chilburn."

Grace could but shake her head in disbelief. "I had no idea. How stupid everyone must think me."

"Not at all, dear. I rather like your order to things. I am usually so very occupied in my observatory. I am awake in the evenings and rest during the day so I don't have the opportunity to see Noah as often as I'd like. Lately I seem to be sleeping more and more, most likely because of the babe. We have spent most of tonight catching up on what typically should be discussed over breakfast. It has been nice to have this time where neither of us has to be off doing other things. Don't trouble over the others. Leave the situation to Catriona. By the time she gets through, you will have set a new trend in seating arrangements."

As if in answer to her cue, the duchess spoke up again. "Lady Rennington, did you not tell me the night of our ball that your grandson, Charles, is quite the poet? I should love to read something he has written; I am such an admirer of verse. I wonder who he inherited the talent from—you, perhaps?"

"Oh, no, Your Grace, I was never one who did very well at poetry, but Lord Rennington, at one time, wrote wonderful verse. It has been so long since he last wrote any, I had nearly forgotten."

"Now, don't discredit yourself, dear. When we were younger, you were quite the poet yourself."

The countess looked on her husband for the first time all evening. A flicker of long-forgotten tenderness passed between them that seemed almost to warm the room around them.

Lady Talbot chimed in, "You know Lord Talbot was also quite the artist at one time. He would send me the drawings he had made while on the Peninsula."

"I was a young fool who was homesick," said her husband, obviously uncomfortable with the soft subject matter.

"The letters you wrote were just as endearing. That is why I married you, Henry."

Soon they were all comparing memories of times and tendernesses gone by. It was astounding. With the mention of one small thing—a grandmother's boast about her grandchild—Catriona had somehow reminded these people of what they had first been attracted to in one another. From then on, conversation was never lacking.

Later, after dinner, they retired to the parlor to play cards. Grace won two rounds, having been taught well by Nonny, who had been quite a cardsharp in her day. Eleanor then delighted them all with her flute playing, accompanied by Grace on the pianoforte. Eleanor's talent was astounding. Grace had never heard the instrument played with such emotion and texture, much less by a lady; women were customarily relegated to the harp or pianoforte.

It was well past midnight when they stood at the door, bidding their guests farewell. Despite its worrisome beginning, the evening had ended up a success.

Grace hugged Catriona as they made to leave. "I cannot thank you enough for all your help this evening. I would hate to think of the disaster it would have been without you."

"Nonsense, Grace, you don't give yourself enough credit. It was you who made the evening so pleasant for everyone. Some of them just needed their eyes opened to it, that's all."

Grace watched them walk to their carriage, then turned to her last guest. The butler Forbes was just helping the old duke on with his coat. Christian, she noticed, had vanished.

"I thank you for coming, Your Grace," she said as he reached for her hand. "I hope your visit was pleasant."

"If only to see that I had been right about you from

the start. I was a bit rough on you at first, but it is as I thought. You will make a fine duchess some day."

Grace smiled at him as he leaned forward to whisper to her, "A bit of advice, though, my girl. Don't waste your time trying to repair something when you don't know how deep goes the break. Some things were just never meant to be."

Thunking his cane, he covered his head with his hat and shuffled off for his waiting carriage.

When the duke's coach had pulled away, Grace closed the door and turned. She started when she noticed Christian standing behind her, leaning against the doorway to his study. His arms were crossed over his chest and his expression was shadowed and dangerous.

"Brava, my lady," he said, his voice bitingly sharp. "You have succeeded in winning the approval of a man whom I had thought untouchable." His eyes grew keen with anger. "Don't make the mistake again of putting me in the position you did tonight."

And with that, he turned, closing the door firmly behind him. What followed a moment later was the uncompromising sound of the lock being turned.

Chapter Seventeen

Grace glanced at the small silver clock that was tucked in the late night shadows of her bedside table. In the single beam of moonlight coming through her chamber window, she could see that its small enameled face read three o'clock. Another hour had passed. A few hours more and it would be dawn—and still Christian had not come up to his bed.

Grace had purposely opened the door between their chambers so that she would hear him when he came in. She'd even made certain to sit in the chair that faced onto his room so that she wouldn't miss him. They needed to talk. She had angered him tonight by inviting Lord Herrick and the duke to supper. After Christian's harsh words to her in the hall earlier that evening, she knew she wouldn't find any comfort in sleep without first talking to him, explaining her reasons, no matter how impolitic they might now seem.

For well over a month now, Grace had picked her way around Christian's sullenness and she was no closer to figuring him out than she'd been that first morning when she'd met him at the marriage altar in Little Biddlington. They were husband and wife, yet he did everything to avoid being with her. Why? Did he disapprove of her, did he think her an incompetent wife? She had tried to do the things she thought a marchioness should do. She took care with what she wore, where she went, whom she saw. Though she sometimes erred, in the long run she felt she was succeeding, for in spite of his negligence, there were rare times when Christian would come to her and take her into his arms, filling her with kisses and touching her more deeply than she could ever have imagined. But then afterward, in the moments when they could be so close to one another, he would always pull away so abruptly and then she wouldn't see him for days. She had tried and tried to figure why, but seemed only to end up asking the same question: What was it about her that continually made him turn away?

The time had come for answers and since Christian was making no attempt to come to her, she would simply have to go to him. Grace slipped on her dressing robe, belting it at her waist. She blew out her candle and headed for the door.

The hall outside her chamber was dark, quiet, the doors on Lady Frances's and Eleanor's chambers long closed for the night. As the tall case clock in the hall chimed the quarter hour, Grace padded her way slowly to the stairs in the faint light shining in through the hall window. When she reached the bottom step, she saw the barest flicker of firelight shining from under the door to Christian's study. She hesitated outside, staring at the door, contemplating what she would say to him. He would be angry. He would resist her efforts to talk, but she told herself she would have to be firm. They simply couldn't go on as they were.

Taking a deep breath, Grace placed her hand upon the door handle, hoping it wasn't still locked. Slowly she turned, and heard it click to open. She took the first step inside.

Christian sat in one of the wing chairs in front of the fire in his study, his brandy cupped in his palm as he stared hopelessly into the sluggish flames. He'd removed his coat and had rolled the sleeves of his shirt over his forearms. His neckcloth was loose and hanging about his neck and he had loosened the first several buttons of his shirt. His hair was ruffled from the numerous times he had raked his fingers through it in the past few hours as he'd sat there, alone in the dark, unwilling to go upstairs lest he should make love to his wife.

"Christian?"

He jerked his head around at the sudden sound of the very woman who was tormenting him. The abruptness of the motion set some of the brandy in his glass to splashing over the side and onto his fingers. He hadn't even heard her come in. For a moment, he wondered if he had completely lost his mind, conjuring up her image somehow in his thoughts.

She moved then and he knew she was real.

Grace stood in the low light from the ebbing fire, her hair curled in blond waves around her shoulders, looking damned decadent in her white virgin's nightrail buttoned up to her chin. She came forward, her toes bare against the thick woolen carpet. She tucked the weight of her hair behind one ear and with just that one simple gesture, he felt the muscles in his stomach tighten as they did whenever he was about to lose all sense and reason and break his vow not to bed her. He had to do something. He had to stop himself from breaking his vow again. He fought to control his desire with the only weapon he had: anger.

"Get out, Grace," he said, almost a growl before he turned back to the fire, waiting for her to leave, vanish, go back by whatever means she had used to come there. He'd been thinking about her all night, thinking about the things that intrigued him about her, and about the danger her life was now in because of him and that damned note.

"No, Christian, I will not leave this time."

He glared at her. "What did you say?"

"We need to talk."

Her eyes had a light of determination in them that told she was not about to be daunted. But he was not in the mood for talking. What he was in the mood for was to haul her to the carpet and take her in front of the fire, lose himself in her goodness and hope and try to forget the misery that had been his life. And she would allow him to, because to her romantic thinking, it meant that he must care—and he knew very well that couldn't be. Caring meant feeling. Feeling meant vulnerability. And vulnerability meant weakness, something he had learned long ago never to fall victim to.

The results could be—murderous.

"Perhaps another time, madam. I am occupied at the moment."

Again he waited for her to leave.

Again she did not.

"Christian, what have I done to displease you so? You are obviously annoyed with me. Is it because I invited your grandfather to supper tonight? You must know I only had good intentions in doing so."

"There are no good intentions where he is involved."

Grace took a step closer. "I do not know what it is that has caused you to hate him as you do. I wish I did. Perhaps then I could understand it. I only know it has something to do with the death of your father."

Christian's vision went black. "What did he tell you?"

He would kill the old bastard if he had dared to—

"Your grandfather said nothing. It was Mrs. Stone who told me that your rift with the duke was struck when you lost your father."

He muttered to the fire, "Servants would do well to remember who pays their wages and hold their tongues accordingly."

"I asked her, Christian. She did not offer the information to me unsolicited. I only asked because I wanted to help you."

"Do not pry into matters that don't concern you, Grace. I don't need your help."

Grace came closer, to where she was standing just beside his chair. He could feel the warmth of her and she wasn't even touching him. Already her scent seemed to fill the air.

"I know what it is to lose a parent, Christian. I lost mine, too."

A strange feeling, like belonging, came upon him at her soft, compassionate words. Could he tell her? Did he dare? He felt himself beginning to yield and fought against it, unwilling to leave go of the painful secret he had kept safely locked within him so long now. If he told her, she would know the truth about him. She would know who she had really married, not the noble heir, but a murderer. He couldn't bear the thought of seeing the look of horror, of loathing in her eyes, she who had worshiped him from the beginning. Instead, he said, "You can know nothing of how I feel."

"Christian, I am your wife. I care about you."

"How can you care about a mu—"

Christian could only thank the benevolence of God

for stopping him before he could finish saying that word. *Murderer.* He closed his eyes, fighting to gain control of the churning emotions that were threatening to choke him. *You must not tell her.* After a moment or two, his pulse began to calm and he was able to breathe more easily again. He said, his voice markedly quieter, "How can you care for a man you know nothing about? Who is my favorite artist, Grace? What is my favorite color? Do you know how I take my tea? Do you even know the date of my birth?"

He looked and saw that Grace's eyes were no longer pleading and soft. Instead she stared at him, utterly resolute, and said, "Milk, no sugar and September the twenty-third."

He stared at her in disbelief.

"I took note of one and asked your sister the other and I might know the other two if you had but allowed me to. I didn't expect to learn everything about you in the handful of weeks since we wed. We were married before we knew each other very well—"

"Very well?" Christian scoffed. "Madam, we did not know each other at all."

"Other marriages have begun with just as little acquaintanceship and they somehow manage to succeed. I knew when I agreed to be your wife that we would need time to get to know one another. I had thought we would spend some time together in order to do just that. Did you not think the same?"

In a perfect world, that might have been true. But Christian's world was far from perfect and he couldn't allow his misery to ruin another life. He had to keep Grace from getting close to him, because getting close would mean getting hurt. Perhaps even killed. She had to stop rhapsodizing on girlish whims of romance and love, marriage and devotion. She had to face the fact that he was not this beau ideal she'd made him out to be in her dreams. She needed a healthy dose of reality. The sooner she realized she had not married the perfect gentleman she believed she had, the White Knight, all the better it would be for her.

"You are too much of a dreamer, Grace. Don't you understand? I did not marry you because of some magical destiny that was written for us centuries ago. I did not read your name in the stars. You did not come to me through the prophetic ether of a dream. I married you because I had to. Not because I wanted to but because you were chosen for me by another." He stared at her hard and finished, as coldly as he could, "Quite frankly, Grace, you could have been anyone."

Every single word struck Grace a telling blow and took a small part of the light from her eyes until all that remained were harsh and broken clouds. Grace blinked a few times as if hoping the clouds would clear. She was fighting back tears and her lip was trembling so hard she had to bite it. She stared at him for several moments, silent, stunned. Finally she said, her voice no louder than a whisper, "I am sorry for having taken your time."

She turned and walked slowly from the room, her step heavy, her arms hanging defeatedly at her sides. And as Christian watched her go, he could only think that his grandfather should be so proud, for Christian had become the very model of him, the man he'd spent a lifetime hating. He was now a heartless bastard, most worthy to hold the title of Duke of Westover.

Chapter Eighteen

When Grace came from her bedchamber the following morning, it was later than her usual waking hour. Rather than breaking her fast in the parlor with the usual biscuits and toast and sometimes eggs, she had taken her morning tea in bed, lingering there, listening to the sounds of Christian moving about in his chamber. She heard his bootsteps on the hall passing her door and her breath caught as she stared at her door and waited to see if he would stop. Still she hoped even as she knew he wouldn't. Instead, he continued past her chamber, down the stairs, stopping to talk to Forbes before leaving. Grace stood at the window and watched through the glass as he climbed into the Knighton coach, ordering Parrott to take him to his club, White's. He never once looked up to see her.

As she stood in the doorway to his study now, it could almost seem as if the things he'd said the previous night had never been spoken. The darkness and shadow that had closed in on her a handful of hours earlier had vanished in the light of day. The fire was naught but a gray pile of ash. No imprint of his body even remained in his chair. Still nothing could take away the memory of Christian's hateful words to her—even now they echoed through her thoughts.

Quite frankly, Grace, you could have been anyone . . .

From the moment Grace had first seen Christian, staring up at him from where she had fallen at his feet in his dressing room the night of the Knighton ball, she had known in her heart that he was the one Nonny had spoken of to her, her perfect knight, the man she would love for the rest of her life. He could chide her for being a dreamer, but no dream had ever been so clear, so absolutely known. It had been just as Nonny had told her it would be—a realization that for as long as she might live, the man who would hold her heart would be Christian. Without question. Without doubt.

Only Nonny hadn't told her what she should do when her knight didn't love her in return.

Christian did not love her; he didn't even like her. Knowing this didn't lessen her love for him in any way, but with the dawning of the new day, her tears barely dried upon the linen of her pillow, came another realization, as clear as the certainty of her love for Christian.

No matter how much she might love Christian, how much she might want him to love her in return, he never would.

Only in the moment that he had spoken those words to her had Grace accepted the truth she had seen shadowing Christian's eyes every day of their brief and unfortunate marriage. There had always been something—something odd, something so obviously missing. Only now did she know what it was. Christian had been forced to wed her by his grandfather, the duke, unhappily and unwillingly. Despite the fact that her uncle had arranged the match for Grace, ultimately, she had made the decision to become Christian's wife. She had wanted it—heavens, she had thrown her all into it. She had never considered that Christian might not have been a willing participant. She had been so taken with the idea of spending the rest of her life with the handsome, charming man she had met at the Knighton ball, so lost to the myth of Nonny's promises, she had never thought of what he might be thinking, what he might be feeling—or *not* feeling.

Now that Grace realized the truth of the feelings he had tried so carefully to hide from her, she was left with but one more thought: How on earth she was going to spend the rest of her life living with him, seeing him, being near to him, knowing he had never wanted her in his life?

It was the thought Grace had spent the early morning hours mulling through in her bedchamber. Over and over she saw Christian's face lit by the fire in his study the night before, the dullness in his eyes as he has spoken those words. It left her feeling emptier inside than she had ever thought possible.

Her parents had preferred to travel the world, leaving her behind to be raised by someone else, stopping for a visit now and again to remark on how much she'd grown as if it were more an obligation than a treat. Uncle Tedric, in the role of her guardian, had sought to dispose of her through the most lucrative and rapid means he could find. Even Nonny, who had been the sole constant in her life, had eventually gone and with her the only life Grace had ever known. And now Christian—Grace wondered if it was simply her lot in life to be forsaken and abandoned by those whom she loved, those who should have loved her.

Much later that afternoon, near the supper hour, Grace sat in the parlor alone. The house was silent, for everyone else had gone out, and the atmosphere was as solemn as if the very walls realized the futility of her future. Her afternoon tea had grown cold in its pot on the table beside her. The book she had been attempting to read the past hour lay face down on the seat beside her. Christian hadn't returned all day and, according to Forbes, he hadn't said when or even if he'd return. For the barest of moments Grace had wondered that perhaps he might be off elsewhere, with someone else, someone whose presence hadn't been forced upon him, someone he had chosen freely. Even though she knew it was a thing considered quite normal among the *ton,* the thought of Christian touching another woman so intimately, bestowing on someone else the only affection he had ever shown her, caused her throat to tighten even as tears came to her eyes.

Grace pushed her troubled thoughts away and took up her book once again, Virgil's *Aeneid.* She sought to distract herself with reading—anything to put a stop to the thoughts that had darkened the entirety of the day. Perhaps Virgil could offer some answers. She promptly opened to a single, telling line: *'Fata viam invenient.'*

She whispered aloud its meaning in English. "Fate will find a way."

In the very next moment, there came a knocking at

the door. Grace looked up from the page just as Forbes opened the door.

"My lady, pardon my interruption, but there is a visitor for you. A Mr. Jenner."

"Jenner?" She shook her head. "I'm afraid I do not know such a person."

Forbes came forward to deliver the man's card on a salver, bowing his head. "He presented this to me with his request to see you."

Grace took the card up, reading its inscription.

Charles Jenner, Solicitor.

"Perhaps you misheard him, Forbes. I would think, given his profession, he would need to speak with Lord Knighton, not me."

"He stated your name quite clearly, my lady. In fact he referred to you as the former Lady Grace Ledys of Ledysthorpe."

Curious, Grace asked Forbes to show the man in. At the very least, the visit would provide a diversion to the despondency that had shadowed the day. She set aside her book and teacup and stood to meet her caller.

Mr. Charles Jenner, solicitor, was a short man, stout, with spectacles that made his eyes appear quite a bit larger than they actually were. He was dressed as a member of his profession, brown frock coat over nankeen trousers, top hat, and square-toed shoes with high quarters lacing up the front. He stopped just after entering the room and smiled, bowing his head in greeting. "Good day, Lady Knighton. Thank you for consenting to see me without an appointment."

Grace nodded and motioned for him to sit, then lowered into the seat across from him. She asked Forbes to bring a fresh pot of tea and waited while Mr. Jenner removed a sheaf of papers from the satchel he carried with him.

"Lady Knighton, I shan't take up much of your time. I have come with some documents requiring your signature."

"Documents, sir? For me?"

"Aye, my lady. It is for the transfer of the property."

Grace nodded then, her initial suspicions confirmed. "It is as I thought, Mr. Jenner. You should be meeting with my husband, Lord Knighton, or perhaps his solicitor. They have handled the particulars of my dower."

Mr. Jenner shook his head, shuffling through his papers. "Oh, no, my lady, it is not a dower property I speak of. I come about a family holding that has been held until now in trust for you. It was previously held by your grandmother, my previous employer, Lady Cholmeley. It was to become yours upon your marriage."

Grace was confused. "But I understood that all of the Ledys family holdings are entailed to my uncle, Tedric, Lord Cholmeley."

"Oh, this is not a Ledys holding, my lady. It is a Mac-Rath property."

"MacRath? That was my grandmother's family name."

"Aye, my lady. 'Tis through her that you have received this, a gift of real property, to be transferred to you upon your marriage."

In all the times they had spoken of the future and Grace's eventual marriage, Nonny had never once said anything to her of any property that would come to her. Obviously, she must have known of it. "Where is the property located, Mr. Jenner?"

"Let me see." He shuffled through his papers a bit more, "It is a Scottish property, called Skynegal. It is the ancestral home of your grandmother's family on Loch Skynegal in the coastal north Highlands area of Wester Ross. Oh, and there is a letter for you here from your grandmother."

Grace took the folded parchment from Mr. Jenner. Her breath caught as she read her name written in the familiar script of her grandmother's hand. She felt a strange sensation, not unlike a chill, that reached from her fingers around the letter.

"Will you please excuse me a moment, Mr. Jenner? I should like to read my grandmother's letter in private."

The man nodded and Grace thanked him, leaving the room. Forbes was just coming from the kitchen with the tea tray and she instructed him to serve their guest while she crossed the hall to Christian's study and closed the door. She sat on a bench near the window and slipped

her finger beneath the imprinted seal to open her grandmother's letter. Her fingers trembled as she began to
read the words contained within.

*My dearest child, if you are reading this letter then
I have gone on to meet my loved ones in heaven. I
hope you are not grieving, dear, because I have long
waited for this time. I shall miss you. You have
grown to be a lovely young woman, very much like
myself at your age. You have been my only happiness since I lost my children, your father and mother,
but I find myself growing more tired each year that
passes. I welcome my eternal rest.*

*Since I have charged Mr. Jenner with bringing you
this letter, you have also just learned of Skynegal and
your inheritance of it. The name of the estate is de-
rived from the native Gaelic 'Sgiathach' which means
the 'winged' castle, and when you first see it, you will
understand why. I had hoped to one day take you
there myself, to see my great-grandchildren running
about the same hills I ran about as a child, but if
that is not to be, then I must charge you with the
task. Skynegal is my own gift to you. It was my home
as a child and a very special place. 'Twas here my
own knight first came to me, where we first danced
and where I knew he would be my only love.*

*Not long after I married, Skynegal was left unoccu-
pied. It was to have gone to your father and mother,
and through them, to you, but as you know, that was
not to be. Over the years, I have received news of
the estate accounts and have done what I can to
maintain it from afar. It is my dearest wish that you
will do what I could not and use your special talents
to see Skynegal restored to the special place it once
was.*

*There is an account of substantial size that has
been set aside to enable you to bring this wish to
pass. Skynegal is a part of you, my dearest—your
past and your future. It is your heritage and it is now
my gift to you. Trust that it is there you shall find
what you are looking for.*

Now as ever . . . your dearest grandmother, Nonny.

Grace folded the letter carefully, but didn't immediately get up to leave. She turned to look out the window, staring at the street, watching the carriages and the people pass by. A bird chirped happily from a nearby elm. A dog barked. Moments passed as she listened to the sounds of life outside and thought over the words her grandmother had written to her.

Trust that it is there you shall find what you are looking for . . .

And in that moment, it all came clear to her. All of her life Grace had felt as if something were missing—some plan, a destiny that she was meant to fulfill. All her life she had known a niggling sense of searching, but she had never known what it was she was searching for. There had been an emptiness deep within her that at first she had attributed to the loss of her parents and then later to Nonny. When she had married Christian, she had thought that she could fill that emptiness with him, with being his wife, loving him, bearing his children, finally being a part of a family instead of someone left behind by memories of one. But perhaps that hadn't been her purpose after all.

Grace believed that for everything in life—from the fiercest lion to the tiniest mouse—there was a purpose. *"Things happen for a reason,"* Nonny had always said. *"They take us further down the road we were meant by God to walk."*

When she had been a child, Grace could recall having come dangerously close to losing her fingers when she'd been playing near some farm equipment. She had been reckless, racing about in the tool shed, upsetting an axe that had been leaning against a wall. But for some reason, when the axe had fallen, it buried its blade but a half inch from her fingers. Grace could recall having stared at the axe blade stuck in the ground so close to her hand and thinking how stupid she had been. For if her fingers had been but an inch further forward, she would have lost them and would never then have known her love of sketching, her joy at playing the pianoforte.

There were other things, too. At a time when young girls played with dolls and tiny china tea sets, Grace had only been interested in building blocks. She had studied the engravings of the master architects—Wren, Adam, Inigo Jones. Later, when she had grown older and she had taken to sketching, it was not birds and flowers that filled her sketchbooks, but buildings, houses, churches—whatever structure that might have captured her eye. At ten years, when she might have been spending her daylight hours learning various dance steps and needlepoint stitches, Grace was designing a tree house. She spent hours planning it, sketching and then resketching it until it was just as it should have been, complete with sash windows and a dumbwaiter. With Nonny's encouragement and the help of some of the estate workers, Grace saw that same tree house constructed atop a grand oak tree along the banks of the River Tees at Ledysthorpe. It had been Grace's special place, where she had gone to dream and reflect while the birds had perched beside her. She remembered how she would look out from her treetop tower with the periscope her father had gifted her with, wishing for her parents to return off the North Sea, miraculously alive once again.

All of her life, no matter how she'd tried, Grace had never been able to conform to the image of what she should have been—the accomplished lady able to sing sweeter than a bird and dance as if the wind was at her feet. She realized now she had spent all that time trying to be a person that in her heart she knew she could never be. It had taken her marriage to Christian, and her failure as his wife, for her to finally realize the truth she had been avoiding for as long as she could recall. Only now it was suddenly so clear.

Use your special talents to see Skynegal restored.

The words her grandmother had written were like the opening of a door, the door to her future. No more would she avoid it, refusing to heed the call. It was time she took charge of her life instead of blithely following the wrong but "proper" path.

It was time Grace embraced her destiny.

Grace left the study sometime later and returned to the parlor where Mr. Jenner still awaited. He looked up from his tea, his mouth crumbed with one of the cook's lemon biscuits, and smiled.

"Mr. Jenner, thank you for waiting. I am ready to sign the papers you have brought to me."

As the solicitor began setting out the documents for her, she went on, "After we are finished, I wonder if I might trouble you to stay a bit. There is a matter I should like to discuss with you."

"A matter, my lady?"

"Yes. I should like to hire you, sir, to act as my personal solicitor for the estate of Skynegal. There is something I should like to do, but I must warn you it is a matter that will require some delicacy and a great deal of fortitude on your part, for there may be opposition from my husband. He is an influential man, sir. His grandfather, the Duke of Westover, is even more influential. I do not know you, sir," Grace went on, "but I can see that my grandmother trusted you and that is enough to recommend you to me. Would you be willing to help me?"

Mr. Jenner didn't immediately respond. For a moment, Grace thought that he might refuse her. The Westovers were, after all, one of the most powerful families in England. Few would dare oppose them for fear of the reprisals. The longer the solicitor remained silent, the more Grace convinced herself he would decline.

A few moments later, however, Mr. Jenner stood and extended his hand toward her. "I have always been a man inclined to a challenge, my lady. Serving your grandmother through the years I did was one of the greatest tasks of my professional life. She was a true and remarkable woman. You remind me of her somehow. Thus, I would be honored to be of service to you, my lady, in whatever capacity you seek."

Two days later, Grace was gone.

PART TWO

Adieu, She cries!
and waved her lily hand.
—John Gay

Chapter Nineteen

Wester Ross, Scottish Highlands

Skynegal Castle lay nestled inland off the Minch, a restless sea channel separating the Hebrides from the western Scottish coast amid a copse of oak and Caledonian pine in a small cove along the pebbled shores of Loch Skynegal. To some, this remote part of northwest Scotland was considered wild and primitive—far too uncivilized for the Bond Street set. But to Grace, it was as beautiful a land as she could have ever imagined, vividly splashed with blues, greens, purples, and pinks—majestic mountains and heather-swept hills flanking a landscape as colorful as any tartan.

She had left London with her maid Liza nearly a fortnight earlier after leading the Knighton servants to believe she was going out on a visit to see her uncle, Lord Cholmeley. They would have found out soon after that she had never arrived at Cholmeley House. Instead she had taken a hackney coach to the offices of Mr. Jenner at Lincoln's Inn and from there had gone to meet the post chaise that would start them on their journey.

The two women had traveled first by land across the midlands of England to Liverpool, then north by sea, since few roads ran through the rocky Highland terrain, and none wider than a pony trail as far north as Wester Ross. It had been a tiresome journey and the weather had only hindered their progress, raining nearly every day since they'd left London. Yet despite her fatigue, Grace found herself standing on the deck of the small packet boat that would bring them to the close of their voyage, captivated by everything around them.

Early that morning, the skies had cleared and a brisk
Scottish wind blew chill against her nose and cheeks,
filled with a scent that seemed to characterize the Highlands—earthy heather, the salt sea wind, and the fragrant pine of the tall fir trees. They passed a scattering of
small whitewashed cottages set beneath heavily thatched
roofs that gave them the appearance of large mushrooms
dotting the rocky shoreline. Word of the sloop's sighting
spread quickly from one to the next, bringing the cot-
tagers outside to curiously watch the unfamiliar vessel
skimming past on the rippling blue-gray waters of the
loch. Dogs barked in excitement and children waved,
running barefoot to the water's edge as if to give chase.
Shaggy orange Highland cattle barely gave them a moment's glance before returning their attention to the pas-
ture beneath them.

Fed by the sea, the vast loch was studded by a string
of small islands, each thickly wooded and ringed by the
mist that skirted the water's surface. Rugged shoreline
stretched farther than the eye could see and several
small herring boats floated like bobbing apples in the
distance. At the farthest end of the loch, like a door-
keeper to this mystical secret retreat, rose the age-old
gray stone towers of Skynegal.

From the moment its silhouette first took shape
through the mist, the castle had brought Grace to drawing in her breath in wonder. It stood in a setting older
than time and looked every bit as magical as she could
have ever imagined it, filled with rich history—*her* family
history. It was a place to which she could finally belong.

Atop a high slope, or *leathad,* the main tower house
was tall and rectangular, with a steeply pitched roof
flanked on either side by smaller rounded towers no
doubt added at a later date. It was these two towers,
outstretched to the sides, that gave the castle its Gaelic
name, *Sgiathach*—the winged castle. The closer one
came, the more vivid the image grew, until it appeared
as if the wing towers were somehow fluttering. Kitti-
wakes and terns were everywhere, hundreds of them,
stark white against the weathered stone, perched upon
the tower parapets, soaring overhead, nesting in the cre-
nelles, calling out in noisy welcome to them.

It was as the sloop pulled aground upon the pebbly beach beneath Skynegal that Grace caught her first glimpse of the castle's crumbling fence lines and overgrown brush. They disembarked, trudging up a weed-thickened path from the shore to stand beneath the tall central tower. Grace craned her neck up at least seven stories past windows with weatherbeaten casements that hung unhappily off their rusted hinges and broken glazing that blinked at them in the fading daylight. She could only think that it was more a ruin than a dwelling and even the cries of the birds looking down on them from the wing towers seemed suddenly mournful as if bemoaning the castle's sad state of neglect.

Grace chewed her lip, but she wasn't discouraged. Perhaps the castle was not as grand as some might expect, but with a bit of work to bring it back to its former splendor, Skynegal would soon soar again.

She looked past Liza, who stood beside her, to the two men who'd accompanied them there from Mallaig. McFee and McGee had met the two women at the dock, bearing a letter signed by the ever-resourceful Mr. Jenner. He had hired the men, he'd written, to guide them along the last leg of their journey into the Highlands. They would remain at Skynegal to help Grace to settle in afterward.

They presented a peculiar picture, each draped in differing ragged tartans, their noses reddened from frequent exposure to the sea winds. The bottom halves of their faces were hidden behind full shaggy beards—one red, the other peppered gray. The only way Grace had managed to successfully tell them apart during their journey was to remind herself over and over again that McFee had the beard that was *fire*-red and McGee had the beard that was pepper-*gray*. A simple method, yes, but it worked.

With them had come the stout Flora, a woman who wore a perpetually serious expression set beneath mud-brown hair that was scraped back beneath a colorless linen kerchief. She was sister to one of the two men and had yet to utter a single word since leaving Mallaig two days earlier. While McGee and McFee would see to the provisioning of the castle with adequate peats for burning and the purchase of necessary livestock, Flora would undertake any needed household tasks until other staff could be arranged for.

"Please, my lady," Liza said to Grace then, "please tell me they've got it wrong. Tell me this broken pile of rocks cannot be the right place."

Grace glanced at Liza before asking politely, "Excuse me, sirs? You are quite certain this is Skynegal?"

McGee grinned at her, scratching his grizzled head beneath his tattered blue bonnet. "Aye, my leddy, I sure ye 'tis *Skee-na-gall,* it is."

McFee nodded his agreement from behind the swirling smoke of his clay pipe, stroking his fiery beard as he said, "Dunna t'ink 'tis changed a'sudden. Been *Skee-na-gall* for nigh hand six hunder years, it has."

"Aye, and looks as if it hasn't been lived in for at least that long either," Liza muttered.

Flora, of course, said nothing.

Grace turned once again to regard the structure, this time looking on what had been her grandmother's childhood home with the even more discriminating eye of someone who had studied a good many structures in years past.

It stood, of course, in dire need of improvements, first and foremost a roof, at least a complete one for what was there seemed to be degenerating in patches. The walls would need immediate repair where they were crumbling and the windows would have to be replaced. Grace could not see anything further of the actual structure because the sun was setting behind them, casting the tower in a bit of a haze. A good deal of what she could see of it was covered by an overgrowth of dark ivy that crept thickly along the weathered stone walls. Grace frowned, her brow knit as she cocked her head slightly to the side, staring at the places where the stone was crumbling away from the curtain wall. She wondered if perhaps it was the ivy that was keeping the castle standing at all.

"Won't make it any better looking at it that way," Liza commented.

"Well, it cannot be completely devastated. Mr. Jenner said there has been a steward living here at all times. Perhaps it is time we met him."

Grace proceeded to the nearest door she could find, small and inconspicuous on such a large structure, with a heavy iron ring hanging from its center. When she lifted the ring, it screeched as if it hadn't been moved since the castle's first stone had been set, and flecks of black paint fluttered from it to the toes of her half boots.

Not a good sign, she thought as she dropped the knocker back against the door with a resounding *thunk*.

They waited to the accompanying sound of the sea and the perpetual *ock-ock-ock* of the birds perched in the various apertures above them. When there came no answer to her knocking, Grace looked to Liza. The maid raised a skeptical brow but wisely said nothing. Grace tried the door again, this time whacking the ring several times hard against the solid wood of the door. Moments passed. Again no response. Grace could hear McFee and McGee shifting behind her. "Odd," she murmured. "I'm certain Mr. Jenner had said that—"

The door scraped open suddenly and a figure presented itself in the doorway. He was short and round and really quite bald, reminding Grace immediately of the childhood story of Humpty Dumpty—a Humpty Dumpty in tartan, she amended, wearing a suit of criss-crossed red and white straining across an expansive girth with skin-tight trews covering his thin legs down to his buckled leather shoes.

The man took one look at them and immediately turned his back to them.

"Hoy, Deirdre," he shouted to the castle interior, "you were right! Someone has come to visit us. Come, come help me to greet our guests!"

He was joined by a petite woman, perhaps four and a half feet tall, who wore an earthy-hued plaid cut long on her slight body, wrapped around her shoulders with the fringed ends of it trailing upon the stone floor. Her face was one by which age was not easily determined— she was somewhere, Grace guessed, between twenty and forty. Her hair was completely hidden beneath an elaborately knotted kerchief and she wore full faded skirts that might once have been black beneath a bluish shirt, cut not unlike a man's waistcoat. Her feet, Grace noticed, were bare on the stone floor underneath.

"Welcome, welcome to Skynegal," said the man of the pair, coming forward to greet them. "I am Alastair Ogilvy, the castle steward, and this is Deirdre Wyllie. Deirdre is a widow to one of the former tenants here and she comes to keep house at Skynegal."

Grace nodded, smiling to the woman.

"And who do we have the pleasure of knowing?" asked Mr. Ogilvy, his curiosity beaming on his rotund face.

"She's the newly come leddy of Skynegal," Deirdre answered even before Grace could respond.

Alastair turned an expression of astonishment on the small woman. "You knew this afore she told it to us, eh, Deirdre? How'd you do it? Was it the sight, Deirdre? Did the spirits tell you this, lass?"

Deirdre shook her head. "Nae, Alastair. I've told you and told you I dinna have this 'sight' you keep buffing aboot." She tucked her hand inside her plaid and took out a folded letter. " 'Twas this letter that was delivered yestreen."

Alastair took the letter and read it quickly, his dark eyes growing large over the top of the parchment. "Och, Deirdre, why did you not tell me afore now that the lady of Skynegal was to be coming?" Before she could answer, he bowed his head reverently to Grace. "My lady, please forgive me for not having greeted you properly afore you could reach the door. I wasn't aware of your coming, else I would have been watching the loch for you to arrive."

Grace shook her head. "There is nothing to forgive, Mr. Ogilvy. I prefer not to stand on ceremony. Might we come in and sit a spell? We've been traveling for some time and I think we're all nearly ready to drop from exhaustion."

"Hoy!" Alastair put both hands atop his head. "Where are my manners? Of course! Please, my lady, please come in! All of you!"

He moved quickly for a man of his width, taking them down a narrow corridor and up two rounded flights of stairs, chattering apologies all the way. They arrived at a cavernous room that rose easily two stories, nearly as wide as it was high. Grace heard several small birds chirping above, where they had no doubt nested in the great oaken hammered beams that traversed the cracked and crumbling plaster ceiling.

The scene of many a Highland feast, the great hall had once played host to Robert the Bruce himself. According to Mr. Ogilvy, the original tower had been constructed in the twelfth century, the side wings centuries later. The tower birds had been residents from the very beginning.

"Legend has it that long afore a castle was ever built at this place, the Celtic goddess Cliodna came to visit. She was beautiful and fair and it is said 'twas she who brought the birds, magical birds whose sweet song would soothe the sick into a healing sleep."

As Grace listened to Alastair's recounting of the legend, she walked slowly about the chamber. The hall was mostly vacant except for the two armchairs and a single crude table set near the cavernous stone hearth. A fire burned low in the grate with a small copper kettle hanging from a chain above it, giving off an earthy scent, most unlike the coal to which she was accustomed. The only other light in the room came from two tallow candles burning in holders atop the table, throwing shadows onto the bare stone walls. There weren't any windows, not a one, on any of the walls.

"Won't you sit, my lady?"

Alastair motioned Grace to one of the two chairs, its fabric worn through in places with bits of horsehair sticking out from the cushioning.

"Please accept my apologies for the meager furnishings, Lady . . . uh, Lady . . . ? Dear heavens, I'm afraid I did not read far enough in the letter to know your name."

"She is Lady Grace, Marchioness Knighton," Deirdre answered as she stooped before the hearth to stir up the fire beneath the fresh peat she'd tossed there.

"Please, Lady Grace will serve adequately."

"Lady Grace it is and please do call me Alastair. Whenever I heard 'Mr. Ogilvy' I tend to think it a designation meant for my father even though he's been in his grave for nearly ten years now."

Grace smiled and leaned back against the cushion of

the chair, suddenly aware of how very tired she was. Already her legs were growing stiff beneath her and she could very easily just close her eyes and fall asleep in this chair with its horsehair poking her bottom till morning.

"Alastair it is, then." She motioned across from her to the opposite chair. "This is Liza Stone, my maid," then to the others, "and Misters McFee and McGee and sister Flora. They've come to assist us in provisioning the castle."

Alastair's eyes again went wide and he nodded slowly. "Provision the castle? So you'll be staying at Skynegal? You'll be making it your home for a while, will you?"

Home. Grace looked at Alastair and said quite without hesitation, "Yes, Alastair. I plan to stay on at Skynegal indefinitely."

Alastair nodded on a smile. "And Lord Knighton? I take it he will be joining you here as well?"

Grace blinked once at the question, a gesture only Liza would have noticed. It wasn't something she'd been prepared for so soon after her arrival and it brought with it thoughts of Christian and London and the life she had left behind. Grace wondered for what must surely have been the hundredth time what Christian had done when he found her missing. Had he rejoiced at her leaving? Had he made any attempt to find her? Grace knew it would only be out of a sense of obligation and not because he held any affection for her. He had made that quite clear that last night in his study.

Still he wouldn't have found her had he tried. With Mr. Jenner's assistance, she had traveled under her grandmother's family name of MacRath so as to avoid the unwanted attention that would certainly come about if it had been discovered that the Marchioness Knighton, kin to the wealthy Westovers, was traveling about the countryside.

But now that she was here, Grace was determined that she should never again look back on what her life had been. She was making a new start and from this day, she would seek her own future, make her own happiness—at Skynegal.

She looked at Alastair, "Lord Knighton shall remain

in London. He is not expected to travel to Skynegal anytime soon."

In fact, Grace continued on a thought, it would be a blessed miracle if he came there at all.

Chapter Twenty

Alastair did not query Grace any further about Christian's absence. If he found it odd that Grace had traveled across country alone with only a maid, he said nothing, nor did he give any indication that he may have suspected something was amiss in her marriage. Whatever his thoughts, Alastair kept them to himself, and instead began to tell her of just how he'd come to his position as steward at Skynegal fifteen years before. He'd spent most of his childhood on a crofting farm on the estate and his subsequent years of schooling in Edinburgh. Grace listened politely, all the while fighting to keep her eyes from closing.

"And after returning to the Highlands, I—"

"Excuse me, Alastair," Grace interrupted finally. "I would love to hear everything you can tell me about the estate and your life here, but I fear our journey has taxed me more than I had thought. I can barely keep my eyes open. If it wouldn't be too much trouble, might we review all this in the morning?"

"Oh! Will you have no supper then, my lady? Deirdre's got us a flavorful stew simmering in the kitchen. And her oatcakes are the finest to be had in Wester Ross. She bakes them with a touch o' honey that is really quite good. Surely you must be famished after your long journey here."

Grace smiled obligingly. "It all sounds wonderful." She turned to Deirdre. "But I fear I am even too tired to eat. If I could trouble you for an oatcake and a pot of tea and direction to the nearest bed, I would be most grateful."

"Beds!" Alastair wrung his hands together before him.

"Oh my lady, I am ashamed to say I haven't had any beds prepared since I didn't know you were—"

"There's fresh bedsheets and coverings on the bed in the laird's chamber a'ready and a truckle set aside it for the maid," Deirdre said. "The others can bed doon here on box beds in the rooms aff the kitchen. I thought Lady Grace would have others with her, so I made ready several of the beds here, too."

Alastair looked at Deirdre, clearly astonished to hear that she had completed all the preparations for Grace's arrival herself and without him taking any notice of it. "But Deirdre, why did you not—"

Deirdre just shook her head. "If I'd have tol' you they were coming, you widna ha' given me a moment's peace a'day. Ever'ting that needs doing is done. Now you take about Lady Grace and show her to the laird's chamber and I'll be bringin' her up her tae and cake of breid."

Alastair stared at Deirdre a long moment before he remembered his duty to Grace. He took up one of the candlesticks from the table, motioning for her to follow him. "Of course, my lady. I will show you abovestairs. If you'll follow me, please."

Grace held up a hand when she saw Liza stand to follow. "Liza, please, don't worry over me. You stay with the others and eat your supper and come up when you are finished. I can manage well enough on my own tonight."

"But, my lady, you've not eaten since midday."

Grace shook her head. "I suspect the rough waters we had just shortly before landing caused my stomach a bit of an upset. Either that or I am simply too tired to have an appetite. The tea and cake will be enough, really."

Liza shrugged and Grace gave her a weary smile before turning to follow Alastair across the great hall toward a far opening in the wall that in her fatigue looked more like a yawning mouth than a doorway. He led her down a darkened corridor that felt a bit chilly away from the fire. The light of his candle threw odd shadows about the walls while their footsteps echoed softly on the bare stone floor. At the end of the corridor, Alastair opened a small arched door and started up a very narrow spiral-turned stairwell leading to the upper floors of the tower.

Alastair chatted while they climbed. "As I'm sure you saw at your arrival, a bit of the castle has fallen into disrepair in years past. We did as best we could to keep it up and we've managed to preserve most of the furnishings, moving the pieces to various other chambers for storage whenever it becomes necessary. I have a full inventory in the estate papers . . ."

Grace yawned on a nod.

". . . But we can go over that in the morning, of course."

He opened a door at the top of the stairs and stepped out into a wide hallway lined on each side with a number of closed doors similar in design to the one below. The walls and the floors were bare, slight discoloration showing where tapestries and rugs had once been. Alastair came to the first door on the hall, lifted its latch, and pushed it open.

A fire was already burning in the stone hearth inside, filling the room with a cozy warmth that enveloped them the moment they entered. Several candles were set in tall holders about the room, lighting a tall oaken bed hung with decorative crewel-work. The bed stood at the very center of the far wall, the coverings upon it already folded down. A small truckle had been set up at the foot of the bed just as Deirdre had said.

Grace walked slowly across the room to a small window that peeked out onto the loch view. Standing ready beside it in the corner was a wash basin and pitcher of fresh water. She dropped her cloak onto a chair and poured a bit of the water into the basin, cupping it into her hands and dousing her weary face. It was ice cold, but even the shock of it against her skin failed to rouse her. She was so very tired, she wondered how she had remained standing this long. She patted her cheeks with a drying cloth, smoothed a hand over her hair, and turned back to face Alastair.

"This is a lovely room," she said, crossing to the fire. The hearth was ridiculously large, nearly as tall as she with no overmantel, merely a break in the wall. Black smudges from fires centuries past marked its rough stone surface.

"I cannot take the credit for the room or the fire, my lady. As you well know, 'twas Deirdre's doing, although I cannot for the life of me think why she would not have told me of your coming."

"She likely didn't wish to worry you."

Alastair shrugged. "I suppose you are right. You probably haven't yet noticed, but there are times when I have a tendency toward excitability."

Grace simply smiled.

"Is there anything I can get for you, my lady? Have you any trunks that you'll need brought up to you tonight?"

"There is other baggage, but you can ask Mr. McFee and Mr. McGee to see to them after they have their supper. All I would like is the tea right now and if you wouldn't mind, I'd dearly love nothing more than to just climb into bed while I wait for Deirdre to bring it."

"Of course, of course." But Alastair made no move to leave, until he realized that Grace meant to get undressed. Then he went wide eyed again. "Oh! Of course, my lady. I beg your pardon. You wish to retire. I will go. I will go see to what is keeping Deirdre with the tea." He bowed his head. Twice. "Good evening to you, my lady." He backed out of the room.

When he had gone, Grace pressed a hand against the small of her back where the ache that had settled there hours earlier had begun to throb. It had been a long and exhausting day. They had risen with the dawn in order to make the last part of their journey up the coast to Skynegal by nightfall. And now that she was here, standing in the midst of her grandmother's childhood home, she was so tired that she could scarcely even consider the significance of it.

Grace dropped her head to the side, rolling it back from one shoulder to the other to ease the tight muscles at the back of her neck. She glanced to the bed that looked so warm and so inviting. She sat in the chair and removed her half boots and then her stockings, flexing her toes before her. She stood and reached behind herself, struggling to unhook the fastenings at the back of her gown, wishing she had worn something easier to get out of. She worked for several moments at the buttons to no avail, and was nearly ready to give it up and retire in what she wore when a soft voice sounded behind her, taking her hands and lowering them to her sides.

"Let me put to a hand, my leddy."

Deirdre set to loosening Grace's gown so that she could easily step out of it. Wearing her chemise, Grace pulled the pins from her hair, giving it a shake and loosening it about her shoulders and back. She turned toward Deirdre. She saw a kindness about the woman's eyes that set her immediately at ease. "Thank you, Deirdre."

"Aye. I'll just be settin' the tae here at the table by the bed so you can take it afore you gae to sleep."

Grace smiled, nodding. She was reminded how, as a little girl, there had been a good many nights when she had taken a cup of warm milk at bedtime while her grandmother had read some fascinating adventure tale to her. She remembered how she had fallen asleep to the soft, comforting sound of her grandmother's voice, and how safe she had always felt there in her bed, tucked against the soft pillows as she had drifted off to sleep. It seemed as if it was a time forever ago, those days of childhood, of security.

Grace stooped to retrieve her gown from the floor. When she looked up again, she found Deirdre standing before her, holding out a white folded garment.

"I thought you might be needin' something to wear this night, so I took this from an auld chest up in the castle garret and washed it for you this morn. 'Twas once your grannam's afore she left from here to wed your grandie."

Grace took the nightgown, holding it as if it had been sewn with threads of gold. Any thoughts of fear or isolation she might have had vanished the moment she slipped the soft linen over her head. The simple shift enveloped her from chin to toe, immediately filling her senses with the scent her grandmother had always worn, a scent she now recognized as touched by the heather of the Highlands. If she closed her eyes, she could almost imagine herself safely tucked away in Nonny's embrace.

"Oh, Deirdre, thank you," Grace whispered, watching as she poured a cup of the tea for her. There was something about the small woman that reminded Grace of Nonny somehow. She couldn't decide exactly what it was, especially since there was nothing at all similar about the two women in either age or stature. Still, the likening between them, whatever it was, gave Grace a small sense of the same comfort she had felt as a child.

Grace slid beneath the bedclothes, tugging the coverings up to her waist. She reached for the teacup Deirdre offered and took a sip from it. It was an unfamiliar brew—herbal, floral, immediately soothing.

"The tea smells so nice. What is it made with?"

" 'Tis valerian with a bit o' *sobrach* and *brog na cubhaig*."

Grace stared at her, uncomprehending of the Gaelic.

"Primrose and cowslip," Deirdre repeated in English as she handed Grace a small pewter dish with a round flat biscuit on it. "It will sure you hae a peaceful sleep, my leddy."

"I remember that my grandmother was fond of cowslip wine sometimes at night."

Deirdre nodded and Grace took a bite from the cake, chewing it lazily. It was tasty, not rich, just right for her travel-weary, unsettled stomach. She took another nibble and then set the plate aside to finish drinking her tea.

Deirdre had stoked the fire and had snuffed all but one of the candles about the room, leaving the one sitting on the table beside the bed before heading toward the door.

"A guid nicht to you, my leddy. If you hae need of anything, just call for me."

"Thank you, Deirdre." Grace set the tea cup aside and eased back against the pillows. They were soft as eiderdown, touched by a pleasant herbal scent. She closed her eyes, so very tired she could barely keep awake. "Deirdre?"

"Aye, my leddy?"

"Thank you for making our arrival so welcoming and pleasant. I know that it must ha—"

Grace was asleep before she could finish her sentence, finally giving over to her exhaustion.

Deirdre smiled and snuffed the candle beside the bed, tucking the coverings up around her before she quietly stepped from the room.

Chapter Twenty-one

Grace's first morning at Skynegal issued in dark and heavy with rain, the wind blowing, thunder rattling what little glass remained in many of the windows, keeping everyone tucked away by the hearth fire behind the castle's heavy walls. Grace postponed the tour she'd planned of the castle's surrounding grounds and McFee and McGee were left to wait out the weather before they could go in search of the additional stock and other provisions they would need in the days to come.

The rain did, however, allow them one occupation—counting the precise number of leaks in the roof of the main tower. There were seventeen.

Sitting in the great hall wrapped beneath the warmth of a thick woolen shawl, Grace contemplated the extensive list they had spent the past hours compiling—the repairs that would be needed and the supplies to be had from Ullapool, the nearest town nearly a day's sail away. Each time they would open one of the doors onto another of the long-neglected chambers, they would discover something more that needed doing—fireplaces to be swept clean of the mice who had taken up residence there; gunholes, unneeded for centuries, to be filled. The work was beginning to appear endless, but not, Grace thought resolutely, impossible. She focused on the first entry on the list, *a secure roof,* and called to Alastair where he stood by the fire, putting on the kettle for more tea.

"I was thinking—are there local men skilled as masons and carpenters who we might hire to begin the repairs on the castle instead of sending off to Edinburgh for the workers? It would seem a more prudent choice, both economically and to avoid the delay. If this rain continues, by the time they arrived, we might be living underwater with the way that roof is leaking."

"Oh, yes, my lady, there are craftsmen close by, most within a half day's journey from here. With the 'Improvements' taking place in the north and to the east, a good many of the Highlanders have had to move from the midlands to the shore and they have had a hard time of it making a living."

Grace looked at him, puzzled. "But why would improvements on an estate force its tenants away?"

"*Improvements,* my lady, do not necessarily betoken a good thing in this part of Scotland. Here it is a term that has come to mean the displacement of many Highland tenants from their homes. Their leases are not renewed and thus they must take whatever they can carry and go, leaving their crops, their homes, their very livelihoods behind. Many of the displaced who can are leaving the Highlands and are emigrating to New Scotland and America."

"But if the tenants' leases are not renewed, then what is to be done with their previous holdings?"

"They are put to sheep instead."

Grace stared at the Scotsman, incredulous. "People are being forced from their homes to make way for sheep?"

"Aye. It is a more profitable means of using the land for many of the landowners."

Grace was appalled. She thought of the feeling of community that had always been so prevalent at Ledysthorpe. "But do the landowners feel no attachment, no responsibility for the lives of their people?"

Alastair shook his head dolefully. "Many of the old Scottish lairds went into exile after the failed Jacobite rebellion, leaving their people here, dependent upon the strangers who came to take over their estates. The new landlords—a good many of them English, begging your pardon, my lady—view their tenants more as an inconvenience than anything else."

Grace stood and crossed the room to stand before the hearth fire. She stared into the flames licking at the peat brick, twisted inside with uneasiness. She knelt to pour a fresh cup of tea and sipped the soothing brew, remaining quiet for some time. She thought of the people being displaced from their homes, forced to leave all they had known and loved. It touched a chord deep within her, the injustice of it, the utter sorrow of it. It was a feeling she had herself been victim to when she had been made to leave Ledysthorpe for her uncle's house in London, and then again when she wed Christian and removed to Knighton House. The only difference was that she hadn't been left without a means of survival. She had been provided with a roof over her head and food on her plate. These poor people had been left with virtually nothing.

Grace turned to face Alastair once again. "I should like you to put out a communication asking for anyone in the vicinity who is interested in working on the castle renovations to come here to Skynegal. Carpenters, stonemasons, plasterers, woodworkers, all. Any who aren't skilled can be taught."

Alastair's eyes went wide as they so often did. "My lady, a good many will come!"

"And we will find work for them. There is much to be done here, not only the repairs to the roof. It was my grandmother's wish that I restore Skynegal to the great estate it once was. But I will need your help in figuring a fair wage for their work. Once we have a preliminary listing, I will write to Mr. Jenner in London and instruct him to forward the necessary funds."

Alastair's expression was fixed for several moments. He just stared at Grace, stunned. Finally his face broke into a smile and he closed his eyes.

"Alastair? Are you unwell?"

The Scotsman shook his head, his smile growing wider still. She saw that tears had come to his eyes. "Oh, my lady, I could not sleep last night for the fear that your sudden interest in Skynegal was for the very reasons I spoke of to you moments ago. Skynegal lies on much good arable land, with oak and pine forests and rich verdant glens. She is not an estate that turns a great profit by her rents, but she could were she to convert to a sheep walk. Factors from the neighboring estates have already come seeking to purchase portions of the estate in order to increase their own holdings for the same purpose. But with the estate held in trust, we could not even consider their offers, at least not until it reverted to its new ownership. And it has now and I praise God that Skynegal has come to you, my lady."

With every moment she stayed at Skynegal, Grace began to sense more clearly her purpose in being called there. "My thanks, Alastair, for your kind words. But I fear I am not as learned in estate management as I will need to be. I will have to rely upon you to advise me on a good many matters. I only know that I cannot abide what you have told me has happened to the tenants on the other estates. My grandmother always said the life-blood of any great estate is its people. I will make a vow never to allow greed for pound profit to overstep my own sense of morality."

Grace set down her teacup and crossed to the window. Outside, on the courtyard, the rain still fell steadily. "When the weather clears, I should like to take a tour about the estate and pay a visit to the tenants of Sky-negal. I would ask that you accompany me, since you are acquainted with the people. I imagine my coming will give them thoughts similar to those which kept you up and worrying through the night. They will fear I seek to evict them. They will not trust me. I want to assure them no such action will be taken here at Skynegal as long as I am lady here."

Alastair nodded.

"Now," Grace finished, "if you would please set to putting out the call for workers, I would like to make use of this afternoon's inclement weather to acquaint myself with the inside of the castle."

"Of course, my lady, I would be happy to take you about and show you—"

Grace put up a hand. "I appreciate your offer, Alastair, truly, but I think I should prefer to explore the castle on my own. Skynegal has been a part of my family's heritage for generations and yet I was never told of its existence. It has been home to people I have never known, setting to events I had never been told. I should like to spend some time getting acquainted with my history privately."

Alastair inclined his head in a gesture of complete understanding.

"However," Grace added on a smile, "if I do not return by nightfall, you may have to come searching for me."

Grace set aside the last of the stack of books she'd found packed away inside the carved wooden trunk, one of several she'd discovered in the many rooms and storage closets of the castle. They mostly contained estate papers, small memorabilia of days gone by, and even some old clothing, long-forgotten and moldering from the damp.

Grace leaned back against the trunk and closed her eyes, rubbing the taut muscles at the nape of her neck. She had placed several of the books apart to study later, texts on estate management and crop cultivation that she thought might prove useful in the coming months. She had been in this particular room for hours, it seemed, her skirts pooled around her, smudged by the dust that had settled over the past century or more. A small timepiece hung from a ribbon around her neck and she took it up, studying it again as she had many times that day.

She had found the piece soon after she'd begun her explorations through the castle earlier that day. It had only an hour hand and did not function at all accurately, its small dial going from sun to moon to sun again several times in the past hours. But that didnt' matter to Grace. She wore the piece for the sentiment of its engraving. Modest, oval-shaped, and cased in tarnished silver, it had inscribed upon its case words in Gaelic.

Is e seo m' uair-sa. Deirdre had given her its translation: *This is my time.*

Grace could have no way of knowing what meaning the words had represented nor what purpose the original owner of the watch could have had for inscribing them. It didn't matter, for the words could not have been any more significant to her had she inscribed them herself.

This is my time.

For the first time in her life, Grace had found a sense of purpose, a feeling that her very existence had reason for being other than to interfere. Her parents, while kind and genuinely fond of her, had seen her as more of an inconvenience to the plans they had mapped out for themselves upon their marriage, a plan that didn't allow for the addition of a third. Nonny had cared for her, raised her in love and security, yes, but doing so was not a decision she had been given any choice in. It was a duty Nonny had assumed in the wake of her children's abandonment of their only *unwanted* child.

Grace's sudden place in the household of Uncle Tedric, a bachelor accustomed to coming and going as he pleased, had left her feeling like a burr beneath his saddle. And then there was Christian, who had made it abundantly clear he had been forced by his grandfather the duke—against his will—to wed her.

All her life, she had known a sense of waiting, of searching, as if the world was spinning past her and she could but watch from the outskirts. But now was *her* time, a time to cease being an inconvenience, to cease being tolerated. Now was her time to pursue her own life's path.

Grace looked to the timepiece once again, then closed her fingers around it as she headed for the door.

Yes, this was her time.

Chapter Twenty-two

The following morning broke to a glorious sunrise that peeked over rugged mist-skirted mountains to the east. After sharing a hearty breakfast of porridge, bannocks, and tea, Grace and Alastair set out on their round of visits to the tenants of the estate. Flora, Deirdre, and Liza set to mopping up the water that had puddled beneath the various leaks in the roof. To help pass the hours inside during the previous day's rain, Deirdre and Flora had baked shortbread for Grace and Alastair to take along with them for the tenants. In doing so, they had depleted nearly all of the sugar and most of the flour and butter Grace had brought along with her on her arrival. McFee and McGee had gone that morning, sailing north for Ullapool to purchase sacks of meal, sugar, and the various other food stores they needed to provision the castle.

They had taken with them a letter that Grace had written to Mr. Jenner at his offices in London with a request for the release of additional monies from the account that had been set aside for Skynegal's restoration. Until then, she would have only what Nonny had given her many years earlier to keep them.

It had been an early spring day when Nonny had come to her holding a small embroidered reticule. "My mother gave this to me when I was a young girl of your age shortly before I wed your grandfather. Women seldom are permitted money of their own and oft are left desolate in times of need. When my mother gave this to me, she made me promise that I should only open it in time of great extremes. I was fortunate in that I never met with such crises and so I am passing this on to you, dear.

I hope you shall never come to a time when you are
faced with misfortune or deprivation, but one can never
tell what Fate has in store. If you should find yourself
in such circumstances, just remember, like Pandora's
box, with this you shall never be utterly without hope."

Grace had never opened the bag, not even to peek,
until just before she had left London to travel to Skynegal. She had known that the bag had contained
money, but she could have had no notion of the amount.
She had been overwhelmed when she had found several
five-guinea coins wrapped within four fifty-pound notes.
Discovering the treasure had removed the last obstacle
to her departure for Scotland, affirming for Grace from
then on that she was indeed pursuing the right course.

Grace and Alastair set out across the heather-covered
Sgiathach hills on sturdy Highland ponies, riding over a
verdant glen carpeted in bluebells, primroses, and wild
anemones. They came across strath and brae along the
River Sgiathach, a peaceful scene touched by the trill
and chip of the bright red crossbills who flitted about
the fir trees as they passed. Along the way, Alastair
passed the time recounting tales of his childhood on this
same land, land on which his great-grandfather had
toiled more than a century before.

"You speak of your love of this land as some would
the love for a woman," Grace remarked, sitting with
ease in the sidesaddle as her pony picked its way along
the narrow glen path. "Have you never wed, Alastair?"

Alastair immediately fell silent—not a thing he was
prone to do—and Grace reproved herself for her too-
inquisitive nature. "I'm sorry, I should not have asked
you something so personal. It isn't my place to pry."

"Nae, my lady, 'tis nothing improper in your asking."
He shook his head. "It is just that I haven't thought of
it in some time. No, my lady, I have never wed. I thought
to once, even got down on my knee to ask her."

"She refused you?"

"Nae, my lady, not at all. Iseabail accepted and we
even made ready to wed the following summer. I had a
year yet to complete my schooling. 'Twas while I was
away to university in Edinburgh that she grew impatient.
She wanted us to wed sooner, but I could not quit my

studies. So she wrote to me that she had decided to wed another." He hesitated a moment, his voice hushing slightly. "Evidently the attachment I had assumed between us was not truly extended to me in kind."

Grace knew well torment of loving another who did not love in return. "I am so sorry, Alastair."

He summoned a resolute smile. "Aye, she's gone to New Scotland these past ten years, but for as long as I live, I'll ne'er forget the first time I saw her. 'Twas at a *ceilidh* and everyone came from hereabouts for dancing and singing. I had never met Iseabail before and when I first set my eyes upon her, she was singing an old Scottish ballad. Iseabail had the most beautiful voice I'd ever heard before or since. I was awestruck, aye. Everyone listening was, too."

A sentimental look came over his face as the ponies continued on their way across the glen floor. Alastair gazed wistfully at the pathway ahead, singing softly in a brogue that he had heretofore kept hidden.

> *Ca' the ewes to the knowes,*
> *Ca' them whaur the heather grows,*
> *Ca' them whaur the burnie rows,*
> *My bonnie dearie.*
> *Hark, the mavis even' sang,*
> *Soundin' Cluden's woods amang,*
> *Then a fauldin' let us gang,*
> *My bonnie dearie.*

They rode along a space, each lost to their own thoughts. Grace listened as Alastair sang, not so much to the words, but to the love that was still so evident in them, the love he bore for the girl who'd broken his heart so many years ago.

A small part of her wondered if Christian ever thought of her as she did him, with a wonder for what might have been had they met under differing circumstances. They were thoughts that stole into her mind far more often than she cared to admit, when she would lie awake at night, watching the moon through her window. She wondered if Christian ever reminisced as she did about the intimacy of what they had shared together, the emo-

tions their union had brought. She knew the passion they
had so briefly shared had touched him—perhaps not as
deeply it had her—but there must have been something
to have made him return to her as he had time and
time again. Grace wouldn't believe that it was simply
the sexual act for if he hated so much the place she'd
come to hold in his life, he could have just as easily
taken his pleasure with another. But he hadn't. Knowing
that was what left the small kernel of hope deep within
her heart.

They steered the ponies across a shallow brook that
tumbled across the glen. A simple stone cottage lay
snuggled close against the hillside in front of them. A
column of smoke rose out of a small chimney—the *lum,*
as Alastair had called it—above the thickly thatched roof
that was weighted down against the Highland winds with
stones hanging from ropes that stretched from one side
to the other.

A handful of small white sheep dotted the verdant
hillside, picking among the moor-grass and heath, their
distant bleating carried on the soft breeze that blew
down from the mountains. As they approached the cottage, Grace spotted a small face peeking at them through
an opening in the wall where there was no window, only
an oilcloth flapping in the breeze for a covering. Dogs
barked, running around the ponies who were so docile,
they barely gave the hounds notice. A low stone wall
enclosed a small byre where a stocky pony and a shaggy
bedraggled Highland calf stood watching them with little interest.

They stopped the ponies and were dismounting when
a man came from inside the cottage to meet them. He
wore a coarse woolen shirt with full sleeves rolled to his
elbows and a tartan belted at the waist and draped from
one shoulder across to the waist on the opposite side.
Woolen stockings with a similar crisscross design covered his legs below the knee, and leather brogues laced
over his feet. Behind him, lingering in the doorway,
stood a woman, her head covered by a kerchief, her feet
bare beneath her ankle-length skirts. Two small children
clung to her on each side.

"*Là math,* Alastair," the man said in Gaelic.

Alastair nodded to him. "Calum, you look well. How is the family?"

The man answered him in rapid Gaelic, eyeing Grace suspiciously as he spoke.

"Calum," Alastair said, "I'd like to introduce you to Lady Grace, Marchioness Knighton. Lady Grace has inherited Skynegal. Lady Grace, please meet Calum Guthrie."

Calum bowed his head respectfully, saying, "My lady."

He no longer spoke Gaelic, but when he raised his head to look at her, she saw again the unmistakable darkness of suspicion in his eyes, suspicion and fear of what her coming to Skynegal might portend for him and his small family.

"It is a pleasure to meet you, Mr. Guthrie," Grace said, smiling openly in hopes of allaying some of his misgivings. When he didn't respond, she motioned toward where the woman still stood framed in the low doorway. "Is this your wife?"

Calum nodded. "Aye, she is. 'Tis Mary. An' the two boys, Calum and Ian."

Grace left her pony and walked over to the others, smiling at the woman. She made to hand her the shortbread they'd brought, wrapped in linen. "Hello, Mary. It is a pleasure to meet you."

But the woman did not look at her, nor did she move to take the bundled shortbread. Instead she glanced uneasily to her husband.

"She disna speak English," Calum said, coming to join his wife. He said something to her in Gaelic and she nodded, then turned back to regard Grace, bowing her head with a tentative smile.

"This is for you," Grace said, holding out the shortbread to her again.

Mary looked to Calum, who nodded, and took the bundle. When she saw what it was, she smiled, although the same cloud of fear that Grace had noticed in Calum's eyes now darkened her eyes as well. *"Taing is buidheachas dhut, baintighearnachd do."*

Now it was Grace's turn to look to Calum in bewilderment. "I'm afraid I do not understand Gaelic yet."

"She gives her thanks to you, your ladyship."

"Please tell her she is most welcome."

As Calum repeated Grace's words to Mary, Grace crouched down and extended her hand to the first of the two boys. He looked to be about seven years old and was tall and thin like his father. She noticed his clothing was tattered and he had no shoes to cover his feet. He did not take her hand, but looked curiously at the fine kid glove that covered it. The other boy did the same, peeking from behind him.

"She disna have a hand, Da," said the first one.

Calum quickly silenced him with a *Hish!* and the child turned to her as if she'd suddenly sprung a second head, one that was coming to swallow him whole. Grace held up a hand and shook her head, saying, "It is all right." She tugged on the fingers of her glove while the boy just stared with a mixture of both fascination and fear. When all her fingers were loose, Grace drew off the glove to reveal her bare hand underneath.

She flexed her fingers. "See, I do have a hand. It was just covered by a glove."

The boy's fear melted away beneath the light of curiosity. He took up the glove Grace offered to him, staring at it as if it were made of the finest gold.

"Will you shake hands with me now?" Grace asked and he did, wrapping his grubby fingers tightly around hers.

"What is your name?"

"Calum," he mumbled, his attentions again focused on the glove, the way it was stitched, the small flower embroidered upon it. He set it up against his hand, comparing the size of it to his own.

"I should have known that your name was Calum because you look just like your da."

She noticed the second boy peering tentatively around his brother's arm. He was perhaps three or four, with a mop of reddish hair and a sprinkle of freckles crossing his small nose. Grace removed her other glove and handed it to him. "And I would guess your name is Ian."

"Aye," he answered in a tiny voice, clasping the hand she held toward him and taking the glove with his other. "You are *vewy pwetty*."

Grace smiled brightly. "Well, thank you, my fine sir."

"What's a 'sir'?"

" 'Sir' is another name for a grown-up boy like you."
He grinned at her, still clutching her glove.

Grace stood then and peered inside the cottage, but
she could see no more than a foot beyond the low doorway, for it was very dark inside. She glanced to Calum
still standing beside Mary. "May I have a look inside?
I've never been inside a crofting cottage."

The two exchanged a curious glance and then Calum
nodded, seeming almost reluctant to allow her inside but
afraid to refuse her.

Grace removed her tall riding derby and stepped
through the doorway into a large room that was at once
a kitchen, sitting room, and bedroom together. Despite
its meager furnishings, it was a place that gave one a
sense of home the moment they entered. A fire burned
in the small hearth, over which an iron kettle hung from
a hook. The far corner of the room was completely
taken up by a huge pine box bed. A crude oaken table
stood at the room's center, covered with numerous
wooden bowls of porridge—at least half a dozen. Odd,
Grace thought, for only four had come out to greet her.

Mary came inside and quickly began taking away the
bowls when she noticed Grace's interest in them. Grace
turned to Calum. "I hope you will forgive us for inter-
rupting your breakfast."

He shook his head. "Nae trouble, my lady. We were
a'ready finished."

"You have a lovely home," she said, noting the small
feminine touches—fresh wildflowers set in a jug upon
the table, a bit of colored cloth fashioned as a curtain
over the window. Grace walked about the room. She
stopped before a wooden peat box to admire a woolen
blanket that lay across its top. Intricately woven, its design reminded Grace of the shawl her grandmother had
given her years earlier.

It was as she was fingering the finely spun wool that
Grace realized there were sounds coming from inside
the peat box, sounds not unlike the whimpering of a
child followed by the distinctive *shh*'ing of comfort.

Without hesitating to ask, Grace took the blanket
away and lifted the cover off the peat box. Behind her,

she heard Mary give a cry of alarm as Grace discovered a woman crouched inside with a small child of no more than two years clutched tightly against her. The woman was trembling, staring at Grace in terror. The child immediately began to cry. Mary shouted something in Gaelic and then buried her face against Calum's chest, sobbing.

Grace turned to Calum. "What is wrong? Why is she hiding in there?"

Calum's expression had grown utterly defeated. "I know I canna expect you to forgive such a t'ing, my lady, but by the grace of God, they had no other place to gae."

"Forgive? What is there to forgive? I'm afraid I do not understand."

Alastair came forward from the doorway to explain. "My lady, the woman inside the peat box is Mary's sister Elspeth and her daughter. They had previously lived on the neighboring estate until they were evicted." He turned to Calum, his expression sympathetic, then looked to Grace once again. "What Calum realizes but you do not, my lady, is that there is an unwritten law among the lairds of the estates and the local magistrates that any family found offering their home to another family who has been evicted will as punishment suffer the same fate." He hesitated. "They fear you will now evict them from their home as well."

Grace looked slowly around the room at the myriad of faces all watching her—Calum, his boys, even Mary, her face wet with tears, and Elspeth, who was now standing inside the peat box. Grace might as well have been the monarch of hell for the look of pure and utter terror they all returned to her.

Anger, fierce and raw, began to burn within her. It was barbarous and cruel that these poor people should live under such a terrible threat every day, fear of simply offering shelter to their own family lest they should be turned out as well. She watched then as the two boys, Calum and Ian, walked slowly to her, their eyes never leaving hers as each of them gently placed her gloves upon the table, returning them to her as if hoping, praying that this one small gesture might keep her from punishing their loved ones.

Grace blinked away the tears that had begun to form in her eyes and turned to Elspeth, who still stood behind her. She was clutching her daughter tightly in her arms, the child's tiny face tucked away against the safety of her mother's neck. Grace held out her hands. "Please let me take her for you so you can climb out of that box."

Elspeth looked confused. Calum spoke to her in Gaelic, nodding, his tone reassuring. Slowly, tentatively, Elspeth loosened her hold on the child, handing her to where Grace waited to take her. Grace took the girl and held her against her while Elspeth quickly climbed out of the peat box with Calum's help. The child looked at Grace and sniffed, her chin quivering. Grace smiled at her and touched her softly on her cheek, wiping away a tear. "It will be all right," she whispered, and pressed a kiss to the soft curls at her forehead before handing her back to Elspeth.

Grace took a deep breath and turned to speak to Calum. "You fear that I will evict you from your home because of the actions of others who hold a position similar to mine. I give you my word, Calum Guthrie, that no such thing will take place. Not today. Not ever. There will be no 'Improvements' such as have occurred elsewhere in the Highlands here at Skynegal. Please be sure to tell the other tenants what I have just said."

Calum stared at her a moment in disbelief and then his face broke into a broad, beaming smile. He quickly repeated what Grace had said to Mary and Elspeth in Gaelic. Mary covered her mouth with both hands in surprise while the boys, Calum and Ian, raced forward and threw their arms around Grace's skirts. Grace glanced at Calum, who had drawn his wife and her sister into his arms. His eyes were closed and he looked as if he were fighting tears himself. She looked to Alastair, standing to the side, spectator to the scene. He was smiling, his own tears glistening in the low light, and when his gaze caught hers, he nodded, mouthing the words "Thank you, my lady, thank you."

Chapter Twenty-three

London

Some people will have a bad day; still others a bad week. Christian Wycliffe, Marquess Knighton was having a bad two months—moving as he was into the third, things weren't looking any more promising.

He had lost his wife—he preferred the term "lost" because the words "been abandoned by" sound so final, so irretrievable, and he had every intention of retrieving Grace, Lady Knighton, if only so he could read her the riot act for having so successfully vanished without leaving the slightest trace.

He would never forget the day he had found her gone. His first thought had been that she had been taken by whoever it was who had left the anonymous and menacing message at his doorstep. The thought that it would be Grace who would pay for his sins had brought Christian lower than he'd ever thought possible. He'd spent the first two days of her disappearance condemning himself for it, until one of the maids pointed out to him that she'd found a number of Grace's gowns missing. As it turned out, only the gowns she had brought with her to their marriage were gone, along with the shoes, the stockings, even the hair ribbons she'd had before becoming his wife. Still, it wasn't until Eleanor discovered her sketching supplies missing too that they knew for certain Grace had left on her own.

While staring at the empty space in her wardrobe, Christian remarked that he had never known of Grace's fondness for sketching. It was a fact Eleanor was all too ready to comment upon.

"You would have noticed," she'd said to him crossly, "had you given Grace even the slightest bit of your attention while she was here."

Christian had been humbled in the face of his sister's indignation, quite simply because he could do nothing to refute her accusation. It had been he and no other who had driven Grace away, and it was a thought he wasn't alone in, either. The servants blamed him, too. In fact, he was beginning to think the cook was purposely oversalting his suppers to punish him. He could see it in their eyes and hear it in their voices even as they tried to pretend she would soon be returning. The maids still brought fresh flowers to her bedchamber, replacing them anew when the blooms withered. Once he'd even found Forbes adding a bit of water to the vases as if by doing so, Grace might somehow turn the corner to notice his efforts as she always had, thanking him for tasks Christian had only taken for granted.

Each morning, when Christian woke to confront the empty bedchamber through the door adjoining his, he would stand on the threshold and stare at her bed, neatly made in pale blue brocade and lace, untouched for weeks now. He wanted to know how she was, where she was sleeping, if she was safe. The thought that she might still come to danger because of his having caused her to flee kept him up and pacing through most every night, pausing every so often to stare out the window to the street as if somehow, some way, she'd magically walk by.

But she never did.

It had gotten so he had begun to wonder if her appearance in his life had been naught but a dream, a brief stretch of his imagination. Flashes of her would come to him from out of nowhere. He could see her brilliant smile the night of the Devonbrook ball when she had walked on his arm for the first time as his wife. He thought of her utter acceptance of him, even when he had treated her badly. He might well have been persuaded to believe she had been naught but an illusion, if not for the melancholy faces of the servants reminding him each day that Grace had been no dream, no illusion, but a gift he had stupidly tossed away.

Not an hour after he had found her gone, Christian

had hired four of Bow Street's best to search for her, each going off in a separate direction. He had expected to have Grace back within days, but thus far the runners hadn't been able to turn up so much as a footprint. Christian couldn't help but begin to fear the worst. The longer Grace remained missing, the worse he felt about her leaving, and the more he knew that when he found her—*if* he found her—of the many things he wanted to do, most important among them was to tell her how very wrong he'd been.

It had taken Eleanor's barbed scorn when they had discovered her gone to finally open Christian's eyes to the fact that Grace was as much a victim in their marriage as was he. He'd been so consumed with his own bitterness toward his grandfather, so angry at his powerlessness, that he'd taken his anger out on her, as if she had been to blame somehow. But he had treated her abominably. Whenever he thought of that last night when she had come to him, practically begging him to care about her, he winced. It was a plea to which he had only responded with cold selfish indifference. He'd been so frustrated with himself because no matter how he had vowed not to allow her to affect him, he had found himself utterly unable to resist her. Grace had been an easy target that night, standing before him in her nightdress, so vulnerable, begging him to give her some small indication of regard. And when she'd finally laid open her heart to him, he had simply stared at her, arrogant and proud like every other Westover before him.

You could have been anyone . . .

He would never be able to forget her expression, utterly cast down, when he'd spoken those words to her. He'd been a bastard and he couldn't fault her for leaving because of it. What he could fault her for was being so damnably good at hiding from him. He wanted to go after her himself instead of sitting idly by, powerless and waiting, but even that was denied him. There was still the current situation with Eleanor to deal with.

With nearly every marriageable nobleman in England in town for the season, Eleanor, it seemed, was hell bent on falling in love with the one man she could not possibly wed, Richard Hartley, the Earl of Herrick. Over the past weeks, Christian had spent his days trying to figure out where his wife might have gone, and his nights doing everything in his power to keep Eleanor and Herrick from forming any sort of lasting attachment. It was not an easy task, for he had to do so without drawing any suspicion from Eleanor. Unfortunately, since the time when they had been children, his sister had always had the uncanny ability of being able to see right through to the heart of a matter, despite any attempts at subterfuge.

She had noticed Christian's reserve immediately and had even asked him directly why he was so opposed to Lord Herrick. Christian had simply responded that he would prefer that she take the season slowly and allow herself to meet any number of young men rather than committing herself to the first one who had noticed her.

In other words, he'd lied.

Blessedly, just that morning Christian had learned that Herrick had been called away from London to his estate in York. His absence would give Christian several weeks respite. Perhaps fortune might even smile upon him long enough to have Eleanor fall in love with another.

Christian stared thoughtfully at a miniature portrait of his sister that stood on the fireplace mantel. If he could only tell Eleanor the truth for his objections to Herrick, she would understand the reasons why she could never marry him. But Christian knew he could never tell her the truth, for if he did, then the even deeper truth would come to light, something Christian had spent his life trying to hide.

A knocking on the study door pulled him from his troubled thoughts. Christian set Eleanor's portrait back on the mantelpiece just as Forbes came in.

"My lord, Lord Cholmeley is here to see you."

Good grief, Christian thought, peering at the timepiece. It was only nine o'clock and he'd barely finished his first cup of coffee. He was certainly not in any frame of mind to face Grace's uncle.

"Tell him I'm not in."

"He is most insistent, my lord. He has, uh, begun making certain threats."

Christian raised a brow. "Threats?"

"Yes, my lord, of the sort that would only serve to further breed scandal."

Christian frowned. He had been afraid of this. His time to repair matters in his marriage without all and sundry knowing about it had apparently passed and the time he had dreaded most was now upon him. He could hide the truth of Grace's absence no more behind excuses of headaches and upset stomachs. With Cholmeley spouting off, soon all of London would know that he had been abandoned by his wife before the ink was barely dry on the marriage documents.

Christian drew a deep breath. "Then I guess you'll have to show him in."

While Forbes returned to the marquess, Christian poured himself a second cup of coffee, adding a splash of brandy to it, knowing somehow he would need it.

Tedric, Lord Cholmeley, came bursting through the door with all the polish and refinement of a violent hurricane. He didn't wait to be acknowledged, but sputtered without preamble, "What the devil have you done with my niece, Knighton?"

Christian stared at the marquess, attempting to maintain a measure of calm. "Sit down, Cholmeley."

But Cholmeley ignored him. "Everyone knows how secretive you Westovers are. What did you do? Kill her? Is she buried outside in the garden, pushing up your pansies even now as we speak?"

Christian looked to the door where Forbes was standing, mouth agape. "You may leave us, Forbes. And please close the door behind you." All he needed was for one of the other servants to overhear Cholmeley's blithering; soon half of London would think he was a wife-murderer.

Christian waited, counting to ten even after the butler had gone. He took two sips from his coffee and looked at Cholmeley again, saying quite distinctly, "Sit down, Cholmeley—now."

The elder marquess shut his mouth and took the chair in front of Christian's desk. His expression, however, remained just as agitated, his fingers gripping the carved arm of his chair.

Christian looked at him. "First, you can quit the theatrics. You know very well I did not kill Grace."

"Then where is she? I know she's not here. I've questioned your servants. No one has seen sight of her for some time."

"No, not since she apparently went on a visit to you. You should have been the last to see her." He looked at the marquess. "Perhaps I should be questioning you about her whereabouts."

Tedric shook his head in disgust. "It is a poor example of a man, Knighton, who can't keep track of his own wife."

Christian couldn't argue against the insinuation, but that didn't mean he liked hearing it, especially from someone like the marquess. "Be that as it may, let me assure you I am making every effort to find her."

Tedric came to lean forward at the very edge of his chair. "Every effort? If you want so badly to find her, Knighton, why the devil are you here?" he pointed to the desk, "instead of out there"—he waved a hand toward the window—"finding her yourself?"

"Yes, Christian," came a familiar and unwelcome voice from the doorway, "do tell us, why are you here instead of out tracking down your wayward wife?"

Chapter Twenty-four

Christian glanced with unfeigned reluctance to the door, already knowing who was there and wishing to the very heavens he were wrong. Surely the saints must be punishing him to demand that he face both Cholmeley and his grandfather together on the same day.

The Duke of Westover stood, cane in hand, listening to the exchange between Christian and Cholmeley. His mouth was turned decidedly downward, his eyes glinting with their usual dark and disapproving light. Christian could almost hear the old man's thoughts as loudly as if they were echoing throughout the room:

What's this, boy? I get you a perfectly acceptable wife and you lose her? What kind of duke do you expect to make if you can't even keep a simple woman happy?

But even as he thought this, Christian knew he could no more hold his grandfather responsible for his predicament than he could blame Grace for having left after the way he had treated her. He and he alone had brought this on.

Christian waited in giving his response until the duke had come into his study, taking the chair beside Cholmeley. They exchanged a short greeting nod before both men turned to stare at Christian with twin looks of censure.

Christian took a deep breath. "Yes, it is true. Grace has left. And yes, whether you wish to believe it or not, I have tried to find her. I have hired four runners to track her, but thus far they have turned up no trace of her."

"She can't have gone far," Cholmeley sputtered. "She is, after all, only a woman."

Only a woman. Somehow it wasn't a designation Christian would ever think again of attributing to Grace.

"I learned quite some time ago, my lord, never to underestimate the fairer sex." Christian exchanged a private glance with his grandfather before continuing. "However, given that Grace had very little if any ready resources to provide for her, I find it difficult to believe that she could have gotten far from London, if she did leave the city at all, which is part of the reason for my remaining in town. I am hoping she is yet somewhere within the city. If she is, I will eventually find her. She must have had some monies available to her to have stayed hidden away as many weeks as she has. Were you aware of her having any ready funds, Cholmeley?"

The marquess shook his head. "No. She couldn't have. I'd have known it."

And spent it, Christian thought to himself.

"Unless . . ."

"Unless what?"

"Unless my mother happened to give her some pin money before she died. It would be just like the old bird to have done something like that. She favored independence in women, confused a notion as that is."

The duke cleared his throat and leaned forward on his cane. "I suppose it is a possibility, but is it feasible to believe that 'pin money' could support a girl and her maid—since I assume she took one with her—for this length of time? Sooner or later she will run out of money. The question is, what will she do then?"

A knocking came to the door before anyone could reflect further on the thought. Forbes came in, bowing his head. "My lord, a Mr. Jenner is here asking to see you."

"Jenner?" spouted Tedric. "Wasn't he my mother's man of business? The one who drew up the marriage contracts?"

"His card does indicate that he is a solicitor, my lord," said Forbes, answering Cholmeley's question.

"He's probably come about something to do with a

provision in the marriage contract that says if the bride disappears, all is null and void," chuckled Cholmeley.

Christian wasn't amused. He said, "In that case you would then forfeit your share of the settlement."

The duke smiled. Cholmeley blanched as Christian turned to Forbes. "Will you tell this Jenner I am presently occupied and ask him if he can leave whatever paperwork he has."

"He says it is an urgent matter, my lord, concerning Lady Knighton and a missive he has received from her."

"Good God, man, why didn't you say so? Show him in."

Christian looked first to his grandfather and then to Cholmeley as the butler left to fetch the solicitor. "Not a word out of either of you until I get to the bottom of this. I will speak to Mr. Jenner."

The duke merely nodded, rooted to his chair. Cholmeley shrugged and stood to help himself to Christian's brandy bottle instead.

Within a few moments, Forbes showed in a small man in plain clothes with ink-stained fingertips. The solicitor glanced nervously at the other two gentlemen before taking the seat previously put to use by Cholmeley.

Christian had no notion of how much, if anything, Jenner knew about Grace's disappearance. He chose his words carefully. "Mr. Jenner, it is good to see you again. I understand you have received some sort of communication from Lady Knighton?"

Jenner looked at the duke and then at Cholmeley, who had come to stand beside him. Both men were staring at the solicitor most intently, unsettling him. They did, however, keep to their word and remain silent.

"Yes, uh, Lord Knighton, I have received a communication from Lady Knighton, but I believe it is a matter that might best be discussed in private, my lord. With you."

Christian waved a hand. "Speak freely, Mr. Jenner. As you already know, these two gentlemen are members of the family. They are aware of Grace's . . ." He paused and said for wont of a better term, *"Relocation."*

Jenner looked at the old duke and then again at Cholmeley. He cleared his throat nervously. "Lady Knighton has sent this letter to my offices." He held out a folded bit of parchment. "It is actually the third such correspondence I have received from her."

Christian took the letter and began reading as Jenner went on. "I cannot forward her any of the funds she seeks without your signature as her husband, even though the account is hers, so I—"

"Account?" Cholmeley broke in. "What's this about an account?"

Christian glanced at the marquess over the top of the parchment. "Calm yourself, Cholmeley, until we know what this is about."

When he had finished reading the letter, he looked to Jenner. "Would you care to apprise me of the particulars of the situation?"

"It would appear I must, my lord."

Jenner shuffled through his papers, handing several sheets to Christian. "The estate was held in trust until such time as Lady Knighton married, although, by its government, it was not to be any part of a marriage settlement. It is hers until her death, when it shall pass to a direct issue of her choosing, since it is not entailed in any way. I had been charged with the duty of informing Lady Knighton of the existence of the trust and her part in it but only *after* her marriage, as stipulated by the trust. I came here to Knighton House many weeks ago and did so."

Christian scanned the pages that formalized the Skynegal trust. "And this account you speak of?"

Cholmeley drew closer.

"Again," Jenner said, eyeing the elder marquess askance, "the account is a separate enterprise from the dower contract, the funds of which can be used only for the betterment of the estate."

"You keep talking of this estate?" Cholmeley said, "What's this about? I know of no estate that isn't already entailed to the Cholmeley marquessate."

Christian returned the trust papers to Jenner. "It seems," he said to Cholmeley, "that upon her marriage to me, Grace became the beneficiary of an estate in northern Scotland, one Skynegal Castle."

Cholmeley began to laugh. "That rotting old pile of

bricks? I know of it. It was some holding from my mother's family. No one has lived there for years. Can't even be reached by road. I'd have thought it in ruins by now."

"Oh, I rather doubt that will ever come to pass," Christian said, "especially since there exists an account of three hundred thousand pounds to ensure its continuance."

"Three hundred thousand!" Cholmeley began to choke on his brandy, gasping for breath until Jenner stood without preamble and clapped the marquess hard twice on the back. It only took Cholmeley another moment to regain his dander.

"You mean to say that little chit has had a fortune at her disposal while I am forced to live in near-poverty?"

"The monies are not *at her disposal,* Cholmeley," Christian reminded him. "According to the trust, they must be used exclusively for the betterment of Skynegal. And from her letter to Mr. Jenner, it would seem that is exactly what Grace means to do."

"With your approval," Jenner interjected, gently bringing the subject back to his reasons for coming there. "As Lady Knighton's husband, all transactions on the account must bear your endorsement."

"Well, at least this trust has some sense to it," the old duke muttered. "Imagine turning three hundred thousand loose to the hands of a woman!"

"In turn," Jenner added, "any transaction must also bear Lady Knighton's endorsement as well."

The solicitor seemed inordinately unsettled in the presence of the old duke, for although he never spoke directly to him, he kept shifting his glance to the old man time and again as they talked. It was a feeling Christian could easily appreciate.

"Well then, let's be done with it," Christian said, taking his quill from its holder and dipping it into the inkwell. He started to sign the document Jenner had given him, authorizing the release of the funds from the account.

"You aren't really going to lend your signature to give all that money to her for that moldering old castle, are you?" Cholmeley exclaimed.

"That is precisely what I'm going to do, my lord."

Christian set his quill back in its holder and returned the documents to Jenner's waiting hand. "If you would please inform me when the transaction is complete, Mr. Jenner, I would be obliged."

Jenner nodded. "Of course. Shall I also arrange for a courier to deliver the news to Lady Knighton then, my lord?"

"She does not know of your visit here today?"

Jenner shook his head. "I did not know of the stipulation requiring your signature until after Lady Knighton had already left for Scotland. That is why I waited so long in coming to you. After receiving her third letter, I grew concerned for her circumstances. I only hope Lady Knighton will forgive me for breaking her confidence. Begging your pardon, my lord, but she wanted no one to know where she was going."

Christian looked at the solicitor. After a moment, he smiled. "No, sir, a courier will not be necessary. I mean to deliver the news to Lady Knighton myself in Scotland."

Chapter Twenty-five

Skynegal Castle, Highlands

Grace stood in her nightdress at her bedchamber window, scowling at the dark cloud of smoke that snaked its shadowed way through the morning sky to the east.

Would the burnings never end?

How she hated knowing that as she stood there, tucked safely within the fortress of these castle walls, yet another Highland family was being unjustly forced from their home on the neighboring estate. It was an event that was happening so frequently of late that the eastern horizon seemed perpetually smoke clouded.

It began with an unexpected knocking on the door. The family would answer, only to find that a company of soldiers awaited them on the other side. They would be handed a Writ of Removal signed by the estate factor and they would be ordered to vacate the premises, refused any time for preparation or reflection. Chaos would lay claim to what once had been peace. They would be given only enough time to grab what little their hands could carry with them before those who had come to evict them put their torches to the vulnerable cottage roof, setting everything they'd worked for, every last thing they owned in the world, aflame.

As the fire began to blaze, the crofters would scramble to save the single most important possession they could claim, the cottage's roof beam. Without it, they might not have the timber necessary to rebuild elsewhere. They would end up like so many of their neighbors, seeking shelter in caves, or worse, forced to live among the elements.

If they were fortunate enough to have their health, the Highlanders could wander to the coast, where they might have a chance to begin life again. The elderly and the infirm, however, fared far worse, for if they were too incapacitated to leave by their own volition, they were simply carried out of their homes without care for their fragile bodies, dropped upon the bare ground, and left to survive against the elements—if they survived at all.

Taken by a sudden shiver, Grace reached for her shawl on the chair beside her, wrapping it closely about herself. The cloud in the distance billowed and grew. She felt a sudden tickle on her hand and looked down to where Dubhar sat, licking her fingers and patiently awaiting a scratch behind his ears. She willingly obliged. For as long as anyone could remember, the long and lanky deerhound had traveled about from croft to croft in search of scraps and a warm fire to sleep beside. Everyone knew him, yet none would lay claim to him. Grizzled gray not unlike McGee's beard, on hind legs the dog stood a head taller than Grace. When he'd first come to the castle one rainy morning not long after Grace's arrival, he'd been weak with a fever that left him panting despite the water they offered him. Beneath the mud that had caked his coat, his body had been naught but hide and bones, his gait sluggish and marked by a pronounced limp. Alastair had suggested the dog might have been bitten by an adder and indeed they found a bite on his rear left leg. The Scotsman predicted he'd likely die, but Grace would have none of it. She'd taken the dog in, staying up through the night with him, and with the help of Deirdre and a poultice she'd made from the rowan bark, the fever had broken the next afternoon.

To see Dubhar now, one would never believe him the same dog. He had added flesh to his bones and could run more swiftly than the wind. They had christened him Dubhar, the Gaelic word for the shadow he had become at his mistress's side, following Grace from one room to the other as she walked about the castle. She had saved his life, and thus he now devoted himself to her.

As Grace stroked her fingers through Dubhar's wiry fur, she looked below her window onto the castle courtyard and the numerous people milling about on the drive. Just like Dubhar, they had come to Skynegal hoping to be saved.

They were most of them crofters from other estates who had wandered to the ancient stone towers of Skynegal, having heard of the mistress there called *Aingeal na Gáidhealthachd,* Angel of the Highlands. Word had spread quickly that the lady of Skynegal had vowed never to allow a single eviction on her estate. They came in droves seeking shelter, food, and clothing, and a touch of compassion. A number of them made arrangements to emigrate to New Scotland or America and simply sought a safe place to sleep until the ship that would take them across the sea departed from Ullapool. Others planned to wander south to Glasgow or the Borders. Grace hadn't the heart to turn a single one of them away, so instead she devoted her days and nights to helping prepare them for their new lives.

After the Scots' rebellion in 1745, a writ had been passed called the Act of Proscription, taking the Highlanders into what was known as "the time of gray." The wearing of the colorful tartans they had so proudly displayed for generations, the teaching of Gaelic, even the playing of the pipes had been forbidden under threat of transportation. Though the proscription was repealed some forty years later, its damage had been wrought through a full generation. When Grace learned of the proscription and its eventaul repeal, she immediately set to work on the design for a distinct tartan, collaborated on with Alastair, Liza, and Deirdre. Its colors were created by using the various plant life found at Skynegal—a lovely dark green made from the heath pulled just before flowering from a dark, shady place; a rich deep red made from the *crotal,* or gray lichen they had scraped from the moorland rocks; and black made from the rich bark and acorns of the Highland oaks. The tartan was used to make the clothing for the refugee Highlanders so that no matter where they might go, be it to other parts of Scotland or the new world, they would always have a remembrance of Skynegal and their Scottish heritage with them.

Since the majority of the Highlanders spoke only

Gaelic, together with Liza, Alastair, and Deirdre, Grace had begun teaching them English, as well as reading and writing and simple mathematics. They had set up pallets stuffed with heather and gorse in the great hall for those who had no homes or family with whom they could stay, and when that chamber had filled, they moved on to the others. A good many of the Skynegal tenants had begun taking in the strangers, echoing the goodwill shown by their mistress.

In turn, those who sought shelter did their share. While the women were employed in the weaving and sewing of new clothing for those in need, the men busied themselves with tending the stock of cattle and sheep in the fields while others contributed to the castle renovations or the repairs needed at the tenants' cottages across the estate. In the space of the handful of weeks Grace had been at Skynegal, this once-abandoned estate, overgrown and in disrepair, had been transformed into a small, efficiently working community.

But Grace knew that a community needed funds to grow and thrive and that was a commodity fast growing scarce. To date Grace had had no reply to the missive she'd written to Mr. Jenner requesting additional funds. By her calculations, he should have received it nearly a month earlier, giving him ample time to reply. After the first couple of weeks, she'd written again, and then she'd sent a third letter for fear that the first and even the second had never reached him. Funds were running short. In keeping the castle stocked with meal and the simplest of necessities, they'd already run through a good portion of the money Nonny had given her. Just the week before, Grace had found herself sorting through her small cache of jewelry, trying to decide which pieces she might sell when next McFee or McGee made the trip to Ullapool for supplies. In the end, she'd decided she could part with almost all of it, with the exception of the inscribed timepiece she'd found her first day at Skynegal and one other—her wedding ring.

Grace turned from the window when she heard a stirring come suddenly from behind her and was greeted by

Liza coming into her bedchamber with an armful of freshly washed clothes.

"I was beginning to think you were going to sleep through the day," the maid said as she set out a fresh gown, shift, and stockings for Grace to wear.

Grace shook her head. "I don't know what it is, Liza, but I am so tired all the time. I can't seem to pick myself out of bed as early as I used to."

Liza cocked a brow. "You work yourself too much, my lady. 'Tisn't right for a lady of your station to be toiling as you do.

"So what should I be doing? Standing around glancing at myself in the mirror when there is so much work to be done?"

Grace took up her hairbrush and began pulling it through the tangles in her hair.

"I suppose your fatigue might have something to do with all the work you do," the maid said. "But it could also have a mite to do with the fact that you're increasing."

The hairbrush clattered noisily to the floor. Dubhar sat up on his haunches, wondering at the cause for the disturbance. Grace turned to stare at Liza, silent and disbelieving.

"Oh, my lady, did you not know?" Then she added immediately, "Of course you did not. No one's ever told you about women and babies and such. But surely you noticed you've not had your monthly since we've been to Scotland."

Grace shook her head, saying at the same time so softly, she barely heard her own words, "There have been times when I haven't bled before and I wasn't—I wasn't—I—"

Grace felt her consciousness threaten to shadow over as if she might faint. She had never fainted in her life, but she supposed if there ever were a time when fainting would be called for, this was it. She braced herself against the edge of the dressing table and waited for the dizziness to pass.

Liza immediately dropped the clothes and came to her, helping her to sit at the edge of the bed. She took Grace's hands in hers. "Oh, I am so sorry, my lady. I thought you knew of it and just didn't want to tell any-body because of the troubles between his lordship and you . . ."

Christian. Good God. Grace closed her eyes against a new wave of what she felt certain now would be a full swoon. Liza squeezed her hand and patted it.

"My lady, I could be mistaken in this. I just figured, what with your monthly going missing and your bodice getting tight like it is—I am a maid, after all, and thus would notice these things."

Grace looked down at her breasts, suddenly noticing the fullness of them swelling beneath the thin fabric of her nightshift.

"Do you ever feel sore . . . there?" Liza asked.

Grace chewed her lip, staring at the maid. She nodded.

"And I've seen you've been needing to use the cham-berpot more often, too. My ma once said 'tis from the babe growing and pressing upon you inside."

Still Grace shook her head against the idea. "But it's been too long since we left London. Wouldn't a babe be more evident?"

Grace looked down at herself, placing a hand against her abdomen. She had noticed a thickening at her waist, but had put it off as too many of Deirdre's oatcakes. To think that it had nothing to do with the oatcakes at all, but that a tiny life quite possibly grew there . . .

"Some ladies don't show they're with child right away. Are you all right, my lady? Are you upset? Does this news of the babe trouble you?"

Grace looked at Liza. At the mention of it, the thought of a babe had frightened her completely, for she knew nothing of raising children other than the scarce bits she'd seen while growing up at Ledys-thorpe. But now that she'd had a moment to reflect on it and get past the shock of it, she found herself filled with a strange sort of warmth that brought her to smiling.

"No, Liza, the babe does not trouble me at all. In fact, it makes me very, very happy."

Liza grinned. "Oh, I am so relieved to hear you say

that! It will be such fun having a little 'un around here, the next generation to carry on at Skynegal!"

"You've come to like this pile of rocks, have you, Liza?" Grace said, remembering Liza's pessimism when they had first arrived at Skynegal.

" 'Tis the sort of place that grows on you," Liza said, tossing her capped head. "But it is only due to the hand you have put to the place, my lady. I never knew your grandmama, but I know if she were here and could see all that you have done, she would be very proud."

"Thank you, Liza."

The maid grinned. "Now when the little 'un is older, can I teach her how to plant a facer?"

"Liza! Girls should not learn to fight!"

"You'd think differently if you'd have been born into my family. 'Twas a means for survival."

"Well, then, I suppose it wouldn't do any harm for her to learn the proper form of it." Grace looked at her. "But what if the babe is a boy?"

Liza thought for a moment, cocking her head to the side. "Then I'll teach him how to darn his own hose."

Grace hugged Liza tightly as they laughed and sat together at the side of the bed, all while the morning sunshine suddenly beamed down through the cloud of smoke in the distance.

Not until the sun was starting to set that afternoon did Grace finally manage to steal a few moments to herself. It had been a long and unusually busy day, filled with small chores and unexpected interruptions.

Another family of crofters had arrived shortly before midday with naught but the clothes they wore and terrible tales of the eviction that had driven them from their home. A man, a woman, and four young children, they had been walking for nearly three days, eating berries and foraging for earthnut to stave off the pangs of their hunger.

After hearing their tale and seeing their sooty, forlorn faces, Grace had promptly brought them in, offered them hot porridge and fresh milk, and arranged for pallets for them to sleep on. She'd spent the rest of the morning updating the record books, adding to the grow-

ing list she was compiling of who had come to Skynegal
and who had gone on.

During a small midday meal of cheese and bannocks,
Grace had done a little refining of her sketches for the
castle refurbishment while she had listened to some of
the children at their English lessons. Later, a disagreement had broken out among two of the workers. When
Grace had happened upon that scene, one of them was
readying to strike the other with a sizeable rock that was
to have been used for the curtain wall. He pulled back
in the moment he noticed Grace staring at him in horror,
the rock just inches from the other man's skull. He himself had sported a bloodied nose and was obviously retal-
iating for whatever wrong the other had committed
before her arrival. After separate explanations from
each, Grace had been no closer to understanding the
cause of their discord, but she did manage to cool their
tempers well enough to have them shaking hands and
retreating to opposite ends of the curtain wall to resume
their work.

Now, having seen that everyone had received their
supper, Grace slipped on her favorite half-boots and
pulled the pins from her hair, letting it billow in the
breeze off the loch as she walked along the brae that
ran north from the castle tower.

Before going out for her walk, Grace had changed
into the new woolen gown and stockings that had been
presented to her earlier that day by several of the
women. It was made of the Skynegal tartan and while
simple in its cut, the gown offered warmth against the
evening chill and its full skirts would allow her to wear
it in comfort throughout most of her pregnancy.

As Grace walked along through the high reedy grass,
Dubhar ambled alongside her, neither racing ahead nor
straying behind, but keeping right at her leg, occasionally
sniffing at a tuft of marram grass. He wouldn't leave
even for a moment to fetch the stick she tossed for him.
The crofters who yet remained in the fields where they
had planted oat, potato, and barley waved to her, calling
out greetings to her in both the English they were learning and the Gaelic they were teaching her in turn. She

called out in response to one of them, Hugh Darsie, when he'd asked if she'd had a good day.

"Glè mhath, Hugh. An danns thu leamsa?"

At his puzzled expression, Grace quickly thought back on her words and realized she had just asked him if he would dance with her instead of how he was faring. She quickly corrected herself with a shrug and he laughed, applauding her for a valiant, if mistaken effort.

A distance away from the castle, there was a small bluff that overlooked Loch Skynegal's cobbled shoreline, where Grace enjoyed watching the oyster catchers as they picked among the rocks for a supper of limpets and sea urchins. At this time of day, with the sun just setting to the west, the water looked like a thousand twinkling diamonds in the distance. A matting of ox-eye daisies and goldenrods waved to her as Grace lowered to sit against a machair tussock. After a few moments, Dubhar meandered a short distance away to poke his snout among the marram grass on the shore.

Grace closed her eyes and leaned back upon her arms, losing herself to the soft wind against her face and the gentle sound of the water lapping at the shore. As she sat, she thought of how very different her life had become in the past few months. No more did she spend her days and nights worrying over the perfect ballgown or the placement of her curls. Instead she clung to the pleasure of simpler things—heavy woolen stockings on a cold Scottish night, the smell of Deirdre's oatcakes baking in the kitchen, the touch of the Highland breeze on her face.

She wondered what the society ladies who flitted from shop to shop along Bond Street for their "necessaries" would think of the Marchioness Knighton, who instead of diamonds and pearls now wore necklaces made of seashells and colored pebbles made by the many children of the estate. Would they gasp to know she drank tea brewed from blueberry leaves? That she forsook her gowns of silk and muslin for the more practical Highland attire?

How curious, she thought, knowing that at this very hour, a world away in London, members of the social elite were busy preening before their looking glasses, fearful of having a single flounce out of place lest it should bring shame and ridicule down upon them. From the moment she had been thrown into that life—even on the outskirts as she had been—Grace had never felt a proper fit, not the way she did here at Skynegal, where she felt truly wanted for the first time in her life. Even more, she did not want to see a babe of her own born into the world of that fickle noble society, growing up cold and unfeeling just like . . .

The sound of a sudden harsh howling broke Grace from her thoughts and she sat upright, searching for Dubhar and whatever it was that was causing him to create such an unholy din. When she spotted the dog, he was not making any noise at all, but was instead sitting calmly several yards away with his head cocked to the side, staring to the true source of the howling, something hidden in the tall grass.

What in heaven's name . . . ?

A leg surfaced briefly above the tall grass.

Goodness, someone was injured.

Grace got to her feet and rushed over to find a man hunched over himself, holding his bare foot, pierced by the spiked head of a rather large and very prickly-looking thistle. Grace acted quickly. She took up a length of her woolen skirts and covering her hand, grasped the thistle head, careful not to stick herself as she jerked it free. The man let out another howl and then promptly became silent. Grace walked several feet away and dislodged the thistle from her skirts, crushing the sharp spikes of it with her boot, before turning to see if the man required any further assistance.

"Are you all right? Those can be terribly sharp and I—"

Grace lost her words as she came face-to-face with the last person she would have expected to see standing there.

It was Christian.

He was there, in Scotland.

He was wearing no boots or hose.

And he was doing the oddest thing.

He was smiling.

Grace found herself wondering if he'd perhaps hit his

head when he'd fallen to the ground and she almost voiced that thought aloud.

Until she saw that he had started toward her.

Grace simply froze, at a complete loss for what she should do.

Chapter Twenty-six

"Hello, Grace."

Christian came toward her, approaching slowly as if he thought she might bolt—a ridiculous thought, really. Where on earth could she possibly go? Grace simply watched him, a small part of her wondering if he was truly standing there on that windswept bluff with her, or if Deirdre had brewed something strange into her tea earlier that day.

But of course Christian was there. She had always known that someday she would see him again. What she hadn't expected was to still be so mesmerized by simply the sight of him. The setting sun shone on his hair, burnishing it a rich sable brown. He wore no coat and the full sleeves of his shirt billowed in the breeze, pulling at his neckcloth as he moved. His eyes were fixed directly on her and Grace knew the moment she felt her heartbeat traitorously quicken that the months they'd spent apart had done nothing to lessen her feelings for him. If anything, living without him had only made her regard for him that much stronger.

Dear God, no matter how she might try to deny it to herself, she still loved him.

Even as Grace admitted this to herself, she knew she could never allow him to know her feelings. The risk was too great, the memory of his hurtful words too poignant even now. She could never reveal how empty she had felt the past weeks without him, how she had longed for his touch, his look, the sound of his voice. How many times would she have endured even his chill indifference if only so that she could see him again?

Grace struggled to focus her thoughts on what had

driven her to leave London, ignoring her first instinct to
go forward to meet him. Instead, she waited until he
stood right in front of her. She lifted her gaze to meet
his and felt her breath catch. He smiled at her again,
damn him. She glanced down at his feet, focusing on his
bare toes peeking out through the tufts of grass, anything to avoid looking into those silver-blue eyes and
getting thoroughly lost once again.

"You're not wearing any boots," she said, absurdly
obvious, yes, but at least it was something to divert him
from staring at her so intently.

"Yes, they are back there near where I stuck my foot.
I had taken them off so that I might approach you quietly." She heard him smile. "Apparently I was so intent
on watching you, I wasn't paying any heed to where I
was walking—or rather what I was walking on."

Grace chanced a look at him—a mistake, for he was
still staring at her and his eyes were so warm she hardly
noticed the chill breeze off the loch anymore. She drew
a quick breath and looked out at the rippling waters in
the distance, crossing her arms before her. *Oh, dear.*

"Deirdre says that there is a legend of when the
Danes had come to invade Scotland centuries ago. Much
the same thing happened. They had come at night and
had removed their shoes so to approach without notice.
They stepped on the wild thistles and yowled so loudly,
they woke the sleeping Scots, warning them of their
coming and allowing them to spring to their own de-
fense. It is said this prevented the Danes from a successful invasion and from then on it was the thistle that had
saved Scotland. Deirdre says it is because of that event
in history that the thistle is so highly regarded among
the Scots even now."

Grace could think of absolutely no reason for her to
have just told him that old folktale other than that she
would do or say just about anything at that moment to
avoid the subject of her having left London, or of his
having come now to retrieve her.

Unfortunately Christian was not a man easily diverted.

"I've missed you, Grace."

His voice wrapped over her like the glow of spring's

first sunshine after months of frigid winter. Grace clung to her fast-fleeting reserve.

"I suppose I should have told you where I was going."

"It is all right."

Could this truly be Christian? Her husband, the aloof Marquess Knighton? His understanding was not something Grace had been prepared for. She had played this scene through her mind so many times over the past months, knowing it would come. But in her mind's eye, it had always been far off in the future, with Christian scowling and angry, railing against her for her desertion. This acceptance and understanding was not at all what she'd expected. In fact, she didn't quite know how to cope with it.

"Yes, well, it is growing late," she said, for want of anything better. "I probably should be getting back."

She turned and started back toward the castle, a direction that unfortunately necessitated a path around Christian. She prayed he would just allow her to leave, giving her some time to gather her wits.

She was nearly past when Christian reached out suddenly and took her arm, gently stopping her. Grace's heart leapt at the touch of him. She closed her eyes and forced herself not to look at him.

"Grace, truly, if I could, I would take back the words I said to you that night."

Damn the tears that were coming even now to her eyes. She blinked them back. "I asked you for your honesty, Christian, and you gave it."

"Do you not think we should at least talk about this?"

Grace drew in a long breath, releasing it slowly, knowing he was right. "Yes, Christian, we should talk. We have much to discuss, but not here. Not now. I need some time. I wasn't expecting to see you here. I need to think about what this will mean to the life I have made here."

She looked at him. He was staring at her, silent, troubled.

"Grace, have you . . . ? He hesitated. "Grace, is there someone else in your life now?"

Grace saw something change in his eyes—was it fear that she had found someone else? Hope that she had not? If only he could know how impossible a notion it was. Just the thought of feeling about another the way she did him was absurd. Grace shook her head. "No, Christian, there is no one."

No one but you.

It was a thought Grace kept to herself as she turned and started walking back toward the castle.

At Skynegal, Grace was met with another surprise when she found that Robert and Catriona, the Duke and Dutchess of Devonbrook, and their young son James had come with Christian. At first she thought it odd that they should have traveled so far, until Catriona told her that their own Scottish estate, Rosmorigh, was located along the coast south of Skynegal on the Knoydart Peninsula, a day's sail away. It was with their assistance that Christian had found his way to Skynegal.

They sat now, the five of them, in the small antechamber set off from the great hall that Grace had put to use as an estate office. While they had waited for Grace's return from the brae, Deirdre had brewed tea for the guests, which Grace now poured into their crockery cups—a far cry from the fine porcelain the Devonbrooks were no doubt accustomed to.

"Please forgive the tea," Grace said. "It is a local blend made with blueberry leaves, and while I find it very tasty, some might think it a bit tart."

"Blueberry?" Catriona took up the cup. "We take blueberry tea often at Rosmorigh, isn't that right, my dear?"

She looked to her husband, the duke, Robert, who nodded from where he stood beside Christian. Grace noticed that Christian no longer smiled as he had earlier when he'd met her on the brae. The frown she knew so well had once again darkened his eyes, but before Grace could consider what she'd done to displease him, Catriona went on.

"One day I must show you how I add a bit of clover to the tea as well." She leaned a little closer, whispering, "I quite prefer it to the China teas."

Grace smiled at her. She had expected such a celebrated society duchess to show disdain for the simplicity they had adopted at Skynegal. She was pleased to find that she was mistaken in that assumption.

"We've already eaten supper," Grace said, "but if you are hungry, I can ask Deirdre or Flora to see if they might yet have some of the stew for you in the kitchen—"

Just then, the door opened and Alastair wandered in. He hadn't knocked—Grace had made it a point that he shouldn't feel the need to, for they were fellows in the management of the estate, not master and clerk. He started when he noticed the others in the room.

"Och, my lady, I didn't know you had visitors."

He made to bow, stepping back as if to leave, but Grace waved him into the room. "It is all right, Alastair. Please, come in and meet our guests."

Alastair wore his usual attire—tartan trews, matching waistcoat and jacket, his spectacles pushed low upon his rounded nose as he always wore them when he was checking figures in the account books.

"Alastair, allow me to introduce to you the Duke and Duchess of Devonbrook . . ."

As she would have expected at such a noble pronouncement, Alastair's eyes went wide and he bowed his head several times in deferential greeting.

". . . and this is Lord Knighton." And then she added, "My husband."

Alastair looked quickly to Grace before turning a bow to Christian. "It is an honor to finally make your acquaintance, my lord. A great honor indeed." And then to Robert and Catriona, "And to you as well, Your Graces."

"This is Mr. Alastair Ogilvy. He is Skynegal's steward and a fine one at that. I don't know what I would have done without him here these past months."

Alastair's face colored nearly as red as his suit of clothes as he beamed under Grace's compliment. "Thank you, my lady. 'Tis been a pleasure, I assure you."

With the introductions done, an awkward silence fell over the room as if no one knew what next to say. Grace endeavored to put an end to it.

"Did you have something you'd come here to see me about, Alastair?"

"What? Oh, yes, indeed, my lady. McFee and McGee have just returned from Ullapool. I've a list here of what they were able to purchase and trade."

He handed her a sheet of paper and Grace scanned the list, nodding. "Looks as if they were able to secure a fair price on the supplies."

"Aye." Alastair hesitated a moment before adding quietly, "My lady, I'm afraid there was a bit of bad news as well." His dour expression told Grace something was very wrong.

"What is it?"

" 'Twas said just before they'd gone that the ship *Prospect* went down afore she reached the coast of New Scotland. It is believed everyone aboard her was lost."

Grace felt her body go instantly numb. She set the list she had been studying atop the desk and turned from the others to face the small window overlooking the courtyard. As she watched the children at play there, she remembered one small smiling face, thumb perpetually stuffed in the mouth, happy blue eyes laughing beneath a mop of blonde ringlets.

Thomas McAllum had had all the innocence and energy of a three-year-old bundle of mischief. He had arrived at Skynegal late one soggy night with his Ma and his Da and several siblings and had immediately stolen his way into everyone's hearts. When Grace would come into the office to work on the castle's accounts, she would often find him curled up in the kneehole of her desk, waiting to pop out his head with an exuberant *"Boo!,"* after which he would throw his tiny arms around her neck and squeeze her tightly as he could. She was "Lady *Gwace*" and he "Knight Thomas," her *"pwotector"* against all things "bad and *scawy,"* just like the knight in the stories she would read to him at night.

When his parents had finally found passage on a ship bound for New Scotland, Thomas hadn't wanted to go. Grace would never forget the way he had clung to her skirts, crying that he wanted to stay there with her. But she had convinced him that all knights one day had to leave on crusade to protect other parts of the world from

the bad and scary things. She could still see the image
of him, standing on the deck of the sloop, waving to her
as they drifted off onto Loch Skynegal bound for Ullapool and their new life—she could still hear his last
words to her before he'd gone . . .

"I *wuv* you, Lady *Gwace,* and when I come back from
my *cwusade* I will *mawwy* you."

When she turned from the window moments later, she
could hardly see Alastair through her tears. "It was
Prospect, wasn't it, that Thomas's family had sailed
upon?"

Alastair nodded but she had known what his answer
would be even before posing her question. Still she had
asked it, hoping she would be wrong.

Grace realized that all eyes in the room were upon her
then and dashed away her tears. She looked to Christian,
Robert, and Catriona where they were still sitting before
her, Alastair behind. She suddenly wanted, needed, to
be alone.

"Alastair, might I trouble you to show the duke and
duchess to the set of chambers across the hall from
mine? Deirdre and Flora should be finished readying
them now and I'm sure our guests are tired after their
journey. And please ask Deirdre to see if she can put
together a bit of supper for our guests. I'd wager young
James would love to try some of Deirdre's shortbread."

Alastair nodded and waited while Catriona and Robert bid goodnight to Grace and Christian before leading
them from the room. When they had gone, Grace turned
to face her husband. "Christian, I—"

"He seems an able man," Christian said in obvious
regard to Alastair.

Grace nodded. "He has been more helpful than I
could have ever imagined. He is a wonderful friend."

Christian looked at her queerly, as if he didn't quite
take her meaning. "Has he been steward here long?"

"Since long before my arrival. He was born and raised
on Skynegal land."

"That is good." Christian nodded. "He ought to do
well in handling things, then, after you return to
London."

Grace stared, utterly speechless, as if Christian had

just told her the sky was green and the moon was made of plum pudding. *Return to London.* He truly thought she should leave Skynegal. She had of course expected this from him, though not so soon after his arrival. It was as if he stood blind to what had just taken place before them, to all that surrounded them in the many faces of the crofters who had watched them when they had returned from the brae.

An anger Grace had never given in to suddenly surged through her. "How dare you? Does your arrogance know no bounds? How dare you suddenly appear here and expect that I would put aside everything to return to London, abandon these people for a life I had willingly left behind? Why? Simply because you expect me to? I will not be returning to London, Christian. I am needed here."

Christian stared at her, stunned.

Grace strove to maintain her calm. She saw now that she had been mistaken in thinking Christian had changed in the time she'd been away, for while he might regret the bluntness of his words to her that night, he still did not hold any true regard for her feelings. If he did, he would know how terrible the words he had just spoken to her were.

"Grace, what you have done here is commendable, but I am a marquess and I have responsibilities that demand my presence in London. I shouldn't even have left to come here now, but—"

"Then why are you here?"

Christian stared at her. "I beg your pardon?"

"Why are you here, Christian? Why did you come all the way to Scotland to find me if your presence is so needed in London?"

"That should be obvious, Grace. You are my wife."

She couldn't keep the scorn from her voice when she said in response, "I am the wife you did not want."

Christian stared at her a long moment. "I cannot go back and change what happened that night."

"Was it untrue? Are you telling me now that you truly wanted to marry me?"

"Grace, don't do this."

But she wasn't about to let it go. Not now. Not when

he was threatening to overthrow everything she had come to care about the past months. "Has my absence in your life suddenly endeared me to you, Christian? Or is it that my leaving you as I did was merely too much of an embarrassment for you? Can you honestly say that you love me, Christian?"

Pressed for the truth, Christian could only fall silent. They faced one another through a long, tense moment.

"I didn't think so," Grace whispered, staring at him hard, suddenly wishing she hadn't gone as far as she had. Her insides were knotted and her throat felt suddenly tight. It was a question she hadn't really wanted to know the answer to—again.

Grace turned to leave. She stopped at the door when Christian finally spoke.

"Damn it, Grace! I don't know that I know what loving someone means, or if I can know what it means. I don't even know you. I need to spend time with you, to learn more about you. There are things about me you do not know. Perhaps once you learn of the true person I am, your feelings for me will change. All I do know is that I am here because I came to realize that I had treated you unfairly in London. I would have come sooner had I known where you were."

Grace turned, staring at him in silence.

His voice softened. "Grace, I cannot know what the future may hold for us. Neither of us can."

She closed her eyes, folding her arms over herself. She wanted so badly to believe him, to believe that someday he might be able to love her as she did him. But could she do what he wanted of her? Could she return to London at the risk of losing everything she had accomplished over the past months here at Skynegal? To Grace, loving someone meant lending support to their ambitions and dreams, yet Christian had been at Skynegal a matter of minutes and already he had asked her to abandon everything. He wanted her to leave the very people who depended upon her here for the uncertainty of a future with him in a place she most certainly didn't want to be.

What if once they were back in England, he cast her aside again as he had before? And what of their child?

If she told Christian now that she was carrying his babe she might never know if he had changed for her or simply because of the responsibility he felt for the child.

It was too great a risk to set the rest of her life balancing upon.

"I am sorry, Christian, but I cannot leave Skynegal. I have begun something here that I cannot abandon. Something I will not abandon."

"Grace, from the looks of things and from what your steward was saying, you are barely making do as it is. Look at yourself. You are a marchioness, a part of one of the wealthiest families in England, and yet you wear woolens like one of your tenants. You drink tea out of crockery cups."

"Does it taste any better, my lord, when drunk from porcelain? Why should you be offended that I prefer the perceived crudities of life here to the falseness of 'polished' society in London? Life here is *real,* not some grand and noble masquerade. The people may not wear imported silk, but they also do not wear the arrogance you do with it. When I look in the mirror, Christian, I see a person, not the rank I was born to. Yes, we have grown short of funds. Feeding dozens of people at a time is costly, but it is only until I receive the monies I have requested of Mr. Jenner from the account set aside for Skynegal. I have written to him thrice now and I hope to hear from him at any time. I—"

Grace suddenly realized how it was Christian had discovered her whereabouts. She let go a heavy breath as if she had just had the wind knocked from her. "Mr. Jenner. It was he who told you where I had gone."

"Do not blame him, Grace. He needed my signature approving the disbursement of the funds you'd requested. He knew you needed the money. He had no choice in the matter."

"But it is an account left to me in trust."

"And as your husband, the management of the account falls under my direction. According to the way in which the trust was written, I cannot use the monies for reasons other than the improvement of the estate, but I can disallow their being disbursed if I do not agree with the purpose of their use."

Grace felt a frightening shiver slither through her. Perhaps it was his use of the word "improvement," that term which signified so much more here in the Highlands than anywhere else. But suddenly she felt as if all she had worked for over the past months was about to take a drastic turn. "Are you saying you will not release the monies to me?"

"I did not say that, Grace. I have only just arrived. I will have a look about the estate, to know firsthand what it is you hope to accomplish here. I will stay for a few days to assess the situation. Only then will I make my decision."

Chapter Twenty-seven

Christian turned from his quiet study of the moon at the sound of someone approaching behind him. In the darkness he could see Robert coming down the pathway to join him on the shore of the loch. He'd been standing there for the past hour, maybe longer, pondering his relationship with his wife, trying to bring reason to this most unreasonable situation. His years of study at Eton could offer no remedy.

"Has Catriona gone to bed already?"

Robert smiled as he often did at the mention of his wife's name, a thing he still did even after five years of marriage. "When last I left her, she and Grace were sitting with James, engrossed in one of Deirdre's stories. I never thought I'd meet another who could spin a yarn as well as Catriona's da, Angus."

A moment passed in silence. Two. Robert said, "Things didn't go well with Grace?"

"Not particularly."

"Tell me, friend, if I'm intruding where I shouldn't be."

Christian took up a flat stone and skipped it carelessly across the surface of the water, watching as the ripples from it fanned outward in the moonlight. "Perhaps it would do me good to hear a differing perspective. God knows I'm at an impasse."

"She won't return with you to London?"

"No."

Robert sighed. "Aye, once Scotland's in the blood, it's a part of you forever. There's no leaving it behind."

"Yet you managed to convince Catriona to leave Rosmorigh to go with you to England."

Robert shrugged. "I didn't have to convince her. Catriona loves me and she knows no matter where we might travel, we will always come back to the Highlands. Devonbrook Hall is a ducal mansion, more a museum than a dwelling, and no matter how I've altered it, it will always hold memories of the fire. The other Devonbrook properties are merely holdings, and the London house is more a convenience than anything else. But Rosmorigh is home. It's as much a part of Catriona as that fiery hair and her Scots' stubbornness. I'd live there with her even if it were as small and poky as Angus's cottage on the moor. But I love her, and love makes a person do unusual things sometimes."

Christian stared at his friend, considering his words. It struck him in the next moment, the very answer to his troubles—how he would convince Grace to return with him to England.

He was going to have to make her fall in love with him.

And he had three days in which to do it.

Early the following morning, after a breakfast of Deirdre's oatcakes and cheese and Catriona's own special blend of blueberry and clover tea, Christian asked Grace if she would take him on a tour of the castle and surrounding grounds. She had looked at him queerly, no doubt taken aback by the request, but then, after a moment's thought, she agreed.

Over the next three hours, she took him through what surely must have been every inch of the venerable old keep, which had stood on this site nearly six hundred years, long before the august Westovers had ever risen to authority. As they threaded their way through each solitary corridor and time-haunted chamber, Grace related to Christian in detail the work they had accomplished in the past months. She showed him the garret where they had repaired the roof and described how they had taken down the ivy that had once liberally covered the outer barmkin. Skynegal Castle was a formidable stronghold. The donjon, or central tower, which housed the residence, rose some sixty feet to the battlements. It was constituted of six storys and a garret housed under a center pitched roof. The private chambers took up the top three floors, the great hall the middle two, and the service rooms were at the bottom, all accessed by a narrow spiral staircase at one corner. Several smaller side chambers had been niched in the twelve-foot-thick walls for use as dressing rooms, storage closets, or wardrobes. The two side towers or wings housed the kitchen and its accompanying chambers, the pantry, bakehouse, kiln, brewhouse, and estate office.

Grace concluded their tour by taking Christian up to the battlements on the north tower overlooking Loch Skynegal. Ordinarily when she came here, she would stand sometimes for an hour or more while the legendary birds of Skynegal soared through the sky around her. The wind blew in harsh off the loch, pulling at her shawl, and if the day were clear, she might see all the way to the Hebrides. She would toss bits of oatcake to the birds and sometimes she would prop her sketching papers on the battlements and draw the crofters' cottages that lay nestled in the distance along the loch shore. But always, whenever she would come here, she would find herself filled with a serenity unlike any she had ever known, a balanced peace that seemed wholly connected to this unique place. There could be no doubt in Grace's mind that Skynegal had been blessed by a beautiful goddess, as legend told.

But today even that peace could not ease the disquietude of Grace's thoughts.

In the short space of twenty-four hours she had discovered she was with child and had seen her abandoned husband suddenly appear. Now she had to face the very real threat of the dissolution of all she had worked for. All through the night before, she had tried to think of a way in which she might convince Christian to grant her the funds she needed to continue her work at Skynegal. She had passed hours in her bedchamber, poring through texts by candlelight, searching for something—anything—that might aide her in her mission until the dawn had begun to break over the Sgiathach Hills, bringing in the start of a new day.

But as she stood with him now on the tower, watching him as he stared out over the loch, his hair ruffling in the breeze, her thoughts were no longer consumed with the future of the estate and the Highlanders. Her thoughts were of Christian.

Many times during the morning Grace had wanted to tell him that she carried his child, but had stopped herself each time from speaking the words aloud. Weighing heavily on her mind was the knowledge that Christian had been forced by his grandfather to accept her, something she had come to accept over the past months. She realized now how foolish she had been to have expected that Christian should fall in love with her, a woman he had never known and certainly had never wanted. Even now, Grace knew his only reason for having come to Scotland was a sense of obligation. If she told him of the child, he might stay, yes, but would he only end up resenting her for it? Or worse, would he withhold the monies in an effort to force her to return to England so that she would give birth to their child there? It wasn't the sort of life Grace wanted—not for herself, not for Christian, and certainly not for the babe.

By the time Grace left the tower and returned with Christian to the estate office it was midday. He had asked if he might have a look at the estate account books so that he could have a full reviewing of the expenditures. Grace fidgeted with her teacup as she watched Christian studying the ledgers across the desk from her. His eyes skimmed each column but he said nothing, his expression absolutely unreadable. What if he decided the estate wasn't in need of further restoration? Surely it was habitable now, but there was still so much more she wanted to do. If only he could have seen Skynegal as it had been at her arrival so that he might better appreciate the progress they had made since.

During that morning, through each chamber and along every stairwell she had led him to, Christian had listened with genuine interest as Grace had pointed out all of the renovations that had already been completed. Would he see the importance of her work here? Would he lend his support to it?

"As you can see," she said, unable to stand the silence any longer, "we were able to avoid a great deal of expense by hiring the workers locally and then teaching the others."

Christian nodded. "It was a provident choice. They have done excellent work."

"And we have really only begun the castle's restoration. The repairs to the roof were finished just last week and the curtain wall is very nearly rebuilt. Once that is completed, I had hoped to begin work on the kitchen." She removed a handful of sketches she had made for an addition to the eastern façade from the desk drawer.

"You drew these?"

Grace nodded. "I've always had a fondness for sketching buildings." She scarcely noticed his amazed expression as she went on. "The kitchen is now too small an area and a potential fire hazard. If we were to enclose the courtyard and relocate the kitchen here, should a fire occur, it would be prevented from reaching the donjon by the passages here"—she pointed to the drawing— "and there."

As Grace nattered on about roof tiles and window glazing, Christian could hear the passion she felt for the work she had done at Skynegal in her words. It was impossible not to. Her enthusiasm was intoxicating. It was in her eyes, bright and alive, and in her expression. And her passion for the plight of the Highland people was equally evident.

Grace had spent a good deal of the morning telling Christian about the clearances taking place on the neighboring estates, describing the evictions and the hopelessness of a people who suddenly found themselves without resources. She introduced him to many of them, young and old alike, and told him what each of them had personally suffered. While their stories did certainly horrify him, Christian, having been born a noble landowner, understood the motive for profit from the land as well as an estate owner's right to do what he wished with his own property. Still, having seen firsthand the impoverished Highlanders' state, he could not morally approve of what had taken place.

The unfortunate fact remained that no matter how she might want to, Grace could not singlehandedly assume the responsibility of feeding and housing every displaced

Highlander in Wester Ross. There would come a time
when the account set aside for Skynegal's support would
run out. He wondered that she had even thought of it.

"Grace, I think it is commendable that you have
found a way to employ the displaced Highlanders with
the renovations to the castle. But you must know the
work will not go on forever. Have you given any thought
to what you will do when there is no more restoration
to be done here?"

If he had expected that she wouldn't have a prospec-
tus in mind, he was to be surprised.

"Actually, I have thought about it and I have even
come up with an idea that will serve to benefit everyone
concerned." She reached into the top desk drawer and
withdrew what proved to be a map of Scotland with
notations and figures drawn upon it.

"Roads."

"Roads?"

"Roads," she repeated with a determined nod. "I have
been doing some reading. Some fifty years ago, there
was an English general named Wade who was assigned
to help keep peace in the Highlands when the Jacobite
threat was imminent. His soldiers had a difficult time
moving through the countryside so he established a net-
work of military roads that would give easier access into
the more remote parts of the country. General Wade
only built his roads as far north as Inverness and he used
the soldiers under his command for the labor. I have
read many of the publications that have been printed by
the landowners who are carrying out the evictions in
favor of the 'Improvements' here in the Highlands. Despite the fact that they greatly understate their measures,
their main motive, they say, is to modernize what they
believe are a primitive people whose only ability lies in
rudimentary farming. There are so many other gifts the
people here have to offer, but there are many obstacles
before them—language is certainly one of them. But one
of the biggest obstacles I can see is the inaccessibility of
the Highlands. Transport of any distance must be made
by water. But if we were to follow General Wade's example—"

Christian stared at her. "You are telling me you want

to outfit the entire Scottish Highlands with a road system?"

Grace smiled. "Not singlehandedly, of course. I was thinking instead of making a request to the Crown for a grant of monies."

Suddenly an image presented itself to Christian, of Grace standing before England's own indolent and arrogant King George IV, dressed in her Scottish woolens, trying to convince the newly crowned king that he should cease spending Crown money on his ridiculous palace at Brighton and instead give it over to the aide of the Scottish peasantry.

Good God, Christian realized—she would do it, too.

Was this the same frightened young woman who had viewed a London ballroom as if it were a lion's den? Or had Grace never actually been that person? Had it only seemed so because it was the role he had *expected* her to play? He hadn't given her credit for the ability to pour a proper cup of tea, yet here he stood, in a castle she had almost singlehandedly refurbished, before scores of people who worshipped her, listening as she exuberantly laid out plans for spending Crown money.

Somewhere in the past months, in a way that could not be attributed to any one feature like a different way of wearing her hair or a new gown, Grace had blossomed. It was in the way she moved about the estate and spoke with the people with confidence, contentment, and ease—and even more, with a happiness that had freed her to smile as he had not seen her do before. He found himself wondering what he might do to make her smile at him in that same way.

All during that morning, he had watched her as she struggled to speak in Gaelic with several of the women who were spinning the wool or as she listened intently while a young child had repeated his latest English lessons. Grace truly listened to what each person who came to her had to say. If they spoke to her in Gaelic, she did her best to comprehend and did not scorn them for not having a grasp of English. Grace knew each one of the crofters by name, from the eldest grandmother to the tiniest babe. She knew if they had been ill, if it was

nearing their birthday. Watching her thus only made
Christian realize his own inadequacy.

He did not know much more than the surnames of
those who peopled his own family holdings. It was a
reserve that had served to keep him apart from them,
detached; it was something he had been taught by his
grandfather from an early age. *"If you become too familiar with them, they will no longer respect you. Without
respect, you cannot hope to rule."*

The difference was that Grace had no desire to rule
these people. Yet the respect they had for her, the allegiance they gave her, was more than he could ever hope
for from his own tenants, people who had lived on and
tended his family's lands for generations. These people
had known Grace for only a matter of weeks and it was
clear they would willingly fight for her, defend her as
they would their own—to the death, if necessary. It was
a fact made even more evident by the distrustful glances
they had given him when Grace had introduced him as
her husband and the new laird of Skynegal.

Christian had never before felt as uncomfortable in
his own clothes as he had when he had stood among
this population of Highlanders. His dress was not preten-
tious by London society's standards, but here in the rugged Highlands, his velvet coat and nankeen breeches
seemed almost flagrant compared to the crofter's woolens, woolens that Grace had adopted in lieu of fine silk.
They all wore the same tartan—the Skynegal tartan,
Grace had told him—modeled after a scrap of the tartan
of her grandmother's family, the MacRaths, which she
had found while rooting around in the castle's upper
garret. To the people of Skynegal, it was a symbol of
their allegiance, of belonging, and it only made him feel
even more the outsider.

What Grace was doing here, rebuilding the estate and
coming to the aide of the people, felt right in every way.
It had reason. It had purpose. If he refused Grace the
funds to compel her to return to London out of financial
necessity, the separation and distrust that already existed
between them would only become worse. He knew in
that moment that he would never be able to refuse her

the money she needed for Skynegal. He didn't want to refuse her. In fact, he wanted to be a part of it.

"Grace, you will have a difficult time convincing the Crown to grant you monies for the road-building project."

She frowned at his defeatism. "I will not know for certain unless I try. And I do plan to try, Christian."

He held up a hand. "You didn't allow me to finish. What I was going to say is that you would stand a better chance of getting a grant if the idea were presented to the House of Lords instead."

"The Lords?" She furrowed her brow. "I rather doubt they would be willing to listen to the whims of a woman, no matter how sensible those *whims* might be."

"Perhaps, but they would be willing to listen to one or more of its members."

Grace looked at Christian, staring at him with an expression that showed she clearly suspected what he was offering to do and prayed she wasn't mistaken.

"Let me help you, Grace. I would discuss your idea with Robert. He also holds a place with the Lords and, as a Scottish landowner, he would obviously have an interest in the project. He might manage to influence some of the other Scottish lords to lend support to the idea as well."

Grace could hardly contain her exhilaration. She came around the desk and threw her arms around his neck, burying her face in his chest. "Oh, Christian, thank you . . . thank you . . ."

The touch of her body, the smell of her hair, impacted upon Christian in an instant. He told himself to step away from her even as he tightened his arms around her. For weeks while she had been gone, he had never once known a sexual thought. Ballrooms filled with variously lovely women hadn't so much as given him a stir. Now as he stood there, he could scarcely breathe and his only thought was that of having her naked and gasping beneath him.

When she tipped her head up to look at him, she wore that same smile he had longed for earlier. It was to be his undoing. The area around them grew suddenly warm and charged with awareness. His only possible response was to lower his head and touch his lips to hers.

It was a kiss that held all the emotions they had both forsaken the past months. It was long and deep and utterly sense stealing. And it was interrupted all too soon.

"Oh—good heavens, my lady, my lord—I had no idea."

It was Alastair, of course, simply following Grace's wish that he should not feel the need to knock before entering the castle office. His face was cherry red with embarrassment.

Grace immediately broke away from Christian's embrace. "It is all right, Alastair. I am supposed to be helping Deirdre with the children's reading lesson now."

She looked at Christian briefly, her smile gone to discontent, before she skirted around him and out the door.

An awkward silence fell over the room the moment she had gone.

"My apologies, my lord. I seem to suffer the curse of bad timing."

Christian shook his head, patting Alastair on the shoulder even as he thought that at that particular moment that he couldn't have agreed more. He headed for the outside courtyard on a hope that the Highland air was brisk enough to cool the fire that was still burning through his veins.

Chapter Twenty-eight

Christian passed the better part of the next two days riding about the estate with Robert and Alastair. He had discussed Grace's idea of putting the Highlanders to the work of building roads with Robert, who enthusiastically supported it. Together, they would prevail upon some of the other members of the House and present a proposal for it at their next session.

It would mean that Christian would have to remain longer at Skynegal to get a more accurate scope of the landscape the estate comprised and to set down a clear plan for the building of the roads. There was still the situation with Eleanor and Lord Herrick to consider, and he had spent the night before doing just that to no happy conclusion. No matter how he tried to find a way around it, he kept coming back to the same inevitable conclusion. He was going to have to revoke the one thing he had always promised his sister she would have. He would have to bring an early end to Eleanor's first season and summon her and Lady Frances to Skynegal. He had no other choice.

As they rode along the brae to the east, Alastair educated Christian on the particulars of Skynegal and its neighboring estates. According to the Scotsman, Skynegal was not a vast holding by Scottish standards such as that of Sunterglen to the north and east, but what Skynegal lacked in proportion, it more than claimed in physical beauty.

Touching on the mist-covered shore of Loch Skynegal, the estate moved inland across a verdant glen following the River Kerry eastward toward Dubh Loch. It was glorious country, mottled here and there with dense deer forest, shimmering loch, and the occasional ancient broch. Along with the beauty, Christian received a first-hand view of the burnt-out cottages that littered the silent and deserted hillside close by to the border of the neighboring estate where the Highlanders had once worked and lived, where stories had been handed down around a smoky peat fire, and where memories had been made.

Christian stood beneath a sober drizzle, oblivious of the rain, caught by the sight of a tattered scrap of tartan waving in the breeze from a tree branch that had been stuck in the ground beside one of the deserted cottages, a last proud symbol of a time that was seemingly gone forever. He wondered at how the British people could know more of what was happening across an ocean in America, but had heard nothing of the injustice being wrought here. The British had fought for so many years to keep other countries and peoples from being oppressed by the likes of Napoleon, yet at home they would oppress their own. The hypocrisy of it sickened him.

" 'Tis difficult for the landlords to understand," Alastair said, staring at the makeshift tartan flag. "We Scots think on our past and our native land with a passionate attachment. Many of us have lived on land that has been occupied by our fathers and grandfathers before us. In the beginning, the landlords promised improvement. They offered lots to replace those that were formerly occupied, but they did this by driving the people from their fertile land in the glen to new homes perched upon rock and moorland, with far less arable land than what they had originally."

"Could the Scots not resist, and apply to the authorities for intervention?" Christian asked.

Alastair shook his head. "Unfortunately, my lord, it is these same landlords and their factors who serve as the justices of the peace. The Scots are a devout people and some of our ministers have even begun to exhort the people to submit and quiet their protest, telling them that the clearances are punishment from God for the sins of the Jacobite uprisings."

As he listened to the Scotsman's words, Christian

began to more fully understand Grace's commitment to
what she had begun here at Skynegal. She was on a
singular crusade to save the Highland populace from de-
struction. "It would seem there must be some way to
bring charges against those who have treated the tenants
so inhumanely."

"Aye, my lord, the people did manage it—once. 'Twas
the most notorious factor of them all, Patrick Sellar,
back in '16. Ne'er a more callous man has come to the
Highlands since Cumberland in the '45. E'en the mention of his name will bring the lassies to tears."

"I remember reading that he was brought to trial for
his misdeeds," Robert said.

"Aye, your grace, and summarily acquitted, too."

Christian looked to Robert. "And you have seen nothing of this at Rosmorigh?"

"We had heard of the clearances, but they have thus
far not extended near to Rosmorigh. Had they, you
could wager your last pound Catriona would be making
every bit the effort Grace is. My wife was raised as a
crofter. It is not until one is faced with it like this that
one can comprehend the fact that such a thing has
happened."

They had been riding at a slow walk, talking as they
made their way around the eastern border of Skynegal
to circle to the north before heading back to the castle.
The horses came around a small copse of oak trees and
Christian spotted something lying discarded in a bog
ditch. At his first glance of it, he had thought it merely a
bundle of rags left behind by one of the evicted crofters.
Looking closer, though, he realized that out of that bundle of rags there reached a single pale hand.

He pulled his mount to a halt and dismounted, has-
tening over to the ditch. He took the outstretched hand
and felt along the wrist for a pulse. He found a faint
beat beneath the covering of icy-cold skin. He called to
the others for help before gently urging the figure over
to face him.

Christian sucked in his breath when he saw what appeared to be a woman, perhaps thirty, her hair matted
and disheveled about her dirt-smudged face, a face so
gaunt she appeared to have not eaten in days. She

moaned when Christian moved her, as if her very bones threatened to crumble. Alastair handed Christian a small flask of water he'd brought along and Christian touched it to the woman's mouth. "Here, miss, drink."

After a moment or two, her eyelids began to flutter and she slowly opened her eyes, squinting against the harsh light of the day. But when she focused on Christian's face, she let out an unearthly howl, struggling weakly to get away from him as she said over and over, *"Oh! Sin Starke! Sin Starke!"*

A moment later, her body went limp in his arms, her cries suddenly silent.

"She's fainted, my lord," Alastair said, shaking his head dolefully. "She must come from Sunterglen many miles north of here. She thought you were Mr. Starke, the factor of the Sunterglen estate, a man as feared as Patrick Sellar ever was." He shook his head. "Poor thing. I fear she's lost her mind."

Christian knelt down and took the woman up in his arms. She whimpered at the sudden movement before she fell silent again. She weighed no more than a child.

"Help me to get her onto my mount, Robert. We will take her back to Skynegal and get her some warm clothing and something to eat."

Grace was standing in the courtyard with Deirdre, discussing the list of food supplies that needed to be purchased when next McFee and McGee made the trip to Ullapool. Deirdre had just set some of the older children to peeling the potatoes for that evening's supper. "We'll be needin' some salt to cure the cod afore the winter comes and—"

The Scotswoman fell suddenly silent, staring over Grace's shoulder with an expression that was in one moment curious, and in the next moment filled with dread.

Grace turned and saw that several figures were approaching down the hillside on horseback, no doubt Christian, Robert, and Alastair returning from their ride. She started across the courtyard to meet them, shielding her eyes against the sunlight. She recognized Alastair first atop his pony, for his bright tartan suit made him the most conspicuous. Robert rode beside him on Bayard, his stallion, but Grace barely took account of him, for she was focused completely upon Christian. He seemed to be carrying something before him on his horse and then she realized it was not some*thing* he carried, but some*one*.

"Deirdre, come!"

Together the two women hurried to meet them.

"Christian, good heavens, what has happened?"

"We found her near the east border. She is unconscious."

He pulled his horse to a halt at the small door leading inside the castle, where Flora at that moment stuck out her head, no doubt wondering what the commotion was about.

As the others followed, Robert and Alastair quickly told Grace of how they had found the woman lying near dead and delusional at the other side of the estate, a distance of nearly two miles. Christian took the woman to the warmest room in the keep, the kitchen, and lay her in the pine box bed that was built into the wall, where Flora usually slept. As Christian stepped away, Deirdre came forward to see to the woman. As soon as she turned her face into the light, Deirdre let out a gasp.

"Gun sealladh Dia oirnn!"

Grace knew that expression. *God have mercy upon us.*

"What is it, Deirdre?"

Deirdre's eyes were wide with fear. "She is Seonag, my Tom's sister."

Just then the woman, Seonag, cried out, conscious now, clutching at her belly. *"Leanabh!"*

And in that instant, Grace froze for she had recognized the Gaelic word for *babe*.

Chapter Twenty-nine

Seonag moaned as another pain tightened within her. For several long moments, it grew and swelled, bringing the bedraggled woman upright on the crude box bed in a shadowed corner of the castle kitchen. Day had given over to night, leaving them with only the light from the fire and a scattering of candles set about the snug room.

"Feumaidh tu dèan laighe," Deirdre murmured, urging Seonag back on the bed. "You must lie down, *piuthar*."

Seonag's cheeks were heat flushed, her hair wet and sticking to the sides of her face. She struggled for a breath, fighting against the contraction as she threw her head back with a weakened wail that echoed up to the rafters of the great hall.

Deirdre spoke soothing words to her in Gaelic, smoothing a cool water cloth over her brow while Flora set to boiling water, fetching clean cloths, lighting another candle, anything to keep herself occupied in the midst of the prolonged chaos.

They had removed Seonag's clothing and washed the mud and soot from her before dressing her in a large man's sark. A sheet covered her from the belly down and a swathe-band had been placed beneath her back and under her arms so that Flora and one of the other women might lift her slightly from the bed to ease when it came time for her to bear down.

It grew late, yet no one inside the castle slept. Upstairs, in the great hall, the people sat upon their sleeping pallets, murmuring quietly to one another until one of Seonag's moans would sound from the kitchen beneath them. They would hush, waiting for that anticipated tiny cry of an infant while holding close to their own children, stroking them softly, cherishing them.

And when that cry did not come, they waited again, whispering prayers of hope in Gaelic.

Seonag was the sister of Deirdre's deceased husband, Tom, and the only family Deirdre had left to her. By Deirdre's estimate, Seonag was not to have given birth for at least another month; she had seen Seonag when she had gone to visit several weeks earlier and all had been well. All would have remained well, too, had the eviction's agents not come in the twilight hours two days before.

Seonag had been alone at the small croft she and her husband, Eachann, worked on the Sunterglen estate, where they had been tenants for the past seven years. Seonag had already retired for the night when the soldiers had come. She could have had no idea what lay in store for her when she was summoned by a sudden and insistent knocking at her door. Eachann had gone from their croft only the day before to take their stock of cattle over the brae to where relatives lived on the other side of the vast Sunterglen estate. He planned to leave them to be tended so that he could keep close to home after the birth of their first child. Eachann knew he would return within ample time of the birth, else he would never have left Seonag alone as he had.

That night, as darkness fell, the eviction's agents ordered Seonag, heavy with child, out of her home, giving her only enough time to gather up the soft woolen blanket she had been knitting for the babe. She was left to watch in terror as the soldiers set their torches to the meager cottage's thatched roof, setting the night sky aglow. When it was done, they ordered her off the estate. She asked if she might stay among the smoldering ruins long enough for her husband to return, but was refused. Seonag had had no choice but to begin the arduous trek to Skynegal, knowing she would find shelter at the home of her brother's widow. Eachann would return to find his home razed to the ground and his wife and unborn child missing.

It was after midnight in the tiny kitchen at Skynegal when the struggling infant's cry finally broke the heavy silence. A relieved cheer went round the great hall and toasts were given over ale around the grand stone hearth, welcoming the tiny new life that had survived despite the terrible circumstances its mother had endured. It was a boy, with a mop of his father's carroty hair and eyes as blue as the clearest Highland summer sky. Both he and his mother, despite her exhaustion, were soon resting and doing well.

Christian and Robert had retired soon after the birth, for they planned to leave at dawn to return to Sunterglen in hopes of finding Eachann to bring him to his wife and child at Skynegal. Flora had collapsed from nervous exhaustion, having fretted her way through the birth of Seonag's child. Deirdre was yet with the mother and child, leaving Grace a few moments to walk out alone in the cool moonlight and confront the emotions she'd barely managed to hold in check during the past several hours.

Witnessing the birth of Seonag's son had given Grace a new reverence for all that life represented—the vulnerability of its beginnings, the wonder at its continuous renewal. Brought on prematurely by the ugly deeds of others and despite great odds, that tiny child had overcome it all. Watching as Deirdre had guided that new life into the world had astounded Grace and frightened her more than she had ever thought possible. Deirdre had been remarkable, knowing just what to do, what to say to ease Seonag's laboring. At the moment that struggling cry was heard, nothing else had mattered any longer. The soldiers, the fire—all of it vanished for the single instant in time. It was truly the most divine moment, an unquestionable symbol of hope for the future.

Grace lowered to sit on one of the flat granite slabs that lay at various places about the quiet courtyard. It was a chill night and she pulled her shawl close about herself while the moon shone down through the stars overhead. For the first time in many days, the sky was clear, the clouds that usually hung about at this hour oddly absent. Grace thought that it must surely be a harbinger of good fortune for the new life that had just come into the world. She rested the flat of her hand against where her own belly swelled so slightly beneath the loose skirts of her gown. She thought to herself that she had never felt the absence of a mother's presence more in her life than she did now.

Grace had been raised to such a sheltered existence, where the things most fundamental to life were never discussed. She had been stunned by the harsh reality of birth, the unadulterated truth of one life begetting another. How she wished she could talk to Nonny, ask her the dozens of questions that were racing pell-mell through her mind. How would she know when it was time for the baby to come? Had anyone ever fainted in the midst of bearing a child? How would she learn how to feed a babe, bathe it?

She heard the sound of footsteps on the graveled walkway behind her and turned to see Deirdre coming from the glowing light of the kitchen. She had removed the kerchief that normally covered her head, letting her hair fall freely down her back in dark rippling waves well past her bottom. As she drew near, Grace noticed that without her kerchief in place, Deirdre looked a much younger woman than she had thought, closer to her own age, which was remarkable for one so knowing.

"You're feelin' a bit of the upset after the birthin', are you?"

Grace shook her head. And then, "Not too much, really."

Deirdre came to sit beside her. "It frichted you, din't it, my leddy, seein' the birthin' up close like that? Makes you feared, does it no', for when 'tis time for your own bairn to come?"

Grace looked at her. She had thought no one but Liza knew of the babe she carried, but then she wasn't really surprised Deirdre had sensed the truth despite her silence. Deirdre had a mysterious way of seeing straight through to a person's innermost thoughts and most heartfelt feelings. It often left Grace wondering that she didn't perhaps possess this "sight" Alastair seemed ever ascribing to her.

"It was a little startling to see. I didn't know it would be so . . . so . . ."

"So messy?" Deirdre nodded. "I would imagine all you've seen of mithers and bairns is wee bundles o' sweetness wrapped in soft white blankets, cooing and smelling like the mornin' sunshine."

Grace nodded, suddenly ashamed at her own ignorance.

"Birthin's an untidy business, my leddy, nocht a bit elegant about it. But doona wirry yourself o'er it too much. Seonag had it worse than most. She was brought to the birthin' a bit too early and the bairn wasna yet ready. I had to turn him and—"

Deirdre must have sensed that Grace didn't have the faintest idea of what she was talking about. She fell silent and set her hand gently over Grace's middle, splaying her fingers outward. Grace could feel the warmth of the woman's tender touch through the woolen of her gown and took comfort in it.

"That bairn you carry now has his heid nestled up here 'gainst your belly. A wee bit afore a bairn is to come from its mither's womb, nature turns him"—she moved her hands—"bringin' his heid doon, to deliver him through the birthin' the easiest."

Grace looked down at herself, wondering at the child she carried, suddenly able to see the babe as more than a thought, a prospect, a dream, but as a reality growing within her. Would it be a boy, or perhaps a girl? Would she be dark or fair? Grace closed her eyes. Would he be loved by the father who didn't yet know he existed?

"I'm so scared, Deirdre."

Awash with emotion, Grace finally gave over to the tears she had kept at bay for so long. Her shoulders shook and she wept freely while Deirdre said nothing, simply enfolded her in her arms, tucking Grace's head against the warmth of her cheek. Grace leaned into the woman's smaller frame and they sat together for some time, neither speaking, neither feeling the need to. The evening breeze blew gently over them, stirring up a tiny whirlwind of leaves as Deirdre stroked her fingers lightly over Grace's forehead, through her hair, smoothing a stray lock of it behind her ear. Twice now, when she had most been in need, Deirdre had comforted her with a mother's touch. And just as on her first night at Skynegal, her touch had put Grace at ease.

"You havna told the laird yet about the bairn, have you?"

Grace shook her head silently.

"How long will you wait?"

"Until I know for certain if he will try to force me to leave Skynegal."

Deirdre's fingers went still against her forehead. "Do you mean to say that the laird hasna come to Skynegal to live?"

"No, Deirdre, he has not. In fact, he has already asked me to leave and return with him to London and the life I left there. I told him I will not."

Deirdre was quiet for several moments. "You think to discover if he loves you by your refusal to go with him back to London."

Grace lifted her head. "If only it were that simple, Deirdre, but it is much more complicated. Christian never wanted to marry me. He was forced to by his grandfather, the duke. His coming here to Skynegal was more out of a sense of duty than any concern for me."

Deirdre shook her head. "I think 'tis more than that."

"Oh, Deirdre, I wish that could be so."

Deirdre nudged Grace into looking at her. She smiled gently, smoothing a tendril from her eyes. "This makes no sense, my leddy, these words you speak. 'Tis obvious he has some bit o' regard for you. You are carrying his bairn, are you no'?"

Grace drew a deep breath. "Deirdre, you have never lived the life I had before coming here to Skynegal. It is so very different. You might find this difficult to believe, especially after the love you shared with your husband, but in some circles of society, a man and a woman couple for reasons other than love or even attraction. In London, it is more often induced by money and the desire for the continuance of that money through a male heir"—she frowned—"no matter how unappealing a chore that might prove to the gentleman."

"Och, my leddy, nature has ensured that for the man at least, coupling is no' a chore. I've yet to see the man who didna think on it both nicht and day. 'Tis in their blood, it is." Deirdre looked at her, one brow slightly cocked. "I'm thinking from wha' you're saying 'tis that the laird cares for you mair than he may like to think."

Grace shook her head against the thought.

"You love him."

Grace stilled, staring at Deirdre deeply. "I do. From the moment I first saw Christian I knew I would love him for as long as I lived."

"Then you must tell it to him."

Grace opened her mouth to give voice to every reason she had against it, but Deirdre held up a hand, stopping her. "If you ne'er tell him that you love him, my leddy, then you will ne'er know if he feels the same for you. Doona wait too long, for there is ne'er a certainty of tomorrow."

Grace felt the weight of a single tear trickle down her cheek. "But I do know his feelings, Deirdre. Christian left me with no doubt of them. He never wanted me in his life. Don't you see? It was for that reason I left him to come to Scotland."

Deirdre simply smiled, shaking her head again. "Nae, my leddy, 'tis you who doesna see. For if he truly didna have a care for you, he wouldna be here now."

Chapter Thirty

There exists a tradition in the Highlands called the *céilidh,* begun in olden times when neighbors and friends would gather together for an evening of food and drink, singing, storytelling, and dancing. It was a celebration built on clan tradition and kinship, characteristics that sadly had faded away during the past half-century or more since the Jacobite defeat in 1745. It was an event that had been looked upon with much anticipation and long after remembered with joy. What better way could there be, Grace thought, than to honor thus the birth of Seonag's son?

The warmth and good spirit that had enveloped Skynegal at the coming of the newly born babe was soon coupled with the blessing of the safe arrival of Seonag's husband Eachann at Skynegal two days later. Christian and Robert had happened upon him soon after he'd returned to his devastated cottage. The crofter's very worst fears at discovering his wife missing vanished behind his joy at hearing that Seonag and his new son were alive and well and being tended to at Skynegal.

They had ridden through the night to return to the castle, coming at dusk the night before, road weary and soaked through from the rain that had showered down upon them during the last leg of their journey. But Eachann had scarcely noticed the damp. He had gone at once to where Seonag lay in a small chamber off the kitchen and hadn't left her side since. Together they named the babe Iain, 'a gift from God,' for indeed he was.

The small family would remain at Skynegal, a part of them all now for clan tradition embraced the bairn born on Skynegal soil. A cottage was being planned for them on an arable plot of farmland in the glen where they might begin anew without the threat of eviction again. Until the cottage was built, Eachann and Seonag would share their first precious weeks as a family in a pair of chambers situated at the far side of the stable, a place previously put to use by the Skynegal groom, a man who had been known to all in the castle's heyday simply as Twig. A Tudor-style cradle had been uncovered in the castle's garret for the babe, and the other tenants, those of the Skynegal estate and those who had come from elsewhere seeking shelter, had all donated clothing and other household necessaries to help replace those destroyed in the fire.

The céilidh was to be held the following week on the grounds surrounding the castle, giving Flora and Deirdre ample time to prepare the traditional baked foods while McFee, McGee, and a party of men went off to the deer forest on a hunt for the feast. It was a perfect time for a celebration. The renovations at the castle and a good many of the tenant's cottages were nearly finished. Summer had come to the Highlands in full regalia of rich heather and primrose and broom. The Skynegal that Grace had looked on at her arrival months earlier was but a shadow of what she was now in her current glory.

Standing atop a heather-swept hillock and looking on the castle from afar, Grace could only think that Skynegal was very much a fairytale place. The sunlight glittered on the water of Loch Skynegal behind her, winking on the newly glazed windows of the castle. In her pastures, reddish-orange shaggy Highland cattle grazed contently on lush green grass while the legendary birds soared in abandon about the castle parapets. Never had Grace felt more at home. She knew now that she had found Skynegal, she could never leave. She also knew that although he had agreed to the release of any funds for her to continue her work, Christian had made no indication that he would stay—but, as Deirdre had pointed out, he wasn't leaving either.

Grace reached to where Dubhar stood at her side and scratched him on his grizzled head, gifting him with a nibble of cheese from her pocket before she turned toward the small grouping of children and mothers who awaited on the haughland ahead. It was a delightful, carefree day, the morning mist having burned off early under the summer sun, the tall grass still damp beneath her feet. She had dressed plainly in a gray woolen gown, her hair simply fashioned beneath a kerchief in preparation for an afternoon that would be spent gathering the blueberries and blackcurrants for the baking they would do for the céilidh.

"Fàilte na maidne ort," one of the women, Morag, called out to Grace as she approached.

Grace returned the greeting and began to hand out the willow baskets she'd brought with her to the eager hands of the waiting children, watching on a smile as they bounded off to fill them. A prize had been promised to the one who gathered the most berries, so they scattered into the surrounding heath, giggling and hunting amongst the ling and gorse, snatching a berry every so often for themselves as they began filling their baskets.

Grace was just starting off with her own basket when she spotted a figure racing up the hillside toward them, arms waving haphazardly, calling, "Lady Grace! Lady Grace!"

She shaded her eyes against the sun and saw that it was one of the boys who tended the ponies in the stables, Micheil. He was obviously upset, but Grace wasn't alarmed, for she knew that one of the mares was due to foal soon and she'd asked to be called when it was her time. Apparently it now was.

"What is Micheil?" she asked as he reached her, "Has Jo begun to foal?"

"Nae, my lady . . ." He came to a halt before her, heaving from having run so fast and so hard. It took him several moments, bent over at the waist to calm himself. Finally he gulped. "You must come right away. The man has come."

"The man, Micheil? What man?"

" 'Tis *Donas.*"

One of the women standing nearby gasped, dropping her berry basket to her feet. Grace looked at her and saw that the woman's eyes were wide and she started babbling in rapid Gaelic to the others, but Grace only caught a few words, her limited knowledge of the language making it impossible to understand. Over and over she heard the word Micheil had spoken—*donas*. And then suddenly Grace remembered that *donas* was the Gaelic word for *devil*.

She took the lad by the arm. "Micheil, what is it? Who is this *Donas?*"

" 'Tis Mr. Starke come from Sunterglen."

Grace felt a chill run through her that had nothing to do with a sudden change in the weather. *Starke* was a name she had heard more times than she cared to count since coming to Skynegal. It was a name that evoked terror when spoken to anyone familiar with it—and there were far too many familiar with it. The fact that he was there at Skynegal was something that could only bode badly.

Grace set her basket on the ground and started for the castle, walking at first, then hurrying faster down the hillside, until she was running with her skirts in hand. Any doubt she might have had as to whether the man had truly come vanished at the sight of the faces of those standing about the castle courtyard.

When she had departed earlier, there had been much laughter and singing. Women were hanging out the laundry to dry and weaving baskets; grooms were mucking out the stalls in the stables. Now no one spoke or even moved. They stood quietly, staring at where two figures were conversing a distance away in front of the castle's barmkin. When they noticed her approaching, the people began to whisper to one another. They had been watching for her arrival.

As Grace strode across the courtyard, she recognized Christian as the taller of the two men, his dark hair and confident stance so very familiar to her now. The other man was not quite as tall as he, but in spite of his height, his manner spoke of his belief in his superiority above everything and most everyone around him.

Grace did not stop for a moment, but continued boldly forward, stopping only when she stood at Christian's side. Dubhar, who had run with her from the hillside, took his usual place at her leg. He did not, however, sit as was his custom. Instead he remained standing, on guard, sensing the tension that accompanied the unsavory stranger.

Starke glanced once at Grace when he noticed her arrival, but briefly, as he might at an annoying midge. It was all the notice he gave her. Given the fact that she was dressed like any of the other women about the estate, her hair unkempt now from her run, he no doubt thought her one of the Highlanders. Grace made use of his inattention to give the man a thorough study.

From the stories she'd heard of him, she would have expected someone more formidable, but in truth he lacked most of the characteristics she would have thought to find in him. His clothing was garish, his manner more plebian than well born, and his prolonged smirk demonstrated a somewhat sadistic enjoyment at the atmosphere his coming had brought.

"My lord," Starke said to Christian, "might I say what a fine effort you have made in restoring the Skynegal estate?" He turned his back on Grace purposefully, as if to regard the castle behind him. " 'Tis amazing what actually lay hidden beneath all that ivy growth."

"Thank you, Mr. Starke," Christian said, "but the credit should go to Lady Knighton, for it was she who undertook the castle's restoration."

Starke was silent a moment, then turned to regard Christian again. His eyes seemed almost to narrow when he noticed Grace was still there.

"Pray tell me, my lord, are you of a mind to sell the estate?" And before Christian could respond, he added, "Perhaps you have heard tell of my employers, the Marquess and Marchioness of Sunterglen? Fine people. They have expressed an interest in purchasing the estate of Skynegal and have charged me, as their factor, with the honor of presenting an offer to you." He stared at Christian. "They are prepared to pay a handsome sum."

His words were so honeyed and so perfidious that Grace had to prevent herself from blurting out that she would never sell the estate. Christian responded before she could.

"I'm afraid, Mr. Starke, that you are speaking with the wrong person. The estate of Skynegal came to my wife through an inheritance from her grandmother, who was born and raised here. While as her husband, I might advise her and manage certain affairs of the estate, the decision of whether or not to sell Skynegal would be entirely hers."

Grace looked at Christian. He had turned to her and she was suddenly reminded of the first night when she had fallen through the wall panel at his feet. A feeling she had spent the past months pushing aside began to reach for her deep inside once again.

Starke nodded. "Indeed. Well then, perhaps you might direct me to her ladyship so that I may present my offer to her personally." He glanced around, completely ignoring Grace who stood not four feet from him. "Is Lady Knighton within the castle? Perhaps we might send someone for her." He glanced at Grace as if intending to charge her with the task of summoning herself, but thought the better of it. "Or perhaps I might just wait awhile for her if she is presently away."

Christian smiled, obviously enjoying the man's oblivion. "No, Mr. Starke, Lady Knighton is not within the castle, but in fact, she is very close by."

"Splendid. Shall we go to her then, my lord?"

Two burly Scotsmen standing closest to them chuckled softly to one another. Starke threw them a quelling look, one he no doubt employed often during his misdeeds.

"There is no need to seek Lady Knighton out, Mr. Starke," Christian said, "for you see, Lady Knighton stands before you even now."

Starke turned to look where Christian had gestured to Grace at his side. The realization of her identity played visibly across the factor's face. She looked no different than she had upon approaching, a handful of moments earlier, but somehow, now that he knew who she was, she warranted his full attention—without the smugness he'd worn for her before. In fact, Starke went so far now as to bow his head reverently.

"Lady Knighton, indeed, it is an honor to make your acquaintance."

Grace did not respond in kind. She might be wearing woolen and her hair might not be properly dressed, but she had been born and bred the daughter of a nobleman.

She was wife to the grandson of one of England's most powerful and wealthy men. Grace had never worn her position in life when dealing with others, not from her peers to even those who served—until now. Her mouth remained fixed as she stared at the man hard, her only thought for the many Highlanders whose lives had been forever destroyed because of his actions. It was because of him that Seonag had been evicted from her home and had very nearly died, her child with her. For months Grace had seen how the very mention of his name brought terror. Even now, on the outskirts of the courtyard, the people hung back in fear.

Starke looked to her. "As I was just saying to his lordship, my employers, the Marquess and Marchioness of Sunter—"

"I heard you, sir," Grace said, abruptly cutting him off. "I decline your offer. Skynegal is not for sale."

Starke frowned. "Perhaps, then, instead of the estate entire, you might consider selling a portion of the lands to the east, the ones that border on the Sunterglen estate—"

Grace crossed her arms before her, raising her chin as she continued to stare at him with all the iciness and arrogance he had her earlier. "Pray tell me why I should sell the land to your employer, Mr. Starke. So that you might turn out my tenants from their homes as you already have at Sunterglen, in order to graze sheep upon the graves of their ancestors?"

Starke glanced at Christian as if expecting him to intervene. He blessedly remained a spectator to the exchange.

"I can assure you, madam," Starke said, his voice steady, controlled, "any tenants we did wish to move would be relocated to alternate plots on Sunterglen."

"Alternate plots? Is that what you call it, Mr. Starke? Just as you *relocated* Seonag MacLean whilst her husband Eachann was away and she in the eighth month of her pregnancy?"

Starke's face turned a shade ashen at the accusation, one he wisely did not seek to refute.

"Look around you, Mr. Starke." Grace gestured to the crowd of Highlanders standing around the courtyard watching the exchange. "These people are the very ones who once peopled the estate of your benevolent employer, those who managed to survive your evictions. Because of greed, sir—greed for land profit—they have been forced to come here to Skynegal to seek shelter from the elements. I am the great-granddaughter of the last laird of Skynegal. This castle and this estate have been a part of my family for countless generations, as it has been a part of the lives and history of the people of Wester Ross. Do you honestly believe I would sell off so much as one ell of this estate so that you might continue your onslaught?"

Starke's face reddened. "I had thought since you come from England," he faltered—

"My great-grandmother, while English, was a Mac-Rath down to her kirtle. She proudly supported Prince Charles at Culloden in hopes of preserving her Scottish heritage. As long as I live, sir, I can assure you I will never disgrace the memory of my ancestors, both English and Scottish, for a few pounds' profit."

Starke simply stared at her, speechless. His eyes, which had before been deferential, now narrowed on her with a scarcely concealed hostility. He looked one last time to Christian. "If you should happen to change your mind, *my lord,* my employer's offer is a generous one."

It had been intended as an affront to Grace, one that Christian was less than willing to allow. He stepped forward, forcing Starke back across the courtyard to where he almost stumbled. When Christian spoke, his voice was hard with warning.

"I caution you, sir, to heed me and heed me well. I do not take insults against my wife at all lightly. In fact, I take them quite personally. I believe Lady Knighton has adequately explained her feelings to you on the matter. You no longer have any business here. I will therefore direct you to your horse so that you may leave the premises. I would further suggest that you refrain from ever returning. If I learn of your having placed one foot on Skynegal soil, I will have you arrested and charged with criminal trespass. Even a self-appointed magistrate must answer to the Crown. Do I make myself clear?"

Dubhar reaffirmed Christian's words with a low growl that came from deep in his belly.

Starke stared at Christian. "With all due respect, you are making a mistake, my lord." He bowed his head slightly to Christian, then looked at Grace, staring at her with patent contempt. "Your ladyship."

Starke turned and started walking to where his mount awaited with the three soldiers who had accompanied him. He pulled himself up and settled into the saddle, tugging on his gloves and setting his heels to the horse's sides before calling to the soldiers to follow.

As he rode from the courtyard, he was followed by the jeers of the very people he had himself once maligned—and when he was gone, the jeers turned to cheers for the laird and lady of Skynegal.

Chapter Thirty-one

The conversation around the fire in the great hall that evening was of nothing else but Grace's swift and just dismissal of the despicable factor from Sunterglen. Those who had been witness to the scene earlier that day related the tale time and time again for the others who had been occupied elsewhere. Each time the story was repeated, the embellishment grew until, by the time they had finished their supper, it had taken on ridiculously epic proportions. No, she had not ordered the factor away at swordpoint, Grace pointed out, nor had she delivered him a blow, or had him seized and thrown bodily into the loch. The more the *uisge-bheatha* flowed, the more elaborate the tale became. Soon some even began composing ballads in her honor. Grace, though embarrassed by the attention, was happy to allow the Highlanders this much-deserved vindication after their recent misfortunes.

When they began making effusive toasts to her fingers and toes, Grace managed to break away from the raucous trestle table and crossed the room to join Liza, who sat holding tiny Iain in a secluded corner. Miraculously the babe was sleeping through the chaos that surrounded him.

Grace smiled at the maid as she took the seat beside her near the hearth. To see Liza now, one would never believe that she had once played the part of the proper English ladies' maids. Echoing Grace's example, Liza had abandoned her prim linen maid's habit for a loose chemiselike blouse over full ankle-length skirts, leaving her hair hanging free and undressed. She looked utterly contented.

" 'Twas a good thing," Liza said, "Your having ordered that devil away like you did."

"I did nothing more than anyone else would have done under the same circumstances."

"You minimize your efforts. It is not just what happened today. It is all you have done here in the past months."

"We have so much to celebrate," Grace said, smoothing a finger over the slumbering Iain's soft cheek. "Everyone has worked so hard and the castle looks—"

Grace soon noticed that Liza wasn't listening to her. She looked and saw that the maid's attention was planted squarely upon a handsome Highlander who was standing across the room on the outskirts of the assembly. He was a great hulking figure of a man with midnight black hair and adventure-filled eyes. Those same eyes, Grace noticed, were fixed keenly upon Liza in return.

He smiled at her, raising his whiskey cup in silent salute. Liza drew in a quivering breath. She broke away from her study of him only briefly when Seonag returned to claim the sleeping Iain. Settling back in her chair, Liza looked once again to where the Highlander still stood watching her with a gaze that rivaled the heat of the fire beside them.

"Goodness, my lady, have you ever seen such a man?"

Grace grinned. "Ah, I see you've noticed Andrew."

Liza never took her eyes from him. Had she been a cat, Grace wouldn't have been at all surprised to hear her purring.

"Noticed him, aye, I have, indeed, and more. Why haven't you told me about him afore now?"

"His name is Andrew MacAlister and he arrived at Skynegal just yesterday. He fought in one of the Highland regiments against Napoleon and has just returned to Scotland from the Continent. His family emigrated to America, but he decided to remain in the Highlands. He's come seeking work and a place to settle."

"Have you ever seen legs like that?" Liza went on, appreciating the fit of his kilt. She actually sighed, giving Grace a chuckle.

"Perhaps I could introduce you . . ."

Liza turned to stare at Grace in abject terror. "Oh, no, my lady, I look so disheveled. My hair is . . ." She smoothed back an errant curl. "And my clothes are . . ."

Grace glanced over Liza's shoulder to see that Andrew was already approaching them. She grinned. "Well, it looks like you won't have any choice in the matter, for he is headed in our direction as we speak."

Liza's eyes went as wide as Alastair's and she froze, too anxious to turn or even move. She remained rooted to her chair, her back to the hall, staring at Grace with an expression of pure panic.

A deep rich brogue sounded from behind her.

"Gude e'ening, Lady Grace. I hope I'm no' disturbin' you. I was hopin' I micht beg an introduction to this fine lassie sittin' 'ere aside you."

Grace smiled, winking at Liza. "Of course, Andrew, it would be my pleasure." She stood. "May I present to you Miss Eliza Stone? Liza, please meet Mr. Andrew MacAlister."

Liza turned about slowly in her chair to face the waiting Highlander. The look on her face as she peered up at him was akin to profound awe. Andrew took her hand and bowed over it, pressing a gallant kiss upon it. "It is an honour t' make your acquaintance, Miss Stone."

"L-Liza," the maid murmured. "You can call me Liza."

"Aye, but only if you call me 'Andrew' in return," he answered on a grin, the sort of grin that would make any girl's knees turn to jelly. It was a good thing, Grace thought to herself, that Liza was still sitting.

"Andrew," Liza repeated.

"Aye." He motioned outward to the hall. "They're preparin' to play a bit o' the fiddle. Would you care to partner me in the dance?"

Liza's face fell. "Oh, but I cannot. I do not know the steps.

"Och, 'tis nothin'. I'll teach it to you, lass."

Andrew drew Liza up from her chair and away with a nod of parting to Grace. Grace stood by and watched as Andrew set his great arms about Liza's smaller frame and slowly demonstrated the movements of the dance. They made an attractive pair, both dark haired, he standing nearly a head taller than she. It wasn't long before Liza had shed her reserve and was laughing even as she misstepped onto his toes.

Grace wondered what it would be like to have a man look at her in the way Andrew looked at Liza, the same way Eachann watched Seonag now with such open and total appreciation in his eyes as she held their infant son to her breast. This was love, she thought—the beginnings of it for one man and woman, the perpetuation of it for another—that indefinable magic that brought two together with the exchange of a glance.

It was indeed the stuff of fairy tales.

"Good e'ening, my lady. 'Tis a fine night, is it no'?"

Grace turned to see that Alastair had suddenly appeared beside her, taking up the cup of whiskey one of the others had brought to him.

"Alastair, good evening. I was wondering where you had gone to."

"I was in the office, going over some figures with Lord Knighton and the Duke of Devonbrook for the proposal they plan to make to the Lords about the building of the roads. The duke has offered to help us find passage for some of the evicted tenants to travel to New Scotland and America and has promised to move others who are willing to his family's estates in the south to fine plots of land there. Also, it seems the duchess's father, Mr. Angus MacBryan, has a small importing venture that he's looking to improve in the coming months and thus will need able hands to help him."

Grace smiled, nodding over a sip of her punch. Robert and Catriona had proven a godsend in their efforts to help the displaced Highlanders. After viewing firsthand the full scope of the people's plight, they had pledged funds and supplies to help see the tenants settled elsewhere. They had offered temporary housing at their estate Rosmorigh as a stopping-off point for those wishing to move south toward Glasgow. They had also given their hand, along with Grace and Christian, to a letter that would be sent to all the noble landowners in the Highlands, Scottish and English alike, asking for their support in the road-building venture.

With the signatures of a powerful duke such as Robert, as well as the heir to the Westover dukedom, they would hold a much better chance of gaining their support. Grace's most fervent hope was that they might induce the landowners to look at the benefits of putting their efforts toward the betterment of their tenants, so they might put a stop to the clearances all together.

"Alastair, do you know where might I find—"

Alastair, however, was no longer standing anywhere near her. While Grace had been lost to her thoughts, the Scotsman had stepped away to stand with the others. His attention was focused at the center of the throng of Highlanders, where it seemed everyone else's attentions were focused, too. Grace hadn't even noticed that the dancing had stopped. The music still played, only now it was soft and low, with a timbre that was as misty as the Scottish hills. There was singing with a sweet lyrical voice unlike anything she had ever heard before. It was the sort of singing that touched one to the heart, the sort that carried one away. Grace listened then to the words of the song being sung.

She on the wings of sacred duty flies
With shepherd's care to bless the untended flocks;
And like an angel missioned from the skies,
They greet her coming from the old gray rocks;
Like the healing birds of Cliodna in the tower high
'Tis the Lady who loves the Highlands . . .
Poor island-dwellers by the lonely sea,
Whom all forget but God in heaven and she,
Of English blood, but true to the Celtic she
'Tis the Lady who loves the Highlands.

It was an ancient Scottish poem that Grace remembered having read in one of the old books she had found stored away in the castle garret, only the words had been slightly changed and were sung to the soft lilting strains of the Highland pipe and harp.

Grace moved from where she stood, drawing closer so that she might see who was singing so beautifully. The torch lights flickered on the stone walls, casting the great hall in an embracing glow. She came quietly to stand beside Alastair. At first, she could not see above the heads of the others, but then someone moved a bit, affording her a view to where there was a woman standing in the midst of the circle of Highlanders. When she saw who was performing, Grace could scarcely believe her eyes.

It was Flora, who rarely spoke above two words at a time, who had as much strength in her arms as most men, who had always seemed so rough and solid and robust, but who was singing with the voice of an earthly angel. Gone was the plain linen kerchief that always covered her head. Her hair was now loose and hanging down her back in thick rippling waves of chestnut. Her eyes sparked in the light from the torch fire, and her hands moved before her as she sang with the gossamer lightness of a swan. With just her voice, she had transformed herself, captivating the masses with her song—a siren who had utterly mesmerized Alastair Ogilvy.

The look on the steward's face was akin to disbelief. He was spellbound by the sweet sounds Flora was creating. When Flora finished the song on one high silvery note, everyone standing in that hall broke into applause. Flora smiled shyly, her cheeks coloring in the light of the fire, unaccustomed as she was to having so much attention focused upon her. Grace watched as Alastair stepped forward through the crowd, bowing his head while asking Flora for the honor of the next dance. The look in her eye as she nodded to him spoke clearly of the beginnings of something tender between them. Grace thought of the story Alastair had once told her of his long-ago love and how he had lost his heart to her after first hearing her sing. She wondered that he might be given a second chance to find that love again.

All around her the enchantment of the evening had woven its way into the lives of the people. Seonag and Eachann, who sat together with Deirdre and the babe Iain, a family so recently threatened, now safely reunited. Liza and Andrew, who basked in the light of their discovery of one another, and now Alastair and Flora, having passed each day over the past months so close to one another, suddenly seeing one another with

new and different eyes. Deirdre's words the night of
Iain's birth echoed softly to Grace's thought.

*You must tell it to him . . . doona wait too long . . .
there is ne'er a certainty of tomorrow.*

Standing as she was, alone on the outskirts of this
scene, Grace suddenly wanted more than anything to
feel a part of the magic that had taken over the night.
She wanted to dance in the arms of the man she loved
and thrill to the touch of his hand and the warmth in
his eyes. This wonderful, mysterious light shared only
between two—his was all that mattered. It was as clear
and as real as the Highland moon beaming down from
overhead and Grace knew then that the time had come
for her to share the truth of the child that lay nestled
within her womb with Christian.

Grace started across the hall, heading for the walkway
that led to the office, hoping she might find Christian
yet there. As she entered the corridor and made the turn
for the office door, she nearly collided with someone
who was coming down the passageway in the opposite
direction.

Grace stopped, looking up at the figure who stood in
her path.

And what she saw there literally took her breath
away.

Chapter Thirty-two

"Leaving the celebration so soon, my lady?"

Christian stood silhouetted by the shadows of the darkened corridor, just outside the great hall, away from the noise and light of the gathering.

"I was just coming to look for you. I—"

Grace's words caught in her throat and stuck there as Christian stepped forward in the muted torchlight. No longer did he wear the carefully knotted neckcloth and high-pointed collar of the stylish English gentleman. Instead he had donned a plain linen *sark* with the full sleeves rolled loosely over his forearms and lace ties opened at the neck. In place of his tailored breeches and perfectly polished Hessians he wore a kilt fashioned in the familiar chequered shades of the Skynegal tartan. And he was smiling, a carefree, contagious, and utterly charming grin that curled his mouth and wrapped its warmth around her like a cloak of summer sunshine.

Grace blinked, twice, but the image didn't fade. She suddenly understood why Liza had been so transfixed by the sight of Andrew MacAlister. She couldn't take her eyes from Christian.

"Christian, you are wearing a kilt," she said. It was laughably obvious, but she was so distracted by the sight of him that she scarcely realized her words.

"I grew weary of being the only one in breeches."

Grace simply stared at him more.

"Actually, I thought perhaps it was time to shed the image of the noble English lord and acknowledge my position as laird of Skynegal."

From the moment Christian had arrived at Skynegal, Grace had held the secret hope that he might realize the virtues of the estate which, while not a financial bounty, had the merits of tradition and kinship and physical beauty that could not be exceeded. She had hoped that he wouldn't turn a blind eye to the people and their plight, that he would realize their importance and embrace his place as their patriarch. Tonight he had surpassed that hope, giving her the most precious gift she had ever been given. Before that moment, Grace would never have thought she could love Christian more than she already did.

She was wrong.

"Thank you, Christian."

"I'll take that to mean that you approve." He presented his arm to her, that strange and wonderful smile still curving his mouth. "Shall we proceed to the hall, my lady?"

Grace gave a wordless nod. It was all she could manage.

As they came into the great hall, most everyone was still taken up with the dancing. They walked across the room and Grace caught sight of Catriona standing with Robert near the hearth. The duke was garbed like Christian in sark and kilt, but in the same tartan that made up Catriona's gown. They exchanged greetings with their friends while one of the women brought them cups of Deirdre's tasty gooseberry punch. Grace found herself wondering how the evening could be any more complete.

She wasn't left wondering long.

A moment later, Deirdre appeared in the entrance to the hall, accompanied by two newcomers.

Christian noticed them first.

"Nell!"

He crossed the distance to his sister in three strides and took her tightly against him. "Still tagging along after Big Brother, eh?"

Eleanor grinned. "I just couldn't resist the sight of you in a kilt."

After greeting her brother, Eleanor turned to embrace Grace. "I am so very relieved to know Christian has found you."

Grace had always regretted having left London without first bidding farewell to Christian's sister, for she had been so kind to her after their marriage. Lady Frances stood beside Eleanor and greeted Grace with a gentle smile.

"Indeed, dear, you had us all so very worried."

"I am sorry for leaving as I did. I . . ." She faltered. ". . . It was just . . ."

Lady Frances took her hand and squeezed it. "Let us not speak of that now, dear. You are here and we are together again as a family. That is all that matters."

Family. Togetherness. How wonderful the sound of those two words were, particularly now that she carried Christian's child.

"But how did you find your way to Skynegal?" Christian asked. "I had posted a letter sending for you, but that was only a few days ago. You couldn't have received it so soon."

"Actually, dear, we were brought here by—"

But Christian had already found his answer, having noticed the arrival of a third newcomer—his grandfather, the duke.

"What is he doing here?"

Lady Frances answered, "Christian, it was he who asked us to accompany him and he was very kind throughout our journey. He seems sincere. Perhaps he has had a change of heart."

Christian's smile darkened to a bitter frown. "How could he, Mother? He doesn't have one."

Grace broke away from them and crossed the hall to where the duke stood, hanging back from the gathering in the doorway of the great hall. "Good evening, Your Grace." She curtsied before him. "What a nice surprise to see you."

The old man raised a cynical brow. "I rather doubt your husband shares your feelings."

Grace refused to be baited by his bitterness. Instead she slipped her hand into his. "Come, Your Grace, join the gathering."

The duke looked startled at the gesture, but didn't refuse as he followed her into the hall.

The others in the great hall soon took notice of their arrival and at the sight of their lord and lady together, in the Skynegal colors. The people stopped their dancing and gave a cheer. As Grace watched on, Christian walked about the room and greeted everyone he met by name. She noticed that he purposely avoided his grandfather.

"Let us give a cheer for the laird and lady of Skynegal," someone called, and everyone hollered out "Aye!"

The piper then struck up a lively reel and the assembly scrambled, forming two large circles in the center of the room, ladies on the outside, men on the inside. As the dancers began to weave in and out, they pulled Christian and Grace along, laughing good-naturedly as Christian struggled to keep in step. Soon most everyone in the hall was skipping and turning, hands clapping, feet stomping, laughing out loud as the music played on and on. Even the old duke seemed to enjoy the merrymaking as he stood chatting with Deirdre near the fire.

Alastair hopped into the center of the circle of dancers and surprised them all as he hopped and stepped to the lively tune with an ease that belied his girth. He rejoined the circle and another took his place as a fiddler then joined the piper. The music was so spirited, the tempo so alive, even the fire burning in the hearth crackled as if joining in the revelry.

Grace had turned about and was making to weave her way back through the line of dancers when she felt a sudden pulling across her abdomen that caused her to falter. Her immediate thought was of the babe and she broke away from the chain of dancers, crossing the room to sit on a corner bench. The tightness in her belly soon subsided, but Grace decided it best that she sit out on the vigorous dancing. A moment later, Christian was kneeling beside her, his face filled with concern.

"Grace, is something wrong?"

She smiled and took his hand. "No, just a little too much dancing, I suspect." She looked at him. "Christian, there is something I must tell you. We are—"

"My lady!" Liza rushed over from the dancing to join her, Andrew coming with her. The maid pressed a hand against Grace's temple. "I noticed you falter. Are you unwell? Is it the babe?"

Christian looked at her. "Babe?"

"A babe?" Eleanor echoed, having somehow appeared beside her.

Suddenly there was an outburst of excited chatter as news of Grace's suspected pregnancy spread quickly around the room.

Grace looked to Christian. His expression had gone blank and he was staring at her queerly.

"Grace, do you mean to say you are with child?"

She could not truly sense if he was pleased by the news. He looked so stunned. She only knew that this was not at all how she had intended for him to learn of the coming of their child.

"Grace?"

Tentatively, Grace nodded. "Yes, Christian. You are to be a father."

The entire assembly seemed to erupt all at once with cheers and hollers of congratulations. Everyone filled their cups, passing toasts all around for the laird and lady's coming child.

Grace watched Christian closely as he accepted well wishes from those around him. He shook their hands and nodded his thanks, but there was something clearly missing. Everybody else was so taken with their enthusiasm, only she seemed to notice that the expectant father wasn't smiling.

When the merriment had fully resumed, taking everyone's attention back to the dancing, Christian turned without a word and started walking from the room. He disappeared into the corridor that led to the outside courtyard.

Grace glanced at Liza beside her. The maid looked close to tears.

"I am so sorry, my lady. When I saw you waver in the lines of dancers, I was so worried about you and the babe, I didn't even think that you hadn't yet told his lordship."

"It is all right, Liza." Grace squeezed the maid's hand and looked at Andrew, who took his cue, coming forward.

Grace stood. "I must go and talk to Christian."

As she started off in his direction, she tried to tell herself that he was not displeased about the babe, but that he was disappointed she had waited so long to tell him. All she would need to do, she thought, was explain her reasons.

Grace found Christian standing in the moonlight in the courtyard, one foot propped up against a rock, his hand resting on his knee. His back was to her as he stared in silent contemplation at the shadowed mountains to the east. If he heard her approach, he didn't acknowledge it. Grace hesitated, searching for her words.

"Christian, I was hoping we might talk."

As she came to his side, she could see in the moonlight that his jaw was clenched tightly, the muscles working as he fought so obviously against his emotions.

Finally he said, his voice frighteningly hollow, "How long have you known?"

"I first suspected the day you arrived at Skynegal."

"It has been many days, yet you said nothing to me."

He was angry that she had kept the news of the child from him. If only she could make him understand the fear and uncertainty she had felt. "Christian, I am sorry I did not tell you before. I—"

Christian turned to face her, his eyes so bleak, it frightened her. "It doesn't matter, Grace. It is too late."

"Too late? Christian, I don't understand . . ."

"Do you not see? He has won."

Christian laughed then, a terrible, bitter sound that carried on the shifting wind. "No matter how I tried, he has still found a way to outwit me."

Grace was only growing more confused. "Who, Christian? Who has won?"

"I would guess he speaks of me, Grace."

Christian turned his back on her to face the old duke who had come out onto the courtyard behind them. All the pain he had endured, the shame, the guilt that had kept him prisoner so long, surged through him in a burst of rage, forcing him to let go of the anger he had kept locked inside himself over the past twenty years.

He rounded on the duke. "You always knew you would conquer me, didn't you, you bastard? From the day I was born you hated me because I was more like him than you. You vowed to make my life a living hell and I handed you the very means for you to do it. And now you have succeeded. You have made my misery complete!"

Christian shut his eyes tightly against the unspeakable anguish that threatened to rip him in two. His hands were fisted and his jaw was so tight, his breath seethed from his nose. A moment, two. Then, from somewhere deep inside, a new and unfamiliar feeling of strength began to rise up inside of him. It swelled and it grew into a conscious defiance against all that had kept him chained to the past for so long. Like the lion who finally breaks free from his chains, Christian gathered that strength, embracing it to him. He could never again allow that man to beat him. He would no longer live as he had before, shackled by a foolish pledge he had made as a child. Not for himself—and not for his future child.

Christian lifted his gaze to the duke again. "You will not win, old man. I don't care what our agreement was. Do what you must, but I promise you now, I will see you in hell before I will every allow you to ruin my son the way you have ruined me."

Unable to stand the sight of his grandfather any longer, Christian turned, looking to draw Grace into his arms, to allow her into the heart he had kept shut away from her so long.

Only she was no longer there.

Chapter Thirty-three

Grace lay in the darkness of her bedchamber, curled brokenly at the edge of the bed with only the moonlight to hold her. Her window was opened slightly and she could hear the sounds of the loch breaking on the shore beneath the castle while the dancing went on in the great hall below. Laughter and merriment continued to abound. Once someone had called out, asking for the laird and his lady. When neither of them appeared, someone else suggested that they had perhaps retired abovestairs for a bit of merrymaking of their own. This had elicited a new round of toasts to the continuity of such a happy union.

It had also elicited a new bout of tears from Grace that even now dampened her pillow.

She felt the brush of a sudden chill against her legs and turned, realizing someone had just entered her room.

"I didn't mean to wake you."

It was Christian, his voice taut with discontent.

"I wasn't asleep."

She watched as he came into the room, approaching her tentatively. "Grace, I need to explain." His eyes were hooded in the moonlight. "There are things you know nothing about, things about me and my past—"

He fell silent, struggling with his words. Grace made to rise from the bed, but he held up a hand to stop her.

"Grace, do you know why I married you?" He answered before she could frame a response. "I married you because I had to, yes, because of an agreement I made with my grandfather. It was not for the reasons you may think. It had nothing to do with money or any of the other reasons. It was part of a debt I owed him made many years ago, a pact I made with the devil that he is."

He paused, gathering his thoughts. Grace simply waited, knowing there was more.

"Do you know how my father died?"

"Mrs. Stone said something to me the night we were at Westover about an illness."

Christian shook his head. "That is what my grand-father told everyone. It was a brilliant excuse. No one ever suspected the truth."

"The truth?"

"Grace, my father did not die because of any sickness, real or imagined. My father was killed defending the honor of my mother against the man he'd learned she had been having a clandestine liaison with." He stopped for a moment and when he spoke again, his voice was ragged with emotion. "The man whose child she likely carried."

The full meaning of his words reached her a moment later. "Eleanor?"

"Yes." He finally stood before her now. "To this day she does not know that we do not share the same father. After my father was killed, I promised my grandfather I would do anything he asked of me if he would never reveal the truth of her conception."

"But she is his granddaughter."

"No, Grace, to his thinking, she was not conceived of my father. Eleanor is simply the illegitimate daughter of my mother, who my grandfather never cared for because my father had chosen her to be his wife against his wishes. After my father was killed, my grandfather was ready to leave my mother penniless and banished from the family. She would have been ostracized by society and Eleanor would have been labeled a bastard. She would never have known the advantage of that same world that had created her."

"But what does that have to do with agreeing to wed me?"

"It was my grandfather's condition, a part of it. In return, he would guarantee his silence and allow my mother and Eleanor the protection and financial support of the Westover name. They were to live in London in a residence separate from my grandfather. He would provide Eleanor with a season and a dowry so that she might marry well. No one would ever know that Eleanor had not been conceived legitimately."

Grace's thoughts turned to Eleanor, and to how willing she had been at the Kinghton ball to accept Grace as her sister. How tragic it would have been had she been punished for the circumstances of her conception. "But what of Eleanor's true father? Wouldn't he have known the truth?"

Christian closed his eyes, his throat working with emotion against the demons that consumed him. Suddenly he was putting words to what had happened while Grace listened on in silence.

"He awoke me before dawn. I can still remember the light from my grandfather's candle stinging my eyes as he shook me from the warmth of my bed. He tossed me a pair of breeches and told me to come with him, that I was about to enter a man's world. I barely had enough time to pull on my coat before he was pulling from my chamber and dragging me along the dark hallways at Westover Hall. He said nothing more of what was happening, and I knew enough of my grandfather's temper to keep silent.

"My father was waiting at the bottom of the stairs, dressed all in black, looking scarcely at all like the man I had called father for nine years. He told my grandfather he shouldn't have brought me. I will never forget his eyes, fixed with a look I only later realized was insanity.

My grandfather refused to listen to him, saying something about how I would learn the lesson my father should have learned long ago. My father had simply shrugged, turning to walk outside. We followed, climbing into the carriage that already awaited on the drive. No one spoke during the short ride, not even when we stopped at a misty moor where my father had often taken me hunting. The sun was just barely starting to rise and I saw a horse there with a lone figure standing beside it. It was then I realized that my father was going to fight a duel.

"I stood watching as my grandfather and my father walked to meet the other man. A pistol box was presented and weapons chosen while my grandfather recited the rules of honor." Christian scoffed. "*Honor.* There is nothing at all honorable about two men agreeing to kill each other.

"The weapons were primed and checked and places were taken. Ten paces were measured out before each man then turned to face the other. In the beating of a heart, a single shot was fired. I saw my father drop into the tall grass. I saw the other man lower his arm to his side beneath the cloud of smoke from his pistol. I ran for my father, crying out when I saw the blood seeping from a wound in his chest. His eyes were already fixed in death and I heard the slow, rasping sound of his last breath leaving his body."

Grace reached for his hand, tears flooding her eyes. "Oh, Christian, I am so sorry."

He took a deep breath. "A short time later, the other man came forward to make sure he had killed my father. He even nudged him with the toe of his boot. I lost all awareness of myself. I remember taking up my father's gun. It was still cocked and primed. I stood and pulled back on the trigger. I discharged his shot. I heard a second shot fire. I watched the man who had killed my father fall to his knees. I looked and saw my grandfather then beside me, smoke rising from the pistol he held. Together, we had committed murder."

If Christian looked at Grace and expected to find disgust for what he had just revealed to her, he was mistaken. Instead tears of compassion were running down her cheeks. She stood from the bed and placed the palm of her hand against his face. Christian closed his eyes, fighting against his own emotions, and took her wrist and kissed it softly. His other hand he gently placed against her belly where even now his child grew.

He whispered against her hand. "No one ever knew the truth." He lifted his head and looked at her. "My grandfather paid the local physician to swear that my father had died of a sudden illness. He paid some men to dispose of the other man's body so that his family would never know what became of him. No one ever knew the truth. Except my grandfather. In order to prevent him from seeing through his threat to my mother and Eleanor, he made me promise my life to him. From that day on, my one sole purpose became that of procreating the next Westover heir. And when a son was born, it would be his."

"His?"

Christian's eyes stung with the tears he had refused to shed for so long. "Grace, he made me vow to give him my son. I thought I could prevent it by never marrying. But then he found you. I thought I could keep him from it by making it a marriage in name only. All I had to do was share your bed once, that night at Westover Hall. I had to take your virginity, but that didn't mean I had to sire a child. I thought I could do it, but my grandfather got the better of me. He had chosen well, because no matter how I tried, I could not resist you. Every time I came to you, I would lose my resolve. I couldn't control it, and I would hate myself afterward because I feared you would become pregnant. Do you understand now why I reacted the way I did at hearing that you carried our child? All I could think was that my grandfather had won, that no matter how I had vowed to myself that I would not give him an heir, in the end, I still had."

Grace touched her hand softly against the ties of his sark. "He will only win, Christian, if you allow him to. If *we* allow him to."

Christian swallowed back his emotions. "I know that now, Grace. It took facing him tonight to come to that realization. As I stood in the darkness of that courtyard, even as I hated him so deeply, all I could think about was all I had done to keep you from reaching me. From the very moment when you came tumbling into my life, you changed everything I had known. I wanted only to keep you from knowing the darkness of my world. I was too blinded by my hatred for my grandfather to see that by keeping you apart from me, I was only preserving that darkness. I should have welcomed you, but instead I hurt you. I blamed my grandfather for the misery I faced each day in the mirror when instead I should have realized that in forcing me to marry you, he had given me the greatest gift I could ever receive." He touched her softly on her cheek. "He gave me you."

Grace looked at Christian, her heartbeat racing.

"You make me a better man, Grace. You gave me your love when I gave nothing in return except anger and pain. I will forever regret having not realized it sooner."

She shook her head, placing her fingers against his lips. "Do not speak of it."

Christian covered her hand with his and kissed her fingertips softly, watching her. "I want to love you, Grace. I need to love you."

Grace blinked away her tears and said on a gentle whisper. "Then love me, Christian. Love me now."

Her words echoed through his consciousness like the whisper on the Scottish wind. Christian closed his eyes, lifting her up and burying his face against her neck. Gently he lowered her to the bed beneath him, her golden hair spilling about her shoulders in soft waves, inviting his fingers to thread through the silken tresses.

Christian took her face into his hands and lowered his mouth to kiss her, taking her tenderly against him. He felt her arms go around his waist, felt her hands run down over the length of him to his legs, her touch filling him with her willing warmth. He felt her fingers slide beneath the fabric of his kilt, running upward over the backs of his thighs. A jolt of desire rocked him as she cupped his buttocks in her hands and he moaned into her mouth, feeling the pressure of her softness against his sex. He felt the fire that had consumed him every time he'd come to her before ignite like wildfire and pulled his mouth away from hers, fighting to maintain his control.

He would not hurry this. They had all night. This time he would give Grace a woman's pleasure. He would show her lovemaking in its truest sense, without pain, without chaos. Tonight he would watch her as she found her release and he would know the reality of an earthly heaven.

Slowly Christian guided Grace back against the pillows, taking up the blouse she wore and helping her to slip it over her head. Her breasts were white in the moonlight and the sight of her nakedness set his heart to pounding, as he took in the perfect roundness of her breasts, the smoothness of her belly that would soon swell with his child. He unhitched the fastening of her skirt and slid the fabric down to her toes.

Christian stood at the side of the bed, just staring at Grace in the firelight, awestruck that she was his, that she would give him the gift of her love again after all that had taken place between them.

He didn't deserve her, but he thanked God for her.

Christian reached over his head, pulling off his shirt. He watched her eyes study his body in the moonlight and felt his sex harden in response as she fixed her eyes upon where it pushed at the fabric of his kilt. He released the buckle at his side and let the woolen fabric fall to his feet.

Grace reached for him, beckoning to him as he stood naked at the side of the bed. It was all the invitation Christian needed. He slid onto the mattress beside her, pulling her soft warmth against the length of him. He took her mouth again, tasting her with his tongue as he took the weight of her breast into his palm, feeling the softness of her skin, working his fingers over her nipple, teasing it to hardness as she murmured into his mouth.

He traced his fingers downward over her belly to the down froth of curls that marked her most passionate place. Lifting her slightly, he urged her legs gently apart. He touched her softly and felt the moistness of her slick against him.

Grace threaded her hands through the thickness of Christian's hair as he slowly rubbed his fingers over her, stroking her, seducing her at the very center of her desire. He felt her body tighten beneath his touch as she knew the beginnings of sexual pleasure. He released her mouth to kiss downward over her neck and shoulder to her breast. Grace arched against him as he suckled her, drawing in her breath and tightening her fingers in his hair as she lost herself to him.

"Oh, Christian, it is so . . ."

Christian nuzzled her belly, knowing what he would do to her, how he would make her body respond to bring her sensations she had only just known a hint of. He kissed her belly and nibbled at her hip as he slid further downward, parting her legs as he moved between them. He drew her hips upward then, gathering her against him, and lowered his head to taste her.

He felt Grace stir, uncertain at such an intimate caress, until her own untested sexual instincts overcame her hesitation and she eased beneath him. Christian worked his mouth over her, tasting her, teasing her with his tongue, tantalizing her as she drew close to her climax. He felt her legs tighten against his shoulders as she sought that which she had yet to find, heard the soft pleasured breaths she gave as each sensation rippled through her. He took her closer, again and again until she cried out and he felt her body shudder against him on the wave of her release.

Grace watched him with eyes that were filled with the wonder of new passion as Christian eased her hips to the bed. He slowly slid his body upward, the muscles in his belly clenching when he touched her with his hardness. He struggled to hold himself in check. He took two deep breaths and slowly, gently entered her, drawing in another slow breath as he buried himself within her. It was the most incredible feeling he'd ever experienced— the tightness of her around him, the joining of their bodies as one—and he drew her up against his chest as he sought to command his desire.

Perhaps it was an unconscious fear of harming the babe, or that he had exorcised the demon of his grandfather from his life, but when he began to move, Christian did so with total control over his body. Each movement of his hips carried him deeper and deeper inside her warmth. His movements began to quicken and he felt Grace lift her hips to meet his every thrust, her fingers gripping his forearms as he rose up over her, entering her deeply, fully, completely, over and over until he felt her take her second climax. He buried himself within her and his own release took him so strongly, so absolutely, that he shouted out words he had no recollection of immediately after, spilling his seed deep within her womb.

"Oh, God, Grace, I love you," he moaned against her neck as he rained gentle kisses over her, tasting the saltiness of her heated skin as they lay with their bodies still joined amid the confusion of bedclothes beneath them.

Some time later, after the fire had dimmed and the night slowly began to give way to the dawn, Christian drew Grace up to him with her back against his chest and her buttocks settled snugly against his hips. He set one hand against her belly where their child lay and brushed the soft tangle of her hair onto the pillow above her head. Clasping the fingers of her hand with his, he breathed in the sweet scent of her neck as together they drifted off to a lover's sleep.

Chapter Thirty-four

The next days were like living a dream for Grace and Christian as they thrilled in the rediscovery of one another. Their waking hours were filled with the warmth and laughter of a Skynegal summer, their nights wrapped in each other's arms, sharing tender kisses and ardent lovemaking.

Robert and Catroina had gone to Rosmorigh in the south, taking a number of the Highlanders with them. Robert had arranged for a sloop that would carry some of them farther south to Mallaig, others onto the islands of Mull and Jura and to a landing point where they could find land transport into Glasgow. Still more would continue to the Borders and to England, to live at the duke and duchess's estate, Devonbrook, in Lancashire.

Before they had gone, Christian and Robert had drawn up a proposal they planned to present at the next sitting of the House of Lords. Christian and Grace realized that presenting the proposal would necessitate that Christian return to England. He had decided, however, to wait until after their child was born.

Since Skynegal had become such an important part of their lives, they made plans for extending the castle with an additional wing to the eastern side. Grace began drawing up preliminary sketches that they would use as a guide while Christian set to making inquiries in Edinburgh for an architect. The mare Jo came into foal and Grace and Christian had watched as the tiny roan-colored newborn had stood for the first time on his spindly legs, taking his first uncertain steps amid a chorus of cheers from those looking on.

Every day at sunset, Grace and Christian would walk

along the shore of the loch with Dubhar ambling beside them, but Grace's most treasured time with her husband was late at night, after they had made love before the light of the fire. He would draw her body close to him, his arms wrapped protectively around her increasing belly. They would talk sometimes until the early hours of morning, about their childhood and about their hopes for the future—the future they would share together.

This morning Grace was seated in the estate office with Dubhar warming her toes beneath the desk. Christian sat across from her, checking the list of provisions for McFee and McGee, who were to leave for Ullapool later that morning.

Grace had just finished her morning cup of tea when she glanced up and saw Eleanor standing in the doorway.

"Oh, Eleanor, good morning," she said, "won't you come in?"

Eleanor's expression, Grace noticed, was unusually serious.

"I was hoping I might have a private word with my brother."

Grace glanced at Christian, who was watching Eleanor closely, then stood to leave. "Of course. I was just going to go through the last of the trunks we found from the garret."

Grace left the room, calling to Dubhar before closing the door quietly behind her.

High in the south tower there was a small chamber that looked out over the restless waters of the loch. Too small to be used as a bedchamber, Grace had begun using the place to organize some of the heirlooms she had discovered while foraging through the castle. As the collection had grown, the chamber had become a gallery of sorts in tribute to her ancestry, spanning nearly the full chronology of Skynegal's history.

Each of those ancestors had their own place where their particular contribution was displayed in a makeshift visual biography. There, near the door, was Hannah MacRath, a young bride who had come to Skynegal from the Lowlands in the days of Queen Mary. Her petite figure was preserved in the small embroidered shoes she'd once worn, with cork wedges placed into the heels to give her added height. Amazingly, Hannah had brought eleven children to adulthood and had lived to the age of ninety-three. Hannah's legacy to Skynegal was a small, leatherbound herbal journal and numerous small bottles in which the ladies of Skynegal had kept dried flowers and leaves to use as medicine.

Sir Roger MacRath's display was situated beneath the window. He had been a fourteenth-century poet whose lyrical verses were scribbled upon everything, from parchment to several window panes. A portrait of Sir Roger's only child, his daughter Mhairi, hung nearby, her thoughtful expression framed by a linen caul. Mhairi was one of Skynegal's most noteworthy residents, for she had made it her life's work to preserve the legend of the "winged" castle and its foundation in the myth of the goddess Cliodna. Some said it was Cliodna herself who had charged young Mhairi with the duty in a dream when she'd been only twelve. Whatever it had been, for the eighteen years afterward, Mhairi had passed every night weaving a tapestry from the finest threads of gold and silver into an image of the castle with the goddess Cliodna watching over from above while her servant birds soared around the castle towers.

According to the legend, on the night Mhairi had fixed the last thread, completing the tapestry, she had gone to her bed never to rise again. That same tapestry stitched by her dedicated hands now hung in a place of honor beside her portrait. It was alleged that as long as the tapestry was kept at the castle, the people of Skynegal would remain under the protection of the Celtic goddess and her mythical birds, safe against any threat of invasion, destitution, or plague. Indeed, thus far, the prediction had held true.

Up in the tower this morning, Grace set aside a small costumed fashion doll that had once been her grandmother's and peered inside the trunk to see what else was contained inside. A small book of sonnets with an embossed cover lay tucked away near the bottom. Grace took it up, reading the inscription inside.

For Grace of Skynegal, you shall forever be the only lady of my heart. Your Devoted Knight, Eli 1768.

Grace drew up, reading the inscription again. Eli? But her grandfather's name had been William. Surely this was her grandmother's book, for it had her name inscribed inside with the date that would put her near her sixteenth year.

As she turned to the first page, something slipped from inside the back cover. They were letters addressed to her grandmother at Skynegal, several of them, tied together with a ribbon. Grace unfolded the first of them, dated April of the same year inscribed in the book.

My love, I find myself counting the days until we might see each other again. I long for the slightest glance from your eyes, the softest touch of your hand. I am sending this book in the hopes that someday I might hear your sweet voice reading from it to me. I am lost without you . . . Your Adoring Knight, Eli.

The next letter, dated six months later, seemed to indicate that some sort of response had been sent from her grandmother. The script of this letter was decidedly more formal in tone.

I will not, it seems, be able to travel to the Highlands as I had planned. Family matters have developed which will require my presence in London. It is, unfortunately, beyond my control. Know I am thinking of you and hoping your are well. I will count the days until I can see you again. Devoted and Frustrated Knight, E.

The next letter was dated early the following year. The handwriting, while still that of the previous author, was less elegant, more of a scrawl.

It is with great regret and a heavy heart that I must inform you of my inability to continue our relationship. Circumstances have arisen that prevent my pursuing anything more than an acquaintanceship with

*you. My happiest days will always have been during
our time together for despite the duties I must assume, my heart will forever remain yours alone.
Your Knight, Now and Always, E.*

When she reached the final letter in the stack, Grace
saw that it was not a letter after all, but a page from a
London news sheet. It was dated April of 1769. She
scanned past the events of that year, noticing nothing of
significance until she reached the very bottom of the
column where an announcement had been printed.

> *It is hereby announced that on Saturday last, the
> 2nd day of April at St. Paul's, the heir to the Duke
> of Westover, Elias Wycliffe, Marquess Knighton, did
> wed Lady Lydia Fairchild, eldest daughter to the
> Marquess of Noakes.*

Grace looked again at the inscription in the book and
the name written there.

Eli.

The truth came suddenly clear. Through all the years
Nonny had spoken of her "one true knight," Grace had
always believed him to have been her grandfather. But
it had been Christian's grandfather, the duke, all along.

So many things made sense to her then—the duke's
lifelong bitterness, his preoccupation that first day in her
uncle's study with her grandmother's portrait. Had they
planned to marry? Had his family prevented it?

Grace struggled to her feet, taking up the book of
sonnets and the letters as she hurried off to find Christian. She wanted him to know the truth about his grandfather so that perhaps he might find some way to
better understand.

As she skipped down the tower steps, Grace nearly
collided with someone climbing up in the opposite direction.

"Oh, goodness—Eleanor."

Eleanor's eyes were red from crying, her cheeks
stained from her tears. The moment she saw Grace, she
collapsed against her, sobbing into her shoulder.

"What is it, Eleanor? What has happened?"

It took her several moments to respond. "Oh, Grace, it is Christian. He has forbidden me to wed Lord Herrick. He refused to listen to reason."

Grace tried desperately to calm her, patting her gently on the shoulder as Eleanor leaned against her. "What do you mean? Lord Herrick has asked you to marry him?"

Eleanor nodded. "Before we left London, he indicated he had something of importance to discuss with me. I received a letter from him just this morning formally proposing marriage. I took it to Christian, but he has refused to give his consent. And Mother has said she will not oppose his decision. I knew Christian and my mother had held some reluctance toward Lord Herrick, but I thought with his proposal, they would see that his intentions are only honorable. No, there is some other reason for their refusal. The worst of it is, Christian won't even tell me why. I know I have not known Lord Herrick long, but I can only think that were we to have more time together, my regard for him would only grow. Christian had promised me, Grace, that I would be given my choice to marry freely. Why would he do this to me now when I have already made my choice? Why?"

Grace shook her head, clasping Eleanor's hands in hers. She looked at her closely. "I don't know, but if you would like, I will see if I can talk to Christian."

Eleanor sniffed into her handkerchief. "Would you?"

"I will go to him right now."

A small smile broke across Eleanor's teary face. "Thank you, Grace. Perhaps he will listen to you."

Grace squeezed Eleanor's hands reassuringly. "You go to your chamber now and lie down. I will come to you there after I have spoken with Christian."

Lady Frances was just leaving as Grace approached the door to the office. The dowager marchioness looked to have been crying as well, but she smiled softly to Grace before continuing out of the room.

Inside, Christian sat alone.

Grace closed the door behind her. Christian looked up at her, his expression stricken and pained. It was killing him to make Eleanor so unhappy. Surely he must have a reason for his refusal. Perhaps Herrick was a blackguard and Christian was simply trying to spare his sister the heartache. Whatever his reasons, Grace decided not to come at Christian about Eleanor immediately, but instead approached the subject from a different perspective.

"I found something in the garret that I thought you should see."

She placed the book of sonnets and the letters she had found on the desk in front of him. She watched as he took them up and read through them, allowing him time to come to the same conclusions she had.

When he was finished, he looked at her. "Where did you find these?"

"They were in a trunk with some of my grandmother's things. I think she might have left them for me to find one day." She paused. "It is your grandfather's handwriting, is it not?"

Christian nodded. His expression was troubled as his lifelong opinions about his grandfather were suddenly challenged.

"Perhaps now you can understand some of the reasons for his bitterness."

"Perhaps. But what I fail to understand is why—if he was made to marry someone other than your grandmother, whom he clearly loved—would he then repeat that by arranging a marriage for me?"

Grace came to stand beside his chair, resting her hand on his shoulder. "I wondered that same thing. Perhaps, in his way, he was seeking to right the wrong he had done my grandmother in abandoning her by bringing us two together."

"Perhaps." Christian was still staring at the letters, no doubt thinking about the man—so different than the grandfather he had known all his life—who had written them so long ago.

Grace knelt before Christian. "Christian, can I ask why you have refused to consent to a marriage between Eleanor and Lord Herrick?"

Christian's expression grew clouded. Grace carefully pressed on. "I know you love her very much and would never do anything to hurt her. Is there something more? Something about Lord Herrick you are not telling me? Is he a blackguard?"

Christian sat forward in his chair, raking his fingers through his hair as he rested his elbows on his knees. He was extremely troubled, more so than Grace should have thought.

Finally he looked at her. "Do you remember when I told you about my father's death?"

She nodded.

"I told you how my father had fought a duel against a man whom my mother had pursued a relationship with. Grace, the reason I cannot give my consent for Eleanor to wed Lord Herrick is because he is the son of the man who killed my father. He is the eldest and *legitimate* son of the man my mother had a liaison with."

It only took Grace a moment longer to realize the import of what he was saying. "Good God, Lord Herrick is Eleanor's half-brother."

Christian nodded, closing his eyes. "So now you see why she cannot marry him. The worst part of it is I must tell her my reasons. I must tell Eleanor of her illegitimacy and the circumstances of her birth. If I don't, she might decide to run off and wed him without my consent. My mother already suspects as much, so she has asked me to tell Eleanor everything. There is no other choice. I will have to tell my sister that I killed the man who was her true father."

"You did not kill anyone."

Neither Grace nor Christian had heard the duke come into the room.

"I should have told you the truth long ago, Christian. I don't know why I didn't. I was so broken after Christopher's death. I wanted you to hate your mother, blame her as I did. It took me twenty years to realize it wasn't her fault. Your father knew Frances didn't love him when he asked her to marry him. Her family was in financial straits. They needed her to marry well. Christopher convinced her that she would grow to love him one day; he thought he could love enough for both of them." He shook his head. "He only smothered her."

Christian looked at the duke. "But what does that have to do with the fact that I shot Lord Herrick's father?"

"Your shot went wide that morning, Christian. I saw it strike the tree behind. It was my shot that killed him."

Christian's eyes narrowed on the duke with loathing. "You allowed me to believe all these years that I had killed him. You are a bastard."

"I will not deny that, Christian. My biggest regret is that it took me twenty years to tell you the truth. I can't expect that you would understand. I was an angry, bitter man. Losing Grace's grandmother was the biggest mistake of my life. Then I lost Christopher, and with him any chance to really know him. We had spent so long fighting each other over his marriage to your mother. I never found the time to tell him that I loved him. *One can never know what it is to lose something precious until it is gone.*"

"You . . ." Christian suddenly said, stunned. "You left that message at the door, didn't you?"

The duke nodded.

"I thought it was Herrick, that he knew that I had killed his father. In fact, I was convinced he was courting Eleanor in an effort to exact some sort of revenge."

The duke shook his head. "No, that message had nothing to do with Herrick or his father. I was trying to tell you not to throw away the chance you had for happiness. I have made many mistakes in my life and I am ashamed of most everything I am. I am stubborn and proud and arrogant. I am also a fool. But there is one thing I am not ashamed of, the one thing I did right in life—bringing you and Grace together."

Chapter Thirty-five

By the time the following morning dawned, Eleanor was gone.

She had slipped away some time during the night, going unnoticed by her maid or anyone else in the great hall. She had taken a small bag with some of her things and Christian's horse, leaving him with only the slower Highland ponies to go after her.

"I should have suspected she would do this," Christian said as he stalked about the stables, saddling the largest of the ponies, a bright bay named Torquil who was just under fifteen hands. "She has several hours lead on me. She could be halfway to Edinburgh by now. I will never catch up to her on this nag."

Torquil quirked his ears at the insult. Grace tried to give Christian hope. "These are the Highlands, not the grasslands of England. Torquil has a surer foot than Eleanor's mount on this terrain and you are more familiar with the landscape than she."

Christian barely heard her as he slammed a fist against the stall post, causing the ponies to jerk up their heads and nicker in alarm. "Damnation! I should have known this would happen. She was too quiet last night when I talked to her, too accepting of the circumstances of her birth."

"You don't think she has gone to Herrick, do you?"

"No. I destroyed any thought she had of that last night when I told her the truth about my father's death. Good God, what have I done? I took away her identity. I blithely informed her she is not the person she believed she was all her life. Why did I leave her alone last night? Why didn't I have my mother stay with her?"

Grace touched him gently on the arm. "You could have no way of knowing she would run."

"I should have realized it, Grace. I told her she is for all intents and purposes a bastard and she never so much as shed a single tear. She just looked at me as if to say I was the one who was supposed to have protected her from all this. I've failed her."

"No, Christian, you did not fail her. You gave her a life and respectability she would never have otherwise known. If not for you she would have suffered the judgment of society."

Christian stood a moment at the stable door, staring out at the hills in the distance. He turned to Grace, taking her by the arms. "I have to try to find her, Grace. If something happens to her, I will never forgive myself."

Grace wished she could do something to ease the burden of guilt that was so obviously consuming him inside. "I know, Christian. And you will find her."

Less than an hour later, Grace stood in the courtyard with Frances, Deirdre, Liza, and the duke watching as Christian hoisted himself into the saddle.

The duke went before him. "Whatever it takes, Christian, we will find her. I've already sent off to Bow Street."

Christian added, "I'll be back as soon as I can."

Grace reached up to him, giving him a farewell kiss. "We will postpone the céilidh until your return with her."

Christian spurred the pony around and headed off at a canter across the courtyard. How long would he be gone? A day? A week? Would he search the ends of the earth until he found her? Grace did not look away until he had vanished into the morning mist. In the moment he was gone, she was seized by a feeling of utter emptiness. Already she wished him back.

Liza must have sensed her despondency because she came to Grace and set her arm around her shoulder. "Don't you fret a bit, my lady. The laird will be back with Lady Eleanor very soon. You'll see. All will be well."

Grace looked at her, this woman who was more friend than maid, and smiled with a flagging optimism. "I truly hope so, Liza."

As they turned to head back inside the castle, Grace noticed Liza staring across the courtyard to where Andrew MacAlister was chopping wood, bare-chested with only his Skynegal kilt to cover him. His sinewy arms flexed and moved as he lifted the axe high above his head, pulling it down to split the helpless log cleanly in half. Andrew caught the maid's stare and gave her a grin that could have melted the mist off the mountains.

"I believe I may have to forbid Andrew from working out in the open like that. Either that or you'll have to start mending my stockings out here!"

Liza blushed at having been caught so obviously appreciating the Highlander's physical charms. Grace smiled. "Perhaps you should see if Andrew would like some cold ale. He looks as if he could use some."

Liza started off across the courtyard and Grace watched as they chatted together. The attraction between the stalwart Highlander and the maid had blossomed into a sweet romance. Andrew brought out a femininity in Liza that she had previously kept hidden behind talk of planting "facers." Liza softened the loneliness Andrew had had to confront after his family had emigrated to America. Most in the castle thought it only a matter of time before the two were wed. Given the fact that Liza had recently posted a letter to her mother asking for "bridal night" advice, Grace would think a proposal very near indeed. As she turned, she saw Alastair strolling past holding a bunch of wildflowers as he whistled a happy tune. Grace wondered whether he and Flora just might manage to see to the task of getting wed before the other two.

The sound of her name pulled Grace from her thoughts and she turned to see the young stable lad Micheil running across the courtyard toward her.

"What is it, Micheil?"

"Did you forget we were to go a'gatherin' today? I've got the pony cart a'ready."

In all the turmoil surrounding Eleanor's disappearance that morning, Grace had forgotten that she had promised to take Micheil with her to the other side of the glen to gather some of the herbs and various other plants she had read about in Hannah MacRath's herbal. He

was just learning how to direct the ponies at the cart
and was anxious to show her his skill. Perhaps it would
offer a welcome diversion from worrying about Christian
and Eleanor.

"Let me change and fetch a shawl and some food to
bring along with us and we shall go."

A half hour later, Grace set the last of the supplies
onto the pony cart before turning to speak to Deirdre
behind her. Since they would likely be digging about on
the forest floor, Grace had dressed more plainly than
usual in gray serge skirts and a linen smock, her hair
twisted up beneath a kerchief covering. Grace smiled in
an effort to mollify Deirdre's uneasy expression. Since
learning of the babe, Deirdre had become more protective of her, growing uneasy whenever Grace wandered
out of sight.

"Do not worry, Deirdre, we will be back by dusk. I
will have Liza and Micheil with me. The grove Hannah
wrote about in her journal is but two miles to the east.
We will simply go and see if any of the plant life from
Hannah's garden still flourishes there."

Micheil clambered up to the driver's seat on the small
pony wagon while Grace and Liza, with Dubhar between
them, settled into the back with the supplies. A crack of
the whip and a "Get on now," and they were rolling
slowly out of the courtyard onto the worn cart path that
traversed the estate to the east.

The three chatted freely as they teetered along the
rutted path. Grace enjoyed the serenity of the summer's
day, the sun shining on her cheeks, and the song of the
crossbills flitting about the pines. As Micheil teased Liza
about her romance with Andrew, Grace's thoughts
turned to Christian. She wondered whether he had
found Eleanor already, if they might at that same moment be riding back across the braes to Skynegal. She
sent a silent kiss his way, imagining the touch of his lips
in return while counting the hours until he would come
back to her.

They had just come over a crest on the cart path when
Micheil unexpectedly pulled the ponies to a halt.

"Micheil, what is it?" Grace turned to look ahead of
the cart at what had caused them to stop. A figure was

racing toward them on the cart path, waving its arms
frantically and calling out to them in Gaelic, *"Cuidich
le! Cuidich le!* Help! Help!"

They climbed down to meet what proved to be a
young boy of perhaps ten years of age. As he neared,
Grace could see that his face was nearly black from dirt
and soot, his feet bare, his body naked except for a ragged shirt that only covered him from shoulder to mid-
thigh. When he reached them, his eyes had a wild light
to them, quite like a caged animal and he was babbling
in Gaelic, shaking his head and swinging his arms.

Micheil spoke to him. *"Dè tha ceàrr?* What is the
matter?"

The boy spoke too frantically for Grace to understand
more than the random word. When she recognized
"fire" and "soldiers" and "Starke" among them, she realized he was speaking of the evictions that were taking
place on the Sunterglen estate.

Micheil quickly answered him, his tone calm. He
pointed to Grace as he said *"Aingeal na Gáidhealthachd.*
Angel of the Highlands."

The boy's eyes went white against the grime that covered his skin. He fell against her, wrapping his arms
around her skirts as he thanked the heavens for bringing
him to her.

"He says the soldiers are marching on the part of the
Sunterglen estate that borders Skynegal. There is an old
widow, his *grannam,* who lives alone and cannot walk
because her legs are too frail. His family are all away
taking their cattle to the hills and he cannot move her
on his own. He fears the soldiers will burn her alive."

Grace stiffened against an all too familiar shiver.
"Then we must go and stop them."

"But my lady," Liza broke in, "that is Sunterglen
land."

"What they are threatening is murder, Liza. We can't
just stand by and allow them to kill an innocent person."
She turned to Micheil. "Can you ask the boy to lead us
while you drive?"

"Aye, my lady, I will."

The pony cart jostled over the rutted glen floor as
they headed for the cottage where the widow lived. By

the time they reached the small croft, two soldiers were already setting their torches to the thatch on the roof. Another stood at the door, pounding upon it and hollering, "We've put the light to the thatch, woman. 'Tis the last time I'll tell ye. Ye'd best get yerself out from there!"

Grace scurried down from the pony cart and ran for the cottage. The soldier at the door glanced at her, his lip curling in disdain. "What d'ye want 'ere, *hizzie*?"

In her coarse clothing, Grace realized he thought her one of the Highlanders. "What in God's name are you doing? There is a woman inside!"

He looked momentarily surprised by her well-spoken English, but quickly changed his expression to one of contempt. "I be the captain of this company and we've come to clear this croft. She was issued a Writ of Removal and has refused to vacate."

He shoved a crumpled sheet of parchment at her. Grace took it, giving it glance. "It is written in English! These people can only speak Gaelic! She doesn't understand why you are here!"

" 'Tis what they get for bein' uncivilized idlers like they are. That old Scots witch has lived long enough. Let 'er burn."

Grace glared at the man in a moment of disbelieving rage before she took both hands up and shoved him hard, knocking him off his feet to the ground. As his company of soldiers stood watching and laughing, Grace flung the door to the cottage wide. Before she could scramble in to look for the widow, she felt herself being seized from behind, locked in the captain's grip.

"Get you gone, you Scots bitch, afore I lock you in to burn along wit' her."

Grace struggled against him, trying to free herself. Dubhar began barking furiously and lunged from the cart. In the next second, he was knocked cold by the butt of one of the other soldiers' muskets. The flames had already spread across to the middle of the roof, licking at the vulnerable thatch as a column of black smoke burgeoned overhead.

Liza scurried up, calling to Micheil to go for her basket in the cart while she pulled at the captain's arms.

"See here, you bloody bastard, free her now! You've no right to hold her!"

The captain let go of one of Grace's arms as he lashed outward, shoving Liza back. In that second, Grace balled both hands together before her and jerked her elbow back, striking the captain hard in his fleshy middle. She could hear the sound of his breath rushing from his mouth and yanked herself free from his hold. She turned just as the man was gaining his feet, drew back her fist just like Liza had taught her, and planted him a facer that knocked him flat on his back in the dust.

One of the other soldiers lunged forward, halting a moment later when Liza took the basket from Micheil and quickly removed a pistol from inside.

"Liza! Where did you get that?"

"Deirdre pressed it upon me afore we left today. I think she might have had a premonition that we could meet with trouble."

Liza trained the pistol's barrel on one of the soldiers who looked to be advancing. "Neither of ye move else ye'll know the wrath of the laird of Skynegal whose wife you have just affronted!"

The soldier hesitated, weighing her words. He turned to his companion, "Hoy, Owen, I'm for leaving'!"

Owen merely said "Aye," and the two of them turned and trotted off for the hills.

The fire was now blazing, tossing bits of burning thatch all about them as the wind suddenly picked up. The air was thick with the smell of the fire. "Liza, come, help me find the widow!"

Inside, the cottage was filled with a heavy veil of smoke that immediately stung their eyes to tears. Grace coughed against the burning it brought to her throat and quickly tugged the kerchief from her hair, placing it over her mouth and nose so that she might breathe easier. She urged Liza to do the same and together they searched, stumbling over the furnishings inside the darkness of the cottage.

"Micheil!" Grace called to the outside, "ask the boy where his grannam is! I cannot find her!"

The two boys came into the cottage then, snaking

through the smoke, flitting toward the back of the dwelling.

"Micheil, no!"

"It is all right, my lady. She is here!"

Grace and Liza shuffled their way toward where Micheil had called to them. In the shadowed corner, they found a crude box bed. Inside lay the figure of a woman too weak to utter more than a struggling cry.

"Liza, help me to carry her outside!" Grace reached under the widow's frail shoulders, speaking very softly to her in Gaelic, assuring her that they were there to help her. The widow moaned when they lifted her from the bed and slowly, carefully, they carried her from the cottage as burning chunks of thatch rained down upon them from overhead.

They bore her across the yard to the pony cart where Micheil took up a blanket and spread it upon the ground for her to lie upon. Grace turned and started to retrace their steps, hoping to save some of the widow's belongings from the fire, but within seconds, the roof had collapsed inside the cottage. She was left to stand, unable to do anything more than watch as the flames roiled out of control, the smoke billowing angrily across the horizon.

"The captain!" Micheil shouted. "He is gone!"

Grace turned from the burning cottage. "Let us get the widow and her grandson into the cart and leave before the soldiers return. We will bring them back to Skynegal with us."

A small pallet was quickly prepared for the widow, made of soft sedge grass and bracken strewn under the blanket in the back of the cart.

"Come, Liza, help me lift her."

But as Grace stooped to take the woman under her shoulders, she felt a sudden rush of liquid warmth between her legs. Her focus blurred and she stumbled back against the pony cart before falling to the ground. She lay there as the darkness closed in, the voices around her fast growing dim.

"My lady!"

"Has she fainted?"

"Oh my God, there is blood!"

"The babe . . ."

Chapter Thirty-six

F *lowers.*

Grace sat in an open field that was filled with flowers—aspodel and primrose of every imaginable hue, brilliant red and orange, pale yellow and pink. The colors were more vivid than she could ever imagine. The wind was blowing in off the loch, whispering through the tall grass that grew along the embankment. The sun was shining. Cliodna's birds in the tower were calling and soaring. Somewhere, everywhere she heard laughter, children, happiness. She stood and the hem of her tartan gown ruffled in the breeze. She laughed. Away in the distance she searched for Christian. He was to return to her today . . .

A shadow fell suddenly across the sun, darkening the sky and blotting out its light from overhead. The wind quickened, pulling at the fragile blossoms around her ankles, hissing snakelike through the grass. The laughter she heard no longer sounded childlike, but instead was wicked and ugly. She frowned at the sudden and unwelcome change and called to the sun to return, but it did not heed her. Instead the wind blew faster and she turned at the sound of someone approaching behind her, smiling for she knew it was Christian. He had come for her, to chase away the clouds, and she put her hand back for him, reaching . . .

A terrible force struck her, throwing her forward. She fell into the flowers, but they were no longer primroses, instead barbed thorns that bit into her hands. She struggled to regain her feet and a blackness came for her, billowing like smoky fingers reaching out to take her. She could not lift her hands to push them away. She could only watch as the darkness drew nearer and nearer . . .

A glimmer then that shone for but a moment's time in the terrible darkness. It sparkled like a guardian star in the midnight sky, a symbol of hope . . . but then the smoky fingers took hold of it, pulling it away. The laughter grew, louder, more frightening, echoing now, thundering above her, threatening her . . . suddenly, softly through the roar, she heard him. He was calling for her. It was her knight and he had come back to save her, just as she had always known he would . . .

"Grace?"

Slowly her eyes flickered open. She stared a moment, waiting for her vision to focus, trying to decide where she was. The field and the flowers were no longer there. Gone was the laughter and singing. Instead she was in her chamber at Skynegal, lying on her bed. Daylight broke inside the windows, casting tiny halos of light about the room, giving it an ethereal air. It was very quiet, not even the sound of the birds outside. Odd, she thought fleetingly, why have Cliodna's birds gone silent?

"Grace, can you hear me?"

She turned her head, wincing when it felt weighted somehow. Christian was there, just as she had known in her dream, but he wasn't her brilliant shining knight. His eyes were shot with red and shadowed underneath. His face was darkened with the beginnings of a beard, his hair mussed about his head. He looked as if he hadn't slept in days.

Grace lifted her hand and touched it to his roughened cheek as she smiled softly to him. The dream, the darkness, none of it mattered. Christian was there with her now. Everything would be safe and good.

"You came back," she whispered to him, wondering why her voice sounded so foreign to her ears.

His brow furrowed and the muscle in his jaw worked as if he were fighting hard against some unknown emotion. He did not smile. He did not speak. Instead his eyes were darkened with torment.

"Christian, what is it? What is wrong. Has something happened? Did you find Eleanor?"

Christian shook his head and clasped her hand, bringing it to his lips and kissing it as he closed his eyes. A single tear fell down his cheek. "She has not been found."

"You are so troubled. But it is not Eleanor, is it? What is wrong?"

Grace thought for a moment. *Remember* . . .

A boy. A wagon bumping along a cart path. She recalled a fire, Liza shouting with fear, the soldier's wicked laughter. "The widow," she said softly. Tears stung at the back of her eyes.

"The soldiers responsible for the fire have been arrested and charged, under direct order of Lord and Lady Sunterglen, who have just returned from London and profess to have known nothing of the tactics of their factor, Mr. Starke. I have their every assurance that the people involved, including Mr. Starke, will be made an example of."

She looked to Christian. "What of Micheil? Liza? The others?"

"They are well. Liza was a bit shaken by it all, but she was unharmed. The widow is convalescing and her family has arrived to be with her. Micheil is very worried about you."

In that same second, Dubhar came to rest his muzzle on the edge of the bed.

Grace smiled. She closed her eyes a moment, collecting her strength. She was so very tired. She looked to Christian again. An image then, a memory of falling to the ground, weakness, a hot and sticky wetness against her legs. There had been a pain deep in her belly and blood, very red, so much blood . . .

Grace felt her breath leave her as the mental images grew clearer. Tears fell over her cheeks and her throat tightened convulsively against the words she feared speaking but could not ignore. "Christian . . . what of the babe?"

Christian bit down on his lip, his eyes filling as he squeezed her hand tightly in his.

Grace swallowed. Why wasn't he answering her? Why wasn't he assuring her the babe was well? "Christian, please . . . tell me the babe is unharmed."

Christian stared into her eyes and silently shook his head, his expression utterly hopeless. "You lost the babe, Grace. There was nothing anyone could do."

Oh, God, no . . .

Grace shook her head against his words, wailing out against a pulling in her chest that she knew had to be the rending of her heart. *No, please, no, not the babe . . . please let him be wrong . . .*

"It cannot be . . . no . . . no . . ."

Christian drew Grace up brokenly against him, muffling her anguished cries against his shoulder as she confronted the terrible reality of his words. He held her there tightly, taking her sobs into himself, until finally his fragile resistance gave way and he lost himself to his own weeping.

Christian stood just inside the doorway leading out to the castle courtyard, watching where Grace sat alone amid the lengthening twilight shadows. He frowned. It had been three weeks since she had lost the babe, three weeks of watching her sit at that same spot, staring off at nobody-knew-what while the rest of the world went on living around her.

She had grown markedly thin, eating barely enough to sustain her each day. She no longer saw to or even cared about the happenings of the estate. She had abandoned all society, shunning the company of others, keeping to her bedchamber by day, only emerging at this time of the night when everyone else was off eating their supper and preparing for bed.

It was just that morning that Christian had come to the very real conclusion that slowly, deliberately, she was killing herself. And he wasn't about to stand by and watch her do it.

Christian stepped out onto the courtyard, watching for Grace to notice his approach while knowing she would not. It was the same every night. He would come and sit beside her. He would talk to her, tell her of the events of the day, read to her the letters she had received from the Highlanders who had emigrated to America, until the moon rose high in the evening sky. She never responded. She never gave the slightest indication she had heard him. She just sat on that rock bench, staring off at the nothingness, willing herself to die.

"Good evening, Grace," he said as he lowered onto the bench beside her.

She blinked, but it was all the response she gave him.

Christian removed a letter he had received earlier that day from his coat pocket, unfolding it. "I thought you might be interested to know we have received a letter from Eleanor." He glanced at her. Nothing. "She sold my horse so that she would have some money. She wanted me to know she does not blame me for telling her the truth. In fact, she thanks me for it. She writes only that we should not come looking for her, that she has gone to a place where we will never find her. She doesn't know when she is coming back or if she ever will."

Christian made to hand Eleanor's letter to Grace as if to allow her to read it. She did not move to take it, but continued to stare vacantly forward. He quietly refolded the page, placing it back in his coat pocket. When he next glanced at Grace, he was startled to see that she no longer stared at the nothingness of the night. She was staring at him. Even though her eyes were dark and lifeless, it was a change.

"Grace?"

"Why do you do this?" Her voice was sharp, not at all her own. "Why do you come here night after night and tell me all these things?"

He stared at her, uncertain how he should respond. "I come to remind you that there is still a world around you, Grace, a world that keeps moving on from day to night to day again. I come because there is still life."

Grace stood without making a response and started walking away from him, arms crossed tightly over herself, dismissing him for the safety of her indifference and self-pity.

Suddenly the despair he had felt over his inability to do anything for her, for Eleanor, overtook him. Christian stood and crossed the courtyard after her, taking her by the arm and forcing her around to face him.

"Let me go, Christian!"

"You are going to listen to me for once instead of blindly ignoring my existence! I have sat by and watched you deliberately destroy yourself over this as if you were the only one to have lost that child. I lost a child, too, Grace, and I feel the pain of it every bit as terribly as you do. Sometimes I feel it even worse because I have to live with the guilt that I feel, knowing if I had been here with you instead of running off to repair the mistakes of my family's past, my child would yet be growing inside of you."

Christian paused a moment to rein in his raging emotions. When he spoke again, his voice was markedly calmer. "I am your husband, Grace. It is my duty to protect you and our children. But I failed in that duty, just as I failed Eleanor. If you want to blame anyone for the pain you are feeling right now, if you want to blame anyone for taking our child away, then blame me. I did this, Grace. Not you. Take that hatred you have for yourself and direct it on me. But for God's sake, stop torturing yourself!"

Grace simply stared through him.

Defeated, Christian released her and turned, heading for the castle, unable to stand the suffering any longer. As he approached the door, he saw Deirdre watching him. He didn't speak to her, just shot her a look as he strode past.

"What you did was good," she said, bringing him up short at the door. "You have brought her to thinking again."

Christian took in a slow and deep breath. "What good will it do, Deirdre?"

Deirdre smiled at him, taking his arm and walking with him inside the castle. "Wait and see, my lord. Wait and see."

Two mornings later, Grace sat at her bedchamber window, wondering why there wasn't anyone in the courtyard below. At this hour, the estate was normally bustling with people seeing to the day's tasks, yet not a single person appeared. Everywhere she looked—the stables, even the fields—all was deserted. Where had everybody gone?

She stood and walked across the room to the door, opening it slightly to peek onto the hallway outside. It was Wednesday, when they always would strip the bed linens for washing and take up the carpets for beating, yet neither Flora nor Deirdre were anywhere in sight. Neither was Liza, she suddenly realized. She hadn't come with Grace's morning tea and oatcake for breakfast.

A niggling of uneasiness began to prick at her inside and Grace slipped silently into the hallway, walking slowly to the stairs. She listened a moment below. Silence. No muffled voices, no clatter from the kitchen. Nothing. She went halfway down the steps and still she could hear nothing but the silence.

When she reached the bottom step, Grace looked on to the vast emptiness of the great hall and knew something had to be terribly wrong. How could dozens of people suddenly vanish without her having noticed? It was almost as if she were walking in a dream.

As she headed down the stair for the service rooms, she thought she heard a sound, a faint keen that seemed to have come from the direction of the kitchen. She looked to the doorway and again heard the sound, slightly louder. Concerned now, she started toward it, entering a room that was normally warm and welcoming and filled with the smells of baking, where a basket of oatcakes was always waiting on the center table, where a kettle for tea could always be found on the fire. But there was no teakettle, no fire in the hearth. Every dish and cup had been tucked away in its cupboard.

Another keen, and Grace turned to where the cradle stood at its place beside the hearth. She felt a tightness seize her deep inside her chest, felt her knees tremble slightly. Cautiously she approached, looking inside to where little Iain MacLean lay on his back, his tiny legs kicking as he stretched and worked his growing limbs.

When he realized she was there, he let out a wail.

Grace looked around the kitchen, wondering why he had been left unattended. "Deirdre?" she called but received no response. What if he were hungry, she thought. What if he needed a changing?

Grace left the kitchen and walked out into the courtyard, searching for someone, anyone, to tell her what had happened. Inside the kitchen, Iain's cries grew louder.

"Deirdre!" she called out. "Seonag!"

No one came in response to her summons. Behind her, Iain had begun to scream.

"Is anyone here?" she called, shouting up to the castle

towers, but again no response. Her heart was pounding inside her chest as she began to truly fear something terrible had happened. Realizing that no one was coming, Grace quickly retraced her steps to the kitchen. Iain had worked himself into a wailing fury, his tiny face now a bright red. Grace knew a moment of panic—she hadn't the faintest idea what she should do. She had such little experience with babies. She quickly grew frightened.

"Deirdre, please " Her voice cracked with her fear. "Where are you? I need your help in here. Please!"

She leaned over the cradle, hoping to quiet the infant's cries. "Shhh, everything is all right, Iain. I'm sure your momma or Aunt Deirdre will be back very soon."

Please let them come back very soon.

But Iain only cried all the louder, and soon was hiccuping harshly on his screams.

In a full panic now, Grace did the only thing she could think of. She reached inside the cradle and took the infant up to her. The moment he felt the warmth of her body, Iain quieted. Slowly Grace began to rock him in her arms the way she had seen Seonag do so many times.

By the time Christian returned, Grace had come to realize exactly what he had done. In the weeks since losing their child, Grace had found herself unwilling to look on the face of a child without feeling a sickness in her stomach. If she'd ever had to walk near Iain's cradle, she would take another direction so as to avoid going near him. She purposely avoided the nursery that had been set up off the great hall, choosing instead to take the south stairs to her bedchamber.

And because of this, Christian had arranged for her to be left alone with Iain, knowing she would be forced to put aside her hopelessness to tend to him.

Grace wasn't angry at what he had done and she told him so when he came slowly into the kitchen where she had just placed the sleeping Iain in his cradle.

When she saw him, saw the anxiety on his face, she could only admonish herself for how she had treated him. "I am so sorry, Christian. I have been terrible to you and—"

"Shh." He drew her into his arms, burying his face in her hair. "I am just relieved to see Deirdre's idea proved a sound one. She said it had taken much the same action for her to come to terms with her own such loss. Still, I worried you would resent me for having allowed this."

Grace shook her head. "How could I ever resent you for giving me back what I thought forever lost? I can only be grateful to you, Christian, for what you have done. In bringing me to this, you have given me back my heart."

Christian felt a well of emotion surge up inside of him—happiness, gratitude, relief, and for the first time in nearly a month, he smiled down into the eyes of the woman he loved more than life, thanking the heavens, the saints, and even Cliodna for giving her back to him.

"No, Grace, it is you who have given me my heart."

And then slowly, he lowered his mouth to hers.

Epilogue

Summer had given way to autumn, burnishing the Highlands in splashes of orange and gold. As was the custom, the festivities for the harvest day céilidh would begin at dusk after the day's tasks had been seen to and the animals had been fed and bedded down for the night.

Earlier that morning, on the bluff overlooking the loch, the sun had cast its dawning light on a ceremony that had joined Andrew and Liza, and Alastair and Flora in marriage. For luck, the brides had carried tufts of white heather in their bridal bouquets and when the vows had been exchanged, there was a rush by the young men in the company to get the first kiss of the newly wedded wives.

Afterward, as the people of Skynegal made their way back to the castle, they'd each placed a stone upon a cairn built to commemorate the day. Christian and Grace, the laird and his lady, had placed the first two stones, followed after by the newly wedded couples, and then the others. When the last stone had been set by one of the children whom Christian had lifted up to reach it, the cairn had stood nearly eight feet tall. The company had cheered *Nis! Nis! Nis!* while the morning sun struggled through the mist and the birds of Cliodna soared overhead, calling out their legendary song.

The mood of celebration had continued throughout the day and with the coming of night's shadows, rush torches had been lit about the courtyard, while small *cruisgeans,* or crusie lamps, shone from the various wooden tables that were set out with food and drink. The children had gathered in a small circle, sucking on sweet aniseed gundy sticks, eyes wide as they listened to McGee telling one of the many adventures of Rob Roy, told to him by his father who'd heard them from his father before. The elder tenants watched on, reminiscing about their own carefree days of youth while McFee and several of his contemporaries assembled at the opposite end of the courtyard, readying to play upon a motley orchestra of fiddles, pipes, and drums.

The darker the night sky grew, the more spirited the gathering became. By the time the moon was high and full above them, everyone had eaten their fill, the ale and whiskey were flowing freely, and a lively circle of dancers were hopping and turning about the courtyard to the hoots and whistles of those clapping their hands.

High upon the near tower, watching down on the merriment below, were the laird and his lady. It was a chill night and they were each dressed in the Skynegal tartan. Christian stood with his arms wrapped protectively around Grace, her head tucked snugly beneath his chin as they looked out onto the scene in the courtyard.

It had been a day filled with celebrations, and there was yet one more celebration to come—over the news of the tiny life that lay nestled inside of her. Deirdre had calculated that the child would be making his appearance some time the following spring. And as Grace looked down on this place and these people that she loved so much, as she felt the protective strength of Christian's arms around her and knew the touch of a Skynegal breeze against her face, she could only think that Nonny had been right all along. Perfect knights did certainly exist, dreams weren't given without the possibility of coming true—and a miracle is always only a belief away from happening.

Slowly Grace turned to face him, this man she loved more than she ever thought possible, a knowing smile lighting her eyes. "Christian, I have something to tell you . . ."

Author's Note

In the course of my research, I will sometimes come across some tidbit from history that will draw my attention more than others. I will often pursue that same tidbit until it eventually ends up becoming a part of one of my stories. For *White Knight*, that tidbit was the Scottish Highland Clearances.

They began as early as the late-1700s and continued in some areas of the Highlands for nearly a century. Imagine that you are living on a small, barely surviving farm. You have lived on this land all of your life, as had your father and his father before him. You do not own this land, yet you were raised with an innate love for it, a respect for the clan traditions of your ancestors and a pride in your heritage. You pledge allegiance to your chief, the great landowner, and for centuries your people have protected him and his kin in times of war and attack, oftentimes sacrificing their lives for him. This pride and love you feel isn't something recently come by; it is centuries in the making.

Despite what hardship may come to your tiny place in this remote ancient land—war, poverty, or disease— the thought to abandon your heritage never crosses your mind.

Now imagine one bleak rainy Highland day. You are a farmer and thus you have already begun cultivating your small plot of leased land to grow the crop of oat, barley, or potato that will sustain your family through the coming year. You have invested everything you have in it—your time, your labor, your money. It is your life's calling, this farming, the work of both your heart and your soul.

Imagine, just as the crops have managed yet again to break their way through the harsh and oftentimes unforgiving Highland soil, your laird's factor comes to pay you a visit. He hands you a document written in a language you cannot read, still he manages to breach the communication barrier enough to deliver the horrible news that your home and the land it sits upon will no longer be made available for you. Even before your precious crop can be harvested, you will be made to vacate with your family and possessions. If you are one of the more fortunate, you might be offered an alternate plot of land on the estate, but it is likely a bare fraction of the size you occupied before. Your sole source of income is now terribly depleted. When you mention this to the factor, he tells you that you should abandon your farming, this work of your heart, and become a fisherman on the coast, only you have never known this work and there is no one to teach you. You make do as best you can, until the day the factor comes again, bearing another unreadable document, ordering you off the land again, only this time there is no alternate plot. You are simply expected to leave, abandoning the gravesites of your family, your heritage, the land you so love, so that the laird may bring in a new tenant to replace you, the sheep that will bring him a tidier profit.

The instances of the Clearances I have illustrated in this story, the evictions, the burnings, are all based upon actual accounts from the time period. Some have argued that the evictions were carried out "for the good of the people being displaced," that the Highlanders were a "lazy, indolent people who were satisfied to live in poverty rather than seek new and improved ways of making a living." What these individuals fail to appreciate is that it wasn't the impoverished state of living the Highlanders clung to. It was the land and their connection to it, a quality as much a part of their character as the mist is to the heathery Scottish hills, a characteristic that has made legend of the personages of William Wallace and Robert Roy MacGregor.

While my heroine, Grace, is a completely fictional character, some of her ideals were shared with other humanitarians of the time, those few who saw the immorality of the "Improvements" and sought alternate ways of nourishing the Highland economy. Dowager Lady MacKenzie of Gairloch was indeed responsible for organizing relief efforts through the building of roads in Wester Ross after the potato famine struck the Highlands in the mid-1840s. From all accounts, this great lady was a woman of character and vision. She taught herself Gaelic as well as ensuring that her sons would learn the language from their Gaelic-speaking nursemaid. She saw that they were then tutored at home instead of sending them away to university so they could better understand their people and thus manage their estates more successfully than the non-Gaelic speaking landowners could. Still other landowners provided housing and food for the displaced Highlanders, taking them onto their own estates as tenants, even if it meant bankrupting themselves in the process, all in the name of humanity.

If you are interested in learning more about the Scottish Clearances, there has been a memorial fund established. It's purpose is purely educational; the founders seek to inform the world of this often overlooked period of time in Scottish history. Their vision is to erect a permanent memorial to serve as a reminder "to the world of this unnecessary human tragedy." I invite my interested readers to contact me by mail or through my website for additional information about the Highland Clearances Memorial Fund.

I hope you enjoyed reading Christian and Grace's story. As many of my readers will already know, this is the third book of what I had originally planned as a trilogy. However . . .

While I was finishing this story, there came a voice from the text that begged to be heard. The voice was that of Christian's sister, Lady Eleanor Wycliffe. She will take us to the mysterious Western Isles of Scotland, a mythical setting peopled with eccentric characters, charming customs, and even an ancient curse. I hope you will look for her story, entitled *White Mist,* in the coming year.

I love to hear from my readers. Please write to me through my website at *http://www.jacklynreding.com* or c/o Post Office Box 1771, Chandler, AZ 85244-1771.

Thank you for sharing your time with me, and with Christian and Grace from *White Knight*. Until we meet again some day, at another time, in another story. . . .

—J.R.

Turn the page for an
exciting preview
of Catherine Coulter's latest
historical romance *The Countess*,
in bookstores now. . . .

Of course I didn't know who he was the first time I saw him. Nor did I really care who he was, not at first. It was only three weeks after I'd buried my grandfather. My cousin, Peter, a major under Colonel Benington during those final days at Waterloo, had been unable to come home from Paris, where he was now serving on Lord Brooks's staff, until, he'd written me, "those officious Frogs can come to some sort of civilized agreement with their rightful, albeit idiot, of a king."

No one was sure that would ever happen. The French, everyone said, were unsteady; their emotions, unlike those of the English, were too flamboyant, too uncontrolled. At the moment, unlike the French, I didn't feel much of anything.

Until I saw him.

I was in the park walking George, my Dandie Dinmont terrier, whom some people believed to be ugly as a devil's familiar on a bad day, oblivious to all the beautifully dressed people driving around in their landaus, riding their prime horseflesh, or simply walking, as I was. George and I were both silent—George out of habit since there had been little else but silence since Grandfather had died three weeks before. He was silent even when I picked up a small tree branch and threw it a good twenty feet away for him to fetch, an activity that usually sent him barking hysterically, leaping and dancing until he clamped his jaws around the branch. He was silent in his chase. He managed to get the branch, but it was at a cost. The man beat him to it, picking up the branch, eyeing George, then giving my dog a blinding smile even as he threw it a good thirty feet beyond where the two of them were eyeing each other. He stood there, hands on hips, watching George, again silent, run so fast his runty legs were a blur. Instead of bringing his owner and his beloved mistress—namely me—the branch, George trotted back to the man, tail high and wagging as steady as a metronome, and deposited the branch at his booted feet.

"George," I said, too loudly I knew, "come away now. You know that you're the diamond of dogs. You have the silkiest topknot of any dog in creation. Come along. I don't want anyone to steal you."

"It's true he's a magnificent animal," the man called out, and I knew sarcasm when it punched me in the nose. "He has an amazing presence, but I swear I'm not thinking of his abduction or a possible ransom. Although, with all that mustard and red hair, perhaps someone would want to steal him in order to blind an enemy."

"He doesn't have mustard and red hair. Mustard on a dog is ridiculous. It's more a fawn to a lovely reddish-brown sort of color." I walked to where the man stood with my terrier. I thought George's colors, particularly the mustard, even though one could call it perhaps unkindly, sickly yellow, were splendid. At least there wasn't all that much of it since George wasn't even twelve inches high and weighted only a stone and a half. I frowned as I looked at him. His coat, a crispy mixture of both hard and soft hairs, needed a good brushing. I hadn't groomed him for nearly a week. I'd been sunk too deep inside myself. I felt guilty for ignoring him.

As for George, the traitor looked besotted. I came down on my knees and patted his large domed head, peeled back his silky hair, and looked him straight in his very large and intelligent eyes. "Listen to me, you little ingrate. I'm the one who feeds you, who walks you, who puts up with your snoring when you've eaten too much at night. I am going to walk away now and I want you to come with me. Do you understand, George?"

George cocked his head at me, then turned to the man who had come down on his knees beside me. The man said, as he tried for a disarming shrug, "Try not to be upset. You see, animals adore me. I was born with this gift, a sort of power, if you will. If I'm not careful, I merely go for a walk on Bond Street and all the frivolous little dogs the grand ladies are carrying about, leap from their arms and chase after me. I try to ignore them. I always return them to their owners, but it just doesn't stop. What am I to do?"

Humor, I thought, something that hadn't been in my life for more weeks than I could now easily remember, hit me between the eyes. I smiled, unable not to. He smiled back at me, took my hand and helped me to my feet. He was big, too big, and too tall. Most of all, he was too young. I immediately took a step back.

"George," I said, growing more uncomfortable by the minute, "it's time to see what Mrs. Dooley has made for our lunch. You know that on Tuesdays, she does something very special with bacon for you. Yes, bacon, fried down to its core, cooked so stiff you can bang it on the floor several times before it crumbles. Come along now. You will ignore this gentleman. He may be nice to you here, where there's an audience who can see how talented he is with you, but he doesn't want you to lick his boots and follow him home. Come along."

I turned then and walked away, praying that George wouldn't stay with the man, wagging his tail and cocking his very homely large head in that cute way he had, his ears at half-mast, that clearly said, "Do you think she's really serious?"

"Wait," the man called after me. "I don't know who you are."

But I didn't wait. I didn't want him to know my name. Besides, why would he care? Didn't he see that I was wearing deep mourning? Didn't he know that being three feet away from him was too close? I even quickened my step. He was big and tall and he was too young. No, I thought, he couldn't do anything here, in the middle of the park, with all these people about. I merely shook my head, but didn't turn around. I nearly shouted with relief when I looked down to see George trotting beside me, his tongue lolling, carrying that branch in his mouth, his topknot flopping up and down. I did turn once I reached the corner.

The man wasn't there.

Well, what did I expect? That he'd unfold his wings
and fly after me, snatch both me and George up and
dump us into a lake of burning sulfur? No, he wasn't a
monster, but he was a man, I thought, young and strong,
and too sure of himself. He was capable of anything.
But he'd made me laugh. Imagine.

George and I went home and I forgot about him.

The second time I saw him, I didn't know who he was
then either.

I was still swathed in black, and this time I even wore
a black veil that half covered my face. When I came out
of Hookham's bookshop, he was standing outside holding an open umbrella, for it had begun to drizzle, and
there was a smile on his tanned face.

I stopped in my tracks. I wanted to ask him how in
heaven's name he could be so tanned when there hadn't
been a ray of sun in over two days, but what came out
of my mouth was, "What are you doing here?"

"I saw you buying a book inside. It's raining. You
don't have an umbrella. Come, I'll protect you from the
harsh elements and see you to wherever you wish to go."

"Excuse me," I said, looking up at that iron-gray sky.
"Harsh elements? Are you mad? This is England."

And he threw back his head and laughed. He'd
laughed at what I'd said. I tried to frown at him. He
took a step closer, but I wasn't worried. There were at
least a dozen people either hurrying through the rain or
setting their umbrellas over their heads.

"Where may I escort you, Miss—?"

I prepared to walk away. He lightly touched his hand
to my arm. I stopped dead, didn't move, just stood there,
waiting to see what he'd do.

"Very well," he said slowly, eyeing me, and I knew
he wanted to pull the veil off my face and stare me hard
in the eyes, but of course, he couldn't. He held his walking stick in his right hand and the umbrella in his left.
"I had hoped that George would prove a suitable chap-
eron and acquaintance to vouch for me that first time in
the park. But he wasn't then and he isn't, unfortunately,
here now. If not a dog, then I must find a human acquaintance to introduce us properly. You are obviously

a lady of rigid moral standards. Do you see anyone you know and trust walking by who would perhaps pause to introduce us properly?"

The urge to laugh was strong, too strong. It was wrong to want to laugh now, very wrong. Grandfather had been dead only a month. No, no laughter. So I just shook my head, nodded, and what came out of my mouth was, "How can you be so tanned? There hasn't been a hint of sun in the past two days."

He gave me a slow smile. "At least this time you've looked at my face, something you refused to do that first day we met in the park. I have some Spanish blood in me, something my father abhorred, but you see, he lusted after my mother, and so I was born. I wonder what he would think of me now, so unlike a pure-blooded Englishman, were he still alive."

"Well, that does explain it," I said, nodded to him, added, "good day," and walked away. I wasn't really surprised when the rain suddenly came down heavy and hard, because after all, it was England, when I realized he was just behind me, the umbrella now held over my head.

I stopped, turned, and stared at his beautifully fashioned cravat, then worked my way up to his chin. He had a dimple in that stubborn-looking chin of his and he was still smiling down at me, all white teeth and good humor. Since the rain was coming down at a fine clip now, I didn't step away from him. I didn't trust him an inch, nor that winsome smile of his, but I wasn't stupid. I didn't want to get soaked. "What do you want?"

"I want to know who you are so that I may meet your parents and all your siblings and the rest of your pets, and assure them that I'm not some devil-may-care rogue bent on ravishing their fair relative. I'd like take you for an ice at Gunther's. I'd like to make you laugh again."

All that, I thought, and knew it was impossible. "I have only one sibling—actually he's my cousin—and he's in Paris, but he would shoot your head off if he saw you bothering me like this."

The man stopped smiling. "You mean bothering you as in keeping you from getting soaked down to your lovely slippers?"

"Well, not exactly."

"That's a beginning. Now, you're in mourning, deep mourning. Does that mean that everyone you chance to meet must be long in the mouth and sigh and prepare to hand you a handkerchief?"

He was hard with muscle, just like Peter. I recognized that even though he was dressed elegantly in riding clothes, which meant, of course, tight buckskins, a frilled white shirt, a jacket no man could get into without lots of help, and highly polished black boots that came to his knees. "I don't want a handkerchief from you. As for you being long in the mouth, I don't think you have it in you. Your mouth is too busy laughing."

"Thank you."

"I hadn't really meant that as a compliment—it simply came out that way, by accident."

"I know."

"I am merely going about my business, not whining or begging for sympathy, or quivering my lips, and you just turn up like—"

"Please don't make me a bad penny."

"Very well. You just turn up like mad Uncle Albert whom we normally manage to keep locked in the third-floor attic, but who periodically bribes the tweeney and escapes."

He laughed. It was such a wonderful laugh he had, full and rich and heady. I hadn't heard a laugh like that in far too long, truth be told. Not since the first time I saw him in the park. Had I inadvertently been funny? I hadn't meant to be. Truly, there wasn't any more humor in my life. When I had thrown the first clods of earth on Grandfather's grave, I decided that twenty-one years of smiles and laughter were enough to grant any human being, more than enough, as Grandfather had been in my life since I was ten when my mother had died and my father had left the country and Peter was at Eton. Grandfather had loved to laugh. To my utter horror, not to my slack-jawed surprise, tears oozed out of my eyes and ran down my face.

They stuck to the wretched net veil. I pulled the veil back and wiped the back of my hand over my eyes. The tears kept coming. It was humiliating.

"I'm sorry," the man said. "Very sorry. Whom did you lose?"

"My grandfather."

"I lost mine five years ago. It was difficult. Actually, though, to be honest about it, it is my grandmother I miss the most of all of them. She loved me more than the sunsets in Ireland, she'd tell me. She was from Galway, you know, where she said the sunsets were the most beautiful in the world. Then, she said, she loved my grandfather so much, she willingly said good-bye to the sunsets, she married him, and came to England. I never heard of her speaking of the sunsets in Yorkshire."

For a moment, I thought he was going to cry. I didn't want him to be nice, perhaps even to have an inkling about what I was feeling. I wanted him to be a man, and act like a man. That way I'd know what he was without having to bother with his name. My tears dried up.

Then he offered me his left hand since his right hand was still holding the umbrella over both of us. It was raining so hard it was as if we were enclosed in a small gray world. It was a good umbrella. I wasn't even damp.

"No," I said, looking at his hand, which didn't even have a glove on it. Like his face, that hand was tanned. I wasn't about to touch that hand. It was large, the fingers blunt and strong. "No," I said again. "I don't want to meet you. I live with my nanny, Miss Crislock, and we have no visitors since we're in mourning."

"How long do you anticipate this blacking out of life?"

"Blacking out of life? I'm doing no such thing. I loved my grandfather. I miss him. I am respecting his memory. Also, truth be told, I am rather angry at him for dying and leaving me here alone, to go on without him, to have no one any more for me. He shouldn't have died and left me. He was old, but he wasn't ill. Everything was fine until he went riding, his horse slipped in a patch of mud, and he shot off his horse's back to hit his head again an oak tree and fell unconscious. He never woke. I protected him from the doctor, who wanted to bleed him every day. I argued with Grandfather, I promised to let him eat all of Cook's apple tarts he wanted, I begged him not to leave me, to open his eyes and smile at me, even curse at me, something he enjoyed as much as laughter, but he didn't. I don't wish to be reminded just yet that life simply goes swimmingly on its way despite the fact that I have lost the single more important person in my life through an idiotic accident, and no one else cares."

"How can someone care if he can't even find out your name?"

"Good day, sir."

This time he didn't follow me. I was soaked within seconds. The veil stuck to my face like a second skin, and itched like sticking plaster. *Blacking out of life.* What a ridiculous thing to say.

And cruel. He'd said it because I'd refused to meet him. Men were hurtful. They thought only of themselves, the important things to them were those that only they wanted and desired.

My grandfather had died. I was grieving. Who would not with a grandfather like him? I was not blacking out my life.

The third time I saw him, I still had no idea who he was. He was speaking with a friend of my grandfather's, Theodore, Lord Anston, a gentleman who still covered his bald head with a thick curling coal-black wig, wore knee breeches—and not just to Almack's on Wednesday nights. He rode with his hounds in Hyde Park, chasing not foxes, but pretty ladies and their maids.

My grandfather had once told me, laughing softly behind his hands, that Theo had worn black satin knee breeches to a mill held out on Hounslow Heath. One of the fighters had been so startled at the sight that he'd dropped his hands for a moment and stared. His opponent had smashed him flat.

Lord Anston grinned to display his surprisingly perfect teeth, patted the man's shoulder, and thwacked his lion-headed cane on the flagstone. He was wearing black satin shoes with large silver buckles. He strolled, I thought, very gracefully for a man walking two inches off the ground.

If I'd moved more quickly the man wouldn't have seen me, but I was looking at those shoes of Lord Anston's, wondering how they'd look on me, then staring at a mud puddle not three feet away, mesmerized, because I knew he was going to step into it, and thus I didn't move in time. He was on me in the next two seconds, smiling that white-toothed smile of his, as he said, "What? No George? Poor fellow, he'll grow fat with lack of exercise."

"George suffers from an ague right now. He's improving, but it is still to soon to bring him out into the elements."

There weren't really any elements to speak of, it being a bright sunny day, but the man merely nodded. He said as would a wiseman pontificating, "The ague is always a tricky business. I'd keep George close until he's able to stick his tail up straight and lick your hand at the same time."

I smiled, damn him, seeing George and that flagpole tail of his wagging wildly when Mrs. Dooley had hand fed him a good dozen salmon balls at breakfast, all small and hand rolled.

"I've got you now," he said, and I took a step back before I realized it wasn't at all necessary. He cocked his head to one side, in question, but I wasn't about to tell him that I didn't trust him or any other man any further than I could spit in that mud puddle some six feet away from me.

"Don't be afraid," he said finally, and he was frowning, perplexed, his head still cocked. "What I meant was if a man can make a woman laugh, she's his."

I was shaking my head when he added, smiling again now, "That was a jest, but not really. Lord Anston told me who you were. I told him not to scare you off by calling out to you. He said, 'Eh what, John? Scare off that Jameson girl? Ha! Not a scared bone in that melodious little body of hers. She sings, you know, which makes for a melodious throat. Perhaps the melodious extends to the rest of her, but I don't really know anything else about her body. Maybe it's sweet, who knows? Yes, that's exactly what Lord Anston said. He also said he'd known you since you were puking up milk on his shirt collar."

"It's possible," I said. "But I don't remember doing that. Lord Anston was a lifelong friend of my grandfather's. I play the pianoforte much better than I sing. My fingers are melodious, not my throat."

"He told me who you were. I must admit that it surprised me. How small the world shows itself sometimes. You're Peter Jameson's cousin. I've known Peter since we were boys at Eton. You're Andrea. Peter spoke of you countless times."

"No," I said. "I'm not Andrea. You've made a dreadful, yet perfectly understandable mistake. Mistakes happen. You will not dwell upon it. You will forget it by tomorrow. Good-bye. I wish you a good day."

I looked back when I reached the corner. He was standing there, just looking after me, his head still cocked in question. He raised his hand to me, then slowly lowered his arm and turned away.

It was the third time I'd seen him and I still didn't know who he was. Just his first name: *John.* A common, ordinary name, but I knew he wasn't either of those things.

That was just fine that I couldn't ever know anything more about him. He was dangerous. Any man who wore laughter like a well-loved shirt was dangerous.